Rise of the Witch Queen

Rift of Realms, Book 1

Geneva Oleander

To the two girls I still see when I plot a new story: all the notebooks full of *Lord of the Rings* fanfiction we passed back and forth in our high school hallways made me the writer I am today.

To all the dreamers: dreams really do come true.

Content Warnings

This is likely an incomplete list, but I am certainly going to attempt to cover all of them:

- Murder

- Violent death

- Unintentional Siblicide

- Child abandonment (off-page)

- Attempted murder of a child (off-page)

- Mention of abortion

- Desecration of the Holy See

- Blood play (copious amounts, in fact)

- Cum play

- Bondage play

- Ends-justify-the-means murder (copious)

- A LOT of vivid sex scenes

- MM, MMM, MMMMF, MF, MMF (etc) pairings throughout

- Missing child (off-page)

- Attempted patricide

- Mental torture

- Mentions of bodily torture

- Mention of sexual exploitation and sexual assault

- Battles (with dead and wounded participants)

- Suicidal Ideation

- Mention of Suicide

Prologue

Battle for New York

Manhattan, New York City, Witch Queendom
May 2160

The rooftop Manhattan bar was abuzz with the presence of five witch royals. Four of them would be married in less than six months in a wedding the world had long awaited. The princesses were surrounded by the queen's guard, but pictures of them laughing and drinking would somehow flood social media despite the wall of armored flesh surrounding their table. This was a planned outing, a sanctioned public appearance Queen Rixana demanded after Princess Nadella's mortalborn lover's identity had made headlines. An engaged witch princess was not supposed to have a mortalborn lover named Maria in Los Angeles.

Tonight was an early wedding celebration. The table was covered with bachelorette favors, and Nadella wore an intricate crown of golden leaves inlaid with heavy emeralds, a clear nod to the fae prince she would soon wed. Anyone who knew her could see through the charade, the painted-on smile and the forced laughter. Heiress to the Witch Queendom, she looked the most like her mother. Her thick red hair hung down her back in a heavy braid twisted with more golden leaves and sparkling emeralds, an odd complement to the black flying leathers all the princesses wore.

Princesses Violetta and Roselle sat closest to each other, engaged conspiratorially in quiet conversation. Anyone close enough to hear them would have heard Acadian words rather than English. They were the only princesses who still regularly used the mother tongue, despite their mother's insistence it isolated their mortalborn subjects. Both sisters wore crowns to represent their own betrothed. Violetta's crown rose and fell like waves with diamonds and sapphires accenting the white gold of the ocean spray. Roselle's crown was black tungsten, curling around her dark hair like shadows with dark garnets inlaid like drops of blood.

Atasia's crown was the most ornate, a golden crown of colorful gemstones and intricate swirls and dips. It sat heavily on her golden head, and the discomfort of the crown showed beneath the smile she faked for the pictures the sisters were supposed to pretend to be avoiding as they discussed their upcoming wedding. All four sisters would marry a prince of the other four magical kingdoms to fulfill the prophecy that would close the rift between the new world and the old, closing the portal that continued to leak darkness into this world of brightest sun.

Only Princess Cordelia wore the crown of the Witch Queendom, a simple black circlet bore black roses studded with delicate rubies instead of arches or spires. She was also the only sister who wore her weapon at the table, a double-bladed battle-ax strapped across her back. She sat quietly as her sisters spoke. Her own father had refused to allow her to be anyone's bride against her will. His demand was made easier by the fact that he was the only of the princess' fathers still around to speak for his daughter, and he was prince consort to the witch queen. There were many other ways in which she was set apart from her sisters, but most of them led back to Prince Consort Darius.

Cordelia looked out past the conversation to the New York City skyline. The rooftop offered a fantastic view of all the ways in which the world had changed in the last century. She'd seen pictures and videos of New York before the rift opened. The dark metallic skyline had been transformed by buildings climbing with ivy and with wide open floors overflowing with plants. The mix of natural and unnatural had melded into a new city entirely, a green city that sustained a new world. What had once been streets choked with cars had become green lanes and moss paths, with the exception of the occasional roads for public rails. Ground cars had been replaced with aeromobile, pegasi, and dragons (depending on the rider, of course).

Cordelia felt Nadella's eyes on her as she snapped her attention to the five pegasi in the corner on the rooftop bar. The princess' bonded mounts were never far. Bay, black, white, palomino, and appaloosa – the mounts were as varied as the princesses themselves, in appearance, demeanor, and power. Cordelia's eyes fell on the appaloosa as the black and white horse tossed his head and neighed. The other four pegasi watched him a moment before following suit. Their restless energy electric across the rooftop, reaching for the witches and ending their facade.

"What is it?" Nadella asked, her eyes on Cordelia.

Cordelia stood, knocking her chair to the ground and unsheathing her battle-ax fluidly. Her sisters had centuries on her, but she was the warrior among them. They came from a world where magic was what made one powerful, and she came from a place where brute strength held just as much power in the right hands.

"Cori?" Atasia this time, her voice desperate.

"Shadowborn," Cordelia whispered.

The queen's guard moved with her as she sprinted across the busy bar, creating a path for her as she ran for her pegasus, Atreyu, and mounted him in a swift motion. Her sisters were a few steps behind her. She felt them building their power inside of them as the queen's guard handed them weapons to strap to their sides.

The bright lights of New York rose to a crescendo as the princess' mounts rose into the air, like someone had turned the volume of the lights up. Cordelia had seen this before. They all had.

"Formation!" she yelled. Her sisters' mounts fell in line, two to each side, forming a *v* with her at the point. *Steady*, she thought to herself as the lights were snuffed out, covered in an inky, unnatural darkness that spread as far as any of them could see.

Nadella's lightning cracked across the sky, revealing a swarm of shadowy figures riding towards them. Most of them rode black pegasi, but the woman at the front rode a massive black, feathered dragon. Fire bloomed to Cordelia's left and right: Violetta and Roselle. Ice built in her own veins, the familiar bite of the luxurious cold that was more home than the warm spring night could ever be.

"Hold formation!" she ordered as the shadowborn approached, illuminated by fire and lightning. There were easily a hundred of them, a large show of force but not the worst odds the sisters had faced.

When the dragon rider was a hundred feet away, Cordelia screamed, "Now!" into the darkness as it approached. Violetta and Roselle erupted first, their flames enveloping a dozen shadowborn. Their screams split the night, and the desperate cries of their burning pegasi ripped at Cordelia's heartstrings. At some point, the shadowborn had chosen to follow the shadow queen, but the pegasi hadn't been given a choice.

Nadella was next by only a heartbeat. Lightning fried scores of shadowborn and their pegasi instantly, short circuiting their hearts and sending them plummeting towards the city below. Cordelia's power continued to build as Atasia surrounded her sisters with a bubble of air before sucking the air from the night around them, a slow death for nearby shadowborn and their mounts. Shadowborn writhed on the backs of their pegasi, helplessly clawing their throats bloody as they fought for precious air.

Cordelia watched as one by one, the shadowborn fell from the sky. She watched as the dragon rider seemed unaffected, unscathed, protected by some deep magic she did not extend to her soldiers. The woman broke away from her other soldiers before she reached the princess, plunging towards the city as the dragon opened its maw.

"Hold formation!" Nadella yelled as Cordelia broke away from her sisters. "Cori! Cordelia!"

All Cordelia could see was a fire breathing dragon flying towards Manhattan. Formation be damned. She was vaguely aware of her sisters following her, abandoning the final shadowborn soldiers to follow Cordelia.

Ice crusted Cordelia's hand, covering her battle-ax as she approached the dragon and its rider. She pulled her right arm back, taking aim at the rider when the dragon stopped its descent suddenly, swinging its large body towards Cordelia and Atreyu.

Cordelia didn't think, she exploded. Ice flew from her in spears. The dragon bellowed as her ice embedded in its wings, the only unarmored part of its body. She called more ice to her a moment before the dragon released the fire it had been holding, blasting it towards her.

Fuck, she thought. She threw up a shield of ice, but dragonfire could not be stopped. It was hotter than the molten core of the planet, and it burned through the ice and slammed into her. The whole world became pain. Liquid, molten pain.

The fire burned through her and into her, and she had to get it out. She screamed as she pushed every piece of ice inside of her against the dragonfire. She imagined a wall of ice, permafrost, a winter neverending, a world of snow–

–and the entire world erupted in flames.

Cordelia

I came back to consciousness slowly, like my senses came back online one by one.

Sound came first. Beeping and a hushed conversation. Familiar voices – mom and dad.

Smell was next. Lavender and chamomile, the smell of incense burning somewhere mixed with the smell of antiseptic and rubbing alcohol.

Then taste. My mouth tasted like I'd swallowed ashes, like maybe my tongue itself had been burned to cinders.

Touch. I was laying on cotton sheets and a thick, heavy blanket covered me from neck to toes. A silk gown hugged my body.

And finally, sight. My eyes were heavy as I opened them, and the conversation from earlier had long since ended. I was alone in a hospital room decorated in posters about mortalborn and magicborn healing. A hybrid room with hybrid healers for people like me.

The fluorescent lights had been dimmed, allowing for late afternoon sun to spill in through the sheer-curtained windows and illuminate the room. I blinked around the room as memory began to seep back into my mind. Dragonfire. I'd taken a direct hit with dragonfire. I should be dead – very dead, in fact. Every part of my body should be ash and bones dropped in some alley in Lower Manhattan.

I held my bare arms up in the sunlight, searching for the maiming the burns would have left behind, even if my mother's healers had somehow brought me back from being barbecued. I turned them over before pushing the blanket and sheets off my body to examine my feet, my legs – every inch of me that I could see.

Impossible. I was dead or dying. This was a fever dream or some afterlife I had always been so sure didn't exist. Maybe they'd found me near death and induced a healing coma, and this was a mirage my subconscious had imagined, the layover between life and death. There was no explanation for me lying in a hospital bed without a single burn on my body after a dragon unleashed his fire on me. Ice princess or not, even permafrost could not stand against dragonfire.

I swung my legs over the side of the bed and placed my bare feet on the cold floor, shivering with delight at the cool touch of the tile. Everything inside of me had always been December.

I wanted to test the limits of this fantasy. I crossed the room and opened the door.

"Your highness," General Sabine, the head of my mother's army and personal guard, bowed as she met my gaze. Sabine was one of the few warriors I hoped to never face on the battlefield. I was arrogant, but she was a different breed of fighter altogether. Six feet tall with the largest biceps I'd ever seen and colorful flower tattoos covering her bald head, she was a wall of solid muscle and her magic was as strong as any royals'. If she was here guarding my room, my mother was somewhere in the building.

"I need to talk to my mother," I said.

"I can have her fetched." Sabine snapped her fingers at one of the guards. "But I insist you return to your room until she can speak with you, your highness."

Noise down the hall caught my attention. I stepped through the doorway and saw someone snapping pictures from a vacant nurse's station halfway down the halfway.

"Seize him," Sabine commanded.

The camera clicked some more before the man and his camera shifted into a crow and flew away from us. A guard a few paces away raised her hands, and we all watched as mud spread out across the floor like a creature with a mind of its own rising up in front of the bird like a wall. The crow cawed and turned to fly into an open doorway, but a moment later, his wings stopped moving and he plummeted to the ground as another guard held her hands up. I heard the bird gasping as he shifted back into a man, his camera around his neck. Air magic.

Guards rushed to him, grabbing his camera and clasping iron bands on his wrist.

"I'm doing my job!" the man yelled.

"You're invading the privacy of a princess of the Witch Queendom," Sabine said, stepping away from me and towards the reporter.

"The people want to know that she's alright, that she's alive," he shouted, turning his wrists painfully against the iron bands that prevented his shifter magic. He turned his eyes towards me, taking me in from head to toe, as if he personally needed to be sure I was alive.

I took a step back into the doorway of my hospital room. Something about how he was looking at me made me shiver. Why did everyone need to know I was alive? What had gotten out about the shadowborn attack?

"How does it feel to be the heir?" he said, his eyes locked on mine. There was nothing cruel in them, only pain and curiosity. How did it feel to be the heir – the heir of the Witch Queendom? Me? The fifth and youngest daughter of the Witch Queen, the last daughter in line for the throne–how does it feel for *me* to be the heir? My eyes met Sabine's, and I knew. I knew why she wanted me to wait in my room until my mother could somehow break this news to me diplomatically, so she could tell me that we would say *this* and *that* to the press. We would attend this event and wear that black dress to make it clear we were mourning, but we were still strong. We were still the unshakeable dynasty of the witches.

Everything seemed to get fuzzy, like there was cotton stuffed in my ears or maybe I was underwater. I saw Sabine step towards me, wrap her arm around my shoulders, and lead me back towards my bed. Another guard closed the door behind us. She must have been talking as she led me to the faux leather chair in front of the window because her lips were moving the entire time. But I couldn't make sense of any words she might have said. My mind was filled with the memory of dragonfire consuming me, but I pushed back with every bit of magic inside of me – pushing the fire out, out, *out*.

What had I done?

Ruyek

Attending a funeral for someone I didn't really know but who should have played the most significant part in my life was strange, to put it mildly. Roselle and I had been betrothed for the better part of a decade, but I'd only spent a few hours with her at royal functions. I think it fair to assume she was not thrilled to have her partner chosen for her. Witches rarely marry and are almost never monogamist – but then, neither was I. I certainly would have shared her frustrations if we'd ever moved beyond pleasantries and duties.

As yet another person told me how sorry they were for my loss, I felt a little guilty that I didn't really feel sad at all. The loss of life was certainly tragic, but I knew death quite intimately. Every vampire did, I suppose. I did feel angry. I think all of us did. Another attack in the world we'd thought our safe haven for over a century seemed like further proof of our continued failure to close the rift. And the four witch princesses were perhaps four of six or seven truly unmatched witches in power, and yet, they'd all fallen so easily in the skies above New York. The loss of that battle stung the most for me, and the loss of any belief we were winning this ongoing war against the shadowborn.

None of us knew what would happen next with our alliances, the war, or the prophecy we had all foolishly staked our hopes upon. I'd never been one to put much stock in fae seers, but my father did, and he was King of the Vampire Kingdom – for now, at least. I was sure of one thing, however: Queen Rixana had certainly already met with the fae seers to scrape together our next steps. There may be no official hierarchy among the magicborn royal households, but the witch queen was rarely challenged when she made a decision that affected all of our futures.

The witch queen was thoughtful enough to hold the funeral at night so my parents and our entire court could attend without too much hardship. Floating flames encircled the courtyard in what my father would call a silly waste of magic, but then, the king of the vampires lived in constant fear of the shadowborn. He'd never admit as much, but it was obvious to anyone who spent more than ten minutes talking about the war, the rift, or the fate of the prophecy with him. I assumed he thought Earth was a fresh start devoid of the shadowborn threat, and their reappearance a century into our habitation here had been a most unwelcome surprise.

The courtyard was full of royals from all five royal households as well as high ranking members of all of our courts. A large castle of black stone walls and turrets stretched out around the courtyard; the Washington Monument still shone above the castle walls, a bit like an old god keeping watch over the land that had once belonged to its creators. Most of our dragons were out hunting, but my dragon and her still-unbridled mate perched atop the castle walls. Isolde flexed her dark feathered wings into the night and rustled her head like a monstrous bird of prey, while her mate, Drystan, watched her every move adoringly, keeping his own red wings tucked in close to his body. They were recently mated and a bit lovesick with one another.

A funeral pyre lay in the middle of the funeral attendees. A pegasus wing, part of a ripped cloak, and what appeared to be trinkets from each of the witch princesses covered the pyre. I assumed there had been little left to gather for a funeral after they'd been engulfed in dragonfire. The other three recently not-quite-widowed princes stood next to me at the macabre affair. Only the mer seemed to be genuinely grieving. I'd heard he and Violetta had grown to be a love match over the years. Though even their love story had seemed more *making the best out of a forced betrothal* than true chemistry the few times I'd interacted with them.

"We should all be preparing for our weddings," the fae boy said solemnly, rousing me from my thoughts.

He wasn't quite a boy, but he'd been born in this world and he was the youngest among the four of us. He certainly looked the part though. His soft red hair curled around the stag antlers that grew from his head, and his skin was fair and freckled. He was leanly built and a bit soft in all the ways I preferred.

"Did you know Princess Nadella well, Ambrose?" I asked, though we both knew the answer.

Ambrose was a few years younger than the youngest witch princess, and Nadella had been born in the old world. She had been the angriest when the betrothals had been announced. Ambrose was still pimply and new then, barely an adult even by mortalborn standards. Rumor had it the princesses had been trying to cover up the story about Nadella's very-public affair the night they died by pretending to be happily celebrating our upcoming weddings.

"I think I would have liked the chance to know her." The fae prince met my eyes. He was shorter than me, though not by much. His deep wintergreen eyes met mine briefly before looking back towards the unlit pyre. Ah. The prince was a romantic. He thought marriage would make Nadella's cold heart grow stronger. A smile crossed my lips as I looked at him. A man who fancied himself heartbroken might be just the sort of entertainment I could use for however long our royal families took to decide our fates.

The crowd hushed as what was left of the witch family stepped into the dimly lit courtyard. The floating flames were only for the few mortalborn among us, but the darkness seemed to heighten the mourning of the whole affair, even if all the magicborn could see well enough in natural darkness.

Queen Rixana was as stoic as ever, her mask of stone fit firmly in place so that no one could read her expression as she moved to stand in front of the pyre and faced the gathered people. Princess Cordelia was not nearly as stoic though. She leaned heavily on her mortalborn father, her cheeks streaked with tears. Her father had been an anomaly at first. The mortalborn man the witch queen had very clearly fallen in love with, but forty years later, magicborn and mortalborn relationships were commonplace. We'd even given a name to the halfling children born of such unions: powerbound. Though, from what I knew, the name was a misnomer. Power and magic were not limited by adding human blood. If anything, I think we all feared it was quite the opposite.

Cordelia's father was handsome, even as an aging mortalborn. His dark brown skin had a few lines and his long black dreads were streaked with gray, but he was still tall and broad, clearly a man who looked after his physique. He cut a striking figure in his Armani suit.

His queen, of course, was only just beginning to show her age, looking like a mortalborn in their mid-forties. She was over four hundred years old, but our kind easily saw seven or eight centuries. She looked a lot like her Nadella once had: long, dark auburn hair, fair skin, and a petite frame. It was a wonder, all of us accepting their doomed relationship with grace to avoid talking about the death that waited for Prince Consort Darius, the inevitability a snake in the grass that could not be avoided with all the magic in both worlds. Though it seemed fair to assume my father had mentioned the prince consort's mortality to the witch queen every chance he got. It was no secret their dalliances had ended when she'd taken up with the mortalborn.

Rixana looked out at the crowd, her eyes betraying the grief her face concealed. A mother's grief. Even my cold heart ached at the thought of losing four children in a single night, a single battle. Battle and loss had been normal in Acadia, but even that kind of loss would have been a deep wound in our ancestral home.

The queen turned her weary eyes back to the pyre. Her general stepped up behind her. The woman was well-known to the royal courts – General Sabine. Tattoos covered her naked head, a feat for magicborn. Our healing powers made any kind of body modifications difficult. Only vampire venom mixed in the ink could have slowed the healing process down enough to make the tattoos last. And even then, it likely took several sessions. A painful process for the aesthetic she was going for, but the effect worked. Her hulking frame and magical prowess were enhanced by the absolute badassery of knowing she'd endured self-inflicted torture for her personal brand.

General Sabine raised her hand, shushing any murmurs left in the crowd. Her voice boomed across the courtyard of mourners, a mix of will and some voice enhancing magic some magician had whipped up for her. *Magicians.* A whole new breed of magic-wielders that no one but the witches seemed willing to embrace.

"All five royal courts and the North American Mortalborn Alliance meet here tonight to honor and recognize the violent murder of four witch princesses," she began. Ahhh – this was to be a call to war then, not a memorial speech. The witch queen was ever clever, calculated – even in how she memorialized her dead daughters. "We gather here to remember their lives, brutally taken by the shadowborn in the name of their false queen, the very woman who drove all of us from our ancestral homeland. We gather here as refugees from their persecution, from the senseless violence that has followed us across worlds–"

Refugees was certainly an interesting way to describe a people who fled one world and quickly subjugated another. It was no secret that the witch queen painted herself as a benevolent monarch who saved the poor mortalborn from their own self-destruction, but even she had to know enlisting the United States military in the middle of a mortalborn world war and then turning traitor and handing over the keys to the planet to the magicborn royal houses wasn't exactly the behavior of poor refugees simply seeking asylum.

"–we gather here as kingdoms and cultures who have come together to mend this broken planet, without ever truly closing the path to the bleeding world we left behind." The general paused for effect, and that effect was immediate. Whispers sprang up in the crowd.

Closing the rift. The promise our betrothals had made to the world. Marriage between all five magicborn houses this summer during a rare hybrid solar eclipse would fulfill the fae prophecy that promised a union between all five houses would close the rift, sealing Earth from Acadia forevermore. But now we were four princesses short and that prophecy seemed like a lost cause.

The general raised her hands again and the crowd silenced. "We gather here to honor Princess Nadella, Princess Atasia, Princess Violetta, and Princess Roselle, and we gather here to promise vengeance in their names, retribution for their murders. We gather to swear to uphold the fae prophecy to close the rift and cease the shadowborn threat to Earth."

There were no whispers this time. Unless the queen was hiding several more princesses, there was no fulfilling the prophecy, but the witch queen never gave up. I met the mer prince's gaze. Tears streaked his face, but there was anger in his eyes. He had come to mourn, not for speeches. We both knew he wouldn't storm off because we weren't allowed such displays of emotion, but I nodded slightly to acknowledge I understood his impulse. I wasn't mourning, but even I thought the political speech was a bit much for a funeral.

I looked over at the fae prince. His face was pure confusion, as if he had no idea just how much of an ambitious monster the witch queen was. The witch queen. My father. His parents.

All of the current heads of the magicborn royal houses, if we were being completely honest. They all allowed Rixana to be their de facto leader, their empress in all but name.

The general fell back to her station behind the queen. Rixana raised her hand to the pyre, to what was left of her children and their bonded mounts, to the small mementos of four dead witch princesses; fire erupted from her hands in a cruel irony considering how their lives had ended.

My eyes drifted to the last witch princess. She didn't have the queen's poker face, that's for sure. Anger. Grief. Disappointment. Disgust. And something else, something with an edge of cruelty to it. In that moment, I desperately wanted to know if it was directed towards her mother or the shadowborn who had murdered her sisters. I felt the sudden urge to speak to her. We had talked on a few occasions. Never for very long or of anything of great importance, but I knew that she was sharp and a warrior through and through. And I knew that the only thing she held of her mother was her golden gaze, and I would bet money on that certainty.

Mortalborn, powerborn – they had something inside them that the witch queen was incapable of feeling. A kind of emotion that she might have felt at some point for my father, but it had been broken out of her and what was left was centuries of anger and heartache. Like most magicborn. Live enough centuries and everything tastes like sand. At least that's what the poets say.

All of us princes turned to each other. We knew each other's names, but I'd only spent any real amount of time with the shifter prince, Savanna – though we'd both vowed to never talk about that night again after we'd been betrothed to sisters.

"What happens now?" the fae princeling asked, his freckled cheeks delicious in the soft glow of the dimly lit courtyard.

"Now we listen to whatever war party or cross-world scheming the witch queen has planned for all of us," I responded.

The mer prince, Caspian, cut his stormy gaze to me. I knew the blue beneath his cheekbones would be lost to most here, even other magicborn didn't have the kind of darkvision vampires did, but I certainly loved the reminder he carried the power of the ocean with him even this far up the Potomac.

"Are you going to argue with me?" I asked. "Is my assessment unfair to our kind and courteous leader?"

"The witch queen is no leader of mine," the mer prince said.

Before I could launch into my usual tirade about all the ways in which Queen Rixana and the Witch Queendom ruled us all in both Acadia and here on Earth, one of the queen's guards stepped up to us.

"Queen Rixana has called for an emergency meeting of the IRC. Your presence is requested," she said.

"If it is a request, can we deny it?" I ask.

Her eyes flared a moment before returning to a look of stone indifference. "You may," she said, "but there may be consequences for your refusal."

She walked away with her hand on a curved blade at her side, a threat that no magicborn needed. If battle broke out in this courtyard, no one would be reaching for a mortal blade.

"You were saying, Prince Caspian?" I turned my head back to the mer with a smile that revealed my fangs in all of their glory. The kind of toothy smile that either sent mortalborn running or begging for me. Earth had been very good to the vampires and our appetites. Before I could muse too long on bloody delights, Caspian turned and stalked out of the courtyard. If I was a betting man (and I was), I'd have bet he'd be the first person seated in the IRC meeting.

Savanna

I stalked along the wall as the magicborn royals and the North American Mortalborn Alliance people of import filed into the large room the witch queen called the Rose Room, watching the procession through the large double doors. The fae prince had returned to his parents' side, almost nestled against his mother. I'd heard he'd been sheltered in the fae court, but he looked so childlike on his mother's arm. He was nearly twenty-five, though a quarter of a century was of little consequence to most magicborn.

Ruyek and his parents could not be more different. All three of them entered separately, and while I watched the vampire king and queen sit next to each other, you could have fit all of Acadia in the space between them. Or perhaps, that was the space they left for Queen Rixana. Everyone knew she'd always been the third person in their marriage, even if she had given up Valdon for the brief lifespan of her mortalborn prince consort.

Princess Cordelia sat next to her father. She was wearing a long black gown but black armor covered her chest and arms, and though her preferred double-headed battle-ax was absent, a short sword was strapped to her side. I noted several daggers strapped along her legs and side as well. The witches definitely had different funeral attire than shifters, but then, she'd just watched her sisters be murdered on a night out that, according to the news reports, had started as an uneventful night of drinking and carefully planned paparazzi. A night that should have been safe. Maybe it was best to always be prepared.

The mer prince walked in with his sister, Princess Adara. Both of them were golden-haired and tan-skinned, eerily physically similar siblings for siblings born to different fathers, planets, and centuries. His mother hadn't left the water since the meeting ten years ago, but then, she had been over eight hundred years old when she came through the rift. Her star was dimming. Magicborn lived long enough that it felt like forever, but it was rare to see a full thousand years. At over nine hundred, she was near the end of her days. Traveling across the world was likely best left to the crown princess.

I craned my neck as the North American Mortalborn Alliance president stepped into the room with her secret service. A look passed between her and the witch princess that it seemed most of the room's occupants missed.

"Oh, sweet boy." Two arms reached for me before I could shift. "At some point, you have to learn to put the claws away for these meetings." I hissed as Ommi stroked the fur along my back. Mom came around my other side and stroked under my chin.

Ommi and Mom had been how me (and then my younger brother) differentiated between our two mothers. Both were our genetic parents. Ommi had broken the golden rule of shifting in an attempt to bring heirs into the world – the golden rule to never shift into another humanoid form. Shifters had the very real chance of losing themselves in other humanoid forms, and Ommi had changed more and more with every shift into a man's form in an effort to have her own children with the queen she loved. She was androgynous now in appearance and spirit. She still used she/her pronouns, but Mom said that the pronouns were out of habit, not a true reflection of who Ommi was after spending so much time shifting between bodies.

Ommi wore a black tunic and loose black pants. Her black hair was cut short and her umber skin shimmered beneath the lights in the hallway. Mom wore a long black dress. Her thick black braids hung down her back, accented with golden beads and thread.

Despite my desire to appear annoyed that Ommi was carrying me into the meeting like a housecat instead of the deadly caracal I'd actually shifted into to watch the procession, I rubbed my head against the underside of her chin. I'd spent the last two years living in an apartment in Berlin, and traveling home to Egypt was far too low down on my priority list. I'd missed my mothers.

Ommi sat me gently in the chair between her and mom. I shifted back, my black suit only slightly askewed from the shifting. Ommi's long red and black tail thumped along her chair rhythmically. It was a nervous tic, though she was loath to admit she had a nervous bone in her body. All shifters had something animalistic they could not shift away, something that was a part of our humanoid form. For Ommi, it was a red and white dire jackal tail. For Mom, it was vibrant green snake scales that ran from the back of her hands to both shoulders. And for me, it was the heterochromic feline eyes I couldn't shift away – one blue, one green – the eyes of a midnight lion. For all shifters, the parts we couldn't shift away were a reflection of the animal we shifted into most naturally, the form we wore like a second skin.

The room fell silent as Queen Rixana stepped into the room. The head of her guard, a woman we all knew as General Sabine, and a mortalborn man with long black braids and a very expensive suit flanked her. The witch queen nodded at the general, who took her post against the wall behind her queen's empty chair. The queen didn't sit like the rest of the congregation, but we were used to her leading the council meetings.

Rixana looked to the still-open doors as two fae women entered the room wearing witch queen leathers and black roses braided into the golden braids that circled their heads like crowns. They were nearly identical. Twins, fraternal by the looks of it – rare for magicborn but less rare for the fae. These fae served the witch queen, not the fae king. The black roses and the leathers were obvious enough, as was their stance next to the general.

"Thank you for joining us after a very long few days," the witch queen said, her golden eyes sparing no emotion as she looked around us. A very long few days wherein her children had been murdered. My mothers would not wear such a painted mask if it had been me, of that I was sure.

"Most of us know each other quite intimately, but President Harmonie Zambrano-Rodriguez of the North American Mortalborn Alliance joins us tonight," Queen Rixana said. Her gaze fell on the mortalborn woman sitting between King Valdon of the Vampire Kingdom and Queen Jassamine of the Fae Court.

"And," the witch queen looked to the man standing next to her, "Marcus Neirling, the head magician of the International Magician's League."

Again with the magicians. The mortalborn learning magic certainly didn't bother me, but I know it ruffled most of the royals around me. Maybe ruffled wasn't the right word – it terrified them. Our magic worked in prescribed ways based on our race and affinity, but magicians could bend magic to their will. The quiet part no one would say out loud was magicians had a very real chance of destroying our dominion over this planet.

The magician bowed his head slightly. He might have spent the money to feel like he belonged here, but he looked like he was about to shit himself. He looked young to be the head of magician's very-new attempt at a structured hierarchy, but magicians valued power over experience. And in the scheme of things, magicians had only learned to harness magic in the last two decades, and only the witch queen had started keeping magicians on staff and working with them. Perhaps that was why she seemed to lead this council – she was always willing to change to stay in power. She did lead us to an entirely different planet to maintain her power.

The other royals all watched in varying shades of interest and disgust as the magician took an empty seat next to Princess Cordelia. Only Prince Ruyek looked amused, like all of this was very entertaining for him.

"Now," Rixana began again. "To the business at hand." The black-clad fae twins stepped up next to her, as if this bit was rehearsed. Maybe it was. "In light of the attack on New York, my seers have reconsulted the prophecy. The deaths of my daughters would mean either all of us were doomed to live in a world with a rift that cannot be closed, or that our original interpretation of the prophecy was incorrect."

The room erupted as conversations broke out.

"Incorrect?" King Taron demanded, his fae prince leaning away from him as his face reddened with anger. "You told us they were certain. We promised our children, broke centuries of laws and traditions to bind our races together in–"

"–how can we ever trust fae seers again after such a misinterpretation?" Princess Adara asked, the blue tones beneath her pale cheeks darkening as her emotions flared.

"Fae seers?" Queen Jessamine responded. "The seers who work for the witch queen no longer belong to the fae court. Our seers are doing quite w–"

"Enough." Princess Cordelia's voice was quiet and the noise did not cease, but I felt the eyes of all the princes in the room turn to her as she spoke. "Enough." She was a bit louder this time, gaining more attention, leaving only King Valdon and King Taron arguing. "Enough!"

This time, the princess' voice carried and the room silenced. I watched as the vampire king considered his retort. Before the death of her sisters, Cordelia was the fifth daughter of the witch queen, and the powerbound daughter of a mortalborn man. Her voice was not even seated at this table. She was an oddity, to be sure, but she was mostly no one. Now, she was the crown princess of the Witch Queendom and the first powerbound set to inherit a magicborn monarchy. The weight of her command was far heavier than it had been before the deaths of her sisters, and I watched as all of that realization crossed Valdon's face before he simply scowled in response, choosing not to argue.

"As much as I am thrilled by the idea of a long drawn-out council meeting on the night of my sisters' funeral, I think we can all agree that letting my mother state her business before we share retorts would move all of this along more quickly." The princess' stare was locked on the vampire king, as if she'd felt all of his fury and uncertainty at her command, and she was challenging him.

Shadows leaked across the table from his hands as his red eyes held her golden stare, and the temperature in the room plummeted as the winter powers of the witch princess enveloped the room. The stare-off was most certainly a challenge. The vampire king's shadows recoiled as ice started to form on his hands and he broke the princess' gaze to look at Rixana, who was still standing behind her chair with the two fae women flanking her.

"Are you going to allow this?" he asked, a definite shiver in his voice.

Rixana smiled a wicked smile. "You show your hand too easily, Valdon. She hasn't even completed the ripening, you know." The queen sighed. "Stop it – both of you."

Valdon's shadows dissipated and the ice on his hands melted instantly, leaving a puddle on the table, but the room stayed far too cold to be comfortable. I met the princess' eyes as she moved her attention away from Valdon. The moment was brief, but it felt intentional.

The witch queen continued the meeting, still standing, as if nothing had happened. "My seers have concluded that it was a misinterpretation. We are certain the prophecy spoke of a single union between our five houses. Our misinterpretation was based on our customs, not through any fault of my seers." Her eyes snapped to Queen Jessamine – clearly, she'd heard her comment about the witch queen's seers.

"A single union?" Mom asked, surprising the whole room. My mothers were usually observers at these meetings, speaking up only when the shifter lands were directly involved or, more importantly, threatened.

"Yes, Yva, a single union between all of our houses," Rixana repeated.

King Taron spoke next. "The fae are not prudes, Rixana. Having a single partner isn't even the norm, but are you suggesting all of our sons marry your daughter?"

A single union. My ears felt like they were ringing. My fiance was dead, a fiance I'll admit I did not know well enough to mourn, but I didn't come to D.C. expecting to be entered into another marriage contract less than an hour after my dead fiance's funeral.

I looked at Princess Cordelia and found her wide-eyed at her father. Oh fuck. She didn't know. Her mother didn't tell her before the meeting. My mothers shivered around me as the room continued to get colder.

Silence. The room fell into silence as the weight of this new prophecy interpretation sank in. I looked to the other princes.

The fae prince looked like a deer caught in headlights with his wide green eyes and curling antlers. The mer prince's eyes were closed tightly, and I couldn't tell if anger or grief was etched in the lines of his face. Somehow, Ruyek looked even more amused than he did when the meeting started. He would be though. This was exactly the kind of chaos Ruyek lived for.

King Taron was the first to speak again. "You took my seers into your court. You took my son, still a boy, and promised him to the daughter you knew was least likely to be happy with him. You asked me to abandon the faeries and come through the rift. Rixana, you have asked too much of me, of the fae court. No. I will not allow this."

"He's right." Queen Madelina's voice shook some as she spoke. I don't think I'd ever heard her speak in a council meeting before. She left the speaking to her husband. The vampire queen looked around the table for support as she spoke again. "Why should we bear the burden of a war we did not start?"

We all watched as Rixana pulled her chair out and sat in it, her seers still standing behind her chair silently. She nodded to herself before turning her eyes on Taron, ignoring Madelina completely. We all felt the heat in her gaze, the heat of her fire pulling the temperature of the room back up. But, to my shock, she responded in Acadian – a deliberate choice that would only exclude the mortalborn in the room.

"You made a choice to come here. You and your fae could have stayed in Acadia with your faeries, Taron, and you could have stayed there until she came for you. And she would have come for you with all of the great powers of the world too far away to help you." The witch queen's voice was a deadly edge, a blade that sliced through the air in the room. "You could have stayed in Acadia, childless and heirless, like you had been for three centuries. You could have denied me when I told you how to close the rift. You knew then that it would seal you off forever from the faeries, and yet, you didn't protest then and you will not protest now out of some misplaced guilt. Oh yes. I've seen the reports. We all know what has become of your faeries, but they had a choice too. They chose to stay and fall under her power. We offered them safe haven too. They're lost to you, and if we do not close the rift, we might soon be attending funerals for your children."

"Stop it." Queen Jessamine said – English this time.

I looked away from the witch queen's face to see tears falling down the fae queen's face.

"I will not stop it!" Rixana's voice roared across the table like the inferno we all felt building inside of her–Acadian again. "I will not spare you the details of what I saw when they pulled the burned bodies of my daughters from the streets of New York. Dragon fire melts everything, you know. Even their bones were molten. If we do not close the rift, we will lose this world as surely as we lost Acadia, but this time, I don't have another planet for safe haven. We are stuck here, and she is coming. Choose this prophecy or choose a war we will lose." Her eyes flicked to Madelina, and as if with a switch, the witch queen brought the whole conversation back to English. "A war that none of us started, but all of us must now face."

"Even if we all agree to this union," Princess Adara said to Rixana, "there are other royal princes and princesses in every monarchy but yours and the vampire kingdom. Why must it be all of these princes again? Have they not faced enough loss?" She was talking about Caspian. Her brother was the only prince actually mourning the death of his fiance.

"Our youngest son is not yet ten." Ommi said, her hand reaching out to grasp mine. "It must be Savanna for the shifter territory."

Queen Jessamine looked at Prince Ambrose before speaking. "Prince Willem is barely ten also. Princess Laurel is married, and Princess Aster is engaged in a courtship that will soon culminate in a marriage proposal. It must be Ambrose."

"And you are the crown princess of the Waterways," Rixana said to Adara. "It is my understanding that Queen Morgana has entrusted the running of her queendom to you in everything but name. I imagine it is your duty to marry mer and stay in Atlantis, rather than enter into a marriage contract with my daughter, Prince Ruyek, Prince Savanna, and Prince Ambrose."

Adara looked at her brother, her eyes filled with sympathy and pain. Caspian's eyes were still closed tightly, but as the attention of the entire room fell to him, he opened them and looked at his sister.

"It has to be me," he said simply.

Adara held his gaze a moment longer before nodding.

"Will anyone stand against this union?" Rixana asked in what was very clearly a challenge.

No one spoke, and somehow, just like that, my momentary freedom was stripped away and I was engaged again. I looked across the room to Ruyek who met my eyes with a smirk I knew all too well.

"The seers have decided the wedding will take place at the autumnal equinox. The prophecy did not specify when this year, but we believe it a fortuitous date," Rixana declared.

And it was a declaration. We all came here like we had a choice to make, but her seers had already set a date for the wedding. Rixana knew this marriage would happen before any of us even knew there was to be a new engagement. I fought the anger that crawled up my spine, the powerlessness that made me furious. This was the way of the new world – and the old world too.

Cordelia

I sat in the room as everyone but my parents and Sabine left us. My anger and grief were living things writhing inside me, pushing against my skin as I stared daggers into my mother. She talked quietly to her general in Acadian. I felt too many things to even eavesdrop. When the door finally closed behind the exiting council, I erupted.

"You will not force me to marry my sisters' widowers!"

My mother held my father's gaze as she spoke to me, as if this wasn't worth her time. "They aren't widowers. None of them married. For all but the mer, it was just a piece of paper that bound them."

"That's what you're focusing on? My word choice?" I slammed a hand on the table.

"It has been decided, Cordelia," my mother said, turning her face back to mine. Her golden eyes were so like mine, but hers had a fiery edge to them that I knew mine did not.

"I won't do this." I looked past her to my father. "Why are you doing this to me?"

"Enough." My mother leaned forward, crowding my vision. "This isn't happening to you. It's happening to all of us. You will do this. I made it abundantly clear *why* you're to do this, why all of the royal houses must agree to this. Were you listening?"

"I won't–"

She interrupted me. "–you will. I am not asking you permission. I was never asking anyone permission. This marriage will happen. The rift will close, and an entire world will be spared.

Your personal emotional comfort with the idea is unimportant in the face of what we must do."

"Please," I whispered, closing my eyes. My sisters' fiances. Caspian – who loved Violetta, who Violetta loved – how could I ever marry him with that between us?

"There is no pleading that will get any of us out of this. They're dead, and this is the only path forward. Accept it willingly or be dragged to it, but the fate of this world cannot be sacrificed for your personal comfort." My mother's voice was that of the witch queen, not my mother. There was no compassion, even when she spoke of my sisters' deaths – the deaths of her children. I knew she was hurting, but she was an expert at putting all of her pain in a box and doing her duty, moving forward – something I had yet to master.

"You have nothing to say?" I asked my father. He had protected me from the marriage pacts ten years ago, refused to let my name be put forth.

My father cleared his throat before speaking. His voice was so deep and soft, so full of all of the emotions my mother was adept at hiding. "We are asking a great sacrifice of you, Cori, and I am sorry for that. But I know you want an end to this war. The seers are sure this is the cost of that peace."

Even he'd fallen in line. If I believed that this union would close the rift, I wouldn't be willing to fight, but it seemed that arguing certainly seemed like I was willing to sacrifice the entire world for my selfishness.

I stood up. "I guess it's decided then."

"I left my world to save the witches." My mother held my gaze as I stepped away. "And that is but one sacrifice over centuries of life. It is the cost of leading them."

I bit down on the need to tell her that I was never supposed to lead. I was fifth in line. I wasn't supposed to and I didn't want to – but I guess all of my own wants and desires were the sacrifice for a crown I never should have inherited.

I instinctively reached for my battle-ax as I walked from the room before remembering my mother forbade me from wearing it tonight. Instead, I rested my right hand on the short sword strapped to my thigh beneath the heavy skirt of my black gown. Nothing felt safe anymore. The attacks on the shadowborn had been increasing since before I was born, but everything was different and I didn't know how I'd ever feel safe again.

"Are you fucking kidding me?" I mumbled as I saw who was waiting for me at the end of the hall.

The president of the North American Mortalborn Alliance leaned against the wall reading a book while her secret service stood a few paces away.

"Cori," she said as I approached, closing her book.

"Madam president," I responded coldly.

She stiffened a bit at my response. "I just wanted to check on you. I'm so sorry. I can't–I don't–" she paused. "I'm not even sure what to say. What comfort can I provide?"

"I don't require comfort from political allies I don't have a personal relationship with, but thank you, I guess."

"Come on." She reached for my arm, but I recoiled. "Why are you looking at me like that?'

"Like what?" I asked, so ready to be done with this conversation.

"Like you hate me." Her words are soft, hurt, and a year ago, it would have moved me.

"I've never had a good poker face."

"I–" At a loss for words, she was still so fucking beautiful that I hated her even more. Her brown eyes dominated her heart-shaped face, and her hair...her fucking hair, thick and black as night, hung nearly to her waist in soft waves. The kind of waves my curls could never achieve.

"Harmonie, let's not do this," I responded. "I am far too fucked up right now to deal with whatever you're trying to do right now. You made a choice and that choice wasn't me. Stop cornering me every time we're in close proximity. And now? Fucking now – if you ever cared about me, don't make tonight any harder than it already is."

"You make it sound so simple. Like I dropped you and chose my career. You know it wasn't that simple." Hurt laced her voice. Hurt that *she* caused. Un-fucking-believable.

"And yet, it would have been that simple to choose me. No one said you couldn't have both. Oh wait! Your campaign manager did. Mortalborn rebellion sympathizers wouldn't vote for you if they found out you were dating the daughter of the witch queen. You made a choice. Live with it. Goddess knows, I've had to." I stepped further down the hall. "And leave me alone. Go fuck your campaign manager. Clearly, he knows exactly what you need."

I left her with tears in her eyes, and I hated that my heart ached despite all the reasons this was her fault, her choice. Six years. We'd been together six years, and it meant nothing compared to her chances of being elected president. Another person who chose me last, just like the fiances I would soon find myself entangled with. My sisters had been their first choice (or at least their parents' first choice), and I was the last princess, the last choice.

My fury led me through the halls and out a side door that led to the back garden. I heard one of the queen's guards behind me, far enough to give me the facade of privacy but close enough to jump in if any shadowborn showed up...not that the queen's guard had been any help the night my sisters died.

Neither had I, though, by that measure. They still died, despite all of my, and our, training and power. They still died.

And no one knows how, a voice inside me whispered – a voice I'd gotten very good at shoving into a box and locking away. Maybe I was more like my mother than I thought.

I walked through the garden towards the stable beyond. More than my sisters had died that night, of course. Five pegasi – five bonded pegasi had died. My sisters' mounts had the good fortune to die with their riders, but Atreyu had died alone, without me. I'd been bonded to Atreyu since I was a child and he was a colt, and while pegasi didn't live nine hundred years, they easily saw a few centuries. His loss was another hole in my chest.

The only salve was a young pegasus with the same parentage, rare for pegasi children. Pegasi didn't mate for life like dragons and rarely recoupled, but Atreyu's sire and dam had three foals over ten years. Aldric was the youngest and had never been bonded. Even with my saddle on his back, he was uncertain of our standing. I'd decided to become his rider out of grief and longing to somehow bridge the loss of Atreyu.

The stable was dark when I entered, but I could hear Aldric pawing at the ground like he sensed my nearness – not bonded yet, but well on our way by sheer will alone. I entered his stall and shushed him as I reached for his brushes. He calmed under my gaze. Neither of us needed light to see each other. Acadia had been a darker world, a world without electricity, and all of Acadia's children could see in the dark.

Aldric was an appaloosa stallion like his brother before him. The black and white patches that covered his fur ended at his large solid black wings. Pegasus wings were massive feathered appendages corded with muscles, strong enough to carry pegasus and rider easily.

I hummed as I ran the brush through his black mane. He leaned his snout against my cheek, and I anthropomorphized his grief, like he felt the loss of Atreyu in the same way I felt the loss of my sisters. It didn't matter that the stallions had rarely interacted and their shared DNA was their only real connection. I wanted someone, anyone, to share my hurt.

My eyes shot open as I heard footsteps outside the door to the stall. I dropped the brush softly in the hay and unsheathed the short sword at my side as the footsteps stopped.

"Are you going to stab me, Cori?" a familiar voice asked.

My shoulders relaxed at Caspian's words.

"Not tonight," I replied, "though the jury is still out if you try to bed me any time soon."

I saw him flinch at my words as he opened the door and stepped into the stall.

"I promise my mind is far from bedding anyone," he replied softly.

"Vi," I said simply.

"Vi," he responded.

I resheathed my sword and motioned for him to grab a brush along the wall. We stood in silence, brushing Aldric down rhythmically in tune to one another's strokes. Eventually, the pegasus was thoroughly brushed and pawed at the ground for our attentions to end. We both put the brushes away and patted the beast a few times before leaving the stall.

My steps echoed Caspian's as we walked back through the dark garden. He motioned at a bench, and we sat next to each other.

"Did you know?" he asked, pain in his voice. "Did you know she was going to do this to us?"

She – my mother.

"I didn't. If she told me before we had a captive audience, I'd have refused her."

He sighed and ran a large hand over his face. "I don't know how we are going to do this. I am broken, Cori, utterly broken. I fear I cannot love you, love any of you."

"Is love required for the rift to close? The fae seers never specified," I responded bitterly.

"The fae seers never specified a lot of things, it seems." His voice wasn't angry. It was resigned. *He* was resigned to whatever fate my mother, his mother and sister, our elders decided for us.

"Were you in love with her?" I don't know why I asked. Of course he was. He had to be in love with her to be so broken over her death. I'd seen them together many times. He'd become my friend because he was around so much, and he was around because he was in love with her.

"I loved her," he said. "I love her still."

I nodded.

We sat on the bench in silence, our legs pressed against one another's. It didn't feel intimate in the way one should feel with their betrothed though. It felt like the intimacy of friends enshrined in loss together. Cas and I were friends, and we were friends because we both loved Violetta. Perhaps our friendship had become our shared loss of her, a dark thing that clung together like a storm.

Ambrose

The vampire prince fell in step beside me as we left the Rose
Room for our chambers. My parents disappeared into a door-

way with the shifter queens to undoubtedly discuss this new arrangement away from the ears of the witch queen. They'd protest together tonight, but I had no doubt they'd already fallen in line.

"Are you ready for this rebound romance?" Prince Ruyek asked, breaking the silence as we walked to our rooms.

"Is romance a necessity for these types of arrangements?" I couldn't keep the disappointment from my voice. I'd built up a marriage and a life with Nadella for the past ten years, and even though she'd never shared the same enthusiasm for our arrangement, I was hopeful love would grow with time. It did for my parents and my grandparents before them. Fae royal marriages were always arranged, but most of the ones I'd witnessed evolved into love matches.

"Romance. Lust. I lose track of the appropriate emotion." Ruyek's ever-present smirk felt hungry as he looked at me.

I shivered. No. No. No. *No.* Four princesses were dead. Romance and lust were a mar to their memories. I didn't speak again until we reached the doors to our rooms, but I did sneak a few glances at the prince walking next to me. He was a bit taller than me, broader too. His sharp cheekbones and almond eyes were artwork come to life, like he'd been carved from stone. I knew he was born in Acadia, and maybe that's why his otherworldliness felt palpable as I looked him over. But then,

I hadn't spent much time around vampires. Everything about them felt *other*.

"Any chance you favor companionship tonight, Prince Ambrose?" Ruyek asked as we paused outside of my door.

"I—I would rather be alone," I stuttered, another shiver running through me that he definitely noticed as his grin widened. Clearly, my protests were not very convincing, even to my own body.

"Another time then." He didn't say it with a lilt at the end because it wasn't a question. I hardened at the sureness of his words.

"Goodnight, Prince Ruyek." I opened the door and closed it hard between us.

I didn't hear his footsteps walk away, but then, vampires could move much more stealthily than even my kind. My heart beat against my chest as I leaned my back against the door. He had to have gone to his room as minutes passed, but still...the thought of him standing there listening to me did something to me.

What was happening to me? I barely knew him, but all my senses were on fire as I thought about his dark eyes and his thick black hair. I imagined running my hands through it, lacing the silk of it between my fingers.

I slid down the door, landing softly on the plush carpet that covered this room. I rubbed myself through my pants as

I strained to listen. And then. There it was: a slight hitch of breath as I freed myself from my soft linen pants.

I bit back a moan at the thought of him listening to me. I couldn't have imagined it. Right? He wanted me, and no one had ever wanted me before. I'd always been too young or too unavailable, betrothed since my fourteenth year of life – I had always belonged to the eldest witch princess. Even if she didn't want me, I'd seen myself as hers and everyone in the fae court had seen the same. I'd had a few offers for dalliances a half a decade ago, but I'd made my position very clear – I was waiting for Nadella. I'd always been waiting for her, and now, she was dead and I had no idea what I was waiting for anymore.

I felt a caress against the inner walls of my mind. *Let me in*, a mass of dark shadows whispered. How did his words seem sensual inside of my head?

You're dangerous, I responded, looking over the vined walls that surrounded all of my memories and thoughts, the sacred part of me I'd been taught to protect from his kind.

That doesn't mean you shouldn't let me in.

A door appeared in the vine walls. It was padlocked from the inside, but it appeared as I looked over the walls at the shadows on the other side. Was I imagining him, or was he really there trying to breach my walls?

Does it matter? His voice was velvet against the thorns that protected my innermost thoughts.

I don't know what you want, I whispered back.

You. Her. Them. Doesn't this arrangement seem like an opportunity for the kind of pleasure you've waited so long for?

The others didn't want me, of that I was sure. The edge of want subsided as I remembered how very little Nadella had wanted me. Would Cordelia be any different? Would Caspian or Savanna?

She is very different from her sister, he said.

How can you hear me? My walls are up!

You're practically shouting your thoughts at me, sweet prince. One of Ruyek's shadows trailed along the wooden door that had appeared between us.

I'm afraid, I admitted, the feeling of fear pounding through me and shaking the ground inside of my mind. What did it mean to open myself up to him? To any of my betrothed?

I won't hurt you. Trust me.

Trusting the dark playboy prince of the Vampire Kingdom seemed like a very naive idea, even by my usual standards. But everyone saw me that way, didn't they? Naive. Childlike. The vampire prince might be the first being to see me like this. Even the few sexual offers years ago had been out of curiosity, an offer to play together like the barely-adult I was then.

You are a man now, Ruyek's shadows said. *And I never really knew you as a child, so this is the only version of you I want to know.*

You're almost a century older than me. My defense was weak in our world. Centuries were decades to magicborn.

Ninety years is not almost a century, surely? he teased. Ninety years of experience, of lovers. What could I offer? *Let me in, Ambrose. I can show you what you can offer me.*

It felt like a command I couldn't ignore, like it hypnotized me. I crawled down the wall of vines and unlocked the chains and locks inside the door with a touch of my hand.

In an instant, he was all around me. I felt his shadows infiltrating my mind with images of his lips on mine, his hands on my cock. In the physical world, I wrapped my hand around my length, but in my mind, it was his hands, larger and rougher than mine. My moan reverberated through my mind and out into my room as his hands — my hands moved up and down my cock.

Think of what I could do to you if you let me inside of your room. His voice was a caress. *Imagine me inside of you, prince—*

I called out as I came in an explosion of pleasure that started in my mind and sprayed out across the soft carpet of the room. Before I could relax, I felt Ruyek's shadows filling my mind, flipping through my memories like a picture book.

No, I whispered as the pleasure ebbed away and panic set in. *No.*

Vines shot out from where I stood just inside the walls of my mind, grasping at shadows that moved too quickly for me to catch.

Get out, I said, softly at first, but as his shadows avoided my vines, my voice grew to a command. *Get out!*

An explosion of flower petals shoved his shadows back through the door, and the door disappeared as the last tendril of darkness crossed the threshold.

You are dangerous, I heaved, out of breath from the exertion of repelling him. Somehow, my victory felt phony, like he'd allowed me to push him back.

His laughter filled my mind, and I wanted to be afraid of him but all I felt was hunger as he retreated. I heard his footsteps outside the door of the room, but I didn't stand up until his door clicked behind him.

What in both worlds had I started by letting him inside my mind?

Ruyek

I fell heavily onto the massive four poster bed in my chambers. Heavy black curtains hung from the sides to block out any sun that may somehow escape the treated windows and the heavy blackout curtains that covered them. Suffice to say, Queen Rixana understood vampire needs quite intimately.

Intimately. My mind went back to the fae prince touching himself while I caressed him inside the walls of his mind. Everything about him stirred me in a way I hadn't felt since the night with Van. Even then, our dalliance had been a fight for dominance more than a claiming. I wanted to claim Prince Ambrose. I tried to listen for him through the walls, but the witch queen had taken precautions with the soundproofing in his castle. I heard only silence.

I awoke in the late morning. My room remained an artificial night as I pulled myself from bed. I hadn't set an alarm and exhaustion weighed heavily as I realized the reason for my awakening. A knock sounded on the door next to mine. *Ambrose's door.* I pulled my pants on from where they lay on the floor and pressed myself against the door to listen.

I heard his door open.

"Good morning," a woman's voice said. "I thought you might want to eat together in my chambers."

Jealousy reared its head as I flung my door open. A dark beautiful head of black curls faced me.

"You're invited too, Prince Ruyek," the witch princess said without turning to me.

I saw red spread across Ambrose's pale cheeks as he looked around her and met my eyes.

"I doubt you have my breakfast of choice," I said as I raked my eyes over the tight jeans and red blouse the princess wore.

At this, she turned to face me. Her golden eyes weren't warm, but I imagined very little about the ice princess was warm – but still, they held an intensity that sparked a fire in me. She had knives strapped to either thigh, and I could see the hilt of a dagger pushing up between her breasts. Dressing down must not really be her forte.

"I have precisely what you prefer for breakfast actually," she replied.

I grinned, sure to reveal my fangs in all their glory.

"Is this a casual meal?" I asked as the princess clearly took in my white tank top and black sweatpants.

"Quite. It's just us, Savanna, and Caspian. I figured we could use a quiet moment after all the noise last night." Her voice was light, but her smile looked forced.

"I think that's a wonderful idea," Ambrose said. He was still wearing flannel sleep pants and a green t-shirt that read *Save the trees for the dryads*. It didn't seem worth pointing out that the dryads had chosen to remain behind in Acadia, and saving trees on this planet hardly helped them through the rift.

"Right." Cordelia nodded and led us down hall after hall in the massive palace. If she was trying to ensure we didn't know the way to her rooms after this journey, she would have to try harder though. I counted every turn and step until we stopped outside of a large, ornate golden door.

"A little gaudy for my tastes," I quipped.

"Mine too," she agreed. "Unfortunately, my parents designed my door and chambers long before I had enough language to explain that to them."

Like so many royals then. Her rooms had been a nursery before being repurposed age after age for her needs. Magicborn monarchs were nothing if not predictable.

The door opened into a large seating room with two black settees and a matching chair around a long rectangular coffee table. A formal table and chairs sat beneath the window at the far end of the room – a window that was most certainly not shuttered and streaming sunlight into the room.

"The windows are treated," Cordelia said as I stopped walking.

"Have the treatments been tested?" I asked, hesitant to trust my skin in a room filled with sunlight.

"Yes. I am assured they passed the most stringent quality tests." Her eyes met mine as I stood frozen to the spot. Our windows were treated in the palace in Venice and my apartments in Rome and Milan, but I rarely tested the treatments by opening the curtains.

"How long has it been since you've seen sunlight?" Prince Caspian asked from where he sat next to Van on one of the settees.

"An age, to be sure." I swallowed the panic in my chest and stepped further into the room.

I felt Ambrose settle in next to me as we walked to the open settee. His magic was plantlife, a forest magic that was surely stifled without sunlight. Suddenly, the growing need I felt for him felt misguided. I was a creature of darkness. What could he ever want with me?

The rays of the sunlight touched my skin as I sat down. I shivered at the caress, but my skin did not blister or burn. Cordelia sat in the empty chair that felt like it was at the head of the coffee table covered in meats, cheeses, fruit, crackers, and vegetables. A carafe of pale wine sat at the edge of the table next to a carafe of thick, sanguine liquid.

A smile spread over my face as I met the princess's eyes.

"I told you I had your preferred breakfast." Her tone was playful, but the plastered-on smile did not reach her eyes.

She was trying then. This was her trying to embrace whatever fuckery her mother threw at us this time. She was doing a much better job than Princess Roselle ever did. We'd been perfect strangers since the betrothal. I reached out to her a few times but was met with only silence.

"Please, eat." Cordelia motioned towards the breakfast laid out before us.

Everyone filled glass plates with food while I poured my breakfast into a large chalice. I sniffed the blood as I swirled it around – mortalborn. They usually fed us bovine blood at royal functions, which sufficed but certainly didn't fully satisfy. Mortalborn blood donors were well-compensated for their part, but a great number of mortalborn balked at the practice of feeding vampires regardless of the competitive compensation.

"So," Prince Caspian said finally after everyone had settled back into their seats with their nourishment of choice. "I suppose we should introduce ourselves properly, maybe attempt to get to know each other."

He looked around to our nods before continuing: "I'm Cas, likely purebred mer, though I've sometimes wondered if I'm powerbound. I spend most of my time in my flat outside of Sydney, but I've spent a considerable amount of time in Philadelphia since...since the first betrothal."

He thought he may be powerbound? What in the name of premature confessions was this? Philadelphia made sense. Violetta and Roselle shared a castle there, or they *had* shared a castle there.

"Can we hear more about you being powerbound?" I asked, never one to miss an opportunity to gather information.

"There isn't much to tell. I don't know my father, and sometimes my magic can be...unpredictable. It just gives me pause." His voice was level, like he wasn't revealing mer court secrets casually over charcuterie.

"Mother dearest uninterested in revealing your sire?" I asked, prodding further.

"Quite uninterested."

Interesting indeed.

"I suppose I can go next with the icebreaker," I said. "Prince Ruyek, definitely all vampire. I unfortunately know both of my parents far better than I'd like. I have a few different apartments in Italy, but I prefer Rome to all the rest. Rome has a hedonistic underbelly that embraces me for who I am."

"And who are you, Prince Ruyek?" Cordelia asked, her eyes boring into me like she'd just given me some test to pass.

"I am everything they say about me in the tabloids, only worse, much worse." My smile did meet my eyes as I met her gaze.

"An insatiable womanizer then?" she asked, a small grin on her face.

"I take offense to that. My exploits descend gender boundaries and *womanizer* completely erases all the men, non-binary, and gender fluid lovers I've successfully *ized* over the years."

"Noted," she said as she popped a grape into her mouth.

I felt Van's eyes flick to mine as Cordelia and I bantered. Yes. He knew about my exploits quite personally, though I also knew he had the same reputation I did in certain circles – just not circles where the princess usually found herself.

"I can go next," Ambrose said meekly from where his leg almost touched mine on our shared settee. "Prince Ambrose, of course. I still live in the palace in the fae court. With the wedding planned for this summer, it seemed wasteful to get my own place."

Ah. So he'd planned to move to Los Angeles with the crown princess after the wedding. Someone should have told her to move her lover out of her mansion before he showed up with suitcases. Was it wrong to think so ill of the dead? I mean, they'd undoubtedly say the same things over my corpse if the roles were reversed. Truth persisted, even after death.

"I prefer Van," the shifter prince said next. "I have spent the last two years living in my flat in Berlin. There's a large magicborn scene in Berlin, and the distance from home allowed me to kind of find my own way, realize who I am and what I want."

"And what do you want?" I asked, genuinely curious.

He cleared his throat before answering. "To see Acadia before we close the rift."

A deafening silence fell over what had been a halfway decent meal amongst not-quite-strangers. I'd been inside the shifter prince before, and I had no idea he harbored such fancies. Going back to Acadia wasn't anything magicborn ever talked about. It was an obsolete desire, a door we'd closed when we crossed the rift. Our only goal for the past century had been to close it permanently, to seal ourselves on this planet.

I looked at him in the ensuing silence, really looked at him. He was a bear of a man, no shifter pun intended. He was well over six and a half feet tall, broad and muscular. Acadian words were tattooed in black ink on his biceps. I'd traced that tattoo with my fingers once and asked him why he chose words about a home he'd never even seen.

He'd chosen mortalborn words for his Acadian tattoo, which seemed even stranger, a Faulkner quote: *How often have I lain beneath rain on a strange roof, thinking of home.* It was easy to forget that Van was the only college-educated among us though. He'd attended a mortalborn university in England and received a degree in literature.

"I didn't think going back was an option," Cordelia finally said, her voice a whisper.

"I don't know if it is," Van acquiesced. "But I still want to go, even if that want is only ever unfulfilled."

"Do you remember Acadia?" Ambrose asked, his eyes on me.

I was the only one here who had ever seen our home world, I suppose. What was there to say? It was a different world in every way that mattered. The sun was small and red, dim enough that I remembered running outside in the daylight as a small child. Two moons filled the night sky, and there were entire species of magicborn this world had never seen: centaurs, dryads, harpies, satyrs, pixies, halflings, and all manner of faerie. It was colder too. Winter was long and summer was brief. A cold sun made even our summers breezy and cool. It was home in a way this world would never be for me, even if I'd found my own place here and learned to fill myself with all the delights this planet had to offer.

I could have said all of that, but I didn't. Sharing Acadia felt like the most personal parts of me laid bare before four people I barely knew. Even my night with Van had been a night of delight, not a night of exploring who we are beyond the physical.

"It has been a very long time, and I was a very young child when we left." My words were true, but the lie by omission was likely obvious to everyone with ears.

"I see," Ambrose said with a nod.

"Cordelia," I said with a grin, "I believe it's your turn for introductions."

She watched me intently a moment before speaking.

"Cori," she said with an awkward wave. "Fifth daughter of the witch queen and somehow, heir to the throne. I am in D.C. only when I am required, and live a few hours south in Richmond."

"Your father's from Richmond, isn't he?" I asked, filing all thoughts of Acadia away.

"He is, yes."

"Is the great scar still there?" Ambrose asked. His voice was inquisitive, like he had no idea what kind of history he was asking Prince Consort Darius' daughter to reveal.

"It is." She threw back her glass of wine after speaking.

We fell back into breakfast silently. I drained the carafe of blood she'd acquired for me before excusing myself.

"We leave after sunset," Cori said as I reached the door.

"We've all agreed on Richmond then?" I asked tensely.

"Maybe not forever, but it seems smart to stay close to D.C. until the wedding."

I looked her over once before nodding and leaving the room. It was decided then: new relationships, new home, new life, all within a twelve-hour period. The witch princess already seemed to hold all of the sway her mother did when it came to reigning over my life.

Caspian

Cori'd fallen in line. Vi had the same look, the same resigned *let's make the best out of this shitshow* look on her face the morning after my first betrothal. That's why we decided to try to love each other, to find something worth loving in a situation that neither of us chose. It was easy to see all the ways in which Cori was different from her sisters, but in this moment, I saw all of their sameness.

Vi and Cori both had thick, black curls and freckles across their cheeks. Cori's skin was a different hue, but her freckles were so like Vi's. They only shared a mother, but the witch queen's daughters all carried more of her than I realized before I saw Cori follow the same path as Vi. They obeyed their mother; for all the fury I'd seen in Vi and now Cori – all the anger they harbored for their mother's absolute control over everyone and everything...they still followed her. To what end? For Vi, it had been an end of no return. For Cori? I guess we'd find out together. I shivered at the thought.

I watched the vampire prince...Ruyek. I guess I had better start using his name now that he was going to be one of my husbands. I watched his demeanor change as the conversation turned to Acadia. I never considered what it must have felt like to leave a world where you could stand beneath the rays of the sun for a world of only nighttime. The first vampires must have suffered terribly when they stepped through the rift. I wonder if they sent word to the others to shield their skin from the deadly rays of this new world.

I watched as he danced through all of those memories in his head and then avoided the opportunity to share any of that with us. He tried to come back from wherever his mind went, but Cordelia brought him right back when she mentioned Richmond. Another choice taken from him, maybe? Just like the choice to leave Acadia?

You need better shields. I heard a shadowy voice in my head as Ruyek left the room.

You need a better poker face. There's no need to read your mind when it's written all over your face, I replied before a wall of water surrounded my mind and pushed the vampire out of my head.

Cori's eyes followed him out of the room. Her poker face was much better. I thought I saw grief, but there was something else there too. Concern? Hurt? Whatever it was, she pushed it away when the door clicked behind Ruyek and turned to us.

"Let's discuss flying arrangements." Her commander's voice seemed to bring all of us back to her.

"I won't need a mount," Savanna said with a smile.

"I can't wait to see what you whip up." Cori's smile seemed a little more genuine than earlier. "Pegasus okay, Cas?"

I nodded.

"Ambrose, have you ridden a pegasus before?" I asked.

His eyes were wide as he looked from me to Cori and shook his head.

"A horse?" Cori asked.

"Many fae can translocate. It's laborious to bring another with you, but we have many in our service who are willing," he responded.

I watched as a flower bud at the base of his antlers began to open its petals. The fae wielded such curious magic.

"Any chance you can translocate?" Cori asked.

"I–well, at least not yet." His eyes traveled down to his lap. Shame, maybe?

"You haven't begun the ripening?" Savanna asked, oblivious to the clear embarrassment turning the fae prince...Ambrose's cheeks scarlet.

"There have been some signs I may begin soon." His voice was small and his eyes stayed downcast.

"There's no shame in that," Cordelia said, saving him whatever damage we were doing with this conversation. "I'm still in it."

"Me too," I offered.

Most magicborn entered the ripening in their mid-twenties. It started slowly. Our magic began to manifest more completely as the depth of our power deepened, and then, months or years or even a decade after it began, it ended. We hit the floor of whatever we'd become and came fully into it.

"Is that why your magic has been unpredictable?" Ambrose asked, his forest green eyes meeting mine.

"It is. It responds in ways I haven't seen other mer magic respond," I answered honestly.

"And you have no leads on who your father is? Truly?" Savanna asked, his mismatched feline eyes turning towards me.

"None. I think Adara might know, but she avoids me so completely when I ask that it's almost like there's a geas on her."

All eyes were on me after that. Oversharing. It's what happened when the nerves set in for me. Or when the grief was too muddy. A lot of both seemed to be happening recently.

"I like Adara," Cori said, an observation that seemed to bring the moment back into focus. "She seems powerful and hungry, like she might eat the whole world if it got in her way."

Vi liked her too, I wanted to say, but cracking open that box with Cori seemed dangerous. I saw all the ways Cori and Vi were alike, but I feared that such a comparison would only keep Vi's ghost closer than she already was.

"Adara is a force to be reckoned with," I said instead.

"So, you can't translocate and you can't ride," Cori said, bringing us all back to Ambrose.

He can ride with me, a voice said in my head.

Fucking stop that, I demanded before shoving the mass of shadows out again. He did have a good point though.

"Let him ride with Ruyek," I echoed aloud.

Savanna tilted his head in thought. "Isolde is a much easier mount than a pegasus," the shifter said.

"And Ruyek won't let you fall to your death." Cordelia smiled again. Her smile was very different from Vi's. Vi's smiles were soft and infrequent, a rare thing, but even in the midst of all this loss and uncertainty, Cori was generous with her smiles.

Ambrose looked a bit terrified.

"We'll make sure you're strapped into the saddle," I offered.

"Right, of course." Ambrose nodded, and I suddenly had the feeling that his fear was not the dragon but Ruyek.

Curious. He hadn't seemed afraid of him when they were sitting next to each other. He didn't even seem uncomfortable, the opposite really. Ahh...so it was fear of what might happen on the back of that dragon then. This time, it was my mouth tugging into a smile.

There was so much hurt and grief in this room, but here was a man in the early throes of attraction. And if I was being honest, his flushed cheeks and the blooming flower at the base of his antlers was beautiful in the ethereal way only fae could be. No witch, mer, shifter, or vampire was the same work of art the fae were, and I'm not sure I ever realized that until I found myself counting the freckles on Ambrose's cheeks the morning after our worlds were upended *again* by the witch queen.

Ambrose

I spent the rest of the day alone in the queen's rose gardens. I assumed the rest of my partners were likely sleeping, preparing for the second long night in a row. *Partners*. It was all surreal. I had never had a single partner, and suddenly, I had four. Better yet: none of them seemed to despise me. They comforted me when I felt ashamed about the ripening.

My heart ached because I would have given so much for Nadella to have extended that kindness to me when she was alive. And maybe she would have. After the wedding, when we returned to the palace that would be our home...maybe she would have *tried*. Her death meant I'd never get to know. She could only ever truly be the woman who rejected me, resented me, hated every second of our engagement. And I ached at that realization.

The garden was a juxtaposition of young blooming roses and tulips closing, their natural bloom completed as they prepared to make seeds for the next generation. It was the middle of May, and color splashed itself around me like a kaleidoscope. I admired the queen's garden for the variety and abundance, but also for the lack of over pruning to extend the blooming stage. Everything had its own natural season, and there was beauty in allowing the flowers the freedom to exist wildly.

This royal garden was not manicured and tamed like the mortalborn preference. It was a window into a hillside of wildflowers, a glimpse of a wilder world lost long before we came through the rift. I'd seen pictures of the rose garden that once stood here against a white mansion and a history so foreign it seemed like a fairy tale. That garden had been one of straight lines and short grass, a portrait of the control mortalborn forced on everything they held power over.

I shivered. Until more powerful creatures bent them to their will. It was easy to see all the good the witch queen had done here. Magicborn, mortalborn, and powerbound alike did not go hungry or without medical care. Children were clothed and cherished in schools that flourished with proper funding. Everyone was housed and strong support programs ensured very few people fell through the cracks of the government machine the witch queen brought with her. But there were sacrifices for this utopia. Mortalborn died beneath her boot if they did not bend the knee, and worse still, shadowborn were merciless monsters unleashed on a world that had never encountered such darkness.

Where we all fit in the scales of judgement always made me shiver. It was easy to see ourselves as saviors to this world. How many animals avoided extinction because my father's court took the lives of poachers and imposed impossible fines and prison sentences on corporate leaders who refused to stop destroying the natural world around them? How many shorelines and coastal communities avoided remapping when rising seas were halted and ice caps refroze?

The cost was not too high for me because I'd never lived in a world where my father was not king and final voice over the natural world. But for a world that had known freedom? Even if they'd often sold it to the highest bidders in the name of democracy – what had losing that freedom felt like? Had that cost been too high? The bands of rebel mortalborn constantly put down or imprisoned (with restorative practices and processes often imposed by vampires with the ability to truly change hearts and minds) thought none of our advancements had been worth the loss of that ideal they held so closely.

What did I know? That's what it always came back to when my mind took these moral detours. *Nothing.* A feminine voice echoed in my head, a voice that had rarely deemed to speak to me but one that had become the sound of all of my self-doubt and loathing. *You know nothing. You never did, just as you are nothing.*

Was it cruel that Nadella's voice lived on only in my darkest thoughts? She'd never been particularly cruel to me. She just didn't want me, didn't want my hand or the prophecy that had chopped up her chances of happiness…had taken her freedom away. I shivered again, though the air was warm and no breeze blew.

Night came and I found myself behind the castle standing in front of a massive stable. Cordelia, Savanna, and Caspian talked about the wind and the riding conditions around me, but I looked for Ruyek. He finally appeared after Cordelia and Caspian saddled and mounted their pegasi.

"Nice of you to join us," Savanna said with a smile I couldn't decipher.

"You know I don't need the flying time you do. Isolde can cover twice the distance in half the time," Ruyek replied with a smirk. His sour mood from earlier seemed to have improved with some rest.

"Want to race?" Savanna said, stepping back from the group.

We all watched as his brown skin melted and popped into another form, a massive form that made all of us flinch a little. The pegasi, at the least, did not seem bothered at all when a large black dragon took shape where the shifter prince had just been. His feathered wings shimmered as they caught the moonlight as his pointed, almost beak-life mouth screamed into the night like the giant bird of prey dragons resembled.

"Show off," Ruyek said affectionately. He whistled and two pairs of massive wings flapped towards us. Ruyek's black and dark purple dragon and the red dragon that followed her every move descended to the ground before us. They were massive creatures and fear bubbled inside of me as the red dragon snapped in my direction.

Drystan, Ruyek's voice whispered in my head. *Isolde's mate is called Drystan, and he will use your fear against you. Dragons are intelligent creatures, and they only bend to those who can control them. If you let him feel your fear, he may very well end up controlling you.*

"Is everything in vampire culture about control?" I asked aloud, pushing Ruyek's voice out of my mind with vibrant blooms and walls of tree of vine.

"You catch on quickly." Ruyek's smile was toothy, a striking display of bright white fangs.

Striking – that was one word to describe the prince before me.

"Come now." Ruyek placed his foot in the stirrup of the massive saddle on Isolde's back and offered me his hand. The moment his fingers closed around mine, I was airborne, swinging up onto the dragon's back as Ruyek's arm slid around me and pulled me in front of him in the saddle. His speed and finesse with the maneuver was something only a vampire could mimic.

My stomach plummeted as I realized how high we were off the ground. Before I could think too much on what falling would do to me, my eyes caught on the black dragon as Savanna shifted again into a large reddish-brown hawk.

"Show off," Ruyek repeated with a chuckle.

A moment later, the pegasi were off the ground as Cordelia and Caspian flew south.

"Dragons are much faster than pegasi. I wasn't lying about that. Let us take the scenic route, shall we?" Ruyek's lips were pressed close to my ear, so close I could feel his breath as his arm tightened around me. And then we were ascending towards the black velvet sky.

I fought the urge to vomit as feathers flapped around us. The male dragon fell back and out of sight as we turned away from the path the pegasi took. I wanted to talk, but I didn't trust myself to open my mouth as Isolde carried us into the night.

A dark shadow appeared along the edges of my mind. *There are benefits to not forcing me out, you know.*

I pulled my blooms in just far enough for Ruyek to step into the meadow of my mind. I was a flower, or maybe a tree; I was something alive and green and scared as I stepped through my springtime gates and faced him.

You can go no further, I demanded, my mind's voice far steadier than my actual voice had ever been.

I promise to go only where I am invited, Ruyek's shadows replied.

Where are we going?

Southwest then east. Have you ever seen the Appalachian?

His shadows wrapped around me as we spoke.

Never, I answered.

Mountains older than the rings on saturn, than life on this planet.

Show me, I whispered. Even in my mind, I felt suddenly breathless.

Anything, he responded before tightening his arm around me as Isolde burst forth with incomprehensible speed.

I stopped counting the wingbeats around the time we surpassed two hundred...also around the time my stomach finally settled down, and I became acutely aware that I could feel an erection pressed against my ass and lower back.

Tell me why you abstained for a woman that made her position on your marriage very clear. His voice was in my head again, but he only stood in the little space I allowed for him. His shadows did not press any further.

She was going to be my wife. Black dahlias bloomed along the space between us in my mind, inching closer to his shadows.

Are you mortalborn? Our gods do not forbid pleasures of the flesh, you know. And even the mortalborn are shit at following any rules surrounding sex.

Gods. Ruyek followed the old gods. I knew some vampires did, but colloquially, everyone only ever spoke about the goddess in mixed company...a goddess who seemed to have abandoned us when we came through the rift.

He waited while I searched for a way to explain, his shadows gently caressing the black blooming flowers on the rich green plain of my mind.

I– it hurt that she never gave me a chance, that she so openly betrayed the marriage we were both bound to, and in my kinder moments, I ached for her. She loved someone else. She didn't want this, and I knew if I fell into any kind of romance with someone else, neither of us would want our marriage. My chest ached at the admission, like I was splitting myself open in finally admitting a sacred truth.

And, he responded when I fell silent, *if neither of you wanted the arrangement, it never stood a chance.*

I answered with silence, but I didn't have to agree. It was the truth. Plain as day when I laid just a little bit of my truth bare. I focused on the steady pressure of his arm around me as warmth pooled in my eyes. Graciously, the wind carried it all away just as we dipped lower. Isolde carried us towards the ground in a terrifying plunge, but she leveled out just as ridges along the earth came into view.

The Appalachian weren't the Andes. The mountains of home were one of the highest mountain ranges on Earth, but the rolling hills and stretches of wild trees beneath us were beautiful. Different but beautiful. They showed their age, a bit like the mortalborn who once ruled over this planet.

"Are you thinking of home?" Ruyek asked, this time his lips were pressed against my ear to ask aloud.

"Yes and no," I responded.

"Hmmm. Let me guess. You always knew you'd be leaving home this year, so this is just the logical next step. Alien mountains. Alien landscapes. This part is the only part you anticipated."

I felt his cheek move against the high point of my ear as his lips surely curled into a smile.

"I did not anticipate riding on a dragon with the prince of vampires. This part is quite unexpected."

"You're unexpected," he said.

"I–" My words stopped as I felt his large hand move lower.

"Can I touch you?" he asked softly. "Really touch you this time?"

I was paralyzed with indecision and...fear, I think. What did I know about being touched by a man who had screwed hundreds of magicborn? What did I know about any of this? What did I have to offer someone with that kind of experience?

"You needn't do anything back. This isn't an exchange of services. I just want to feel you, really feel you. Last night was barely a taste."

Last night when he'd wrapped himself around my mind while I touched myself.

"Okay."

"I need an enthusiastic yes, sweet prince."

"Yes. Please, yes," I whispered, but my answer felt like a beg I didn't intend.

His hand traveled lower, slowly. So slowly I didn't know if he was teasing me or holding back. I was aware of his fingers as he lifted up my shirt and laid his hand flat against my belly, just as I was aware of his lips against my ear and his dick pressed against me. But all of those sensations muted as he slipped his hand into my loose pants, and all I could feel was long, soft fingers dancing against my length.

A sharp intake of breath – mine and his – as he gripped me.

Fuuuccck. His voice echoed in my mind, the shadows dancing over the flowers between us now, caressing them as he moved his hand.

What do you want? he asked me, but I couldn't answer as my breaths came quicker. No one had ever touched me, and I had never touched myself the way he was touching me. His wrist rolled as he stroked me fast and faster, pressing me against his palm and squeezing my tip as he moved.

What do you want? he asked again.

"I want–" My words trailed off. I was too close to manage mindspeak. His hand was moving so quickly, so firmly. I wanted him to keep doing this, that's what I wanted, but I couldn't find the words as I clenched, breath stopping as every sensation narrowed to my pelvis. I came with a gasp, a desperate wanting I had never felt in my life before.

You want me, don't you? he asked as my cum poured across his hands and into my pants.

My defenses weakened as euphoria burst through me, pleasure taking over every muscle in my body. I felt his shadows reach deeper in my mind, but I was too liquid to fight back. He showed me a dream, like a memory of a moment I hadn't lived through – we were naked on a massive bed, and he was even more gorgeous than I imagined. I watched as he moved behind me and pressed a pierced cock against my entrance.

You want this? he growled through my mind as he entered me – and I was cumming again, warm against us both as he pulled me out of my mind and into reality.

"I want you too," he whispered against my ear as Isolde climbed higher again, changing the direction of our flight.

The Appalachian Mountains were beautiful, but I was far more interested in the dark prince with red almond-shaped eyes behind me.

Savanna

It took a little over two hours for me to reach Richmond. The city came into view slowly, a sprawling metropolis surrounded by suburbs. It looked different than before my kind came through the rift, but then, the whole planet was different. Greenery climbed out of windows and along buildings and every building had solar panels atop it. Abandoned highways had been replaced with communal gardens that criss-crossed and circled the architecture of the city.

The personal car had been the first to go when our parents established their dominion over this world. Buses, trains, communal aeromobile flying vehicles, and mounted animals had replaced them under new environmental protection laws. Animal welfare laws came next, assuring that the horses that suddenly found themselves a major mode of transportation were well-cared for and the witches and vampires ensured heavy sentences for those who broke these laws.

Richmond was different from all the other cities transformed by magicborn laws. When I arrived that night (somehow ahead of the pegasi and dragon, by my own observation), what had only been revealed through pictures and paintings was far uglier than even a crisp photograph could reveal.

The scar ran the entire length of the city north of the river on the eastside. The ground was black and barren, without a single light to illuminate it in the darkness. No houses or stores sat on the land Queen Rixana had blasted the full strength of her power into in the final subjugation of this world. The burned ground hadn't been empty a century ago though. Houses, schools, businesses, and approximately thirty thousand mortalborn soldiers had been standing in the East End when Rixana burned all of it down with molten fire hotter than dragonfire.

She burned every structure, being, tree, and blade of grass to the ground so completely that nothing had ever regrown. Fae magic could certainly have encouraged the earth to regenerate in the area, but Rixana insisted the scar remain, as a reminder of what she would do if the mortalborn rose against her ever again.

Somehow, a mortalborn man whose family had been from the East End had fallen in love with Rixana over half a century later. He was a young politician then, from what I understood, who meant to stand up to her and demand his community be rebuilt. Instead, he was the one who fell...into her and in line.

I perched atop an ancient clock tower that connected to a train station. The station still had people in it this time of night. Without personal cars, people were always coming and going at train stations. Aeromobile taxis flew above the city, their solar panels using energy stored from the day to move them in the darkness.

The scar wasn't exactly empty tonight. I ruffled my feathers and watched with keen hawk eyes as two vampires spoke to a mortalborn man in the otherwise desolate burned space. I shifted into a barn owl as I moved closer to hear well enough to distinguish their conversation.

"Please," the mortalborn begged. He was young and his cheeks were hollow like he hadn't eaten well in months. His blonde hair hung down his back in a limp curtain of messy curls.

"What will you give us in exchange?" the taller vampire asked. His red hair was cut close to his scalp, highlighting his high cheekbones and moonlight white skin.

The second vampire moved behind the mortalborn, tracing a pale hand along the mortalborn's spine.

"Anything," the mortalborn pleaded again, "please."

What happened next made sense once I realized the emaciated man was a thrall. Feeding directly from mortalborn was frowned upon in polite society, but it wasn't illegal. The pain and pleasure of a vampire's venom was intoxicating – something I knew quite intimately. Magicborn could usually experience it without the addiction, but mortalborn did not possess such strength.

I watched in awe as the black-haired vampire behind the mortalborn lifted him easily, pressing him against his vampire companion. In one swift movement, the mortalborn's pants were off and the vampire's cock was free and covered with his own saliva and venom, no doubt. The vampire paused before entering the man, nodding to the redhead. The vampire cradled the man against him a moment before sinking his teeth into his neck as the man behind the mortalborn pushed into him.

The sound of the mortalborn's pleasure seemed to tear into the night as he leaned against the vampire feeding him while the other held him up and pounded into him. It might not have been illegal to feed directly from mortalborn, but as I watched the vampires take turns feeding from and fucking the mortalborn, I began to think that it should be. Vampire venom was a high no mortalborn drug could come close to, an addiction that drove mortalborn to madness.

Eventually, the mortalborn thrall would refuse all necessary sustenance and exist only in yearning between vampire encounters. And one day, the thrall would disappear from these streets. Whether he would die of emaciation or succumb to the inevitable blood loss from being constantly available to bloodsuckers was a mystery the magicborn authorities had invested no resources into figuring out.

When the two vampires finished with the mortalborn, they dropped him to the barren ground and left him in his inebriated state. I could hear him pleading still for more. He was so thin, so strung out that I was sure his life was numbered in days. I watched a moment more as a third vampire approached the mortalborn. She was smaller than the ones who had come before her but the six inch heels she wore certainly gave her a similar perspective.

I'd seen enough.

I turned my back and flew towards the castle built on an island on the south side of the city. The mortalborn had called it Belle Isle, and it had transformed from military-era prison to a preserved outdoor space over the centuries before we came through the rift. Now, a massive castle of dolomite walls, high towers, and gothic architecture stood on the island. The gray stone was local to the area, and it set the castle apart from the glass, metal, and red brick of the rest of the city.

Shortly after I landed on the top of a high tower, the pegasi flew into view. I waited for them to land in front of the stables behind the castle before flying down to join Cori and Cas.

"Change of clothes?" Cori asked as she dismounted and took me in as a barn owl.

I shifted back into my humanoid form. "Barn owls hear better than hawks, and there was a very interesting interaction in the scar, one worth hearing clearly."

"Peter?" Cori asked, her eyes sympathetic.

"Excuse me?"

"The mortalborn thrall who frequents the scar is named Peter. Did he have blonde hair?" she asked.

"He did. I hate to tell you this, but I don't think he has many nights left." My voice was sympathetic now that I knew she knew him well enough to know his name.

"We tried to get him treatment, but he refused to go to rehab."

Cas crossed the distance from the pegasus he rode and placed a hand on Cori's shoulder. "Treatment is almost never successful for thralls."

"It certainly can't be successful when he refuses to try," she responded with a downturn of her lips.

"We should get inside," Cas said, looking at the black sky ominously.

Cori nodded. We traveled without a farewell to avoid any news coverage of our journey. After the deaths of the four witch princesses, it seemed prudent to keep our movements quiet when possible. Everyone had known where the witch royals were when they'd been attacked. A watching world was dangerous with shadowborn passing through the rift.

Cori gave us a tour of her castle. It was different than I imagined. The outside screamed traditional Acadian royal, but the inside was all modern. Clean edges, whites and blacks with minimalist decor punctated every room. Art hung on the walls, but it was all paintings of pegasi, dragons, and Acadia. Nothing particularly grandiose. It all seemed thoughtfully curated and selected.

"This is my own wing. There are five bedrooms around common areas. The four I used to keep for my sisters have been cleared out and redecorated for all of you." Her voice did not betray emotion, but the twitch of her mouth did. She wanted to frown again, to sink into the despair I knew she was barely keeping at bay.

"Are you sure?" Cas asked, his voice soft. "There are other rooms in the castle. We don't have to occupy their rooms."

"I am sure. They rarely stayed anyway. The rooms were more symbolic than anything. Now, at least, I will not be surrounded by four empty rooms." The twitch of her mouth was gone and a mask of strength slipped back into place.

"Which one was–" Cas began.

"–you don't want to know that," Cori interrupted. "Please do not ask or try to figure it out. For your sake and mine."

His ocean-blue eyes held her golden gaze a moment before he nodded. Knowing which room had been his fiance's would eat him alive. I agreed with Cori. He didn't want to know, and while I had never been close with Atasia, I didn't want to know either. It was easier to focus on the here and now.

The wing beats of dragons forced us away from the ghosts.

Cori picked up with her tour when a very-disheveled Prince Ambrose and a very smug Ruyek entered the castle. Rue was wasting absolutely no time with the fae prince apparently. I doubted anyone else could smell the proof of his escapades, but even in this form, my senses were all heightened. I met Rue's eyes and he smiled.

We could both take him, you know. He'd let us, Ruyek said in the tiny clearing of jungle I saved for his mindspeak conversations.

Just because he'd let us doesn't mean we should. He's starved for attention, I responded.

Wrong. His family heaped attention on him. He's starved for touch, for wanting, and he deserves to be adored.

He deserved to be adored? I'd never heard the vampire prince talk about anyone like that. I pushed him out and returned to the conversation all of us could partake in.

"The gym is here," Cori said as she opened a massive door into an even more impressive room.

The gym had a large empty space in the middle, exercise equipment circled the perimeter of the room, and weapons racks covered every bit of reachable wall surface. A rack of ten different double-sided battle-axes was mounted closest to the door. The battle-ax across Cori's back had a wooden handle but a variety of materials were used in the weapons selection on the wall.

I stepped towards the weapons reverently. I'd always been a fan of blades. They had the finesse of Acadia in them. Guns and bullets had been the weapon of choice for the mortalborn before the magicborn had confiscated and outlawed them. The artillery was only a minimal threat to the magicborn, but they remained a constant threat to the mortalborn of all ages. Despite the law, I noticed a rack of long-barreled guns at the back of the gym.

I picked up a battle-ax with a smooth, black metal surface and tested the weight in my hand. It was lighter than the wooden one on Cori's back. I was sure of that. The material was lightweight and strong.

"Titanium," Cori said, stepping up next to me.

"Seems like a better choice," I responded, nodding to the weapon on her back.

"My weapon is made of Acadian ash wood, reinforced with druid magic," Cordelia answered. "No mortalborn metal can mirror its strength."

"And you're sentimental." Rue smiled as he spoke, stepping into our proximity with Ambrose close to his side. Cas was across the room inspecting the guns. Curiosity was always a pull for the mer prince.

"Aren't we all?" Cori responded, her eyes raking over Ruyek's body curiously.

Whatever tension had existed between them that morning had dissipated. We weren't directly talking about Acadia, but we were certainly skirting the edges of the conversation that led to Ruyek storming out of breakfast.

"Tis the fate of refugees," Rue replied.

Cordelia answered with a *hmmm* before running her hand along the handle of the axe in my hand. "I can't argue with the craftsmanship though, this weapon is beautiful. You're welcome to it if you want," she said to me.

"I'm more of a claws and teeth kind of guy," I chuckled.

"Surely you're weapon trained?" Ambrose asked, pulling all of our eyes to him.

"Extensively," I answered, "but it is still not my preferred mode of defense."

"Or attack," Rue grinned.

"Are you weapon trained?" Cori asked the fae prince.

"I–the fae leave the weapons to their warriors, but I know that is not the case in other courts." His cheeks were red beneath the smattering of freckles that I certainly understood Ruyek's attraction to.

"Kingdoms, not courts," Rue replied.

"Queendoms," Cori argued with a tilt of her chin towards the ceiling.

"Point taken," Ruyek obliged with a nod.

We all slowly dispersed around the gym, inspecting the weaponry and equipment. Ambrose stayed close to Ruyek, but the rest of us spread out. Just as Cas started to put reps up, a mortalborn servant opened the door and stepped into the room.

"A visitor, your highness," the dark haired mortalborn bowed dramatically toward Cori before realizing we were all *your highnesses* and bowing in each of our directions in turn.

"It's nearly midnight," Cori said with a frown.

"There's a Maria Flores to see you, your highness. She says it's quite urgent," the servant replied.

"Nadella's lover," Cori said with a guilty flick of her eyes towards Ambrose. "We'll meet her in the throne room."

"Bringing out the throne room for an intimate meeting with your sister's girlfriend?" Ruyek asked.

"I've never spoken to Maria before in my life. If she's here after what happened to her source of support, I am sure she's here for a royal audience." Cori's words weren't cruel but they were direct. The mortalborn was likely adrift in the world after Nadella's death, and this call was most certainly a plea for royal charity.

Cordelia

There was only one throne in my throne room. This castle was mine, just as Richmond was my own foray into ruling.

Since it was usually just me, the singular throne had never mattered, but as the four princes stood behind the large obsidian throne, I wondered if it was time to install a few more – since they'd be my *husbands*. I wanted to shiver at the thought. I hadn't been with any man in years, and I never imagined tying myself to one, let alone four, magicborn men. I'd always stuck with mortalborn lovers – though I wasn't entirely sure why.

A servant and a guard escorted the mortalborn woman into the throne room once we'd all settled. Maria Flores wasn't anything like I'd imagined. Despite being nearly three hundred years old, Nadella had looked to be in her early to mid-thirties. Magicborn aged, as was evidenced in my mother's wrinkles and graying hair, but the speed at which magicborn telomeres broke down was glacial.

Maria was not the pristine, young woman I'd imagined when I heard Nadella had kept her mortalborn lover, despite the political reasons not to after being engaged to Prince Ambrose. Maria looked to be in her mid to late forties. Her thick black hair was streaked with gray, and her deep brown eyes were framed with a few lines. She was short and curvy, with the natural weight of mortalborn decades settled on her frame. She was beautiful, but she was not the L.A. model I'd envisioned.

"Your royal highness," she said as she reached the bottom of the dais my throne sat on. She curtsied low with a sureness of having knelt between royalty before.

"Ms. Flores," I said with a nod of my head. "What brings you across the country to my home?"

Her confidence and sureness did not waver, despite the underlying tone of annoyance I couldn't stifle when I spoke.

"I am sure you know of my relationship with Nadella," she said, her brown eyes boring into me like she had some accusation to make. "But I am not sure you know the true nature of it." She looked to the fae prince before continuing. "Nadella was my wife. I have all the legal documentation to prove it, if you need to see it."

"Wife?" Ambrose whispered behind me. I felt his hand grasping the top of my throne like he might stumble without the support.

"Ms. Flores, my sister is not here to speak for herself, and as we all know, she was legally and politically bound to Prince Ambrose of the Fae Court. I find it hard to believe she was married to a mortalborn woman without my mother knowing of it," I responded, my eyes locked on her.

"Queen Rixana was well aware of our marriage, but as you know, polygamy is not illegal and she simply told us to keep it quiet until Nadella married Ambrose. She had some vision of us all working it out together after their wedding."

"Impossible," Ruyek said behind me. "There is no way the witch queen kept this quiet."

Maria held up her hand and with a flick of her wrist, a paper appeared in her hand. Not just a mortalborn then. Maria was a magician. I nodded for the guard to bring me the paper. I felt the eyes of the princes over my shoulder as I read the marriage license.

"You've shown your hand too easily," Ruyek said again before I could speak. "We all know you are fully capable of forging a very clever looking contract since you dabble in power that doesn't belong to you."

"Your prejudice against magicians doesn't change the fact that Nadella and I have been married for seven years, and we have three children together," Maria responded. "We used a powerbound donor, but she's their mother just as much as I am."

Nadella had children? Mostly mortalborn children at that – and I had no idea. How – how was that possible? I couldn't make sense of what she was telling me.

"You'll understand if we have to speak with Queen Rixana before believing you," Cas said as the silence stretched on without a word from me. What could I even say?

"I don't really care if you believe me. I came to warn you." Maria's gaze was harsh. Was she angry we didn't easily believe that Nadella had an entire family we – *I* – her own sister – had never known existed?

The guard stepped closer to the woman, her own power brimming below the surface as if ready to strike the magician if her warning turned out to be a threat.

"You have our attention," I finally said.

"Is there a place we could talk more–" Maria looked to the guards in the room and the servants before continuing. "–privately?"

I felt a mass of shadows pushing against my mind. I didn't even pause at Ruyek's intrusion. Instead, I opened up a small clearing for him outside of the walls of solid ice and permafrost that protected all the secrets of my mind from him.

Bind her magic if you take her away from this room, and bring us with you. I do not trust her, the vampire's voice whispered in my mind, as if Maria could hear our mindspeak if it was not whispered.

I know how you feel about magicians, and it is prejudiced, I responded. *But you're right to be cautious. We don't know anything about her or why she's here.*

"We can speak in my council room, but you must consent to binding," I said aloud.

Maria's lip twitched, her only tell before nodding in agreement. The binding was simple enough. A guard left the room before returning with a green, acrid-smelling vial of green liquid. I could smell it the moment the guard reentered the room.

My own magic recoiled inside me at the scent, trying to push away from the fae magic that could stifle anyone's magic.

Maria kept her eyes locked on me as she took the vial and drank it in one gulp. Her eyes watered, but she did not gag. I'd trained under the influence of magic binding. It was a normal training routine to ensure I learned to fight hand to hand, weapon to weapon, without the use of my own magical abilities. I gagged every single time the liquid passed my lips.

My guard led the six of us through a door behind the dais. We passed through a long hallway before coming to a large door made of the same stone as the castle itself. The guard opened the door and then stood next to the entrance as we all entered my council room. It was similar to my mother's. A long circular table with twenty chairs dominated the space. The walls were white and the furniture was modern white and black lines. The only decoration was a beautifully painted map of Richmond before the East End had become a black scar on the land.

We all sat quickly. Cas and Van sat to my left while Ambrose and Ruyek said to my right. Maria sat a few empty seats away from Van, like she wanted some space from all of us. The guard closed the door behind her, staying in the hall where she couldn't hear anything from this soundproof room.

"Warn away," I said finally, after all of us had exchanged a few uneasy glaces.

"I don't owe you anything, your royal highness," Maria started inauspiciously. "But, for all the issues Nadella had with your mother, she loved you. She loved all of her sisters, and I know she'd want you to know what's coming. Before she died, she started to have nightmares. She even consulted a fae seer because they felt more like a vision, but they all confirmed she did not have the sight. It was not a vision, but it was still real.

"Someone was communicating with her in her dreams. Someone incredibly dangerous. It started as a mass of black flames, but it turned into a woman Nadella knew from Acadia. Your people like to call her the shadow queen. We think she was trying to convince Nadella to join her cause. She told her all kinds of things that contradicted everything Queen Rixana and the others told us about the shadowborn. I think it had to have been a trap because Nadella knew they were coming to New York, but no one was supposed to die."

Silence. Absolute fucking *could hear a pin drop* silence followed Maria's insane proclamation – no, her accusation. There is no way on Earth or Acadia that Nadella conspired with the shadow queen and knew the shadowborn were coming to New York.

Clearly, Caspian was of the same mind. "You're lying," he said flatly. "I don't pretend to know Princess Nadella well, but I do know she would not have endangered her sisters or the innocent victims killed in the Battle for New York."

Maria's eyes locked on mine as she spoke. "No one was supposed to die. It was supposed to be a chase, a hunt to take all of you to a secure location where the shadow queen could speak to you."

"We were all prepared to fight, to kill the shadowborn," I argued. "Nadella *killed* shadowborn in that battle. I was there."

"Nadella could be a very convincing actress when it was demanded of her, and she was certain her choice and the sacrifices of innocents would lead to peace," Maria answered, her voice soft. Honest. She sounded like she was being honest.

"What were these contradictions? The secrets the shadow queen shared to win Nadella over?" Van asked, his eyes looking from me to Maria as he spoke.

"I don't know the whole of it, but I know that Nadella believed there was much more to the shadowborn and the exodus through the rift than what Queen Rixana told anyone." Maria folded her hands in front of her, as if gesturing she had nothing more to share.

"What do you expect us to do with this knowledge?" I asked, my own voice fighting back all the emotion that came with the betrayal setting into my bones. Nadella's betrayal. If she had told me, told us – I wouldn't have broken formation. I wouldn't have done whatever it was I did that led to the annihilation of my sisters.

Murderer, the voice in my head whispered, but this time it wasn't only talking about me. If I was culpable, where did that leave Nadella? I closed my eyes and remembered her screaming my name, begging me to hold formation. Had she really been leading us somewhere? Leading from behind was something Nadella had always done. Even though I physically led our formation, she directed us with her words, her power, her–

"Is that the warning?" Ruyek interrupted my spiraling thoughts. "That the shadow queen isn't the big baddie in this story, and we all need to what? Be on the lookout in our dreams for black flames? Are you saying she is going to come to us?"

Maria moved her gaze from me, finally, locking eyes with the vampire prince. "I don't presume to know what the shadow queen will or won't do, prince of darkness, but I thought you should know there is much you do not know, and that Nadella died trying to steer her sisters towards the truth."

Prince of Darkness. Just as Ruyek held prejudices against the magicians, the magicians held them against him. The powers of vampires were often seen as the most sinister, and the blood drinking certainly gave most mortalborns pause.

"Your children," I asked, steering us away from that can of worms. "Are they cared for? Well cared for?"

"Quite. Queen Rixana respected Nadella's wishes enough to ensure we could stay in our home and live comfortably for the rest of our lives." Maria's sharpness ebbed away a bit and the weight of her loss slipped through the facade of strength.

"I'm sorry for your loss and the children's loss," Ambrose said, surprising all of us. "I can't imagine losing a mother as a child."

I cleared my throat before speaking again. "Did my other sisters know about you? About the children?"

"Would knowing that bring you peace or hurt?" Maria asked gently.

"I don't know, but I need to know." It felt like I was pleading, but I needed to know.

Maria nodded. "Atasia knew, but she was sworn to secrecy. Nadella never intended for anyone to know, but secrets can be hard to keep in families, and Atasia and her were always close. It was hard to keep it from her for long. If you ever want to see them, Princess Cordelia, I'd be happy to introduce you. Marcos is three, and Estrella and Leandra are five. Their biological grandfather was a male witch, so their powers are just starting to manifest."

A second generation powerbound descended from a rare powerful male witch and a mortalborn magician. Their existence was uncharted territory.

"I'd like that," I said before standing and wishing Maria safe travels back to California while I mentally tried to make sense of the absolute bomb she'd just dropped on us.

Caspian

Cori kindly selected a room for me with a large tub built into a massive bathroom. A large bag of sea salt leaned against the side of the tub. On the ride here, Cordelia led me on a short detour down the Potomac to the coast of Virginia. The Atlantic might not be my home ocean, but I still felt at home in any body of salt water.

She hadn't stopped me when I landed on an empty shore, stripped, and dove into the waves. In fact, Cori kept watch and didn't even comment on my tentacles. Violetta never warmed to my mer form. It was too alien for her, too *other*. Vi loved me, but I knew she loved me most in the humanoid form I chose to wear around non-mer.

Some mer had beautiful fishtails like a cinematic mermaid princess, but most of us had a combination of sea creature appendages. My sister and I both had eight tentacles, though our mother had a glorious golden tail that shimmered iridescent in the sunlight. But even Queen Morgana's tail was far from the human proportions of legend. Her tail was a long, serpentine thing that was three times the length of her humanoid upper body.

I stripped and then stepped into the deep bath with the memory of the ocean swim still alive on my skin. I smelled like salt water. I slowly turned the knobs until the water was warm enough to remind me of home, then tore open the bag of sea salt and liberally poured it in the water. I sunk into the water and closed my eyes, transforming my legs into eight long tentacles of varying shades of blue.

I kept my eyes closed as the door to my room opened. I caught Van's scent immediately. Our friendship felt like the anchor in the great ocean of grief that threatened to consume me. I heard him walk towards the bath and listened as his clothes hit the ground. The air shifted and a soft splash echoed across the bedroom.

I opened one eye to see what sea creature he'd chosen. I smiled as a small brown otter swam through the rising water of the massive tub.

"Good choice," I said, though I wasn't sure if he could hear me beneath the water.

We stayed in that comfortable silence while the tub filled up. The sea salt was authentic, so if I closed my eyes and ignored the sound of the faucet, I could pretend I was home. It had been a long time since I'd been home. Home was Atlantis, the queendom my mother built on the bleached and dying Great Barrier Reef. Her power, care, restorative efforts, and worldwide ocean protection laws brought the bones of the reef back to life. In my twenty-nine years of life, I had only ever known a thriving tropical paradise.

Vi had visited Atlantis only once. She was a fire wielder and the water stifled her. There was plenty of magic to help her travel underwater safely, but she said she felt like she was drowning even in the open air parts of the Atlantis Palace –

like the knowledge she was leagues below the air dampened her spirit.

So, we stayed away after her only visit to meet my mother, Queen Morgana. I don't know that my mother was very impressed with her either. Queen Rixana had decided who would marry who, insisting the matches were all based on the prophecy. We now know that had to be a lie, or at the least, severely misguided.

"Are you thinking about her?"

I felt the air shift a moment before Van spoke, and I opened my eyes to see him lying nude in the tub in his humanoid form.

"I am," I responded.

He shifted his legs a bit, giving me a wide open view of *everything*. I wasn't sure if it was on purpose or not, as his mind too seemed to be somewhere else.

"Happy memories, I hope."

"Some happy, some not-so-happy. I loved her, but it wasn't a perfect match. You know that." Guilt laced my voice. How could I handle this grief if I did not examine all that I lost honestly? The good and the bad. I had to run through all of it if I was going to marry in four months.

"You and Vi tried your absolute best to choose happiness, Cas. Never be ashamed of that. It's okay if it was more trying than natural chemistry. Arranged marriages rarely work out well. That's why they rarely happened in Acadia."

"I guess you're right. Look at King Valdon and Queen Madelina. Doomed from the start," I responded, stretching my tentacles out across the tub as I spoke.

"Valdon loved someone else," Van responded somberly, and I could see him calculating what that might mean for me.

"And he refused to try when he couldn't have her. I'm going to try, Van. You know that."

Van reached under the water and ran his hand softly along one of my tentacles. "You really are a sight, old friend. You almost never let anyone see you like this, and I don't know why. You're beautiful."

Why? That was a loaded question. I'd seen Violetta shudder when she first saw me in my true form. She was ashamed of her initial reaction, and she tried to explain it away—but the fact remained that she shuddered like I was some eldritch horror come to life. I couldn't unsee her face, the disgust in her eyes. I limited my shifting in front of her, and we were never intimate in this form. It was better for both of us if I kept the mer part of me separate from my princess of fire.

"Not everyone finds me beautiful. Some people even find me repulsive," I admitted. Some truth, without all the other layers of self-doubt and self-consciousness shoved in there.

I watched in awe as Savanna shifted. His long, brown legs transformed into black and silver tentacles and black scales gathered along his arms and ribs in the same place blue scales covered my body.

"Isn't it dangerous to take another humanoid form?" I whispered reverently, but my body betrayed me as I reached out and stroked his tentacles.

"Dangerous in that adopting this form could change me, could make me long for the ocean if I do it too often. But if it helps my future husband, my best friend, understand his magnificence, it'd be worth it."

Future husband. Best friend. The words hung between us as I moved closer, running my hands along every tentacle and every scale. He was beautiful, and it was glaringly obvious he modeled his mer form after mine. How could he be beautiful and I be repulsive?

I was entranced as I climbed over him, our tentacles mingling as I moved over his chest until we were face to face.

"I want to love you," I whispered, the deepest secret buried in the grief and guilt that threatened to consume me.

"Then love me," he said. "Love all of us. Open your heart to the great possibilities of this new future. Hurt. Grieve. Rage from time to time if you need to – but Cas? Choose love again. It's that simple."

"Shift back," I said as I looked into his eyes, my own lips inches from his.

"I'm fine. I don't have to do it often–"

"Shift back, Van," I interrupted. "You made your point, and I like you as you are. You don't need to be part-mer for me to want you."

He shifted, jostling both of us a little with the change in space. Tentacles took up significantly more space than legs. I wanted to kiss him, but I knew I wasn't ready. Not yet. Reading my face, Van pulled me closer and leaned his forehead against mine.

"You'll be ready. Not now, but you will be. I believe that," he whispered.

I stayed like that a moment before shifting positions so my head laid on his chest. I felt him hardening inside the web of my tentacles as I rested there. I knew he couldn't help it, and though I had no intention of going any further than this at that moment, it felt good to be wanted in this form–in my true form.

Cordelia

I had never been so exhausted in my life. The moment my head hit the pillow, I fell into a deep dreamless sleep. A mercifully dreamless sleep. Dragonfire, shadowborn, and my sisters' ghosts let me rest undisturbed for the first time since the night in Manhattan. They'd started calling that night the Battle for New York, and because I lived and repelled the shadowborn temporarily, the world had proclaimed a great victory with me as the obvious heroine.

Four of my sisters were dead. An entire family was very nearly wiped from the face of the planet. My mother's legacy was destroyed in more ways than anyone would admit. I was all she had left. Her powerbound daughter who had been so far from the throne, my ascension was an impossibility when she took a mortalborn as her lover and bore his child. These were the thoughts that flooded me the moment I awoke. My sleep had been peaceful, but my waking was far from it.

These thoughts followed me through a cold shower (my preference) and the grueling training session I inflicted upon myself in the gym. Several miles into my uphill treadmill run, the gym doors opened. Savanna and Ambrose entered. Van was anticipated, but Ambrose was not.

"Good morning, princess," Van said with a smile, his perfect white teeth gleaming against the dark umber of his skin. His smile was vibrant and alive, happy in a way that I longed to be.

I nodded and continued to run.

Ambrose gave me a little wave and a half-smile. White lilies bloomed around the base of his antlers this morning, and he wore loose sweatpants and a dark gray t-shirt that had the words *Proudly plant-powered* across the front with the white outlines of flowers surrounding the slogan. Everyone knew the fae were all strictly vegetarian, and the shirt was clever.

I continued to run as Van and Ambrose circled the room, admiring the weapons racks. Van was explaining the different weapons to Ambrose and letting him hold them and ask questions. Our fae prince must have decided not being weapon-trained made him defenseless when the shadowborn came for us.

Nadella believed there was much more to the shadowborn and the exodus through the rift than what Queen Rixana told anyone. Nadella's mortalborn lover – her wife's voice filled my thoughts. There was no reality in which I could accept the shadowborn were anything but our enemies. Nadella had been played by the shadow queen, and the price for losing that game was her life.

Did the shadowborn kill your sister? A voice inside my head asked. It wasn't a voice of shadow flames. It was my conscience. I had been consumed by fire, and then I had thrown every ounce of winter inside me to push it out of me and–

"Cordelia? Cori!"

I looked up to find Van running across the gym towards me, concern etched in his face. I looked down at my hands and my legs and everything around me. Ice spread out from my hands down across the treadmill, so cold and thick that it had stopped rotating. The ice spread out a few feet on either side of me, creeping along the equipment that surrounded me.

"What the fuck?" I asked.

I pulled myself free of the ice and stepped off the treadmill. The ice I apparently created remained where it was. I looked up to meet Van's gaze as he shifted into an arctic fox and easily moved across the ice to me. He couldn't speak in his animal form, but he herded me off the ice with gentle nips and nose touches until we stood on the unfrozen gym floor.

He shifted back into his normal form and met my eyes with that same concern I'd heard in his voice.

"I don't know what happened," I said honestly, my voice a bit shaky. "I was just running and thinking and–" I trailed off.

"It's the ripening. You are coming into your true power, and it can be unpredictable. Particularly in the beginning." He placed a large hand on my shoulder, and while I knew he was just offering comfort, his touch centered me, grounded me.

"My power doesn't feel like my own sometimes. It feels *other*," I responded.

"It can feel like that. I couldn't shift nearly as much before I started the ripening. It would exhaust me for days to shift into a large animal, and I got the shift wrong sometimes." He smiled again as he spoke, and it warmed the coldness inside me.

"What does that mean? Got the shift wrong?" Ambrose asked as he stepped into our bubble of refuge, the safe space I was suddenly finding myself in beneath Van's touch.

"Ever seen a dog with cat ears or a snake with legs?" Van chuckled. "It wasn't always hilarious, but it was always a little funny when I got it wrong. Sometimes my body just wouldn't bend and restructure like it was supposed to. It happens to all shifters before they finish the ripening. Only my homeostatic form was easy before then."

"A midnight lion?" Ambrose asked, his curiosity palpable. A midnight lion, a creature that doesn't even exist on Planet Earth, was somehow Van's go-to shifted form.

Van nodded. "It's funny. I never even saw one, you know. Mom and Ommi had pictures and paintings of them from Acadia, but our most natural form is innate. It's a part of us. Even if shifters never see Acadia again, the life there is a part of us."

"Can I see?" I was surprised at the sound of my own voice. I hadn't meant to ask Van to indulge my curiosity aloud. It just slipped out. I'd never seen a midnight lion either. The only one of us who might have was Ruyek, and it seemed unlikely he was being introduced to massive predators as a toddler in Acadia.

He nodded and stepped away from us, giving himself enough room to work with. His shift was fluid, like water, like it was the most natural thing in the world. It was hard to imagine him ever struggling with any shift, but I believed him about the ripening. His eyes relaxed as he shifted too, like moving into that form was like going home.

A massive black lion stood before us when his shift was complete. He had the same heterochromic eyes in this form: one green and one blue. He didn't have a mane like an African lion. He looked more like a massive black mountain lion, but even that was only an approximation to what a midnight lion was. His body was a mass of muscles and his eyes were more cat-like than lion-like, just like they were in his humanoid form.

I found myself drawn to him. Ambrose must have too because we both took a step towards the lion that was Savanna. His head was as high as my chest, and I was tall for a woman (five foot ten the last time my mother had forced me to get a physical). I raised my hand in front of his face like he was a house cat, like I was asking permission to touch him. He shoved his head into my hand in response.

Ambrose stepped up next to him and ran a hand along his back. Neither of us spoke as we touched him. His fur was softer and thicker than a short-haired house cat's. I'd never touched an African lion before, so I had no frame of reference for comparison. My mother kept many house cats over the years though. She was very fond of them, which was quite strange for a magicborn. Pets weren't usually a thing in Acadian culture (and no, mounted pegasi are not pets).

"You're magnificent," Ambrose finally said, breaking the silence.

Van responded by moving his head to nuzzle Ambrose affectionately. Right about then, my stomach growled loudly. The protein bar I'd eaten before my workout felt like ancient history, and apparently I was starving. Van rubbed his head against Ambrose once more before stepping back and shifting into himself again.

"It seems like we need to feed our princess," Van said with a grin.

"You feel up to going into the city?" I asked.

"I thought you'd never ask," Van responded.

Savanna

I'd seen plenty of cities around the world, but Richmond was wholly unique. Like most modern cities, it was no longer the concrete jungle the mortalborn constructed. There was green everywhere. The highways from a century before were blooming with the colors of community gardens and large expanses of open greenery for animals to roam. The largest highway had become a grazing ground of tall grasses for cattle and pegasi alike.

Few, small roads remained for public transit buses, and the train lines were constantly bringing citizens between cities. Solar panels were mounted on buses and trains. Gone was the time of burning dead dinosaurs to fuel a planet quickly heading towards extinction herself. This was the only planet we had left, and we took a vested interest in preserving it.

Buildings were bursting with greenery on balconies and solar panels on top. There was a hydroelectric plant just outside the city for any needs that solar could not provide. Hydroelectric was heavily monitored and mer and witches with water power offset the natural toll hydroelectric plants historically caused to water ecosystems.

What made Richmond different was the scar. It was so garish by the light of day, a jagged expanse of black, burned ground with no vegetation growth after over a hundred years. Where buildings, homes, schools, and hospitals once stood, only burned black rubble remained.

I watched it as we flew towards downtown from the castle. Cas and Cori rode pegasi while Ambrose rode me. I'd transformed into a massive black dragon again for ease of transport. Ruyek was uninterested in testing clothing with new sun-blocking tech installed. I know that stepping into the light filtered through treated windows had already been quite the task for him mentally. He'd grown so accustomed to the darkness in this world with a merciless star at its heart.

We landed in the courtyard of a brick building older than our existence on this planet. Much of the original brick buildings had remained. Upgrades to reduce environmental impacts and convert to clean energy were mandatory for all buildings, but the historical bones of much of the downtown and Carytown neighborhoods had remained.

This cafe was located in the Shockoe Bottom neighborhood along the James River. The neighborhood had been reimagined, of course, with mer businesses and homes built along Dock Street. The National Museum of Mer History had been constructed next to the Holocaust Museum that still stood a block from the water. Cas promised to take me to both soon.

"Heads up," Cori said after I shifted and they'd all dismounted. "You know I'm powerbound and my father's family is from here. What you may not know is that my mortalborn cousin owns a restaurant here."

Cas looked from Cori to the restaurant, and she nodded with a smile.

"You're going to love her," Cori said as she opened the courtyard door and led us into the restaurant. Her smile was muted, but it was genuine as she led the four of us to the bar.

The restaurant was small but homey. The door we entered led us past a hallway with three bathrooms and a few unmarked doors. We came out in the middle of the restaurant. To our right, booths lined a wall opposite a massive wooden bar with a mirror wall that read *Cali's Caff*. To our left, booths lined either side of the restaurant and four two-top small tables sat in the open space between the booths. Everything in the restaurant was rich, dark wood, black leather, and gold accents.

"Oh, Cori," the woman behind the bar rushed towards us and enveloped Cordelia in a tight hug. "I'm so sorry, baby. I can't imagine."

The woman was older than Cori by probably a decade, and she was nearly as beautiful. Her skin was a rich brown like Cori's father's and long black braids were twisted around each other into a big bun atop her head. Her eyes were a light brown and dark freckles covered her cheeks. She was tall and strongly built like Cordelia.

"I'm okay," Cori whispered, her own arms clinging tightly to the woman. The woman kissed her cheek and grabbed her in for one more tight embrace before letting her go.

Only a few patrons were in the restaurant, but it was the time between breakfast and lunch on a weekday. I felt their eyes on us as we walked across the restaurant and sat at the bar. Everyone knew who we were, and while I'd avoided the tabloids since our engagement was decided upon by the IRC, there was undoubtedly a lot of talk.

I honestly didn't want to know what the mortalborn had to say about it. I barely understood what I thought and felt about my new engagement. The last thing I wanted to do was read the opinions of people who weren't sitting in that meeting being told it was this or certain annihilation. But, the reality was, Richmond was Cordelia's home. That wasn't a secret, and our presence here was going to get out sooner or later (it likely was already out since Rue's very-well-known dragon and her mate were very visible creatures). I guess it might as well happen over a delicious meal.

The woman went back behind the bar and handed all of us a menu before introducing herself. "Hi! I'm Calliope. This is my restaurant, and if you leave me a bad review, I will crash your wedding." She smiled widely as Ambrose coughed awkwardly.

"It's a joke," Cas said to Ambrose.

"Of course." Ambrose nodded.

We were seated Cas, Ambrose, Cordelia, then me at the bar.

"Vegan or vegetarian?" Calliope asked Ambrose, clearly taking in his pointed ears, antlers, and t-shirt slogan.

"Vegan – except for cheese." He smiled. "I do prefer to know it's humanely sourced though."

"Everything is humanely sourced by law," Cori responded.

"And corporations would never break the law," Cas teased.

Cori frowned, as if she truly did believe her mother's laws ensured humanity in the dairy industry. Was it humane-r than a century ago? By far. Was it as humane as the witch queen had all of us believe? Debatable.

Calliope pulled a green menu from under the bar and handed it to Ambrose. "This is the vegan one, but I can add cheese to anything. My cheese *is* humanely sourced *and* local. You can see the cows grazing on the old I-95 and the goats live on my own land a county over."

When she smiled, I saw the similarity to Cordelia again. They were similar builds, but Cordelia had a lot of the witch queen in her facial features and lighter complexion. Their smiles were magnetic in the same way. I had to remind myself I was engaged again. I could absolutely not flirt with my fiancé's cousin.

Calliope took our orders and then went through a door next to the bar to talk to the kitchen. She came back with a charcuterie board devoid of meat but piled high with cheese, crackers, fruit, and vegetables. We all dug in while waiting for our individual plates.

I laughed easily as we all talked about home. Ambrose and Cori were the only ones among us who had grown up with more than one sibling, and I listened as Cori told stories about her sisters without the familiar mask of grief snapping into place.

I was acutely aware of people coming in and out of the front door. No one sat at the bar, but the number of whispering patrons had grown since we first entered. I smelled only mortalborn coming in and out. No shadowborn or powerbound among them, so it seemed safe enough. I still watched everyone who entered and left because being alert and cautious was natural for a shifter – especially for a shifter who had grown up in a world on a knife's edge of interplanetary war.

When the final empty booth was filled with mortalborn, I met Cas's gaze down the bar. It was nice to feel safe and cocooned in our own little world at the bar, but even Calliope's smile had fallen as more and more patrons crossed her threshold at ten in the morning on a Thursday.

"I think it's time to go, princess," I whispered to Cordelia, my hand on her arm.

She looked around with wide eyes, like she'd allowed herself to drop her guard for the first time in a long time.

"I think it's plenty safe, but I think it's just time we go," I assured her.

"I'll send you the bill," Calliope said with a smile as we all stood to leave.

"Put it on my mother's tab," Cori said back, though her smile didn't reach her eyes.

"Always. See you soon?" Calliope's eyes were locked on Cori, far away from the sudden business of her restaurant.

"Absolutely," Cori responded to her cousin.

I nodded to Cas, who led the way from the bar back to the door to the courtyard where Cordelia's appaloosa pegasus and the palomino pegasus Cas had been riding since D.C. were waiting. I took up the rear, keeping close to Cori. I could see cameras and phones snapping pictures silently as we walked, like everyone had agreed to silence their shutter sounds before entering the restaurant.

"Fuck," Cas said as soon as he stepped through the door into the courtyard.

Paparazzi. Everywhere.

I could feel Cori's pulse quicken at the sight of a courtyard full of photographers and reporters. The crowd spilled out all the way to the river's edge, where a few mer looked at them curiously from their shop windows and doorways.

"Stay calm," I told Cori. "I have no problem getting them to move."

Cori clung close to my side as I shifted into my midnight lion form, her energy panicked.

"Princess Cordelia," a reporter yelled. "Are you expected to bear children for your husbands? Is that even legal under Acadian laws?"

"Prince Caspian," another yelled. "Do you feel like you're betraying Princess Violetta by being engaged so soon?"

Another: "Was your relationship with Violetta even a love match?"

Another: "Prince Ambrose, does it feel strange to be engaged to four people you haven't seen since you were a teenager?"

Another: "Who are you going to wear for your wedding, Princess Cordelia?"

Another: "Will the wedding be here or in the capital?"

Another: "Some people are saying the princesses were murdered to cover up the misinterpretation of the prophecy. What are your thoughts–"

I roared a ground-shaking, window-rattling roar into the crowd, and it silenced immediately. Another started to ask a question, and I roared again before shifting into a black and bay pegasus to get Cori the hell out of here without having to cross the sea of people.

I felt her arm land on my withers a moment before the air around us started shifting. She was screaming and her body was changing, elongating and bending. The crowd looked on with horror as the witch princess did something impossible for witches: she shifted into a pegasus with the same black and bay marking as me.

"No time for questions," Cas said. "Fly."

He gently smacked the pegasus that was somehow Cordelia on the croup. I watched as she shook out her wings a moment before running towards the crowd. They all parted, diving out of the way as she managed to flap the unfamiliar wings enough to be airborne. She didn't ever get very high, but I passed her, leading the way just above the crowd and then the river on the short flight back to the castle. Soon, Cas was behind us on his palomino and a terrified-looking Ambrose was behind us on Cori's mount.

I landed easily on the front lawn of the castle and shifted back into my humanoid form. Cori landed much less gracefully, nearly falling to the ground. Her equine eyes were terrified. So many things had just happened to her. The first few shifts are agonizing for a shifter. It took time to learn how to shut off the pain receptors in your brain as you shifted. She'd felt her body break apart and remake itself without the forewarning to expect it. And now, she likely had no idea how to shift back.

I caught my breath, my own calm ebbing as I heard Cas and Ambrose land and dismount behind us.

"What just happ–?" Ambrose began, seemingly moments before realizing Cori was still not herself.

"Cori, you shifted into this form. You can shift back," I said, stepping towards her cautiously. "You have to imagine your normal form, your true form. Imagine yourself standing here in front of us and then throw every bit of your power at that thought. It takes training to learn how to use less magic reserves to shift."

We all watched as she tried to do just that, but the only magic that appeared was the snow that began blowing all around us underneath the warm sun of the late spring sky.

"What if," Cas began behind me before stepping up next to me. "What if she used your magic?"

"What the hell are you talking about?" I asked.

"Touch her. You send your magic into her shift," Cas replied, his eyes large with wonder.

"How would that work? What does that even–"

"Just try," he interrupted. "We need to bring her back. Try."

So I did. I walked up to Cori and ran my hand through the hair of her mane a moment before laying my palm flat. I willed Cori to shift back into herself, to shed the pegasus form and become herself again.

Then she was neighing, then shifting and screaming again. She fell heavily onto the ground once two legs were beneath her again, sobbing. I knew how she felt, but I'd felt that pain as a young child who had been prepared for it and trained for it as all shifters were.

I didn't think. None of us did. One moment, Cori was lying on the ground sobbing, and the next, Ambrose, Cas, and I were on the ground too. All of us holding her. I cradled her against me while Cas stroked her face and Ambrose held one of her hands with both of his.

We stayed that way for a while. A million questions ran through my head, but I didn't voice any of them. Guards and servants ran towards us soon enough, but Cas sent all of them away except for the guard who seemed to be in charge of things.

"I need you to contact Queen Rixana. Tell her what you saw here, and tell her to get her ass on a pegasus immediately," Cas said, angrier and harsher than I'd ever heard him in all our years of friendship.

Ruyek

Clearly, I missed a lot due to my biological aversion to Earth's particularly unforgiving star. I was sitting in the common area between all five of our bedrooms when the noise coming closer from down the hall turned into Cas, Ambrose, and Van (who was carrying Cori) pushing into the room.

"What the fuck?" I asked as whatever I missed came storming into the room.

Van laid Cori on one of the sofas. A moment later, guards and servants entered the room, clearly feeling they needed to do something, but they didn't really know exactly what that was.

"I repeat," I said louder. "What the fuck?"

Ambrose looked like he was about to fill me in, but then the witch queen's general stepped into the room.

"The queen has arrived," Sabine said.

"Why is the queen here?" I asked, getting quite annoyed that no one was telling me anything.

A moment later, Queen Rixana stepped into the room. I hated that somehow all the light and attention seemed to bend towards her when she entered. Her power, her presence, was magnetic. Even my own eyes, who very much wanted to continue to search Ambrose's face for answers, turned towards her. She commanded even reluctant attention.

"I got your summons, Prince Caspian, though I felt translocation a much faster choice, given the urgency of your message," the queen's voice was curt. I definitely needed to know what message Cas had passed on to her about whatever the hell was going on.

A fae woman stepped in the room behind her. Ah– the source of her translocation travel then.

"I won't ask you to excuse my frankness because I will not – I *will not* lose another of your daughters, Queen Rixana," Cas bit back. The mer had balls then. Noted.

If looks could kill, I'd be down a fiance as Rixana stared Cas down. After a moment of a look that could slice steel, she lowered her eyes to Cori.

Yes, remember your daughter, you old hag. My shadows appeared in Ambrose's mind.

His eyes grew large as he looked across the room towards me, clearly taken aback.

What the fuck happened? I asked him.

Cori – Cori shifted.

Excuse me? Come again. She did what now? He couldn't mean what I thought he meant. She was a witch – a power-bound witch at that. Impossible.

"It's my understanding that Princess Cordelia displayed some unexpected power today," Queen Rixana said.

Oh right. All the servants and guards here reported to her first, not Cori and definitely not us. That and whatever message Cas sent clearly filled her in enough.

"When I think of displaying unexpected power, I think of the moment in the IRC when Cordelia made the vampire king back down," Cas said, clearly taking point on this confrontation (because yes, it felt like a confrontation). Cheap shot at my father though. I approved. "I don't think of a witch shifting into a pegasus without even their consent, intention, or understanding of *how* that happened or how such a thing is even possible."

Rixana's face softened a bit and she looked to her general. General Sabine looked back, a question in her gaze.

"Tell them," Rixana said. The queen closed the distance between the door and her unconscious daughter, shooing Savanna away and sitting next to her. We all watched in silence as she tenderly ran her hand along Cori's forehead before taking her daughter's hand in hers.

Rixana looked up expectedly to General Sabine, who seemed to be trying to sort through the order she'd just been given. Her flower tattoos stood out in the warm sun coming through the treated windows, highlighted against the plain black of her uniform and sword hilts. She had a short sword on either hip and a knife strapped to either boot. I bet she shaved her head every day for that kind of shine.

Sabine didn't sit. Neither did the fae woman, who stepped up next to the general and gently put a hand on her arm. The fae woman was slight and wiry, a sharp contrast to the solid wall of muscle the general was cut from.

"We have seen this before," Sabine finally began. "But not very often. Some call the witches with this power a syphon."

"I knew it," Cas whispered, his tone angrier than I understood.

"What do other people call this power?" I asked, picking up on what Sabine wasn't saying.

"A magic eater," Cas answered, meeting my eyes. "A magic eater is what they call the shadow queen, who has the same ability to steal magic and use it however she wants."

"It isn't stealing magic," Sabine snapped back, her knuckles flexing at her side. "It *can* be, sure, but much of the power a siphon uses is given freely. The shadow queen *can* take power, but she has an entire army, an entire kingdom willing to give it freely."

"Can we back up a smidge?" I asked, my own eyes hardening as I spoke. "Are we now to believe the shadow queen has dedicated followers who perhaps work for her willingly, rather than enslaved shadowborn she can control? That perhaps there is much we do not know about the shadow queen's war with us?"

"Do not ask questions you are not ready to hear the answer to," Queen Rixana snapped in my direction.

"Oh. I am ready, your majesty. We are all ready to know what you know about the shadow queen and why she will not cease in her pursuit of the magicborn who came through the rift. What does she want with us?" My words were a growl and the shadows in the room raced towards me and pooled around my legs, moving in dark, menacing waves.

"Perhaps you should ask your father that question," Rixana responded without backing down an inch. "Because I will not be sharing war secrets with people not actively engaged in combat against the shadowborn."

"Has Cordelia not been actively engaged in combat against the shadowborn? Did your four daughters not die actively engaged in combat with the shadowborn?" Van asked, his voice eerily quiet.

"She should not have been in combat with them. We have armies for that, and she is now my only heir. She will not be in combat again." Rixana's words sounded like an order, though I wasn't sure the shadowborn gave a shit about her proclamations. No one had expected a battle that night in Manhattan either.

"What do we need to know about Cordelia's power? Her syphoning?" Ambrose was the only one who didn't look pissed. He looked – well, he looked scared – like he was terrified of whatever was happening to Cordelia.

Rixana looked to Sabine before answering. "Sabine has studied the shadow queen's power extensively. She will stay here to help train Cordelia and to train all of you to help hone her skills. She will need to know how to utilize all variations of power so she is never caught unaware again."

"What do you mean *caught unaware*?" I asked.

"Syphons are considered invincible, impervious to magical attacks. When hit with magic, they can simply cast it out. Without proper training, the casting it out part can be disastrous. She will need training and support. Is it fair to assume all of you will be of assistance?" Rixana asked, looking at each of us in turn.

What was she asking? Would we freely give our power to Cordelia? I don't fucking think so–

She's asking if we will help Cori learn how to wield this deadly, terrifying power, Ambrose said. My shadows were still curled up in his mind and clearly, my thoughts were projecting very loudly inside his head. *We have to help her, Rue. We have to.*

Okay.

Just like that, Ambrose silenced all of my arguments, all of my fight. In part because he is the one who said it, but also because the witch princess was someone beginning to endear herself to me.

"We will," Ambrose said. "We will help her train, help her learn."

Rixana squeezed Cori's hand before standing up.

"It is my desire that she be proficient in her gifts by the wedding. I know four months is not very long, but Sabine is an excellent teacher, and you will train extensively," Rixana said, her words another command.

None of us argued as she said goodbye to Sabine before taking the fae woman's arm and disappearing from the room without another word to any of us.

"Move her to her bed to rest," Sabine said to Van. "Training begins in the morning."

"It can take a few days to recover from your first shift," Van argued.

"We do not have a few days. We will begin in the morning," the general said before turning and leaving the room.

Once she left, Van scooped Cori up like she was a small doll, not a tall, muscular woman who was rock solid.

"Now what the fuck do you know about syphons?" I asked Cas once Van returned from tucking Cori into her own bed.

All of us had moved to sit on two couches opposite each other. I sat with Van while Ambrose sat with Cas.

"Not much except that the shadow queen is one. She is the only one anyone has ever heard of," he replied.

"Until now," I said.

"Until now." Cas nodded.

"Is what they say about the shadow queen–" Ambrose trailed off and looked toward the closed door, like Queen Rixana or General Sabine might be listening.

"What do you know about the royal conspiracy theory, Prince Ambrose?" I smiled, feigning shock.

"I don't know – I mean I don't know anything really, not for certain. I just know that there are some magicborn who say things," Ambrose whispered, his voice shaking a bit.

I wanted to poke at him more, but all of us were a little frightened to mention the royal conspiracy theory aloud. Queen Rixana had eyes and ears everywhere, and she'd left her most trusted general and adviser here with us. Her eyes and ears were *very* close at hand.

We all fell into an uncomfortable silence. I suspected we all knew different parts of the same truths. We just had to find a safe place to lay the pieces out and put the puzzle together. That place was most definitely not here in this palace.

Ambrose

For the first time in a long time, I was scared. I don't think I was scared of the shadowborn or even the witch queen. I think

I was scared for Cordelia, scared to think through what all of this meant for her, for us, for the future of this world. And clearly, my fear was present on my face.

Cas and Van turned in for the night first, leaving me and Ruyek sitting opposite each other. Ruyek looked like he was studying my face, trying to read me, when I heard his voice in my head.

Stay the night with me.

I–I never–

None of that matters. If you want to stay, stay. I'll take care of you. His voice, his shadows danced with all the pent-up anticipation I knew we both shared. I'd purposefully spent last night alone with the walls of my mind fortified. We had moved so quickly. I didn't want our connection to be because I was starved for touch, and Ruyek was Ruyek – a player. I want it to be real and genuine. We were going to be married. I couldn't just be another notch on his bedpost.

I need it to be real, I finally said. *I've waited too long, turned down too many for this to mean nothing to you.*

Ambrose, I'm marrying you. We all signed the papers. It's done. I wouldn't have done that if I didn't mean to keep good on my promise. And I promise I don't have another spouse or family anywhere. There's only you – and Cas and Van and Cordelia, but you know that.

I did know that, and it didn't make me jealous. It didn't give me pause at all. Somehow, it made sense that all of us would find room in our hearts for each other – like this was the true intent of the prophecy all along, and this wasn't Queen Rixana grasping at straws when the original interpretation literally went up in flames.

Okay, I said. *But I need you to be gentle.*

Ruyek's smile darkened and his eyes looked like the eyes of a starving man who'd just had a feast laid out before him.

I don't plan to ravage you tonight, sweet prince. I just want to explore each other.

He led me into his room. The curtains were drawn, but night had fallen so he crossed the room and opened them. A glorious full moon stared back at us. It felt closer than ever, like an old god leaning in close as fate shifted with Cori's new powers. Her powers *were* world-altering. To be invincible, to be able to use the magic of all races of magicborn. It was beyond comprehension.

I stood awkwardly near the closed door as he took his shoes off and laid down on the bed, his arms folded behind his head.

"Come here," he whispered.

It felt like a command, and so I did. I came to him, pulling my shoes and socks off and laying in the bed next to him. My breathing was heavy as he looked down at me, his head propped up higher than mine.

"You lead," he said softly. "We can do whatever you want tonight."

He was so calm, not shaking like I was. I wanted this. Goddess be damned, I wanted all of Ruyek, but that want and that need terrified me too. I'd never *wanted* like this. I had forced down every bit of attraction I had because I was waiting for Nadella. And though I was ashamed to admit it, I felt like her death unshackled me. It freed me; it led me to this moment and this room with someone who actually wanted me.

I shivered.

"I don't know what to do," I whispered, looking up at his deep red eyes, so dark they were nearly black in the soft light coming from the few lamps in the room.

"You can do whatever you want, Prince Ambrose. I consent to everything you can dream up." Ruyek's smile was toothy – as in, his fangs were on full display when he looked at me.

Starving. We were both starving.

"Can you–can you touch me? If that's what I want?" I asked.

He moved so quickly, it felt surreal. His ethereal vampire speed was breathtaking in action. He straddled my hips, our faces level as he leaned down and kissed me. Though, it couldn't really be described with the word *kiss* – this was a devouring. His tongue parted my lips and explored my mouth thoroughly. I felt the bite of his fangs as I explored him back, my tongue scraping over the razor-sharp edges. I felt the drop of blood well up on my tongue a moment before Ruyek moaned, and then I felt him swallow the blood down.

Divine, he said in my mind. *You taste as divine as I dreamed you would.*

His words gave me courage I'd never experienced before. I pulled my mouth away and gently pushed his shoulders down, making it very clear where I wanted his mouth. He moved slowly this time, stopping to pull my t-shirt over my head before pulling his own off.

I was unprepared for the feast his body would be for my eyes. He was muscular but svelte, and a trail of black hair led down the center of his belly to the top of his pants, just as black hair curled around his nipples.

My own chest was hairless except for the tiny bit of red hair that trailed between my belly button and my pants. I was covered in freckles too, a kind of sun-kissed that felt alien next to Ruyek's alabaster skin. His eyes roamed over me, and I felt him harden against me, his crotch a little south of where my body was responding in kind.

His almond eyes, slanted slightly downward near the bridge of his nose, held mine intently as he moved his mouth to one of my nipples. His tongue lavished me with attention in a way I didn't even know could be pleasurable.

If I bite you, you could go mad, you know – become addicted to the pleasure of it, he whispered in my mind.

"Please," I begged aloud. He lowered himself over me, my dick digging into his stomach as he sucked.

He moved to the other nipple, and this time, I felt the pinch of his fangs. He hadn't broken the skin yet, but I shivered with the sudden need I felt to feel his teeth piercing my flesh.

Even the anticipation can drive someone crazy, he said. *But I have bit a few magicborn before, and they managed to control themselves. Our willpower is much higher than mortalborn.*

"Rue, please," I begged again, my voice more desperate than it had ever been.

And then he struck. His teeth sank into the skin around my nipple. I cried out in pain at first, but only seconds later, the pain subsided and pleasure coursed through me. I strained against my pants as I heard him gulp my blood down his throat.

Without pausing his drinking, he reached down and pulled my dick free and began to stroke me. I was going to fucking cum from him drinking my blood and barely touching my cock. I was going to–

And then he pulled away, taking his mouth and his hand away from me. He gently licked where he'd bitten me and the wounds closed up.

"Are you ready for this?" Ruyek asked. Shadows crossed his red eyes as he met my gaze. We were both hungry for this, and I was as ready as I was ever going to be.

He moved down my body and pulled my pants completely off before settling with his mouth over my dick. He took me in his mouth slowly at first, stopping to lick my head before taking more of me. I wasn't a small man, no magicborn were, so I was surprised when he swallowed all of me down, my dick digging deep into his throat.

"Fuck," I whimpered as he began to move up and down. "Fuck. Fuck. Fu–"

And then he pulled his mouth away from my dick and ran his hand along my thigh, his fingers dancing lowered until I felt them against my asshole. He looked up at me for permission, and I nodded.

What happened next was not what I anticipated. He sank his teeth into my thigh. I cried out a moment before the pleasure returned, coursing through me until a little cum leaked from my dick. He took a few gulps before pulling back and covering his fingers with my blood. He licked the wound closed just as he pressed his fingers against me.

I'd never – no one had ever – even in my own explorations of my body, I hadn't done this. It felt like something intensely personal, something to be felt with someone else. He started with one finger. He entered slowly, languidly. I was stiff at first, squeezing hard on his finger.

Holy gods, he whispered in my head, his eyes closing in pleasure as my body squeezed. The pleasure in his voice somehow allowed me to relax enough for him to slip another finger inside me. I jumped as he touched my prostate, running his long middle finger down it just as he pushed a third finger inside.

My breathing was ragged, like I was running a marathon, rather than absolutely losing myself in the vampire prince's touch. His fingers continued to move inside me as he took me back into his mouth. This time, he was not slow or exploratory. He took me deep and I felt the slight bite of his fangs against the sensitive skin of my shaft, and I broke.

I came in a rush of feeling I'd never encountered when touching myself. I squeezed around his fingers as he swallowed me down, drinking every bit of cum I offered up.

"Ruyek," I whispered, panted, as he pulled his fingers out of me and his mouth away from my dick.

"Is it my turn now?" he asked.

I had no idea what he meant, but I was in. I nodded as he pulled his own pants off.

Holy gods indeed, old gods and the goddess save me. He was massive, every bit of ten, thick inches. More impressive than his size though, was the two piercings on his cock. One piercing went through the hole of his dick with the other ball peaking out just under his broad head. The second was along the underside of his shaft, a straight bar through the skin with two metal balls on either side.

"How?" I whispered, my mouth hanging open in awe.

"The same way magicborn get tattoos despite our regenerative healing: venom. My own, in this case," he responded as he moved over me.

He put another pillow under my head before placing his knees on either side of my neck.

"Can I face fuck you, Prince Ambrose?"

I just nodded, not because I was being submissive but because I wanted him. I wanted him in any way he was willing to give himself to me.

I struggled as he pushed himself into my mouth. The cold of the metal piercings against my teeth was shocking at first, but I was even more shocked when he gave me no time to adjust to what was happening. Ruyek put his hands on either side of my head and pushed himself all the way into my mouth until I gagged.

"Swallow," he demanded. "Take me deep and you won't gag."

He didn't wait for me to attempt anything though before he pulled out again and slammed back into my throat. I felt my dick hardening again as he fucked my mouth and my throat mercilessly. He didn't stop when I gagged, he just pushed in further, forcing me to swallow and move past the reflex.

Every ounce of my attention and sensations narrowed to the feel of the bruising pace he set, using me in a way that I never thought I'd like – I'd love – I'd *crave*. He pushed his dick down my throat harder and harder, and I felt the tension building in him as his legs tensed around me.

Without thinking about what I was doing, I moved a hand between us and ran my fingers along his balls just as they too started to tense. And then it was his time to break. He came in a rush of warm liquid pouring down my throat, and I swallowed him down. His cum tasted a little like iron, just like I would have imagined cum of a man who subsisted on blood would taste if I'd ever let my own fantasies take me this far.

He pulled out of my mouth and collapsed against the bed, breathing heavily. I was hard again, but I didn't think Ruyek was up to helping me with that again. And I guess, Ruyek agreed with my mental assessment.

"Touch yourself," he demanded between heavy breaths. "Now. I want your cum all over me."

I straddled him this time, and he watched me touch myself, biting his own lip as I moved my hands up and down my shaft.

One day, he said in my mind as I worked. *One day I am going to fuck you like you never thought possible, Prince Ambrose. I am going to break you and remake you into someone else entirely.*

I came at the words he growled in my mind, my cum spurting across his chest just like he wanted. When I collapsed next to him this time, he pulled me against him, my back to his chest. We were both covered in cum and blood, but nothing had ever felt more right in the world. He loudly breathed in my scent, and all I could think about was the next time I'd feel his teeth in me, feel the pleasure of his venom coursing through me. Maybe that feeling was an addiction, but I wasn't very sure I minded. I thought about it without pause as we both fell into a deep sleep.

Cordelia

I was somewhere between consciousness and unconscious-
ness when I heard my mother's voice in the same room. She

was talking to all of my fiances and maybe Sabine? I couldn't understand what they were saying or why they were here, but I could hear their voices. Angry at times, fearful at others. I was still floating in a sea of agony. I knew the pain was gone, but the memory felt strong enough to break my mind apart.

I remembered touching Van in the courtyard. I was terrified and my power was awake, tingling beneath my fingers, but it felt different than the usual bite of the ice that lived inside of me. It felt like something else entirely. And then there was only pain. A flood of pain, a drowning as my bones broke and stretched, tendons and muscles stretching until they snapped and then reformed, making new connections as my body morphed into a black and bay pegasus that mirrored Van's shifted form.

I could barely remember the flight as new muscles flexed and carried my foreign body in the air. Pain. Everything was pain. Every flap of my wings, every bob of my body beneath them. We were back in front of the castle and Van was telling me how to shift, helping me understand what I needed to do – but I couldn't. I didn't know how, and it didn't make sense. I wasn't supposed to be able to shift.

Cas was talking, and then Van was touching me and I felt my body changing. Bones broke anew. Muscles and sinew tore and snapped. I was screaming. I was screaming in my mind and then aloud, as I crumpled. I was screaming and screaming and my entire body was on fire with pain receptors on overload.

And then I was in this space between conscious and not. I wondered if my body had gone into shock, or if maybe I was dying. I didn't know what was happening, and in this liminal space between reality and nightmare, I didn't care. I wasn't even sure I wanted to be alive anymore. My sisters were dead. I thought it might be – no, it *was* my fault. Somehow, the ability to use Van's magic seemed to solidify my fear that *I* had sent that dragonfire out into the sky that night, that I had pushed it away to save myself, and in doing so, killed my sisters.

Murderer. Nadella's voice filled my head. *I was trying to save us, save all of us, and you didn't listen. I told you to stop. I told you to stay in formation. You killed us, all of us.*

The ice walls of my mind were down. They'd crumbled beneath the pain of shifting, and I felt a darkness rolling across the frozen ground and thick snow that blanketed my mind. It was like shadows, but it burned like fire – like pitch black flames made of death itself.

Nadella's voice was gone and somehow I knew that it was my own mind being cruel to me, but the dark presence was very real. Something, someone was in my mind, my unprotected, shattered mind that was still reeling from pain worse than any I'd ever endured.

I looked down at myself. I wasn't a blizzard personified any-more. I wasn't winter and ice. I was myself. My own physical body naked on the frozen ground, shivering for the first time in my memory. Cold never affected me before. My entire life, my mother had to force me into coats and long pants, reminding me that frostbite didn't care if I didn't feel the cold, the nerve damage would happen nonetheless.

I watched as the black flames began to take the shape of a woman. She was tall and thin, and she wore shadows for clothes. Her skin was fair, but her hair was as black as the void of the next world. She was death. I knew it. Somehow, I knew it.

She chuckled. *I wish I had the power reserves that the goddess of death has.*

Her voice had the Acadian lilt to, the accent unmolested by living on Earth for over a century.

You're her, I whispered back, never leaving where I was crumpled on the snow, but raising my eyes to meet her – golden eyes. Eyes so like my own but different too: a bit of red splattered around her pupil like blood before fading into the golden color.

What are you? I asked. What did shadowborn even mean? I knew she was the first, but how had she become the boogey-man? How had she made thousands more, tens of thousands more shadowborn over the many centuries of her life.

Your mother knows, she responded. *She knows everything, but she will only feed you selective truths because she is ashamed of what she's done, of all the horror she unleashed on both worlds.*

Just like Maria had said. My mother knew so much more than she was telling us, but–

I don't believe you, I said defiantly. *You're a liar and a murderer. You have killed so many innocents. For what? What reason could possibly be justified?*

I am not the monster you think I am, Cordelia. I am not even the monster you should be afraid of. I am nothing in comparison to her. Her voice was so melodic for exactly the monster I knew her to be.

I turned my head as I felt someone else in my head. No flames this time, all shadows.

I knew you were keeping her here, Ruyek said. *Leave her the fuck alone.*

Do you even know my name, sweet boy? the shadow queen asked.

I don't fucking care what your name is, he growled back.

My name is written many times inside of the king's archives, archives you are forbidden to enter until you are King of Vampires.

You're a liar, a master manipulator, and you need to fucking leave, Ruyek said as his shadows surged forward and pushed the woman to the ground.

I shielded my face as shadow and black fire exploded across my mind.

Snap out of it and build your fucking walls back, I heard Ruyek scream as his shadows continued to wrestle with the shadow queen's.

Build my walls up? I felt incapable of doing anything but lying down in the snow and waiting for the real death to come. I had nothing left. But then something happened. The black fire circled the mass of shadows that I knew was Ruyek.

He was screaming. His howls of pain pulled me out of the bottom of the well of pain I'd been wallowing in just enough for me to stand. I felt ice building to a crescendo inside me until my very blood felt frozen, and I shoved it all towards the flames and shadows. I willed the ice not to harm Ruyek. I'd never been able to control it like that, but I begged for my ice to freeze the flame and not the shadows.

A feminine scream of pain and the flames were gone far faster than they'd come. It was like her mind had translocated out of mine.

Build your fucking walls up, Cori, the shadows panted; Ruyek was clearly in pain from whatever he'd just endured. *And thank you.*

I turned back to the broken fortress of my mind and poured every bit of power left in me into rebuilding the walls of ice. The broken ice lay on the ground outside the new structure, like it could not be repurposed after whatever shifting had done to me, but the new walls looked different, somehow.

I turned to the mass of shadows to see Ruyek's power pushing into me, feeding me as I built my defenses back up. His shadows danced inside the frozen blocks of ice. When we finished, my walls were stronger than they'd ever been before, and I felt a single moment of safety before being dragged out of my mind into consciousness.

Ruyek, Ambrose, Caspian, and Savanna were all sitting on my bed, while Sabine stood just inside my door, frowning. Wait. Why was Sabine here?

I looked out the window at early morning light and had no idea what day it was or how long I'd been out. When had my windows been treated?

Yesterday, Ruyek said in my mind.

"Two days," Van said, watching me assess the window light.

"The general was convinced you'd be ready to train yesterday, but I told her I know a bit more about shifting than she does. I knew you needed to recover. Thanks for proving me right," Van said with a smile.

"What happened?" I asked, my head swimming with the bits of information I had pieced together. "Was my mother here? Why is Sabine here?"

Cas filled me in while everyone else listened – everyone but Sabine who huffed loudly and left the room while we talked.

I was silent after he explained what I was, what I could do. I knew then, I *knew* that I'd killed my sisters with the lack of control I had over this syphoning power. *Power like the shadow queen*, Cas had said, explaining how that power made her unkillable.

Everyone can die, Ruyek shadows said in response. *Blades or bullets work just fine. If you can bleed, you can die. Magical means though? That gets tricky.*

"We have to start training today," I said, pushing myself up in bed.

"You need to rest," Van said. "The first shift is the hardest. You have to rest before you can even attempt anything like that–"

"Untrained, I am dangerous," I interrupted. "I am a liability, making me an asset to the other side of this war. I have to be trained."

I watched Van look from Cas to Ambrose to Ruyek before nodding.

"Can we at least eat first?" Ambrose asked.

"I made protein shakes," Sabine replied as she stepped back into my room. "Drink them on the way to the gym."

Caspian

The protein shake was actually quite good. It didn't feel
like a well-rounded breakfast (and Ambrose had insisted on

knowing the ingredients before consuming it), but it was good and filled me up enough for the grueling workout Sabine was about to put all of through. Sabine ordered all of us to start with cardio before moving to weights, while she moved with Cordelia into the center of the gym.

The general explained that starting with witch magic would be less strenuous for the princess. I ran on the treadmill and watched as she talked through various things with Cordelia. She seemed to know exactly how to train her, and I couldn't help but wonder how she'd gained so much knowledge about the shadow queen's syphoning.

Magic eater. That's what my sister had told me the shadow queen was. She'd whispered it late one night when we were alone, like she shouldn't be sharing this with me. I didn't understand then why all the knowledge the Acadians had about the shadow queen had been kept under lock and key when we came through the rift. Wouldn't arming us with knowledge increase the odds of defeating her? If this prophecy to close the rift suddenly fell on our shoulders: didn't we deserve to know everything?

I upped the speed on the treadmill as anger pushed me forward. Anger that was quickly devouring the grief inside of me. I couldn't escape the feeling that Violetta should not be dead, that none of this would have happened if our elders had been honest with us. I wished Ruyek was a bit older, so maybe he could remember whatever it was they were hiding from us.

We had all moved on to lifting when something happened. Apparently Sabine's power had something to do with earth because when she grabbed Cori's arm for the hundredth time, Cori screamed as the entire gym, the entire castle, began to shake.

I watched as Ruyek grabbed Ambrose to him and cocooned them both in a mass of shadows so thick they were like a solid wall of protection. Van shifted into a bird and flew from the room in a hurry, while I threw a wall of water around me. The power in me, that alien power that didn't feel like the ocean, pushed at my insides as I stood there. I heard equipment falling around us. I feared the entire castle was falling down, and still, that alien power pushed and pushed and screamed to be let loose.

And then the shaking stopped.

"What did I tell you?" Cori yelled. "I'm fucking dangerous. I should be put down before I turn into the fucking shadow queen!"

I let my wall of water come down just in time to see Cori stomping from the room, tears streaming down her face.

"Here isn't going to work," Sabine said to the three of us who remained. "Pack a bag. We leave at dusk."

"Can she just order us to leave?" Ambrose asked.

"Either we trust her to train Cordelia or we don't," Ruyek said. "If we trust her, we need to pack a bag."

Luckily, the shaking had been isolated to Belle Isle. The city itself had felt only a small tremor, and no one had been harmed. The castle needed some repairs, all of which Sabine coordinated before lining us up outside after nightfall. We all had a bag. She'd been kind enough to tell us to pack for a tropical location (and assured Ruyek he'd been protected from the sun).

A familiar fae woman appeared on the lawn beside us.

"Are you a taxi?" Ruyek asked, clearly still pissed that Sabine had insisted Isolde stay here because where they were going was a place with limited food sources for hungry dragons.

"Don't be rude," Sabine said, stepping up to greet the woman. "Everyone, this is Autumn. She will be taking us to one of the most remote places in the world. Cordelia has to train, and we have to ensure no one is harmed during her training."

"Prince Ruyek." Sabine offered him a heavy cloak with a hood and sleeves that zipped. "It will be daylight when we arrive there."

"Are you fucking kidding me?" he asked.

"Remember," I heard Ambrose whisper softly. "We trust her or we don't."

"I'm beginning to lean *don't* on that scale," Ruyek said, but he pulled the cloak over himself and pulled zips and layers up until he was completely engulfed in several layers of heavy material.

"If you allow him to burn alive in the sun, his father will drink you dry," Van said gravely, his eyes meeting Sabine's.

"And he'll fuck your goddamn corpse when he's done," Ruyek added.

"We are very interested in keeping Prince Ruyek alive. The prophecy demands it," Sabine said, never flinching at any of the threats hurled her way.

"All at once?" Ambrose asked.

"Two at a time is easier for Autumn," Sabine said. "Prince Caspian, you will go first with Princess Cordelia."

How had I drawn the short straw to go first? But if I was going with Cori, I wasn't going to argue. I stepped up to her side and reached down for her hand.

"Hey," I asked quietly. "Are you okay?"

"I'm not," she whispered back. "I'm not okay at all."

A moment later, Autumn placed a hand on each of us, and we were spinning through reality. Wind, sunlight, and darkness swirled around us in inky layers until we hit the ground hard. Cori remained standing, but I slammed into the sandy ground beneath us.

"Welcome to Malden Island," Autumn said. "An uninhabited island quite literally in the middle of nowhere."

"Ruyek is going to love this," I responded as I looked around at the tropical island around us.

"We will ensure he has proper protected lodging when I return," Autumn said.

She was gone a moment, but just long enough for me to stand up and wipe the sand from my pants. Ruyek was going to hate this, but I was in paradise. I looked down the expanse of open beach. We were in the Pacific. I knew Malden Island. It was four thousand miles from Atlantis, but it was still close compared to many of the islands in the Pacific.

Then Autumn was back with Ruyek and Ambrose. Then, finally, Van and Sabine.

"Do not take your cloak off," Ambrose said to Ruyek urgently.

"I can smell the ocean. Trust me when I say I wouldn't fucking dream of it," Ruyek responded.

Cordelia found a large boulder to sit on. I sat next to her in silence while I watched Sabine, Autumn, and Ambrose (who'd been recruited to help) build a shelter. Sabine used her earth power to pull up dirt and sand with her powers to build a large rectangle that would apparently serve as our home. Ambrose was tasked with reinforcing it with plants. Luckily, he could conjure plants because the plantlife on this island left a lot to be desired.

Soon, the rectangle was covered in vines that dug through the earthen frame Sabine erected. He layered vines over vines over flowers over moss, until the walls were so thick an ounce of sunlight couldn't enter, except through the wide open space they'd left for a door.

That's apparently where Autumn came in. All fae had interesting qualities, almost like shifters. Autumn was a tall, willowy woman with ears far more exaggerated in their point than even Prince Ambrose's (which were impossible to miss). Her brown skin and long black hair were elegant but not uniquely fae. It was the two long black antennae and two short smooth black horns sticking out of her head that seemed very fae.

I watched as Autumn walked down the beach until she came to a particularly long, flat boulder that did look about the right dimensions for the door opening. Without even straining, she reached down and hoisted the massive boulder up and carried it back to us.

"Huh. A rhinoceros beetle then?" Van asked as Autumn carried the boulder back and placed it against the open doorway.

Ambrose nor Sabine looked shocked, as if they'd seen this sort of thing before. Maybe super strength and insectoid features were normal in the fae courts. Sabine and Ambrose worked their magic to create vine hinges and to fill in any cracks the boulder door left. When Sabine led all of us inside and closed the door, we were in utter darkness.

"You can take it off now," Ambrose said to Ruyek.

Ruyek only hesitated a moment before trusting the fae prince enough to reveal his skin to whatever lay around him.

"Still smells like the sea, but it will do," Ruyek said, a smile clearly in his voice.

All of us could see well enough in this darkness (except perhaps Cordelia, who didn't say much and just stood near the door while we worked). Ambrose made rooms using vines, deciding (like no one would notice) that he would bunk with Ruyek, I would bunk with Van, and Cordelia would bunk with Sabine and Autumn. The room was cut up into four rooms before long: three bedrooms and a main living area.

By the time the redecorating was done, Autumn translocated outside and then threw the door open. Nighttime. We all stepped outside one by one into a beautiful star-filled night. The moon was still mostly full. Only a tiny sliver of shadow proved it was starting to wane towards a new moon.

Autumn disappeared and reappeared with a box full of rechargeable lamps. A moment later, she was back with bedrolls and pillows. Clearly, Sabine had told someone to prepare everything we needed for a quick grab after the house was built. Autumn came in and went several more times, but I was drawn away from everyone else.

My feet pulled me towards the waters of my birth, of my life, and I could not fight the siren's song of the ocean. It was louder than it had been the night we stopped on the beach on the way to Richmond. This water was home. All the voices behind me were drowned out as I focused on the sound of the waves and the few animals on the island.

I stripped naked and walked into the water, shifting when I was deep enough. I took a deep breath through the gills on my sides and dove into the water. I swam and swam, stopping only to eat seaweed that passed by me or the occasional small fish. In that moment, I was far away from all the shadowborn, the wars, and the witch queen's iron fist. I was home, and I was myself in the waters that never stopped calling to me. I was mer, as mer were intended to be.

Cordelia

And so, we trained. We all attuned to Ruyek's needs and became nocturnal creatures. We wouldn't sleep until late in the morning after breakfast inside the make-shift house and some conversation. Sabine and Autumn had the foresight to let us eat and talk in private, making themselves scarce during the morning meal.

I tried to focus on the routine, pushing away all the thoughts that threatened to consume me, but the reality of my own culpability in my sisters' deaths never went away. Their voices screaming in my head did not quiet. It was my fault. I killed them, and it felt like there was nothing I could do to forgive myself for that.

I threw myself into training because it was something that could take up at least most of my brainspace. The island was roughly the shape of a triangle, with a ten mile perimeter. At nightfall, Cas, Van, Ambrose, Ruyek, and I started by running a five mile stretch of beach. We often spent time investigating the Polynesian runes and the faded memorial to the barbaric testing of hydrogen bombs the mortalborn detonated on the island two centuries ago.

I mastered Sabine's magic after just a week of trying. Witch magic was familiar. It was a language I understood, even if the dialect proved different from my own ice magic. Ruyek, Cas, Van, and Ambrose watched as I erected another hut after syphoning Sabine's magic. There wasn't enough earth on the island for the test I'd set for myself, but just like with my ice, I could create what I needed.

This hut was larger than our first with earthen walls separating the space into six equal-sized rooms. My fiances cheered as I finished construction and collapsed on the beach. I lay there in the sand, heaving heavy breaths as Ambrose reinforced the structure with vines, making a bamboo door covered in moss this time, rather than using a stone.

This structure was three miles from the first, and I listened as Van and Cas coordinated moving all of our bedding (and books – Ruyek had insisted Autumn bring us a small library for down time) to the new hut.

"Sabine and Autumn can stay in the original structure," Ruyek instructed. "I think it's high time we have our own space on this gods-forsaken island." To a vampire, I imagine an isolated tropical island *was* a gods-forsaken place.

After my first training milestone that night, we started a fire behind the new home I'd somehow built of earth. It felt surreal, whatever was happening to my magic. I'd added a layer of ice that would not melt to the outside of the structure as a feeble attempt at magical air conditioning. It was certainly cooler inside this structure than the last.

Sabine and Autumn had left the island for more supplies, leaving us alone in the endless night and silence of Malden Island. Simple conversation turned more serious as Cas' eyes met mine.

"Are you okay?" he asked – a normal question that everyone who was not okay answered with a lie, but I was tired of lying, of hiding the absolute wreck I'd become.

"No," I answered, my eyes holding his. They were so blue, as blue as the ocean, the water that was as crucial as breathing to him.

"Do you want to talk about it?" he asked.

Goddess be good, I did not want to talk about it, but something about his gaze and the earnest faces around the fire made me believe I could.

"I'm dangerous. We all know that I can train and I can learn how to use everyone's magic on this island, but I'll always be dangerous," I responded quietly.

"What are you not telling us?" Van asked gently.

I shook my head. "It's the truth. Without any more explanation, it's the truth. And if the shadow queen gets her claws in me again, I am a liability."

"What are you saying?" Cas asked, his eyes tender.

"I'm saying that something like me, like her, shouldn't exist, and if I wasn't the only witch princess left to inherit my mother's crown, I think everyone would agree with me."

Silence permeated around us. Even the crackling of the fire seemed to ebb as four worried stares tracked me.

"Everyone powers up during the ripening," Van finally said. "We all have to learn how to wield the store of magic we find ourselves with. You are not a liability, Cori. You're just young."

"Firstly, twenty-eight is only young by magicborn standards, and none of us know how many years I'll get. Secondly, everyone has powers that make sense, that are natural and predictable," I argued. Just because he was fond of me, it didn't make me any less dangerous or any less deadly.

"Mine aren't predictable," Cas said so quietly that mortalborn ears would have missed it. We all watched as he stood up and looked to the sky. It wasn't clear what he was doing at first, but soon, thunder roared in the distance. Heavy, black clouds blotted out the last quarter moon.

Van's mouth fell open as heavy raindrops started to fall and lightning streaked across the sky. This wasn't mer magic. Mer controlled water. They could create water, use it as a weapon or a life-giving force. No mer I'd ever heard of could call a storm into creation. That sort of power was–

"Incredible," Ruyek said, as if he was reading my mind – and it was entirely possible he was, so I reinforced my mental walls as warm rain began to drench us, drowning the fire quickly.

"How is this possible?" Ambrose asked, his eyes half-closed as the water fell.

"I don't know," Cas said. "I've searched archives and talked to the oldest mer in Atlantis. This shouldn't be possible. I feel like I am mer and something else entirely."

"Something this world has never seen before," Ruyek said, his tone ominous.

"What do you mean?" Cas asked.

"I– I need to consult our archives in Rome. I need to be sure," Ruyek said. He looked at Ambrose. "Fancy a trip to Rome? I'm sure my parents would be delighted to host us."

"Hey, I want to go," I said.

"You and Cas, it seems, need to train. You're right. You are dangerous as long as you're untrained," Ruyek replied. "You can choose to be far less dangerous if you learn how to control your powers. I mean that for the both of you." He looked from me to Cas.

Autumn returned before dawn. Ruyek explained they wanted to return to Richmond, where they would rest until nightfall before flying onward to the west coast of Ireland in a small castlehold the vampires had restored atop the Cliffs of Moher.

Isolde was the fastest dragon on Earth, but she still couldn't fly almost five thousand miles in a single nightfall. Even County Clare would be pushing her limits.

"You better both be in fighting shape when I return," Ruyek said, all of us standing around for our goodbyes before their departure.

"How long do you plan on being gone?" I asked, frowning without meaning to.

"A few weeks at least. There is something else that needs to be tended to, something that has been a long time coming." Ruyek's voice was low, ominous in a way that didn't make sense to me.

"I imagine things will be different before I return, but I will return. No matter what the tabloids say. I'm sure they'll latch on to the idea of a breakup once they spot me and Ambrose separated from the three of you." He took my hand in his as he spoke, a smirk on his face.

I realized then that he'd never held my hand before. Not like this. We'd all trained and cohabited together, creating a homeostasis that would be disrupted with Ruyek and Ambrose gone.

No matter what you hear, I will be back and I will keep us safe. Ruyek's voice whispered on the edge of my mind. I had secured my mind so thoroughly that whispering was all he could manage.

I nodded. He stepped up and wrapped his long arms around me, engulfing me in his essence. Iron and midnight surrounded me, drenching me in the otherness that had begun to feel a lot less *other* somehow.

Ambrose came next, replacing darkness with springtime. Jasmine and nectar. An image of a field full of wildflowers permeated my thoughts as he held me, looser than Ruyek had, more timid and unsure. I squeezed him harder at his reluctance and was surprised to feel him relax under my touch.

Everyone hugged and said their goodbyes before Autumn whisked the two of them away.

"Now what?" Cas asked. "Everything will be different now."

"We do exactly what Ruyek told us to," I answered. "We train. We learn to control whatever the fuck is inside of us."

"Good call," Sabine said. "The vampire prince is gone, so we can train at all hours of the day. I think a good ten mile run is in order. We can watch the sun rise."

"Awesome," I mumbled, but I fell in line after Sabine, who took off first, leading all of us in a run along the beach. Luckily, Cas and I practically lived in our running shoes since coming to Malden, and Van, per usual, shifted into an animal that did not need running shoes and would lap the island several times before we finished (a gazelle this time).

Ruyek

We arrived in Ireland moments before daybreak the night after we left Malden. My internal clock was fucked beyond compare, and I was suddenly grateful for the sun blocking technology the witches had deigned to share with me. The cloak kept me safe as the sky lightened. This world's sun was ruthless, even in tiny doses.

Isolde's poor mate had fallen behind not far into our journey. He was younger and slower, but she would keep me safe first. We both knew he was not far behind. Dragons were powerful magic wielders in their own right. Their fire was not a chemical reaction or some biological development. It was fire magic, and they had intricate, emotional lives just like magicborn and mortalborn. While they did not have a language we could perfectly understand, we easily communicated through feelings and intentions in each other's minds. It was well-accepted that dragons had their own language they could mindspeak with each other, which is perhaps why we'd created our partnership centuries earlier in Acadia. We were alike, dragons and vampires, both feared omens of death and destruction.

Isolde unloaded us right near the front entrance of the castle. I'd called the castle staff before leaving so they knew to air the place out and prepare the castle. Our staff lived nearby and worked here full time, just like they did when we took up residence, but their duties to an empty castle were far less involved than they were when one of the royal family was present.

Guards, maids, and cooks would alternate between day and night time shifts when we were there (though, the cooks were usually for show or non-vampire guests, which were rare). Luckily for Ambrose, we did keep cooks in residence just in case they were needed. Several guards stood outside the door as we arrived. The daytime guards were all powerful shifters, while the night time guards were all vampires.

Most of the household staff were mortalborn. We paid them well for what amounted to very little work when we were not there and ensured they were compensated extra when we did show up. Mortalborn were always nervous around vampires, but few vampires wanted to work as household staff in a castle that was abandoned the vast majority of the time. My father had only fed from and fucked a mortalborn maid here once to my knowledge. I was told it was consensual, but my mother insisted on accompanying my father every trip after that. Powerbound born of vampire and mortalborn unions were rare (very rare) but not unheard of in this strange new world.

The castle itself was attached to what had been O'Brien's Tower before we arrived on this planet. The tower had been restored and reinforced to its nineteenth century glory, and my father commissioned the sprawling castle of the same Liscannor flagstone as the original structure.

I helped Ambrose dismount from Isolde before rushing into the safety of the castle. Unlike the treated windows of the witch castles, most of the castles we built on this planet had no windows. Inside was an eternal night lit with LED candles that drew power from the windmill farm further up the coast.

It looked like an ancient castle from the decor, but it had all the modern amenities needed to be comfortable.

Ambrose shivered as we walked in the door into the front parlor. It was filled with modern, comfortable furniture and books on every wall. He looked around at all the books in shock, and I couldn't wait to show him the actual library here. He shivered again.

"Cold?" I asked.

"Freezing," Ambrose said, his lips shaking.

"I prefer the cold, you know. All vampires do," I replied.

A mortalborn man met us in the parlor.

"Your highness," he said with a deep bow and even deeper Irish accent.

"It's good to see you, Seth." I smiled. I'd never drank from the man, but we did have a dalliance two years earlier that made the summer I spent here absolutely delicious.

He blushed at my greeting.

"Please turn the air conditioning down a tad. My fiance is much more of a springtime creature," I instructed.

"Yes, your highness." Seth paused, straightened, and then bowed to Ambrose. "Your highness."

I watched as Ambrose watched him leave, as he looked from me to Seth like our interactions gave something away. Perceptive. I wasn't ashamed of having lovers during my previous engagement. There was no love there, no connection at all. Ambrose was different. Cas, Cori, and Van were different. I decided to make it a point to prove that to him – to all of them – soon.

"Seth?" I called after the mortalborn.

Ambrose stiffened next to me as Seth walked back into the room.

"Would you be willing to stay here with Prince Ambrose? I'm told the cliffs at sunrise are worth seeing. I wouldn't want him to miss out on them because of me."

Seth looked at me curiously before answering quickly. "Of course, your highness."

"Excellent," I responded. I leaned into Ambrose's space and kissed his cheek. "I'm told it's quite the sight at sunrise. You'll have to tell me all about it when you return."

Hours later, I heard the door to my chamber open. I'd been dozing, but I recognized the sound of Ambrose's steps as he walked toward the massive bed that dominated one of the walls of my chamber. A settee, a large desk, and shelves and shelves of more books completed the decor of my personal room. There were three doors: one led to the hall, one led to the bathing room, and one led to my own dining room.

The bed shifted with his weight as he crawled in behind me and pressed his front against my back. He wrapped an arm around me and kissed my neck, chasing any remnant of sleep away with touch.

I turned to him and looked into his vibrant green eyes. He was so beautiful, and yet, so unlike the sort of man I usually found myself attracted to. I usually craved rage and power. My affair with Van had been a fight for domination, a fight that had ended with both of us covered in blood and venom as my shadows bound his wrists while I fucked him. We'd both consented, of course, but that was the sort of sex I usually preferred with other men.

Even Seth, mortalborn and far less powerful than any magicborn, asked to be chased along the black cliffs at night. When I finally caught him, he'd punched me square in the jaw before opening for me. We both wanted to feel like we had to work for it, like there was actually a chance Seth could overpower me.

I thought of chasing Ambrose, of pushing him into the earth and fucking him until he screamed my name and shivered. That would be fun, more fun because I don't know that Ambrose would have the heart to fight back once I caught him. It would be an entirely different kind of connection with him. And even more importantly, I knew he'd be offering me more than his body. I had no doubt he'd offer me his very soul if vampires were truly the undead monsters of mortalborn legend.

I turned to Ambrose and met his lips. Our mouths met hungrily. I knew we'd missed this on the island. We'd been unsure of how to proceed with the eyes and ears of everyone so close. He moaned against me as his hand tangled in my hair. I'd taken the braid out I wore while riding, and my long hair was free and unbound over my shoulders.

I felt him stiffening against my abdomen.

"Ruyek," he whispered against my mouth. "Ruyek, I want this." He reached his hand between us and squeezed me through my briefs (the only clothing I was currently wearing).

I did too, but something about the timing felt off about it. He'd just spent time walking the cliffs with my former lover, a lover who he'd seem to clock for exactly what he'd been to me. No. No. Jealousy or fear of abandonment or whatever was going through his head would not be the reason we fucked for the first time.

I pulled away. "What are you doing?"

His cheeks went scarlet under my gaze. Even in the complete darkness of the room, I could see every feature clearly.

"I–" he stuttered and pulled away quickly. "I thought you want–"

"Do not confuse me, Ambrose. I want you unequivocally. Body and soul, I want every drop of you. Every wonderful and terrible thing you have to offer: I want it. But why now? Why after your walk with Seth? Talk to me."

He pulled away further, moving to the side of the bed and turning the lamp on the bedside table on. He could see well enough in the darkness, but his dark vision was nothing like mine. He looked down at his hands, his eyes so far away from mine that I worried my bluntness had hurt him.

"I–" He paused and looked up at the ceiling before pinching the bridge of his nose. "I want you to want me, Rue. I want you to want me like you've wanted so many others, and I want to show you that I have what you need – that I can be what you need. I've never really wanted to do that before. I didn't honestly think I could with Nadella, and now, we both know I was right. She loved someone else, had an entire family and life without me in it."

"You are what I need. You are precisely what I need, and if I wasn't worried that this timing was going to cheapen what you have to offer me, I would fuck you right now without hesitation," I responded gently.

"It won't–" he started, but I interrupted.

"Lay back on the pillows, Ambrose," I instructed.

He did as I asked, his eyes so uncertain. I moved to reach over him, pulling a bottle of lube from the drawer next to him.

"What are you doing?" he whispered, his voice trembling.

"I always imagined I'd take you first, you know. I so enjoy the taking, but I am an equal opportunist when it comes to sensation," I responded. "Are you sure you want this? Here? Now?"

He nodded, though I had the distinct impression he had no idea what he was consenting to. I straddled him, my cock trying to free itself from the hold of my briefs as his cock pressed against the soft silk pants he wore. He'd changed since we landed.

I pulled his t-shirt over his head and kissed him. My fangs itched the moment I tasted him again. I wanted his blood inside of me, all of him inside of me. I'd never been more sure. I stopped kissing him long enough to pull my briefs off and let myself press against his skin. It was still buttery soft, but his muscles were so much more defined after just a few weeks of training.

Taking the hint, Ambrose reached down and pulled his pants and boxers off. I lifted myself up to make it less awkward.

"Are you sure?" I asked again.

He nodded.

"Can I bite you?"

"Please," he begged.

I moved myself further down his body, straddling his thighs as I rubbed lube over him.

"Oh," he whispered, his eyes wide as he seemed to realize what was happening. "Rue," he moaned as I touched him.

I moved back over his chest, lined him up to my ass and breathed in as I lowered myself onto him. He was impressive, like all fae males I'd encountered – long and deliciously thick as he pushed into me.

I felt the burn of the stretch as I pushed in the first inch, and I met his gaze. He looked wild with need for me, and then, as if to prove it, he whispered again: "Please."

I took his mouth with mine, purposefully raking a fang over his lip and licking the blood that welled up in his mouth. I drank him in, poised just as I'd been with only an inch of his cock inside me.

Take control, I said inside his head.

I–I don't– he stuttered, his green walls trembling like an earthquake was shaking the foundation of his mind.

You do know. Do it, I growled inside him.

I pulled my mouth from his as he placed his hands on my hips and cautiously pushed me down another inch. I watched his eyes as they rolled back in his head, feeling himself inside of me, stretching me, and his pleasure made me come undone.

I moved so fast he would have no idea what was coming. I buried my teeth in his neck. He cried out in pain, but then his pain turned into pleasure as he moaned. I pushed myself down in a single movement, taking every inch of him until I was the one moaning.

Fuuuuck, I said in his mind. *Fuck. Fuck.*

My pleasure rippled between us as I drank his blood into me, sending warm tingling sensations through both of us as we shuddered against each other. And then I moved, riding Ambrose as I drank his blood slowly, savoring every drop just as I savored every inch of him inside me.

I refused to let myself cum as he came apart inside of me, his pleasure screamed into the castle so loudly that everyone inside must have heard him.

"Rue," he panted as he came down, realizing I had not cum.

"Get on your knees," I panted. "I want more. I want all of you. I don't have the self-control to wait."

Ambrose

I caught my breath a moment before following Ruyek's command. I wanted this. I wanted him, but I was terrified of everything, of all of it. I was ready, but I had no idea what to be ready for.

He moved my hips where he wanted them and pushed my face down into the pillow from where he was positioned over me. I realized then that he hadn't sealed the wound on my neck and blood was staining the silver pillowcase beneath me. Somehow, the thought of me bleeding all over his bed turned me on and I felt myself hardening again.

Goddess above. He was going to unravel me. Everything I never knew I wanted was right here, right behind me he rubbed lube on my ass and slipped one finger inside of me. He leaned over me again, sinking his teeth back into my bleeding neck just as he shoved two more fingers inside of me at once.

I stiffened at the intrusion, at the stretch.

Relax, he said in my mind.

I tried to listen to him, but I felt I was going to short circuit as the pleasure from his fangs mixed with the pleasure of his fingers pumping inside, pressing against my prostate as he moved.

I'm ready, I said back to him. His shadows were still coiled in my head, and I knew he was waiting. *Please. I want this. I'm ready.*

He licked the wound on my neck before repositioning himself. I felt him press against me, and the cold metal of one of his cock piercings reminded me that I had to take more than just his dick.

I breathed in and out slowly as he pressed against me, my body tight against the sensation.

"If you don't relax, it will hurt," he instructed, one of his hands rubbing my back as I remained tense.

"I–" Goddess. What *did* I want? I wanted to relax so I could enjoy this, but I also wanted him to fuck me, to hurt me deliciously.

"Do you want me to hurt you, Prince Ambrose?" Ruyek's voice was a low growl, a sensual promise.

I nodded into the pillow. Yes. Yes, I very much wanted Rue to destroy me, to unravel me in ways I never imagined.

And by the goddess, *he did*. He pushed himself into me, forcing himself past my initial resistance in a single thrust. I shuddered as the pain and the pleasure of his invasion rolled through me in waves. The metal of his first cock ring rubbed against my prostate as he slowly moved before pulling back out.

"Please," I begged again (in what I hoped was not a pathetic plea).

I felt Ruyek's hands on my hips as he lined himself up again and then, in a single thrust, buried himself inside of me.

I screamed. Pain. Pleasure. Pain. Pleasure. The pressure inside me threatened to tear me apart as he moved, both of his piercings rubbing against my prostate as he took me in long, deep thrusts. He pulled almost all the way out before thrusting back in and the room was filled with the sounds of his moans and my gasps.

I had no control over the sounds that came out of me as he leaned in close and pushed himself in as deep as he could go, his hand shoving my face into the bloody pillow as he pushed in deeper, deeper, *deeper*.

I could hear the cadence of his moans changing as he neared his peak, and just as his free hand wrapped itself around my cock, we both came. His warm cum filled me as my own covered the sheets below us.

We both stayed like that for a beat, our heavy breathing filling the air as I felt him going soft inside me before pulling out and throwing himself on the bed next to me.

"I need you to promise me something," Rue said as I lowered my ass and moved to face him on the bed.

"Anything," I said, my breaths still ragged.

"Never doubt how desirable you are again. Not to me. Not to Cas or Cori or Van," he whispered. "You could cut the sexual tension on that island with a knife, and one day, all of us are going to be in the same place at the same time in the same mindset. I don't know about the accuracy of any prophecy, but I do know that we are going to have a delicious fucking future together, and that you are going to spend the rest of your long life being thoroughly desired and properly fucked. Promise me that you won't ever forget that."

I nodded, feeling sure of myself for the first time in forever. "I promise."

"Now, let's go shower so we can wash ourselves off before I fuck you again." He smirked as he looked at me, his fangs on full display as his red eyes held my gaze. I shivered in anticipation because that sounded like the best plan I'd ever heard.

Savanna

One day of training ran into the next on the island, and
Sabine was a relentless trainer. Without Ruyek here to slow

us down during the sunlight hours, she pushed us harder than ever. Beyond his sensitivity to light, it made me wonder for not-the-first-time how terrified the witch queen and her guards were of Ruyek. He was more powerful than his father by leagues, and he could take the throne whenever he wanted. Power was what chose the monarch of the vampire kingdoms. The royal family had been stacking the deck for centuries with arranged marriages to extremely powerful vampires, ensuring the crown passed from father to son.

Though it was not always the oldest or only son and the succession was almost always covered in blood. Women were notoriously disallowed to inherit in the vampire kingdom. It was the only such domain left in the magicborn world (though of course, there had only been one short-lived witch king in Acadia's histories).

Cori mastered water easily, pulling Cas' power into her and manipulating it as quickly as she had Sabine's magic. His storms and newer abilities, they were both struggling to wield with any degree of finesse. Cas could call a storm without issue, but he struggled to get it to stop at times. Other times, it was only there a few minutes before dissipating back into clear skies.

Cordelia hadn't tried to shift since Richmond, and I felt like we were saving that for last. We spent long hours into the night talking about how to put the pain of the shift into a box, to contain it inside yourself so that you could not feel it.

One such night, a week after Ambrose and Ruyek left, Cas, Cori, and I sat around another fire, our voices low despite us being far from the prying ears of Sabine. Autumn was on the island far less frequently over the last week, only coming by with fresh supplies and reports from Queen Rixana for a short time each day.

"If you can conquer mer magic, you can conquer shifting," I told Cori, her eyes staring straight ahead into the flames.

"Why?" she asked quietly without looking up. "Why do I have these abilities? This curse?"

Cas responded, "Few would think your abilities a curse. I bet people would kill for–"

"People have already died for it," she whispered.

Cas looked from me to Cori as silent tears fell down her face.

"Are you talking about New York?" Cas asked.

Cori nodded. "Did you already figure it out then? Already realized you don't get to marry the woman you love because of me?" Her voice was angry and hurt, the grief written all over her face.

Cas sighed and looked up into the night sky at her words. He just – didn't respond, and I could almost feel Cori's heart breaking in the silence. I think we'd all figured it out. The way she clearly shouldered the blame for the deaths of her sisters, despite them being attacked by the shadowborn. Maria's insistence that none of them were supposed to die that night. The dragonfire – it all felt like a cosmic, tragic accident that Cori couldn't forgive herself for.

"They attacked you, Cori," I finally said, my voice soft. "You were fighting for your life, and no one ever even bothered to tell you this kind of power was possible. You have to let go of this blame you keep–"

"I've been afraid to really talk about her," Cas interrupted me, like he hadn't heard me at all. "I don't know how to talk about all the ways in which we did not love each other, all the ways in which I am beginning to love both of you."

I snapped my eyes to him. What in both realms was he saying?

"I did love Vi in my own way. We both learned to love each other because we believed we could choose happiness in a way that none of the others did," he continued, his eyes still on the sky. I watched as Cori moved her own gaze to where he was looking, like they were both seeing something I was missing. "I found a way to be happy with her, and I am sad and angry and broken at her loss.

"But spending this time with you, with all of you – Ambrose and Ruyek too – has made me realize that the prophecy *was* wrong the first time. Vi shouldn't have died because the seers were wrong. None of them should have, and I don't know if their deaths were designed by the goddess to set us on the right path or just a fucking tragedy that forced us to reexamine the prophecy.

"I miss her. I'll always miss her. I grieve for her, but I had no chance at true, soul-deep happiness with Violetta." He snapped his eyes from the sky to Cori, and I watched as their gazes met. "I forgive you, Cori. Even if you cannot forgive yourself for that which you had absolutely no control over, I forgive you.

"I'm not glad they're dead. I wish they weren't, but I need you to know that even if Vi was alive, I would have found my way to you, to this reality where everything makes sense. It would have broken her heart and mine, but I know now that if I had spent any more time in your vicinity than I did in the last decade, I wouldn't be able to deny what is happening right now."

Cas looked at me now, meeting my eyes. "Van, we have been friends for so long, and at the first suggestion we were destined for marriage, I knew that the love between us was more than friendship. It has always been more than friendship. I never wanted to hurt Vi. I wanted to be able to give her all of me, but I never did.

"To be quite frank, she didn't want all of me either. I was too *other* for her. She looked at me like an animal when I was in my mer form, in my natural, real form. And it wasn't her fault, but it made me ashamed of myself, of who I am.

"Me and Vi made the most out of a situation we had no control over, a situation none of us truly wanted. I'd much prefer to deal with breaking her heart than burying her, but all of that is beyond our control now. It is and was beyond your control, Cordelia. I need you to believe that."

Tears poured down Cori's cheeks as she looked at Cas, looked at him like she desperately wanted to believe him.

Our moment was broken by the sound of Sabine's voice carrying down the beach.

"Atlantis is under attack," she yelled as she ran towards us.

Autumn appeared next to the fire a moment later.

"What do you want to do?" Her eyes met Cori's, awaiting the command of the highest ranking witch royal on this side of the world.

"Cas?" Cori asked, sniffing and wiping her face as we all stood.

"I have to go," he looked at Autumn frantically. "You have to take me to Atlantis."

"Us," I said. "Take us to Atlantis."

General Sabine paused a moment, as if remembering Queen Rixana's insistence that Cori would not be on the frontlines of this war again, but then she met Cori's eyes and nodded.

Her agreement to follow Cori's orders over Rixana's felt like a cosmic shift that would ripple across time and space.

Autumn reached out her arm, and we all grabbed onto her. A moment later, we were falling through water. I shifted into a great white shark as we fell through the ocean towards the castle below the waves and watched as Caspian pulled the water from around Cori, Autumn, and Sabine (who I had honestly not expected to come with us), creating a pocket of air for them to breathe as we sank.

We only fell a few moments before the water around us was a blur or shadow, tentacles, and fish tails. The water around the Great Barrier Reef was not very deep, and the mer castle spread out across the ocean floor in front of us, the highest towers breaching the surface easily.

I knew Cas' powers would be diverted keeping fresh air bubbles around three people, so I nudged Cori with my snout. She'd seen me shift, so the massive shark in front of her didn't cause her any alarm. She looked into my eyes and nodded before placing her hand on me. I pushed my power towards the surface of the smooth skin of the shark.

She held her eyes tightly as she pulled the power from me. The pain of the shift rippled through her, through the water as her skin stretched and stretched and stretched into a massive black and white orca.

The orca shook a moment before feigning left and closing her mouth around a shadowborn with long green tentacles. Black blood and thick shadows filled the waters as she shook the shadowborn. I flanked Cori, biting through what looked like shadowy mer. I knew the shadowborn could take the forms of any creatures, but I didn't know that there were any mer left in Acadia to corrupt.

The water darkened as a storm rolled in, tossing all of us around with its might, with the fury that rolled off of Caspian as he pulled lightning down from the sky and fried shadowborn after shadowborn. The water crackled with the electricity, even though he was clearly working hard to concentrate the strikes on our enemies and keep all of us from being electrocuted in the process.

Cori and I stuck together, fighting around the perimeter of the castle as shadowborn poured in from all directions. Mer fought next to us: tridents and spears working alongside their water magic against the shadowborn. The water grew darker as the storm raged and the shadowborn filled the waves with thick, inky darkness.

A flash of golden hair descended from above, and I looked up as Cori turned to face the shadowborn approaching her. Cori shifted back into her normal body, her cheeks full of air that would run out too quickly as she faced the woman heading straight for her.

The water around her froze, catching mer and shadowborn alike as it traveled through the waves towards the shadowborn woman. Was this the shadowborn general she'd spoken of? The golden-haired woman who attacked her that night in New York? It had to be.

Black fire, an impossibly hot shadowfire that boiled the water around us, erupted from the woman as she faced Cori. The fire couldn't burn through the layers of ice radiating from Cori. Her power rumbled through the ocean like an earthquake as she approached the woman.

I knew Cori could destroy the shadowborn general, but I feared she'd run out of air before she did. But the lack of air did not seem to slow her down as shackles of ice wrapped themselves around the woman. The general pushed them away with her fire, fury burning in her eyes as Cori approached her, the ice getting harder and harder to burn through as the distance between them lessened.

Cori was a gods-damned superhero. She seemed unstoppable as she sucked the woman's fire into herself, swallowing all of that power down into wherever she kept all the power that she could syphon, could take from others and wield herself. Ice froze the woman's legs and arms as she screamed into the sea, wasting what little air she had left in defiance of the most powerful witch on this planet. Rixana's fire be damned. Cori was a goddess as she froze the woman in place, cocooning her in ice just as her eyes shifted to meet mine. Cori nodded a moment before closing her eyes and falling towards the ocean floor. Her air, it seemed, her final bit of oxygen, had finally run out.

Caspian

I swam through the palace. The battle raged outside its walls, but my mother was inside. I saw Adara fighting the shadowborn, but my mother was absent, distractingly absent. I couldn't call the storm off after I called it. Carefully wielding the lightning had been the absolute limit of my control over that strange power.

The castle was so empty, like every available mer was outside fighting in the battle. I heard voices as I swam towards my mother's throne room. The doors to the throne room were closed, and they didn't budge as I shook them.

"Show me my mother," I yelled as I shook the doors that were clearly secured from inside the room. "My mother." I sobbed. "Please."

"Prince Caspian," a sing-songy voice called behind me.

I whipped around to see a horror I had only ever read about, only ever seen in childish nightmares. The creature that faced me was not a mer. It was an abomination, a creature created with dark magic. It had a long black fishtail similar to the tails of some mer, but the tail was so long, serpentine and monstrous in a way that was distinctly not-mer. Hooked spikes of black bone ran down the length of its tail, hooks that I knew contained a deadly venom with no antidote.

But the creature's face and its torso made it very clear I was not looking at a mer. The face was skeletal, with empty eye sockets and gray flesh that hung from its bones. The rest of the humanoid upper half was similarly rotted and decaying, an undead horror created in the depths of Acadia.

"Siren," I growled. "You do not belong here. This planet is not yours."

"So angry," the creature said, curling her lipless mouth of black and broken teeth into a smile. "Just like your father, I suppose. He has always been angry. Angry that the strongest of you left, abandoned him and his to a grim fate. Angry that he could not convince your sister – wait, sister? That's not right. Angry that your *mother* would not come back with him when he came through the rift for her. You were fated for Acadia, you know. Some savior for the people from her dark designs, but I hear you're going to close the rift and leave everyone there to us, to *meeeee*."

She – he – it – the thing that swam before me drew out the *me* with another wicked smile.

"Where is my mother?" I growled. I had no time for whatever riddles the siren felt like playing with.

The siren looked back down the hall. "I imagine she's outside where you left her," it said. "But Queen Morgana is in her room just like the coward she's always been."

Enough. I lunged for the siren, wrapping my hands around its boney neck and squeezing. The creature laughed as the bone cracked beneath my grip.

"If she wasn't a coward," it croaked out, "she'd have killed you the moment Adara brought you to her."

I screamed into the quiet castle, so quiet compared to the roar of the battle only moments before and snapped the siren's head from its body.

"It'll have to be burned," Adara said, her appearance surprising me from further down the hall. Her eyes were wide, as she was stunned and maybe – frightened? "Take it into the dry dungeons and burn it, Caspian. Now."

"But mother–" I began.

"My mother is dead," Adara said, putting a strange emphasis on *my*. "Burn the siren. Your fiances are waiting in the witch chambers. Recovering, I hope. I'll meet you there."

She swam away without any more explanation than that.

Ruyek

The first few days in Ireland were a blur or sex and sleep. I
eventually came out of my room to comb through the castle

library for information, but I only found two books of any interest. One was on Acadian prophecies and another was on Acadia before the old gods were abandoned for the goddess.

"It's interesting," I said, drinking a glass of blood in bed with Ambrose pressed against me, his eyes closed in the afterglow stupor of post-sex bliss. "There's a prophecy that claims the only son of Phorcys will descend from–" I paused. The book was ancient, written in Ancient Acadian. I'd studied it as a child, but it was a dead language and much of it was lost to time.

"Ascend?" I tried again, setting the glass down on the bedside table. "Hmmm. The son is definitely coming from somewhere to do something."

"Who's Phorcys?" Ambrose asked with opening his eyes.

"One of the old gods," I said. "The god of the sea, I think, and maybe drowning and other terrifying ocean things."

"Cas would love him then. All the terrifying things that are only really terrifying to non-mer," Ambrose mused. "Why did we turn away from the old gods?"

"*We* didn't turn away from the old gods. Vampires have held fast to the old traditions. Everyone else did, and for all the reasons people worship new deities: someone more powerful stepped onto the scene," I answered.

"What?" Ambrose opened his eyes at that. "You think the old gods and the goddess were corporeal? That they had real power?"

"You can have power and not be corporeal, but yes. The goddess was most definitely corporeal. She visited the monarchs for centuries before retreating to Tirnanahg. Maybe she died, maybe she just grew tired of us." I shrugged. "But if she was a real being who could deign to show herself, eat, drink, and fuck: why not the old gods?"

"How do you know she ate, drank, and fucked?" Ambrose asked.

"You really don't know anything." I shook my head. "The stories. The songs. Everyone knows she made merry with the magicborn when she visited, enjoying all the delights of the flesh. My father even claims her blood is in our royal line. He says that's the reason we are monarchs. Divine right of kings apparently transcends worlds."

Ambrose sighed. "Why do you know all of this? And more importantly, why don't I?"

"When people take over new places, they often forget where they came from. They forget the ills of the old world and steal the customs of the conquered, molding them into some amalgamation they can claim is a compromise of cultures. You think gods and goddesses are magical beings up in the sky because the mortalborn believed that for thousands of years.

Everyone from Acadia – everyone born in Acadia, remembers the truth. We just choose to forsake it because we feel removed from it, like we can be someone else here – a new people entirely. But I remember. All the heads of state remember. The historians, the learned among us, all know so much we just don't talk about it."

"Is it because you're scared?" Ambrose asked, his voice suddenly somber. "Scared that the old world is creeping in to take this world from us?"

I laughed dryly. "I can't say we deserve to keep this world we stole from the mortalborn, but yes. All of us are afraid of going back to how things were. We ran headfirst into the great unknown to escape the old world. We can't go back, Ambrose. Whether it's right or fair that we took this world, we can't go back."

His green eyes held mine. Moonflowers and evening primroses were blooming around his antlers, and it didn't seem like an accident that since our bodies found a rhythm together, the flowers he favored all bloomed at night.

I traced my finger along the flowers gently, felt him shiver when my knuckles brushed his antlers. We'd learned very quickly that his antlers were erogenous. I turned towards him and wrapped my hands around each antler, gingerly rubbing them up and down until he was nearly panting.

I pushed the books away and positioned myself over him, pushing his legs against his chest as I pushed into him again. We were both so covered in lube, blood, and cum that there was more than enough moisture to lead me in.

It didn't get old. We fucked hours and hours of every day, and I never tired of him, never tired of his body around mine. He was just as tight every time, always clamping down in hesitation as I pushed into him and past the resistance.

My bite marks on his neck had begun to scar. I wanted to mark him, wanted to brand him with my venom and my fangs. Just as I hoped to leave my mark on Cas, Cori, and Van when we returned. Ambrose and I had gotten a head start together, but they were never far from my mind. I missed them, but I knew Ambrose needed this time to come into his own sexuality before opening up to them.

I leaned down and bit him again. His blood was effervescent, sweet and young and addictive. He tasted like he smelled, like a sunny meadow I could only imagine in this world, a ray of sunlight that did not burn me when I felt it bursting inside of me.

My strokes were greedy as I pounded into him. His moans, his nails digging into my arms, made it very clear he didn't mind the unforgiving pace. I felt him tensing beneath me as I hit deeper and deeper, opening up every part of him as I claimed him.

Don't cum, I whispered in his mind.

Please, he begged. *Please, please.*

Don't cum, I commanded again just as I went over the edge, filling him for the third time since sunset.

I knew his body was raw from our efforts, but I also knew he would heal quickly. A few hours rest would make him good as new. I pulled out of him and moved my mouth from his neck to his dick, taking him into my mouth. I felt him fighting the urge to cum as he filled my mouth, my throat, and then I pulled away and looked up at him.

"Do you trust me?" I asked.

He nodded, his eyes pleading for release. He'd let me do anything right now. He watched me as I pushed three fingers into his ass, rubbing his prostate until precum dripped from the head of his dick.

"Please, Rue. Please let me–"

I interrupted him with a bite. My fangs sunk into the head of his cock. He cried out at first, tensing up beneath me, but then the venom sank in and he closed his eyes in pleasure as I drank his blood and precum down. One, two gulps, and I knew he was losing the fight against his orgasm.

Cum, I commanded in his mind. *Fill my mouth with all of you.*

He obeyed. Cum and blood flooded my mouth, a sensation I savored. He came and came, dumping what felt like several orgasms worth of cum down my throat as he emptied himself. I knew this would be the last round tonight. In the morning, we'd translocate to Rome. I wanted to ensure my father had no idea we were coming.

The next leg of our journey was very carefully planned. I needed my father to be caught unaware. He no doubt knew we were on vampire kingdom soil, but he'd be watching for us to leave at night on Isolde. I explained to Isolde as clearly as I could that she could head to Rome with her mate at sundown.

My father knew the fae in his territories who could translocate. They were all registered and knew they could be called on at any moment. We all preferred to travel by dragon, but sometimes there wasn't time. I sent Seth out the very first day we arrived to find someone my father didn't know about who could take us quietly to Rome.

It had taken a week for Seth to find a powerbound of fae heritage who had only discovered his ability to translocate within the last year. Seth assured me that he could translocate others without issue and that my father had no idea. Apparently, my father had some unwritten rule about powerbound being unable to register to do much of anything in his kingdom. If nothing else, the bastard was as prejudiced as ever.

"Your highnesses," Seth said as he introduced us to Aodhán.

The boy looked like what I imagined a powerbound young man with a fae mother would look like. He wasn't the ethereal beauty most fae were, but his facial features were still delicate and soft. His was shorter than most fae and his body was strong and stout, giving away his mortalborn heritage more clearly than his ears; his ears came to a slight point, but they weren't the severe, sharp points of Ambrose's ears.

"Your highness," Aodhán said, bowing awkwardly in our direction.

Seth had told me the man's fae mother lived on a quiet farm with her aging, mortalborn lover. Clearly, she'd raised her son like a mortalborn because he looked absolutely terrified as he avoided my eyes.

"Have you shown him my chambers?" I asked Seth.

"Of course, your majesty – pictures from every angle. He knows where we're going." Seth bowed again, cutting his eyes to Ambrose with a smile. He was absolutely smitten with my fiance. I knew it. Ambrose knew it, and we'd both turned down a threesome several times over the last week.

We have three other fiances who will definitely care if we bring someone else to our bed. I'd told him.

Do they have to know? he'd asked, putting on his most charming smile.

You're being impertinent. Dismissed.

Seth'd walked away from me like a puppy with his tail between his legs. I didn't blame him, of course. Ambrose was so very pretty.

"Have you paid him?" I asked Seth.

"Half now, half when you let me know you've safely arrived," Seth responded, holding out a cell phone for me to take.

I hated them. Most magicborn did. It took all the charm out of life, the mystery. The need to know where everyone was every second of the day was unsettling.

"Fine," I said. "Then let's get to it."

Aodhán held out an arm for me and Ambrose. Ambrose hesitated only a moment before grabbing on. A blur of winds and darkness, and we were standing in my empty chambers in my father's castle.

"Your majesty," Aodhán bowed in my direction, and then he was gone again.

"Did he just call you *your majesty*?" Ambrose asked.

"I need to tell you something," I said, putting up shields of thick shadows against every entrance and exit to my chambers to block any prying ears.

"I know," Ambrose said, frowning slightly. "I know you think I'm a ditz who doesn't notice anything, but I'm not an idiot."

"What? I don't think you're an idiot. I just–"

"Stop trying to protect me, Rue. We're in this or we're not. You brought me here knowing how dangerous this is," Ambrose interrupted, his usual cheerful demeanor replaced with severity. "You don't need to tell me. I know. I just need you to promise me that you know you can win."

"Without a doubt." I nodded. "I've known for a long time, maybe twenty-five years or so."

"So what now?" Ambrose asked.

"First, I'm going to let Seth know we're here safely, and then I'm going to fuck you until we're both so exhausted we fall into a deep sleep until sundown. Then we're going to take what is mine," I said.

Cordelia

I was drowning. I'd used the last of my precious air to bind the shadowborn general in ice shackles that would not melt.

Even if I died, they would remain. Death was cold, just like I preferred. I fell into it easily, my burdens slipping away as cold fingers closed around my shoulders.

It felt like I was being pulled onto someone's lap. And I was small, so small. Was it my mother's lap? I couldn't remember her ever holding me like this. My father? Yes. But my mother? No, never.

"Soraeda," my mother's voice rang out in my head.

I felt her lips on my forehead, but I couldn't see anything. Everything was impenetrable blackness, but I could hear and feel.

"Don't leave, Mother." A voice came out of my mouth, the voice of a child, but it wasn't *my* voice. It had never been my voice. The lilt was clearly Acadian.

"I'll be back this time next month, my girl."

"Please, Mother, please–" not-my-voice pleaded. I felt myself shaking, fighting sobs.

"And your father will come with me when I return. You haven't seen him in so long."

"Please–" the small voice coming out of me pleaded.

And then she was gone. I was gone – or whoever I was in that moment was gone. I felt like I didn't have a body, like I was a soul floating down a cold river.

It was peaceful, floating towards what came next. Mother talked about Death like she was a person, rather than a place.

Father talked about Death like it was Valhalla, some place souls went to drink and be merry together in the next life. Maybe it was both or neither. I could feel someone with me, but there was no wine or singing like my father described.

If I was dead, I didn't have to close the rift. I didn't have to learn to wield the magic of others, and most importantly, I didn't have to wear my mother's black crown. She would have to find someone else powerful and hungry to prove herself, to be adopted as the next heir to the Witch Queendom. I could just stop all of this. Stop fighting the voice that told me I deserved to die for killing my sisters.

I forgive you, Cori. Even if you cannot forgive yourself for that which you had absolutely no control over, I forgive you. The memory of Cas' words broke the silence all around me.

Cas. Van. Ruyek. Ambrose. I stood up, digging my feet into the clay bottom of the river. Everything around me was black, nothingness, but their names grounded me.

I forgive you, Cori. His words rang out loudly, and I wasn't sure I wanted to go back but I wasn't sure I wanted to die either. So I just stood there, letting the water move around me and holding on to four names: Caspian. Savanna. Ruyek. Ambrose. Caspian. Savanna. Ruyek. Ambrose. Caspian. Savanna. Ruyek. Ambrose. Caspian. Savanna. Ruyek. Ambrose. Caspian. Savanna. Ruyek. Ambrose. Caspian. Savanna–

Cori! Cori, please. You have to wake up. You have to. It was Savanna's voice ringing out in the silence.

We need a healer! Another voice, this one I didn't recognize.

Feet shuffling around me. Someone was carrying me, holding me. My back was pressed against someone's chest, and then my lungs were burning and the darkness around me shattered as I vomited salt water everywhere.

I blinked at the brightness of the room, of this reality that had colors and sounds and feelings. And my lungs *burned*. Goddess be good, I felt like every breath was on fire as I gasped air back into my body.

I was lying against Van's chest, his arms wrapped around me, and a fae healer leaned over me, her eyes still wide with concern as she checked my pulse. We were in rooms filled with air, but I could see the ocean through the windows. The witch chambers in Atlantis then.

"I thought I was dead," I croaked out, my throat burning.

"Shhh," Van whispered, pulling me further up his chest and burying his face in my neck like a cat. "Don't speak. You need to rest."

"You were dead," the fae healer said. "Clinically, at least. Your heart stopped beating, but only for a few minutes."

"How are you here?" Van asked, pulling his head out of my hair to look at her. "Why are you in Atlantis?"

"Autumn came for me," the healer said, looking over her shoulder at the fae woman they'd all grown to know quite well. "She told me my services might be needed and brought me here."

"Autumn–" Van started, but she interrupted.

"I serve the witch queen, Prince Savanna. There was no way in this world or the last, that I was going to allow the only heiress to Queen Rixana's throne to fight in a battle with the shadowborn without healers."

"Thank you. Whatever your reasons, thank you." Van held me close as he spoke, like he was afraid I was going to slip back into that dark river if he didn't ground me here. He didn't know, of course, didn't know that he *had* grounded me here.

Caspian. Savanna. Ruyek. Ambrose.

And whatever that fact meant for me, for us – I wasn't going to forget it.

"Goddess above." Cas' voice pulled me away from any thoughts of staying in Van's arms and drifting into much-needed sleep. I'd shifted and apparently been momentarily dead after expending a lot of magic. I was tired.

Cas shifted his tentacles away as he stepped through the door of the room. It was so strange to see a hallway filled with water that wasn't seeping into this waterless space. And then, he ran to me, throwing himself across my lap, pulling me and Van into him and sobbing.

"I'm okay," I croaked, my throat somehow more sore than it had been when I'd come to. A good sleep was definitely in order if I was ever going to talk again.

"She came back to us," Van whispered, his eyes watery as he looked down at me. "She came back. She's safe."

We stayed like that a while, Cas crying into the blanket someone had been kind enough to cover me with (because I still didn't know how to shift my clothes back with me) while Van held me tightly and kept his head buried against the crook of my neck.

I woke up in a strange bed, unaware I had fallen asleep at all. I remembered leaning back against Van and thinking about how nice it would be to sleep, and then I was here in a large bed in the witch chambers. They were empty now, except for Van and Cas who were sleeping on either side of me.

Light filtered in through the window, but filtered through a quarter mile of ocean, it was different from the sunlight I was used to. It made me think about Ruyek. He could stay here without burning alive in the sunlight; all the UV rays were dispersed within fifteen feet of water.

Cas turned over, still asleep, and draped an arm over me, and I leaned into him. He was warm, so unlike the cold river I dreamed about. I snuggled into him and breathed him in. He smelled like salt and summer, and long ago memories of a day at the ocean pulled at my memory. Violetta and Roselle had taken me. Their laughter was music as they watched me run into the water and then run out, squealing like young children do through the excitement of a new experience.

A few of the queen's guard stood a few feet behind them, watching as mortalborn and magicborn on the beach gave us a wide berth; they were all most certainly aware of what would happen if they approached the youngest witch princess uninvited.

Violetta. My eyes snapped open.

"The general," I said aloud, pushing Cas' arm off and sitting up in bed.

Cas and Van jolted away.

"What?" Van asked sleepily.

"The shadowborn general. Where is she? Is she alive?" I asked as I scrambled out of bed. Someone had slipped a nightgown over my head. Without shame, I ripped it off and grabbed the pair of silk pants that looked like it had been set out for me and pulled them on.

"In the dungeons," Cas answered. "She's locked up, Cori. Bound in ice shackles that will not melt and iron chains."

I stopped my frantic dressing and looked at the two of them. They were wide awake now and desperately trying to avoid staring at my naked breasts.

"Come back to bed," Van whispered, his voice a dark promise. "Please, Cori. Come back to bed."

I hesitated only a moment before pulling the silk pants back off and climbing into bed completely nude between Cas and Van. This was it, right? We were getting married, and whether or not I felt guilty about it, it wasn't wrong to want them. We were engaged.

I could see both of them reacting beneath their sleep pants as I wriggled between them. They were both shirtless.

I pushed my ass against Van's crotch as I settled against him. Cas moved closer, sandwiching me between them.

"I'm not ready for everything," I whispered, like speaking at a regular volume would burst the moment, "but–" I paused, breathing heavily, "you can both touch me – if you want to, I mean."

All my bravada seemed to fade when attempting to actually speak the words – to speak my intentions, my desires aloud. I don't think it was shame that had me bumbling like an idiot, but fear of rejection. Fear that I was not the same grounding force in their world that they were becoming in mine. I'd heard

Cas when he told me we were *it* for him, that this marriage was his destiny. But I still found myself doubting all of this, everything that was growing between us on what felt like irredeemably barren ground after heartbreak and grief molded me into someone I didn't recognize.

Van answered with his hands. Large fingers caressed my side before moving to my breasts, cupping one and then the other before rolling a nipple between the rough pads of his fingers. All I could think about was his name grounding me, all of their names bringing me back to life when every other part of me wanted to drift into eternity.

He didn't linger long on my breasts before moving his fingers down my stomach. He purred against me, sending vibrations across the three of us as he slipped a finger between curls and flesh to touch my clit.

I jolted to attention in response, my back going rigid against him. It had been a long time since someone touched me. The last person to touch me was Harmonie, of course, before she became the president of the North American Mortalborn Alliance, before she was told to cast me aside for votes.

"Stay here," Cas whispered, as if he could follow the train of my thoughts moving to Harmonie. "Stay with us."

So I did. I focused on where I was. In bed with Cas and Van and feeling all the right things. Van began to rub my clit, and the moan that escaped me was unconscious.

Cas moved even closer, his lips hovering above mine. His ocean-colored eyes bore into me, like they were searching for something.

"May I?" I whispered as I looked at his lips.

It was enough. Me asking for consent was enough for him to close the distance between us. His lips pressed against mine. He was so much gentler than I thought he'd be. His kiss was delicate, thoughtful, as he pressed his tongue against the seam of my mouth. I didn't hesitate at all. I let him in, let him explore me with his tongue – his very long, very adept tongue.

I gasped as Van slipped a finger inside me. It had been so long, so long since a man had touched me like this. I thought I'd marry Harmonie, thought we were end game, and after she left me, I hadn't wanted anyone. I became a person who didn't seek pleasure or release. I trained. I trained and trained and trained to get my mind off the matters of the heart.

I felt Van's finger move away from my clit, but before I could complain, Cas' hand moved down my front and pressed down where Van had been, and Van pushed another finger inside me.

Goddess. Goddess. Goddess. They were moving in sync, Van's fingers moving inside me, pressing at all the sensitive places on my walls, and Cas rubbed my clit while he continued to kiss me, never breaking for a breath as he consumed my mouth.

Everything rose inside me: sensation, hope, love, lust, and most importantly, an orgasm to end all orgasms. I came loudly, my cries muffled by Cas' lips as I broke apart. Cas moved away and motioned something to Van, but I was still flying, tremors running through my body as Van repositioned me on my back.

I realized my eyes were closed when I opened them to see Van crawling down the bed. He hooked an arm around each thigh and held his face just above my pelvis. His eyes were asking permission, and my nod of approval was far more enthusiastic than intended.

Yes. Yes, please.

Shifters were unique in a lot of different ways. I knew that from simply interacting with the world, even if I'd never slept with one. The moment Van ran his tongue between my lips, I realized a new way in which this particular shifter was unique. His tongue was rough (but not unpleasantly so), and he definitely had the smooth keratin papillae of the feline family.

As he swirled his tongue around my clit, I realized just how grateful I was he was a shifter. It snagged just the right amount, pulling on me like a nature-made suction fucktoy as he lavished attention on that sensitive spot.

I felt the air shift around me as Cas picked up my head and laid me on his lap–his very cool, smooth, be-tentacled lap.

"Is this okay?" he asked. He didn't need to tell me he was asking about his mer form being in bed with us.

"Yes," I moaned, nodding as another wave built inside me. I wanted to tell him that I thought his mer form was beautiful, that I thought he was beautiful in every version of himself.

Cas wrapped a long blue tentacle around each one of my breasts, using them just as nimbly as fingers as he squeezed. Gently at first, just enough to pool blood and sensation where he tightened. I came in a rush. All of it, both of them together – it was exquisite.

Van chuckled against me before tentatively licking me again.

"Too much," I whispered. I was all sensation and my clit felt electric with a second orgasm in such short succession. Cas loosened his hold on my breasts and I breathed heavily, completely sated – but also very aware I had not returned the favor.

"Come here," I said to Van, still breathless.

His cock was straining against his pants as he moved towards me. Van leaned next to us, and I didn't move from the comfort of Cas's tentacle back brace as I pulled Van's dick free from his pants. To say he was large would be an understatement. I genuinely felt concerned about our ability to ever fuck. It was thick and beautiful with thick veins running along its length.

I moved my hand up and down a few times before curiosity got the better of me, and I repositioned myself between his legs.

"Wait," he said just as I was about to take him into my mouth.

I looked up, unsure what he was going to say.

"I– you–" He paused uncomfortably and looked over at Cas before continuing. "You need to be careful. I have a knot."

Goddess be good. I knew not *all* male shifters had a knot but particularly powerful ones did. Somehow the thought of it inside of me both terrified me and made me wet all over again.

"I'll be careful," I said as I lowered my mouth to the head of his penis.

I understood the basic mechanisms of a knot, even if I'd never seen one up close and personal. I kept my hand on his shaft before my mouth as I took more and more of him in, stretching my mouth in ways that were exhilarating and a bit concerning. He was so big – so much bigger than the few mortalborn men I'd taken to my bed before Harmonie.

I moved my hand and mouth in tandem, being careful not to take him to the base as I started to feel his knot swelling as his breathing got quicker.

I locked my eyes on his just as he began to reach between Cas' tentacles. I slowed down, delaying his orgasm as he seemingly reached inside of Cas and pulled out *two* cocks. All my work stopped as my eyes grew wide. Caspian had two dicks. Like a snake or a lizard – or *a shark*. Cas had octopus and shark traits, apparently. The scaled pattern on his arms made sense now, at least. He had parts from a variety of sea creatures.

Van grinned at me as I watched him alternating his strokes between the longer penis on top and the only-slighter-shorter one below it. I had so many questions, but I put them all away as I turned my attention back to Van.

We all moved synchronously. I focused on the head of Van's penis as I felt his knot growing *and fucking growing* beneath my hand. I was full of curiosity, but I had no desire to be choked to death by his penis.

His legs tightened beneath me, just as I realized Cas had moved to his side so Van could move both of his hands along the mer's dicks. I moved my free hand between my own legs, my body coming to life at their sounds and scents. I gently rubbed my clit as I sucked Van harder and harder, faster and faster.

Van's noises seemed to heighten Cas's proximity to release as both of their panting filled the room, each of their breaths picking up speed just as I came, moaning against Van's dick moments before they both fell over the edge together.

Van's cum filled my mouth, his ever-present scent of grass and wild sage filled my senses as I swallowed him down. Cas came loudly, and *fuuuuck,* how I loved a noisy man. I swallowed Van down, my hand suddenly only able to stretch around half of his knot's inflated size. Cas's cum glistened on

Van's chest, and all of us collapsed in the warm, tingly bliss of satisfaction.

We lay on the bed, naked and content, for a while. I felt myself drifting in and out of a nap. Cas was still in his mer form, tentacles wrapped around my waist as I snuggled against him. Van pushed against my front, his hard cock and inflated knot staying erect long after we had finished. I imagined feeling that inside of me, of holding him inside of me after he came and shivered at the thought.

Just as it began to dawn on me that I had (briefly) died and then cum three times in the last twelve hours *and* I was fucking starving, a knock sounded on the door. We all jolted awake. Cas didn't shift back into his humanoid form, but his penises had apparently returned to wherever they hid inside his tentacles. He moved easily even without water, his tentacles pulling him across the floor in fluid motions.

Cas watched as Van and I jumped under the heavy blankets on the bed and covered ourselves before opening the door. Adara stood there. Her eyes widened briefly as she looked between Cas and the bed, but she hid whatever thoughts she had quickly.

"We need to talk," she said, apparently cutting straight to the point as she stepped from the water of the hallway into the open air of the room. Water pooled around her pale blue tentacles over the intricately designed tile floor.

Interesting that Adara and Cas had tentacles while Queen Morgana had a long, slender gold fish tale with bioluminescent blue spots along the sides. I'd only seen the ancient Queen of the Waterways once, but she'd left quite an impression.

"I'd say we do." Cas nodded and then sighed. "Any chance you could have some breakfast sent in and let us shower before we jump into that?"

"Of course." Adara turned to someone in the submerged hall and spoke quietly in Acadian. "I'll be back in an hour. It's up to you if we need to have this talk in my chambers or here."

Her eyes moved from Cas to me and Van. Ah. It was up to Cas if he wanted us to hear whatever it was they needed to talk about. Dying before the battle ended definitely meant I'd missed a few things.

The chambers were much larger than the bedroom with its massive bed, two wardrobes, and desk. A sitting room lay beyond the bedroom with several large chairs and sofas, and a dining room was through a door in the sitting room.

On the other side of the sitting room was a massive bathroom. Ten people could easily lounge across the floor of the stone-bottomed shower and eight shower heads were positioned around three of the sides of the shower.

The side of the shower that faced the rest of the room was covered floor to ceiling with a massive stained-glass sliding door. A mer woman with a long fishtail was depicted in the elegant glass doors, surrounded by the sea and a sea floor covered in wavy seaweed. A variety of aquatic creatures shared the painted glass ocean with the mer.

"The mer certainly know how to impress their guests," Van said as both of us took the glass art in awe.

"To be clear, these chambers were only ever occupied by Queen Rixana, and once, Violetta. There's a reason we call this the witch chambers. We don't get many guests at the bottom of the ocean floor," Cas said.

"Seems like it's their loss then. This is exquisite," I replied.

Cas pulled the doors open when we'd finally had time to take in every detail of the scene.

Despite all the sexual tension that still hung in the air like a heavy fog, we managed to clean ourselves (and only ourselves) before getting out of the shower. The wardrobes were filled with clothes of various sizes and cuts. I found a flowy blue dress of thin gossamer fabric. Van pulled on a pair of joggers that were more like capri pants on his six foot seven frame and a plain black t-shirt. He then graciously braided my hair for me as several servants brought breakfast into the room.

Thin raw slices of salmon, tuna, and mackerel were piled between strips of barbecued eel, sea urchin wrapped in seaweed, and roe. Different flavored seaweed and a bowl of rice were piled on the plate next to several kinds of sauces in what had suddenly become my favorite charcuterie board of all time.

We all stuffed ourselves with the smorgasbord in front of us before Adara's presence brought us all back to reality – whatever reality we were in that led the shadowborn to directly attack Atlantis with a host of shadowborn who'd been mer before their corruption. I might have missed the end of the battle, but I saw enough to know there was something much larger going on here that might finally give us some answers.

Caspian

My sister had changed since we'd seen her just an hour earlier. Her tentacles were gone, and she wore flowing black pants,

a black halter top, and most interestingly, a coral crown with a large pearl just below the highest peak in the center of her forehead. My mother's crown.

"Is she really dead then?" I asked, taking in the tired lines of my sister's face.

The hours and days after a long-reigning magicborn monarch died and her heir took up the throne were exhausting. Even though such a transition had never happened on Earth, I knew enough of our histories and monarchies to know that Adara would not get a full night's sleep for a very long time.

"She is," Adara said simply, sitting down in an empty chair.

Cori and Van sat next to each other on a couch facing the chair I inhabited. A long table with the remnants of breakfast lay between us. Adara's chair faced all of us at an angle, giving everyone what was undoubtedly a caricature of the saying, *heavy is the crown*. She looked *so* tired. Absolutely exhausted. I'd never seen her that way, and it was a reminder that she was two centuries older than me.

"You know what I need to know," I said, my voice as level as I could keep it with the anger and hurt of twenty-nine years of unanswered questions bubbling up inside me.

"You want to know who your father is?" Adara asked. She looked resigned, maybe even somber.

"I want to know who my parents are," I corrected her. "I want to know if everything that monster said yesterday was true."

Adara shifted in her seat a moment, looking down at her hands.

Why was she in her humanoid form? She didn't have to pretend here, didn't have to be anyone else, and yet, she could be a witch or a shifter if it weren't for the golden scaled pattern along her forearms and exposed stomach. Golden where mine were blue – where Queen Morgana's had been black. I didn't know who Morgana was to me anymore. Mother for so long and now–

Adara looked at the three of us before speaking. "Are you sure you want everyone here? I know you are recently engaged, bu–"

"Yes," I interrupted. "They will stay, and you can be completely transparent with all of us."

She nodded. "Alright then. I never wanted to keep this from you, Caspian. I need you to know that from the beginning, I did not want any part of this charade. But when three shadowborn infiltrated Atlantis and attempted to kidnap you at only a few hours old, mother won me over. You weren't safe unless who you were was hidden. From you – from everyone.

"There's a prophecy, a different prophecy than the one about the engagement, that foretold your birth. It wasn't one of ours. The seers were shadowborn who'd been fae before their corruption. The shadowborn were particularly interested in acquiring you because of the weapon you'd be one day."

"That doesn't make any sense," I argued. "I have odd powers, but by the goddess, Cori is a far more powerful weapon than me. Ruyek and Ambrose's combined powers? So much more than being able to call a storm and control lightning, and I use the word *control* very liberally here."

"Cas," Adara's voice was nearly a whisper, "what you know of your power is only a taste. Your father placed a geis on you after the attempted kidnapping. You are so much more than you know. That geis and Morgana's plan to hide your true identity was enough to keep the shadowborn away until now. But even with the geis dampening your powers, the ripening is awakening parts of you I thought would be hidden."

"Who is my father?" I cut straight to the point. He put the geis on me, so if I could find him, he could remove it.

Adara sighed. "How long do you have?"

"What's that supposed to mean?" Van asked, speaking for the first time since Adara entered the room.

"There is so much that was lost before and after we came to Earth. Ruyek likely knows much more than all of you, but we all agreed to leave the most unsavory parts of Acadia behind when we started over. Explaining all of this will take time." Her vibrant blue eyes held mine as she spoke, like she heard Van but her answer was only for me.

"Tell me everything," I said. "Tell us everything."

Adara nodded tightly. "The old gods were far more removed than the goddess so many of us now acknowledge. We rarely saw them. They lived in Tirnanahg far from even the most remote cities in Acadia. Rarely, they would grace magicborn with their presence, and every few centuries, a story about the child of a god or goddess would surface, and a very powerful magicborn would take the throne from someone else, like they had some god-given right to power because of their demigod status.

"A lot of times, the turnover of power was much needed. When a magicborn royal household had become too inbred in their attempt to keep the bloodline pure, or corruption of power lasted several generations, a demigod would pop up and create a new world order. That was one of the only ways in which the old gods interacted with us. Our worship was really an acknowledgement of their true immortality and magical superiority.

"We did not go to churches or temples to light candles for them. Sometimes a seer would request an audience with the gods and ask for some favor on their or another's behalf, and sometimes, the gods would grant it, but most times, they would not. That was the extent of our communication.

"A few thousand years ago, something changed. The gods stopped answering any summons and there was a lack of demigod warriors that was felt as monarchies reveled in their corruption without consequence. And after a few centuries of quiet, the Goddess visited the witch queen and explained that she'd imprisoned the old gods and was the only true deity left. She made an example of the monarchs who opposed her recount of events and changed the power structure, and we all quickly fell in line.

"The Goddess visited us often, and she was well-known for asking for powerful sacrifices for whatever she was doing in Tirnanahg. She meddled in our politics and marital alliances frequently, but something was wrong about her from the beginning. We all knew that she had done something to gain her power. Some said she devoured the other gods. Others said she was a–"

Adara glanced at Cori apologetically before continuing. "Some said she was a magic eater and that the powerful sacrifices and missing gods kept her fueled up, so to speak. No one ever opposed her until – well until the shadow queen three centuries ago. She was relentless in her pursuit to destroy the goddess, and maybe that laser focus is what drove her mad, drove her to turn on everyone around her.

"The shadow queen's power was inexplicable too. She could corrupt people with a bite of her fangs, like the mortalborn imagined vampires turned people before we arrived. Her venom changed them, made them into something new that she could control and command. We left Acadia because *she* had become a threat we couldn't live with. The goddess was dangerous, but the shadow queen was a whole new level of threat."

Adara paused and looked down as if she was done speaking. This was a lot to take in, to decide if we believed her or not, but it didn't answer any of my questions.

"Who are my parents, Adara?" I asked pointedly.

"Right." She nodded. "We now know that at least some of the old gods were only imprisoned, rather than syphoned to oblivion. It's possible the Goddess still took from their magical cores, of course, but some were still alive.

"Well, I guess I'm not sure if *we* as in the entire magicborn community knows, but *I* know. Queen Morgana knew, and now, you know. Your father is an old god, Cas. His geis made you seem nothing more than the half-mer you are and put a vice on your powers. He came through the rift with some prophecy that claimed his son would save Acadia, that he would destroy the Goddess.

"But–" She paused and took a deep breath. "The prophecy stated the exchange would be a life for a life. Your life for her life, if the seers were correct."

I knew who my mother was. The look on her face, the hurt in her eyes. It all made sense. Everything I had ever known about myself, believed wholeheartedly about myself was a lie.

"You're my mother then," I said softly.

She met my gaze. "I am. Your conception and birth were a well-guarded secret. Phorcys stayed until you were nearly a year old, disguised as a mer serving at the hands of Queen Morgana. When the shadowborn tried to abduct you, his relationship with Morgana was painted in a new light as she presented her new son to the world. He was just some mer lover, some nobody who had done what the lovers of mer monarchs always do: provide an heir and then disappear into oblivion.

"When you were a year old, he returned to Acadia. I haven't seen or heard from him since." Adara's eyes were wet with emotion.

She'd loved him then, the god who was apparently my sire. The man who had created me to be a weapon for a world and a war I had no stake in.

"I thought all of this, this war and realm-shattering fight against evil was against the shadow queen," Cori said, her voice accusatory. "Who is the real enemy here?"

"We are facing more than one enemy, Cordelia," Adara responded. "The shadow queen is a psychotic genetic anomaly who murders, schemes, and kidnaps in the fight against a Goddess who was always far less a threat to us than she herself was. And yet, the Goddess can come through that rift and subjugate this world whenever she wants to.

"Our fate and our future is perilous because of both of these powerful women. One is just as much a threat as the other, objectively speaking, but the shadow queen is the only one sending soldiers through the rift right now. The Goddess has been absent since we left."

"You're my mother," I said like I was several minutes behind in the conversation because suddenly my entire life was coming into focus.

Morgana claimed me as her own, but Adara was my lifelong companion. She was never away from my side. She helped tutor me and train me. She'd been the most steadfast person in my entire life, and somehow, I'd accepted that my mother was simply old and tired. I never considered that the very foundation of my life was a facade.

"I'm sorry you didn't know, Cas. I really am, and I'm sorry that you had to hear any of this from a fucking siren. I should have told you as soon as you came into manhood. You deserved to know." Adara's eyes were apologetic. Adara, my mother.

"This is a lot to unpack," Van said, his eyes full of concern as he looked at me. "Can you give us some time to process this?"

"Of course," Adara stood quickly, but she didn't leave immediately. She took a few steps towards me and cupped my face. "You have always been my son to me, Cas. You don't have to forgive me for lying to you or for keeping so much from you, but I need you to know that you have always been *my* son in *my* heart."

"Wait–" I said as she pulled her hand away. "How can I find Phorcys? How can I get him to release me from this geis?"

"You'll have to go through the rift and find him. I imagine he returned to Tirnanahg, but he didn't really leave me with instructions on how to find him. He told me he knew that you would come and you would find him because the prophecy foretold it."

Adara turned away then and disappeared through a door on the other side of the sitting room. I knew it led to a hallway without water in it, a safe passageway for any non-mer visitors, but beyond that, I had no idea where she was going or what the fuck was even happening in the rest of the palace.

"I can't be a demigod." I shook my head as I spoke. "That's fucking ludicrous, right?'

"I don't think she was lying," Van said.

"Me either," Cori added. "I just think we have to figure out what this means for us, for the rift, and for whatever we are supposed to do next."

Ambrose

We didn't sleep nearly as much as we'd hoped to on our first

day in the vampire palace. Ruyek was a ball of nervous energy, and apparently fucking me was the only thing he could do to keep his mind off what was coming. I happily obliged. Ruyek dominating me had become the heartbeat of my life. It felt like it was life-sustaining nourishment. His fangs, his cock, his fingers – all of him was an addiction. It went far beyond just the feel of his venom in my veins.

Spending centuries intertwined with him felt like a paradise I never thought I'd be worthy of. I'd hoped for Nadella to even acknowledge me as her husband, to deign to touch me in any capacity, but Ruyek worshipped my body. He treated me like I was a gift – like I was someone he'd been waiting for his whole life.

Ruyek told me to come with him to his father's throne room, but he also told me to leave if I was ever in any danger. I shivered as we walked to the throne room. It was just after dusk: the normal receiving time for King Valdon.

We walked past a line of waiting vampires and mortalborn alike, stretched down a long hall that ended at the double doors into the throne room. I noted there were even a few fae among the magicborn. These were Valdon's people, come to make their case or share their recommendations. Magicborn monarchies did allow their people a voice, but how much or how little that voice was listened to sat entirely with whoever wore the crown.

Bows and echoed cries of "your highness" followed us down the line. There was visible shock running through the crowd, and it was obvious to me that Ruyek did not usually pay his father a visit this way.

Just before we reached the doors into the throne room, a vampire woman stepped directly in our path, forcing us to both stop walking. The hall was long, but there was not much wiggle room between the line of citizens and our pathway. The woman looked like a vampire even without her fangs showing. Her skin was so white it looked like spun silver moonlight, like a skin that had never seen any sun (not even the sun in Acadia), and her hair was the midnight black of most vampires. And her eyes were as red as Ruyek's, the dark, deep red of blood.

Before either of us could respond, she sank to her knees, placed her forehead on the ground, and splayed her hands out in front of her in what was the deepest bow I had ever seen.

"Rise," Ruyek said. It sounded like this interruption left the word a bit clipped, like maybe all this fanfare was unnecessary.

"Your majesty," the woman said, her face still turned towards the floor. Any mortalborn around her wouldn't have heard her words, but every magicborn ear near us certainly picked it up. "Your majesty has come to deliver us."

Ruyek stiffened. Prince Ruyek was not *your majesty* yet. He wouldn't be unless tonight went as smoothly as we hoped. And what exactly was Ruyek delivering the peoples of the

Vampire Kingdom from? Or who, may be the better question? King Valdon was not an immensely popular man, but I'd never heard of any overt cruelty. The witch queen would not have allowed it – right? She was tough as nails, but she also insisted the mortalborn and magicborn communities be well-cared for by their heads of state.

"Rise," he said again, more softly this time. "I trust you know what to do."

She rose this time, meeting his eyes with the full weight of her gaze and a barely-there nod. She was beautiful in the same way that Ruyek was, attractive like the sharp edges of a blade – like the promise of a bloody death.

Vampires weren't undead like the mortalborn myths insisted, but they were in close communion with death and they were incredibly difficult to kill if you didn't encounter them in the daylight. And I knew, though I did not want to think about it, that young vampires in the midst of the ripening were known to lose any semblance of control when drinking from anyone. All vampires had some accidental deaths on their hands. They were the living, breathing embodiment of death, a species who needed the very life essence of other living creatures to survive. I shivered again, my thoughts at war. Who had Ruyek killed when he came into his powers? Had he killed anyone since?

Stop it, his voice said in my head. *Put your damn shields up and don't wander down a path of ghosts you don't want to encounter. I am what I am, but I need your shields the thickest they've ever been every second we are in this kingdom. Do you understand?*

Yes. Of course. I'm sorry, Rue.

And I was sorry. How many people had heard me questioning what kind of monster Ruyek was?

"Return to the king's line," Ruyek said to the woman in front of him. "I hope that his majesty gives you everything you need."

The woman dipped her head in a semi-bow once more before stepping back into line.

Ruyek led the way through the doors. His walk changed as he stepped into the room with her father, swagger and bravado etched in every step. His smile was wide and toothy as King Valdon looked down from where he sat on a black throne on a raised dais. Queen Madelina sat on a matching, albeit lower-backed throne next to him.

The entire room was red and black. Deep sanguine was painted on the walls, and a vibrant red sun and black clouds was painted on the ceiling. The intricacy of what had to be Acadia's sky gave the Sistine Chapel a run for its money. The floor was a pattern of black and red marble, and the only decor was a massive painting of the royal family hanging on the wall behind the two thrones.

"Father, Mother," Ruyek's voice boomed, his smile wider and more wicked than I'd ever seen before. "It has been such a long time since I visited the throne room. I've quite missed it."

At his proclamation, King Valdon stiffened in his seat.

I followed Ruyek as the vampire standing in the middle of the room, about to address the king, stood still and silent. Ruyek stood at the bottom of the dais and smiled at the man.

"By all means, continue," Ruyek said to him with a motion of his hand.

The man went into a long winded explanation about the scarcity of human blood for any vampires who traveled outside of the vampire kingdom. He asked that the king raise the pay for donors and ensure there are places to buy blood in the other kingdoms. His daughter, apparently, had moved to the Witch Queendom. While there was blood available, it was not as readily accessed as it was here, and he was scared to travel without the security of guaranteed nourishment.

Valdon promised the man that he'd send a missive to the other monarchs about ensuring there was blood readily available in all major cities. He also suggested shipping blood to his daughter before traveling to ensure he had a supply available. The man bowed low, first to Valdon and then to Ruyek.

The next person was a fae woman with quite the opposite problem. She was requesting more businesses hire mortalborn or non-vampire magicborn to man their shops during the day. She loved living in Turkey (she'd come a long way for this request, apparently), but she couldn't adjust to a nocturnal lifestyle. King Valdon promised to incentivize businesses to have daylight hours as more and more magicborn left the borders of their own kin to live in different territories.

The woman who had fallen on the floor in front of Ruyek was seven people into the line. I had an idea of what she offered Ruyek and what he'd accepted when she called him by his father's title and he acknowledged that she was going to do something. I checked and rechecked my mental shields as the vampire woman looked from Ruyek to Valdon.

"I invoke the power of the blood rites and officially submit my request for a blood war for the vampire throne," she said, her voice sure and booming around the room like the call to action it was.

Ruyek told me that this request was made a few times a year. It was well-known that the most powerful vampire on Earth no longer held the throne, but Ruyek was never in the room when the request was made and while there was some official paperwork sent to him every time this request was made, he'd refused to fight his father for the throne until now.

It wasn't uncommon for a prince to wait until his father was in his sunset years to challenge him for the throne as a sign of respect, but that respect had been discarded many times before when it was apparent one of the heirs had surpassed the king in power. The secret was Ruyek didn't really want the throne, but his request for full access to the royal archives and the king's archives had been denied before we ever left Ireland.

He left me no choice, Ruyek had said when the denial appeared the following day. *He knows his position is precarious, but he thinks I'm too much a fool to want the throne. He's half-right. I don't want the throne, but I am no fool. He has made his decision, and I must make mine.*

Ruyek had been sure his father knew his intentions the minute he translocated onto palace grounds, but he hadn't given his father enough time to stock up on powerful blood to give himself any kind of advantage. He said he wanted the fight to be as fair as it could be.

Valdon did not respond, but he did blanch (which was quite a feat given how pale he already was). Madelina's face was quite different. I watched as a small smile tugged her lips. It was well-known their marriage wasn't a love match, but did she hate him so much she wanted to see him fall?

"Do you accept this challenge, Prince Ruyek, or will you pledge your allegiance to King Valdon?" Madelina said.

It was supposed to be Valdon who asked, Ruyek had explained that much to me, but clearly, the king was still reeling from the challenge. He likely suspected Ruyek's intentions, but at least some part of him had to have been hopeful his son wouldn't dare, that maybe he would come to reason.

"I accept the challenge," Ruyek said simply. His small smile was a mirror of his mother's.

The guards sprang into action at his words. They ushered everyone back into the hall. One of them tried to pull me along, but I refused. The guard gave me one uncertain glance before nodding and returning to the crowd of petitioners, a crowd that was suddenly electric with the historical event about to unfold.

Win or lose, vampire kings were rarely challenged. King Valdon's last challenge had been centuries earlier, long before the migration through the rift. A cousin to the king who was certain he was more powerful, but Valdon had cut him down swiftly.

Against the wall, Ruyek said in my mind. I'd made just enough room for him to talk to me, and I worked hard to ensure only he could enter.

I obeyed, moving swiftly to the wall nearest the exit just as I heard the guards on the other side locking the door. Only one guard had remained to witness the duel. He'd be the lone account that was written into the historical record when it was over.

When it was over – and Ruyek was either king or dead. I shivered.

"Is this what you want?" Valdon said without leaving his throne.

Madelina sat next to him, still as a statue. That small upward turn of her lips remained as she looked only at Ruyek. Ruyek, who had told me how much he adored his mother and how much he hated his father for all that he made her endure. Ruyek, who had vocally supported the end to the vampiric patriarchy and promised to elevate women in the vampire kingdom once he was king. His positions on gender equality were well-known, and the vast majority of the populace supported his progressivism. We lived in a world that bent to the will of the witch queen. Male-led politics had no place in this new world.

"You cannot run from this," Ruyek answered his father after an uncomfortable silence.

"I will give you full access to the archives," Valdon said, the smallest amount of pleading in his voice. His fear wasn't going to be a secret then. He knew his time was up if Ruyek did not bend the knee.

"It's too late. You denied me when you thought I would not challenge you. You had an opportunity to avoid this. Your hubris will be your downfall." Shadows leaked from Ruyek as he spoke.

Valdon looked crushed for only a moment as the look of betrayal and realization slammed into his features. Without warning, the room was drenched in the inky magical darkness that even magicborn eyes could not penetrate. I heard a body slam into the wall next to me and a grunt I recognized permeated the thickness of night around us.

Fuck. So a cheap shot from Valdon was how this was going to start?

A sound like grinding stone filled the room, and then an earth-shaking crash sounded. The throne, I realized, as my other senses filled in for my lack of sight. Ruyek had hurled his father's throne to the wall behind the dais. Had he still been in it?

A moment's respite, and then the room was filled with movement as the duel truly began. Grunts and crashes, a whimper from not-Ruyek. Actually, as the room filled with the sound of their fighting, the grunts and groans seemed to *only* belong to King Valdon. Goddess above: Ruyek was destroying his father.

"I do not want to kill you," Ruyek yelled over the sound of another throne hitting the ground while shadows thick as smoke whirled around us. Even in this darkness, there were heavy layers of black as Ruyek and Valdon's power whipped around us.

Valdon didn't answer, but suddenly, the shadows were building around me, pushing me against the wall as unfamiliar magic wrapped around my body. My throat constricted. Oh gods. I couldn't catch a breath as the king's darkness shoved its way into my mouth and nose, obstructing my airway completely.

A moment of frantic drowning passed before I realized I was dying. Ruyek had feared this, had told me to make myself small and unimportant because his father was a cheating snake. He'd kill me, then, to try to force Ruyek to bend the knee.

Just as my mind was beginning to fog over, as the darkness extended beyond the room and into my very existence, the room erupted. Ruyek was an earthquake, a reckoning for his father, as the ground split apart and the walls themselves crumbled as he roared.

The darkness flinched away from me, and I breathed in heavy gasps as air filled my lungs in a rush.

"Do not touch what is mine," Ruyek roared. The entire room shook anew with fury.

Madelina's frantic gasps filled the room a moment later. Valdon'd been using us both as leverage then, hoping the threat of one of our deaths would stop the duel, would stop the darkness that was Ruyek.

Light leaked back into the edges of the room. I could see Ruyek, rising above the destroyed dais and throne as he sucked in his father's artificial darkness. His eyes were solid red without even a sliver of white, and his long, black hair whipped around his face. He looked like a god, like death incarnate, and my own magic shook at the realization that Ruyek could kill everyone in this room in an instant. He'd clearly allowed his father to fight back then, allowed him to fight with dignity until his tricks turned cheap.

Blood leaked from Valdon's mouth and nose as shadows constricted so tightly that the sound of breaking bones permeated the air. Ruyek was killing him. Goddess above, he was going to have to live with his patricide. I knew that he was prepared for what he had to do, but this?

"Ruyek!" Madelina cried, her voice raspy from her husband nearly choking her to death. "Ruyek, offer him leniency. Let him bend the knee!"

Madelina, a powerful vampire in her own right, a queen who had nearly been killed by a husband who could never love her like the witch queen. Gods – two worlds' worth of magicborn knew he and Rixana were forbidden lovers. Rixana wore his bite on her neck for everyone to see. It had been an open secret. How could she not hate him?

Suddenly, the room tilted and fell away.

I was standing outside the vampire castle. It was the hazy blue-purple-black of the hour just before dawn outside. I looked up at the sound of beating wings. A bay pegasus carried a figure cloaked in black towards the ground. The animal landed a few feet from where I stood, and the rider dismounted.

"Valdon," the voice cried – a voice I recognized. "Valdon!" Queen Rixana's voice boomed, magnified with magician's magic. The sound seemed to shake the very foundation of the castle as the witch queen threw her hood back. Her wild red hair flew behind her as wind blew around the castle.

A door creaked open. A door that I hadn't even realized existed because it was so well camouflaged against the stone facade of the castle. Madelina stepped out into the darkness. She was wearing the same sanguine dress she'd just been wearing in the throne room, but her breathing was calm and her voice was steady as she spoke.

"This is it then?" Madelina asked. "You've finally come for my husband?"

"I don't want to do this." Rixana, for the first time in my memory, sounded tired. "He is not welcome in your son's kingdom. I will welcome him in mine."

"Why did you wait for this moment, Rix?" Madelina asked. *Rix.* That was a nickname I'd never heard anyone call Queen Rixana before. "You could have had him the moment we came through the rift and stepped out of the shadow of her laws.

You could have had him the moment we took our thrones in this new world. We did not need this facade here. Gods know you had no problem taking a mortalborn as your prince consort. Why did you wait? Why did you make me wait, knowing that you would come – that one day, you would come and take him away for good."

"We never wanted to hurt you," Rixana responded gently, so gently for a woman who had always been steel. "Please don't do this, Del. Not tonight. He will have safe harbor in my queendom. You have to let go of all of this hate, and you have to let him go."

"I have never kept him against his will. You must know that there was a time when he loved me too – not like he loved you, but there was a time when he came to me willingly and not just for duty. A time when we both thought we could escape the shadow of whatever it is that's between the two of you." I could hear the tears in Madelina's voice, centuries of heartbreak and anger in every word.

"Rix," Valdon's voice called from behind his wife.

Queen Madelina held Queen Rixana's gaze for one long uncomfortable moment before stepping aside. King Valdon stumbled into the darkness. He was covered in his own blood and limping, but when he saw Rixana, he seemed to pick up his pace. It was uncomfortable watching them embrace, watching both of them fall into each other with so many mortal lifetimes of longing and wanting between them.

"We have to go before the sun rises," Rixana said so softly that it didn't seem like I should have been able to hear it, but I did. "I have a safe place for us to lay low while you heal."

Lay low. The uncontested ruler of the world was talking about laying low. From who? From Ruyek? A shiver ran through me as I realized how wrong all of this was. How did I get here? It couldn't be nearly dawn. Why did no one notice me standing there watching them?

The vampire throne room poured back into focus. At first, all the colors seemed to be in the wrong place, but then the scene righted itself. Ruyek stood above the dais, his shadows a solid wall beneath him as he looked down at his father. Valdon was constrained by shadows, but Ruyek must have stopped breaking bones long enough to allow him to speak.

"I would rather die than bend the knee to you," Valdon spat, blood falling from his mouth as he stared up at Ruyek. There was no love in his gaze, only relentless fury.

"You've made your choice then," Ruyek said just as his shadows swarmed back in, smothering Valdon as he screamed in pain. The sound of ripping flesh tore the room just as everything came into focus for me.

Thoughts rushed through my head. What I saw, where I'd been – none of it had come to pass yet. I had seen something that would be – or could be – free will made the truth of visions murky. But I didn't have the sight – or I didn't until this moment. And Valdon was going to die. Ruyek was going to kill him and everything I saw was never going to happen. Goddess. Queen Rixana would not rest until Ruyek was dead if he killed Valdon. Valdon *had* to live. He had to make it safely to the Witch Queendom–

"STOP!" I yelled, and yelling *hurt* after being choked half-to-death.

My voice stilled Ruyek immediately. His shadows fled from his father, bringing his broken body into clear view. There was so much blood on the dais, blood that was even more important for vampires than it was for any other magicborn. His left arm hung limp, nearly torn from his body. He was dying. He was going to die if he didn't see a healer.

"Valdon," I started, walking towards the dais. Ruyek's shadows swirled harmlessly around me as I walked. "If you live, she will come for you."

His eyes went wide – eyes that were much more like Ruyek's than I ever realized. I didn't even know if he could speak in his current state, so I made myself perfectly clear.

"Bend the knee and Queen Rixana will come for you; before dawn breaks, she will come."

Everyone in the room stopped moving – everyone except for Valdon. We all watched as he pushed his body up from where he lay on the dais, losing more blood as he pulled himself to his knees.

His eyes looked up at Ruyek, and the expressions on their faces made me think they were talking mind to mind. Maybe Valdon was unable to speak due to his injuries.

Ruyek nodded. "I accept your plea for mercy, Valdon. You will be stripped of your titles, your rank, your every possession, and your family. From this day forth, you are no father of mine, no royal in my kingdom. You will leave my castle and my lands before dawn, or you will be strung up at the castle gates to meet the sun's light."

Valdon nodded before collapsing back on the dais.

Tears streamed down Madelina's face as she rushed to his side. I guess we truly cannot help who we love. Even in the face of centuries of cruelty, love persists.

Ruyek lowered himself to the ground and instructed the lone guard to fetch a healer for his father. My body shook as Ruyek walked toward me. My Ruyek. *King* Ruyek. I shook and shook, my body a parade of tremors.

"Ambrose!" Ruyek cried as he rushed the last few steps to me and pulled me into his arms as my body went limp and my vision went black.

Savanna

The morning after Cas' entire worldview shifted, he told us we should go back to Richmond. I didn't really want to leave him, but I knew that he had some things to sort through with his sis– mother. He and Adara needed space. He promised to return to us within the week and kissed both of us nearly senseless before Autumn was summoned to collect us.

She deposited us outside of Cori's castle on Belle Isle. It was so strange translocating across time zones. It was yesterday in Richmond, about dinner time, when we arrived.

Richmond looked the same as it had when we left. The accidental earthquake had caused very little damage, and magic (both magicborn and the magician variety) mended what little damage it had caused. Autumn kept us in the loop about all things *the rest of the world* while we were training, coming often enough that we knew the only shadowborn attack since the Battle for New York was the one in which we'd just fought.

"The prisoner next," Cori said to Autumn. I'd never heard her command many people, but something about it sent a shiver through me. "To my dungeons, not my mother's. I'd prefer she not know about this."

I watched the war going on behind Autumn's eyes. Her face made it very obvious that she was trying to decide who she'd hedge her bets with: the witch queen or her only heir. After a moment, she nodded.

"I give you my word," Autumn answered before disappearing. Wise choice. Anyone with a brain and understanding of magic levels would put their money on Cordelia.

"What are we going to do with the prisoner?" I asked as Cordelia led us into the castle.

"I'm not going to do much beyond demanding some answers. I don't have the stomach for much more. But Ruyek?" She chuckled. "I am going to ask Ruyek to break open every single door in her mind until everything she knows, we know."

I didn't point out the fact that destroying the sanctity of someone's mind was its own kind of torture because I didn't disagree with the ends our means would justify. We had to know what was happening in Acadia, and we had to know before we made the decision to try to close the rift.

Cordelia ordered Chinese food just as we entered the central sitting room that connected all of our own quarters. The growing connection between Cori, Cas, and me had shifted when we'd all explored each other the morning after the battle. It had been a quiet intimacy between us, but I knew (I think we all knew) that walls around our hearts crumbled as our fingers and mouths learned the most intimate parts of each other. Cori, who had felt so lost when we first arrived on Malden Island, seemed to have centered herself around our growing affection.

I need you to know that even if Vi was alive, I would have found my way to you, to this reality where everything makes sense. Cas's words from the island resonated through me as Cori shoveled lo mein into her mouth. Her world-bending powers ravaged her body, stole from her bones and her muscles as alien magic syphoned through her. She had to be absolutely starving all the time.

I knew that the love between us was more than friendship. It has always been more than friendship. Did I know what Cas knew before the witch queen reimagined our futures? I felt like I did, like my decade of running from the prophecy that bound me to a witch princess I didn't know (much less love) muddled me too much to stop and examine why Cas and I were such fast friends, why our quiet confidence felt like more than brotherhood.

"What are you thinking about?" Cori asked, her mouth still full.

"Us, this," I said simply.

She nodded gently.

"It feels like everything is different now," she replied. "Like all the fight I put up when it came to y'all dissipated. I'm still full of so much guilt I could burst, but I want this. I want us." Her eyes glistened only a little as she spoke.

"Me too," I agreed. "We are in such unknown territory here, but in all of the uncertainty on the *how* and *why*, I know that this is where I always should have been."

Cori set her now-empty carton of lo mein on the coffee table between us. "Do you want to train," she asked. "The magic's been fun, but I've really missed my axe."

Her double-headed battle-ax collection was impressive. So many different materials of shafts that made me consider an axe instead of my preferred claws and teeth.

Half an hour later, we were both in workout clothes in the massive gym her castle housed. We both started with a double-headed battle-ax. I chose one with a smooth metal handle while Cori selected one with a hickory handle. Her Acadian weapon stayed strapped to her back as we sparred.

She was more adept with the weapon, and I soon realized the metal handle transferred the vibrations of the impact to my hands. My wrists were aching after only a few parries. She was faster than me too, moving swiftly away from my blows without a need to parry.

After half an hour of absolutely wearing me down, I shifted into a midnight lion. Slipping back into the muscular black lion felt like coming home, like shedding a costume. I roared, shaking the ground between us with the deep thunder of the sound.

Cori sighed before running toward me and shoving the ax handle at my chest, holding my claws at bay a moment as she touched my shoulder. I paused at the feel of her fingers in my fur, unsure of what she intended. A moment later, the mystery was solved as I felt a pulling sensation from my magical core. Cori gritted her teeth as her body shifted into the form of a massive lioness. This was no Acadian species, but a Masai lion from East Africa. Her long legs and curved back made the breed distinct and apparent.

The battle-ax clattered to the ground beneath us as she lunged for me, snarling and snapping her teeth as she pushed me to the ground. I let the shock get me only for a moment. Then I found my feet and swatted a clawed paw at her.

Our fight was brutal. Claws and teeth, pouncing and pinning each other as we fought for domination. My midnight lion form was all muscle, but just like in human form, Cori was fast and lithe, easily avoiding many of my attacks. We tussled until both of us had crusted blood in our fur and our chests heaved with exhaustion.

Shifting was beautiful on her. I'd spent the last decade only engaging with male partners to avoid any unintended heirs before my wedding. Atasia had her own partners, but human birth control was far more reliable for witches than it was for shifters. Something about my kind was too alien, too other, for the biology to work perfectly with the medication.

Thinking about sex and Cori led to me pinning her as I grew hard. I knew enough about my anatomy as a midnight lion to know sex in this form would likely be unpleasant, though the curiosity of it lingered as I shifted back to my humanoid form.

Cordelia didn't hesitate and quickly shifted beneath me. Her golden eyes held mine for a heartbeat, two heartbeats and then I devoured her. My lips crashed into hers and she opened for me immediately. My tongue explored her mouth as she shivered beneath me. I knew the rough papillae on my tongue were a unique sensation. Mine were rounded rather than spiked like a true feline, and I'd been told they were quite pleasant. As if in confirmation, she moaned against my mouth.

I lowered my hips over hers, letting my erection push against her. I wanted to fuck her right here on this gym mat, but that didn't feel right. Wait – she managed to shift with her clothes (though for once, I sincerely wished she hadn't).

"Can I take you to bed?" I asked as my hands explored her muscled body, soft in all the right places.

She nodded eagerly and wrapped her arms around my neck. I pulled her up with me as I stood and cradled her long body against mine. It had been so long since I'd felt the warmth of a woman against me, beneath me. I enjoyed the fight and hardness of men and had full intentions of taking everyone in our betrothal to bed in time, but Cori was a sensation unto herself, an anomaly in our relationship that made me feel like a starving man finally offered food.

I bolted towards my bedroom, cradling her against me as my speed carried us swiftly there. We encountered no servants or news on my flight to the large, soft bed that dominated an entire wall of my room. I laid her down gently, my chest heaving as I climbed over her.

"Are you sure?" I asked. She knew I had a knot, but she'd also spent the last several years in a romance with Harmonie Zambrano-Rodriguez and had only ever been sexually involved with mortalborn men.

In answer, she stripped her sports bra off and shimmed out of her workout pants and underwear. Goddess above, I watched as she pulled herself from beneath the cage of my body and got on all fours, looking over her shoulder at me with a grin.

"I'm ready when you are," she teased, and I pounced.

Cordelia

I don't know what came over me, but everything had shifted for me after the battle. I'd spent weeks fighting what was growing between us, but my brief journey through death grounded me in the reality that Van, Cas, Rue, and Ambrose were endgame. They were a kind of life I never thought I'd have in a world dominated by death and misfortune, a precarious future not promised to magicborn, powerbound, or mortalborn as long as the rift was open. And now – maybe not until some goddess we'd never met was stopped.

Everything was uncertain and bleak – everything except us, the five of us against both worlds, Earth and Acadia. Us against a merciless shadow queen and a goddess of unfathomable power. I knew in my heart that some of us (or all of us) would likely die pitted against these impossible odds, but I also knew that we were alive *today*, in the only healthy relationship I'd ever seen *today*, and I wanted to know the limits of everything: of my body, my heart, and my desire.

Van ripped his pants and boxer briefs off behind me as I watched him over my shoulder. His considerable length and width hardened between us. Fuck. Fuck. I was doing this. We were doing this. He lowered his head between my legs and dragged his tongue between my lips, parting me smoothly and finding my clit.

A shudder ran through me as the keratin nodules of his tongue snagged on my clit. I wanted him inside of me though, I wanted him buried to the hilt and stretching me wide.

"I want you," I moaned as he continued to lick me, building pressure inside me with each swirl of his tongue.

He paused to answer. "I need you incredibly wet, dripping, so you can take me."

Oh gods, his fucking words pulled me closer to the edge as he continue to taunt me with his tongue, to pull and release, to snag my clit deliciously before licking again. I was dripping. I felt the puddle between my legs forming just as I was about to cum, and then he pulled away and lined himself up before sinking inside me.

I came in a rush as my body stretched for him, pain and pleasure mingled as my body clamped down around him in an orgasm. He paused inside me as I came apart around him.

"Are you ready?" he asked, a bit tardy since his hips were already flush against me.

"Fuck me," I said as way of response. And he did. He pulled out again before thrusting back in, setting a harsh pace as he moved inside of me. A delicious ache grew between my legs as my body molded around him, stretching to accommodate his size and speed.

He was so big, so fucking big, and I knew it would be so much more when he came. I felt his knot growing as he fucked me roughly, felt his penis struggling against the limits of my body as he grew closer to his own release. He slowed down as his breaths grew quicker and quicker, holding fast deeper and deeper inside me as his knot stretched me more and more. It was a sensation of fullness I'd never experienced, a stretch even my most ambitious sex toys had never brought me.

My moans turned into his gasps as he pushed himself against my cervix, filling me from top to bottom, wall to wall as his knot stuck my body to his. He came loudly inside me, his hot cum rushing into my body just as his knot stretched me to the brink of what I could handle.

I breathed heavily as we stayed like that, my body stretched around him in pain and pleasure, a stretch I couldn't have dreamed up before this moment.

"Fuck," I panted.

"Tell me what you're feeling," he whispered.

"Pain, pleasure – everything," I responded, my eyes tightly closed as my head hung between my arms. He was so deep in this position, as he fucked me from behind and filled every centimeter of my vagina to nearly the breaking point.

He showered kisses on my back as we stayed like that, stuck together by the mechanics of his body. Just as my legs grew tired from holding me up, he shifted us, rolling us down to the bed. His chest was against my back, his dick still buried inside of me swollen from his orgasm. He reached a hand over my stomach and down to the curls between my legs.

I didn't know if I could take any more sensation, but as his finger rubbed against my clit, I realized I could most definitely take more. I could take him endlessly, without stopping, because my body came alive beneath his touch. He rubbed and pinched gently, pulling me towards another orgasm as he touched me.

I felt myself tightening around him, clamping down on his swollen knot as my body pulled taut between us. I came with a scream. Pain mingled with pleasure in an indescribable feeling as I gushed.

He moved his hands up to my breasts, gently teasing my nipples as I came down from the peak. We stayed that way a long time, him gently touching me as his knot deflated enough for him to pull out of me. And then we just lay there as he cradled me in his arms like the most precious thing he'd ever held.

So this is what it felt like? To be loved? To be cherished in a way that did not come with strings or demands? This is what my future could feel like if we survived this war. Centuries of cherishing each other, of pleasure and love and happiness. The thought was almost too much as tears fell down my cheek. *If* we lived. *If* this world survived what was coming. Maybe then, we could have a future without fear, a happily ever after I never imagined for myself.

We slept in far later than was usual for either of us. After the stress of the last few weeks, the intense workout, and sex, we were apparently exhausted. Van woke me with a kiss. My soreness from the night before was gone, healed. Though I couldn't remember my dreams, I knew I was drenched with anticipation as he crawled over me. He looked down at my naked body and smiled.

"What are you smiling about?" I asked.

"I never imagined this was a possibility. My whole adult life, I was going to marry a stranger, and now I have you. I have all of you, and I feel like I know you as well as I know myself."

I admired his body too, his thick, solid body and beautifully deep brown skin. His hair was short, but I wondered what it would look like a bit longer. I wondered if he'd ever worn it braided. He looked almost mortalborn as he looked at me, a mortalborn in the NFL or a UFC champion, but a body I recognized as akin to mine. Only his eyes made him distinctly shifter. His vibrant mismatched cat eyes made it clear he was not mortalborn, that there was power inside him that was ancient and alien to the world of my father.

Van opened my legs wider before pushing himself inside of me, stretching me with his girth as he moved slowly. He sighed as he buried himself inside of me. I felt him in every inch of my body, like his size and power radiated out from where we were joined. He slipped a hand between us as he started to move, rubbing my clit as he fucked me.

His fingers easily helped his dick find my climax. I came apart loudly, suddenly very grateful we weren't on a small island with dirt walls anymore. After I came, his gentle strokes grew harder and deeper, nearly bruising with their intensity. I felt my pleasure building again, a tightening across my body as he wound me up. We came together. His knot filled all the way up and locked us together again with a sensation I was already beginning to crave. He stretched me to the point of breaking and then he took more and more as his knot grew, until I didn't know where I ended and he began.

Just as he settled his weight against my chest, sucking the skin of my neck as we settled in to wait for his knot to deflate, a knock sounded on the door.

"What the fuck?" I asked.

"Do not open that door," Van growled against my neck, the deep tone of his voice reverberating against me.

"I am so sorry to bother you, your highnesses, but Sabine says it is quite urgent," a small voice said from the other side of the door.

"Tell Sabine that whatever it is will have to wait," I responded.

Why the fuck didn't Sabine go back to D.C. already? I didn't need her anymore, and I certainly didn't want her in my castle and my city, the perfect little spy for my mother.

I heard the woman's feet carry her away from the door and sighed as Van moved his head lower and started sucking on my nipples. His hand slipped between as he sucked and licked my breasts. I spread my legs even wider, expecting him to rub my clit, but I stiffened when I felt a finger press against my ass.

"Can I?" he asked, his eyes meeting mine.

"I–I never–" I felt embarrassed that I'd never done anything anal, but I was curious. "Yes." I finally breathed.

I felt his fingers move up a moment, likely covering them in the cum dripping out of me before pushing one inside of me. I went rigid as he pushed into me. It was uncomfortable, my fear of the unknown was making me clench.

"Relax," he whispered as he moved his head a bit lower on my stomach for a better angle. "I just want to get you somewhat prepared for Cas."

Heat spooled in my core at the thought of Cas fucking me with both of his dicks, stretching me in ways entirely different from Van. The thought loosened me, and I felt my body unclench around Van's finger as he pushed it in further, tentatively and gently stretching me as he pushed another finger in.

Oh gods. I was going to fucking cum from his fingers in my ass and his dick locked inside of me. My breath picked up as he moved his two fingers in and out, slowly pulling me open until a third finger joined. He moved his fingers in and out expertly, pulling them out then pushing them back in until my body felt like liquid, like he could do anything he wanted, and I'd let him. I was vaguely aware of his knot going down as he continued to fuck my ass with his fingers.

I felt him slip out of me, felt both of our cum dripping out of me as he pushed my legs up. He pulled his fingers out of me and met my eyes as his dick pushed against my ass, now primed and ready for whatever he offered. I looked down and watched as he rubbed our cum across the head of his dick until it glistened with moisture.

I nodded, still afraid but ready to feel everything. My breath caught as he started to push into me, so much bigger than even three of his massive fingers. The stretch hurt but somehow I knew the feeling of him all the way in would be life-altering.

Another knock on the door.

"Did someone fucking die?" Van roared at the door, the head of his dick not even all the way inside of my ass yet.

"Yeah, fucking sort of." Sabine this time, no servant running errands. "Prince Ruyek is now King Ruyek, and you might want to stop fucking each other long enough to be prepared for the shit storm that is coming."

Caspian

I stayed with my – with Adara and helped her rebuild. We
didn't talk anymore about my father or who I really was, who

she was to me. She named me as next in line in the succession without the usual caveat of "until I have a living heir." It was the closest she came to publicly acknowledging me. The closer I looked though, the more I was certain most of Atlantis's inhabitants knew. Many of them had been around long before I was born and long before the rest of the world was presented with Prince Caspian, the second child of Queen Morgana. The ruse was to fool the rest of the world and any spies who made their way back to Acadia, not the mer. I was the only one left in the dark apparently.

And so, we worked side by side the day that Cori and Van left. Magic made the work much easier and several fae and witches had joined us in their scuba gear. We were done by evening. The physical structures of Atlantis were easy to fix. It was the loss of life and the terror of a shadowborn attack that would take much longer to heal.

Adara's coronation was later that evening. It was an intimate affair, only the queen's council members and a few distant relatives attended the event. The fae and witches who helped us rebuild were feasting in the witch's chambers while we stood around at the solemn affair.

The shifting of the crown and queenly responsibilities happened the moment Morgana died, and the coronation was only a shifting of powers. Every ruler of one of the kingdoms was endowed with a power boost, an extra few kernels of power tied to the office of king or queen. The ceremony was a ritual that shifted that power, but it hadn't been performed since we came through the rift.

I could see the stress on Adara's face, the very real fear that this ancient magic was tied to the land in Acadia and could not be shifted here. For all we knew, none of the monarchs retained that extra power when they crossed over. None of them would have admitted a loss of magic to even their heirs.

The council chanted in Acadian, their bodies swaying in the chamber. This was a true mer throne room. We were all in our fins and tentacles, a celebration the likes of which I hadn't attended in so long I ached. The chanting rose and fell like the peaks and valleys of the ocean floor, telling a story of the first mer queen and her ascension to the throne, her seizing of the powerful heart of the waterways in Acadia.

Councilwoman Mira stepped out of the half circle chanting around the throne. She carried the mer crown, the *true* mer crown. It was a heavy thing made of coral, seashells, and pearls. Seaweed that never seemed to wither hung from the uneven, natural peaks of coral that made up the majority of the crown.

The voices rose loud again. This time they were singing about the ancient power bestowed by the passing of the mer crown to the next monarch. The room was filled with the boom of their voices. Men and women mer council members sung as if the words possessed them, like they were in a trance.

Mira extended her hand face up to Adara when she reached where she clung to the pearl and coral throne with her blue tentacles. No one wore bikini tops or clothes like they did in mortalborn princess movies. We were all naked, ourr genitalia covered or hidden away by our mer anatomy.

Adara laid her hand palm down on Mira's offered one. In the blink of a moment, Mira replaced her hand with the sharpest spire of the crown, a sharpened pearl blade that extended at the peak. The pearl sliced Adara's hand open and blood spread in the water around the crown. Adara grasped the crown with both hands and closed her eyes as Mira let go and stepped back just as the song ended.

Adara's eyes were closed, and I wondered if she was praying to my father, to the ancient god that mer must have been patrons to long before the goddess came. We waited so long that everyone started to glance around. Morgana had been crowned many centuries before Adara or I was born, but this wait time felt wrong.

Finally, Adara opened her eyes. There was no rush of power into the room, no glowing light from the crown like I'd read in history books.

"The power of the mer queen has been lost beyond the rift. If you follow me now, it must be because you choose to, because you choose me. This throne will no longer be held by ancient power." Adara's voice filled the room with so much confidence and certainty.

How was she not reeling? I think I was reeling. The power was truly lost, left behind in Acadia. Tens of thousands of years of magical tradition gone. Another casualty of this planet, of this place where we were all truly orphaned.

Mira bowed her head first, just beyond Adara's reach. "All hail Queen Adara of the Waterways." Her deep voice was just as sure and confident as Adara's. I watched something pass between the two women, something that looked very much like affection.

Mira's smooth brown skin bled into a muscular shark tail and her fingers were clearly webbed. Her black hair was braided down her back with seashells and pearls embedded artfully in the design. Was she my true mother's lover? Would Adara name her princess consort once the dust had settled from her new reign?

The other council members followed Mira one by one, until I was the only one without my head bowed. Adara met my eyes, pain and sorrow pulsing between us like a living thing.

"Prince Caspian, heir to the Waterways, do you accept me as Queen of the Mer?" Her voice was small and far less sure than it had been when she spoke to a room of her council members.

Did I accept her? Did it matter if I didn't? But then, of course I did. Whatever she'd kept from me, all the lies she told me over a lifetime of questions, she was the only person I'd ever bow my head to in Atlantis.

And so, I did. I bowed my head low just as the council members yelled in unison, "Long live the queen!"

There was no feast or party afterward. I think there used to be, but the former queen was not usually deposed in the middle of a battle that claimed the lives of many. I joined Adara and Mira in the small royal dining room for dinner. Raw fish sliced thin floated just above the table, held still by the mer guard's control of the water, and there were no less than four mer guards armed with tridents and several pearl-handled obsidian knives strapped across their bodies.

We ate in near-silence, talking intermittently about my up-coming wedding and the changes Adara wanted to make in Atlantis' infrastructure in an effort to modernize it. Apparently, Morgana was terrified of human tech and even more wary of all the comfortable magic having a magician on staff would bring.

Just as I was about to push away from the table, a mer woman with short brown hair and the long, thick tail of an eel swam in through the open door.

"A message," she said without ceremony, "for Prince Caspian." She paused.

"Well, let's hear it," Adara finally said.

"Prince–King Ruyek is still in the Vampire kingdom, and Princess Cordelia wishes you to return home as swiftly as you're able," the woman said.

King Ruyek. Had Ruyek gone to Rome to challenge his father? Of course he was stronger, but he'd actually won! He was king now, and what did that mean for all of us? Adara looked as stunned as I was by the news, so apparently being engaged to Ruyek ranked higher than being the mer queen.

"Is there anyone who can translocate available?" I asked Adara without hesitation. Home. I had to get home. And for now, that was Richmond, but really, that was anywhere my fiances were, anywhere in this world or any other world where I would find them.

"Yes, I keep a fae on staff," Adara said.

Within ten minutes of the news, I was deposited on the front lawn of Cori's castle on Belle Isle. It was the middle of the night when I arrived in Richmond, and I had to remind myself it was the middle of the night prior as I rushed to the front door of the castle. I found Cori and Van sitting in her council chambers. Autumn and Sabine were there too, along with a few witches I didn't recognize.

"What in seven hells do we do now?" I asked as I sat heavily into the chair next to Van. He was seated to the right of where Cori sat at the head of the table.

"Ruyek taking the throne is certainly one issue to make sense of," Cordelia said. "The other issue is my mother. Apparently she offered Valdon safe harbor in the Witch Queendom. We believe they're in D.C. by now."

"Ruyek and the father he just dethroned are going to be basically in the same state?" I asked.

"Please never tell someone in D.C. they're basically Virginians, but yes. I think it best we all head to Rome." Her head snapped to Autumn. "And no, I won't be translocating. I am a witch, and I will travel by pegasus. I have no desire to forget that about myself simply because translocating is faster."

Ruyek

Defeating my father was one thing. Dealing with the shit-show that came with actually being king was a very different experience. The mer pretty much kept their councils monarch to monarch, but that was expressly forbidden by vampire law. Every single person on staff, from the guards and the maids to the council members and my own mother had to reapply for their positions.

This was particularly important because I had taken the coward's way out and decided not to murder my father. If I'd had the foresight to realize how much work that made for me, I might have ignored Ambrose and killed him to save myself the trouble. The *trouble* was loyalty. Every person on staff and every person allowed to remain in the castle in any capacity (like my mother) had to be vetted. Their loyalty to me and their acceptance of my father's deposition had to be guaranteed.

What did that look like in practice? It looked like me being allowed to pry into the minds of thousands of employees and high-ranking vampires before they could remain. They could refuse the mind-prying, but they'd be walked out of the castle immediately and banned from ever working in the royal household again.

As one could assume, most of the guards and servants didn't give a shit who was king. They cared that they got paid and hoped I'd better compensate them than my father (which I did, immediately, one way to win loyalty is better wages).

The council members were not as easy to read. One of them, Lord Havis, allowed me into his mind but used his own power to jumble any chance at figuring out his inner thoughts. I dismissed him as soon as I discovered his game. Two others left of their own accord, until only four remained.

All men, ancient and Acadian like my mother, and seemingly loyal and accepting when I looked into their minds. When I declared my mother would lead the council, two of those four left after mumbling about progressive politics under their breaths. Two stayed: Lord Emmil and Lord Aurel.

They were both Acadians who had grown up with my father, but their minds revealed a shifting loyalty over the century we'd been on this planet. Aurel's memories showed him stirring up vampires to back me if I ever challenged my father, a quiet rebellion that made it clear that checking in on the minds of my council members regularly would be crucial moving forward.

Emmil seemed loyal to power, and at the moment, that was me. Though I wondered what all the women vampires of my kingdom would do when they were able to challenge me for my throne. My mother, for one, was an incredibly powerful wielder cowed into domesticity by tradition.

I declared the rest of my council would be representatives from the other four magicborn kingdom, and then reminded everyone that I had four fiances to fill those roles. And oh look, we had a council. Emmil bristled a little at the thought of a council that was dominated by non-vampire voices, but he also wanted to keep his job so he didn't push back once I'd made it clear this wasn't up for debate.

We were discussing how much of my time would be spent here versus in Richmond when a guard let me know that my fiances had just arrived. I hugged my mother and then dismissed the council. Ambrose was a constant by my side, through every interview and early council meeting, he was a shadow I never felt the urge to wield.

"Take them to the king's chambers," I told the guards stationed outside of the council room. The council room shared a wall with the throne room, but the king's chambers were the entire west wing of the castle. Once rehired, the staff quickly made the chambers mine and my mother moved into my former rooms.

A lot had happened in just a few days. Word took a little while to reach the other kingdoms, and the pegasuses needed a few days to travel to Rome. It was just enough time to do all the grunt work necessary to get this castle mine enough that it wasn't my father's anymore.

One of my favorite changes was the bed large enough for eight people Van's size to sleep comfortably in. This was the only bed in the king's chambers. I'd thought about conjoined rooms like we had on Belle Isle, but I was done pretending I didn't want to sleep with (double entendre intended) all four of my lovers. We had guest rooms if someone was unwilling to take this leap with me, but I felt like we were all already coming around on the gods-forsaken island.

The first thing I noticed was the shift between them. Something had happened between at least two of them, maybe all of them? Ambrose's eyes widened like he saw it too, the way they all stood so close together naturally, like the distance between them had been crossed while we were separated.

"Alright," I said. "First, we are all heading to the shower. Somehow, all of you smell like pegasi. Then, you are spilling the details of every kiss, hug, and tug over dinner."

Cori rolled her eyes, but I saw the slight smile pulling at the corner of her lips.

"Like one singular shower?" Van asked, looking at Cori like she'd be uncomfortable.

"Precisely. If that's too much, I can have a servant lead you to the guest room showers," I answered.

"I don't care as long as I get clean very quickly," Cori answered, her eyes seeming to reassure Van as she spoke.

I led them through the bedroom and into the massive bathroom that had to be magic-ed to fit my specifications. A massive open floor shower dominated half the bathroom. Several different shower heads (more than we could ever use, even if we all took two) surrounded the tiled floor. The floor sloped slightly towards the drains at the back of the shower, but the rest of the bathroom was flat – except for the salt water hot tub deep and wide enough for a mer with very long tentacles to spread out with a few friends.

The toilet was in a different room through a door opposite the shower, along with mirrors and a very long, ornate sink. Vampire castles had very few toilets installed, since we did not need them, but we had enough non-vampires around to have a few. Installing one for Ambrose was high on my list before taking over the king's chambers. I already had everything he could possibly need in my old chambers, as every kind of lover had graced my bed before I got my own apartments fifty years ago.

"Was this like this before you became king?" Cas asked as he walked over the hot tub and turned on the faucet.

"Absolutely not. My father was not a man of imagination. The most interesting thing he ever did was fall in love with a witch," I said. I didn't need to point out who the witch was. We all knew. Everyone knew.

"May I?" Cas asked, his eyes full of something that looked very much like adoration as he looked from the tub I'd installed just for him back to me.

I turned my back to him and activated the wall screen, choosing a few options that made the hot tub start bubbling and the shower heads start spitting out warm water.

Without a moment's hesitation, Cas pulled his clothes off, his legs shifting to blue and black tentacles that pulled him over the side of the hot tub and into the bubbling water. Just like the shower, the hot tub would be drained and refilled after use, so it was meant for the scrubbing he immediately started doing with the bar of goat milk soap in a basket adhered to the wall.

I felt like I could watch him all night long, the mer in his true form enjoying the salts I'd had translocated from the waters near Atlantis. He was solid muscle and skin tanned from his time training in the sun, and his dirty blonde hair was streaked with more blonde than it had been before we'd started training. The blue hue beneath the skin of his cheeks and the blue scale-shaped patches on his arms remained visible, even beneath the fawn hue of his tan.

Soon enough, Van, Cori, and Ambrose were stripping and my attention was torn away from Cas to my other three glorious fiances. I was intimately familiar with Van's naked form, but as he stepped into the hot spray of the shower, I was still struck by his sheer mass. He was a giant of a man with all the finesse of a feline. He moved easily, like he wasn't lugging around nearly three hundred pounds of solid muscle.

Cori though, gods– Cori was tall and lean and muscular. Looking at her chiseled thighs made me imagine her squeezing me to death while I licked her to orgasm. What a delicious way to die.

Ambrose was as lean and beautiful as he always was. I'd seen him naked more times in the last few weeks than I might have ever seen anyone naked (my former flings never developed into anything long-term), but every single time he stripped, I felt like the luckiest vampire in either world.

It took everything in me not to propose a shower orgy. I knew they'd just traveled a long way, and a lot of political changes had happened in the last few days. Two newly crowned monarchs within days of each other was rather unheard of in the annals of Acadian history. When monarchs lived eight to nine hundred years, change was rarely swift. A few coups across heads of states were the exception, but one being challenged and one being murdered in uncoordinated decisions this close together? I had no doubt the witch queen thought this was all connected. She was probably doing mental gymnastics between rounds of fucking my father to try to figure it out.

I wondered what Cori thought of all this. Where did her father fit into whatever was happening between Rixana and my dear old dad? The witch queen was never one for quiet defiance, so I'm sure she'd make some sort of public appearance or proclamation to defy my rule in her own way. She no doubt knew this day was coming, but everyone likely thought I'd wait until after the wedding. I would have waited if my father hadn't barred me from the archives, of course.

"We need to search the archives tomorrow," I said aloud, stepping away from my own thoughts to loop everyone in. "I also plan to go through my father's office. I've been a little busy since the duel, but he kept it locked up tight since before we left Acadia; now, I have the only key."

"Are we talking archives that historians have access to or just your father? The difference will determine what we may or may not find," Cori responded.

"Both. We have the historian curated archives and my father has personal archives. They're both in Vatican City. The royal archives are in St. Peter's Basilica and the king's archives are beneath the Sistine Chapel," I answered, a little breathless as I watched Cori lather herself with a bar of soap I sincerely envied.

I imagined my own hands running over her body, my fangs sinking into her neck and her breasts. How I yearned to see her stiffen with the momentarily pain of it before relaxing into the pleasure. I wondered what she looked like when she orgasmed. Did her back arch? Did her eyes fly open or close tightly with release? I'd seen many a witch in the throes of orgasm, but none were exactly the same.

The rush of chasing someone else's pleasure was half the reason I was a certified slut. I loved to watch someone fall apart beneath me. When I'd fucked Van, his rock hard body became jelly beneath me when he succumbed to orgasm. It had taken him a full hour to be ready to return the favor. I shivered at the memory of his knot inside me. What an absolute thrill that had been. He was the only alpha I'd ever fucked, though he was not the only shifter.

My thoughts roamed to Ambrose. What would he look like with Van's knot expanding inside him, pushing him to the limits in ways I simply couldn't. We'd used a few extra large dildos over the last week, but the real thing was a totally different experience. Van and I were similar sizes otherwise, but his knot was an experience no toy could replicate.

I slipped easily into Van's mind. A thick jungle wall of vines covered with lizards, snakes, and goliath bird-eating spiders greeted me. His mind was definitely well-guarded. I felt all the animals on the wall turn their attention to me at once, like they were all collectively Van's consciousness.

The hoot of an owl and the screech of a monkey filled the otherwise silent space.

You're here. Van's voice almost purred as his midnight lion appeared at the top of the walls and pounced down in front of my mass of shadows.

Of course I'm here. I've wanted to be here since we were first engaged.

You've been quite busy with the fae prince. The lion chuckled and shook its head so much like a housecat I wanted to reach out and pet him.

He came to me first, and I'll admit I am absolutely taken with him. He's eager and soft in all the right ways. I felt my shadows writhe at all the memories of me inside of Ambrose.

Do you love him? the lion asked.

Do I love you? That's the real question. There's no room for jealousy in this marriage. Yes to both questions. I've somehow started to love all of you. The old cold heart has grown four sizes bigger in the last month. The thought struck me as I spoke it. It had only been a month, about five and half weeks if we were being precise, since we'd been engaged. And somehow, everything had changed.

I want you, the lion's voice was a deep growl this time, the promise of a roar building.

Then have me, I answered. *But I really want to see you have Ambrose.*

The lion shook its maneless head. Midnight lions were most similar in size to an African lion, but they looked much more like a black mountain lion. The animal had no mane, but it was larger than the African counterpart and every inch of the creature rippled with muscles (maybe even more ripped than the humanoid version of Van, which was saying something).

"Are you two having a silent conversation?" Cas asked, pulling me roughly out of Van's head at the interruption.

"How can you tell?" I asked with a grin.

"You're staring at each other very intently, and you're both suddenly hard. I can imagine where the tide of that conversation went." Cas chuckled as he spoke.

I hadn't even realized I was staring.

"Watching you two fuck is definitely on my bucket list," Cori said, "but I think we should sleep tonight. It's been a very, very long few days."

"Cori died briefly," Cas added so nonchalantly I nearly choked.

"Excuse me?" I snapped.

"It's okay, she found her way back to us," Cas responded, still very calmly for the absolute bomb he'd just dropped on me.

She couldn't die. The only way I'd be able to bring her back was blasphemy, illegal in both words, but by the fucking gods, I'd walk the path of necromancy and make her a shade if it meant I could keep her in some form. There were very legitimate reasons for outlawing that kind of magic, but Death herself would not keep me from Cordelia. I had no doubt that Morana would claim Cori for herself, that winter-loving bitch, but I would do whatever was necessary to bring her back. I'd destroy Nefthys with my bare hands before I let her take her into Hel's domain.

Cori crossed the distance between us. We'd all been staying in our bubble thus far, but she moved across the shower to me.

"I'm okay, Rue. I came back because of you. All of you anchored me here, like unbreakable threads," Cori said, her hand on my arm.

Fuck. My dick was so hard I might cum with a single caress and she was right in front of me in all her naked glory, but she had *just* told us no sex tonight. I swallowed.

"Do you have piercings in your dick?" she asked, sounding more curious than turned on, unfortunately. She sank to her knees in front of me. "May I?" she asked before her fingers made contact.

"Please." My voice was a beg, a plea for anything she was willing to give me.

Her fingers found the Prince Albert piercing first, pulling gently on the curved bar through the head of my dick. Then the frenum piercing, running her hand along the straight bar on the underside of my dick beneath the head. I felt her mouth drawing closer, and she looked up for consent again. Touching and blowing me were two very different things, but fuck yes.

I nodded my consent, closing my eyes as she took me into her warm mouth and sucked gently.

"Gods," I moaned as she took me in deeper, twirling her tongue over each piercing as she swallowed me down, down, down until I was down her throat and her eyes were watering.

"Let me fuck you," I pleaded. "They can watch."

Her watery eyes went wide with shock from the implication but she didn't stop moving her head, taking me deeper and deeper until my entire dick was in her mouth. I reached down and ran my fingers along her head.

"May I?" I asked.

She nodded and moaned slightly as I pulled my hips back before slamming into her mouth, her throat. She took all of me greedily and eagerly, like she was as hungry for me as I was for her.

I paused deep in her throat and looked at the other three. "Any objections to watching me fuck Cori in this shower?"

Cas shook his head vigorously and was quickly echoed by Van and Ambrose. I think everyone was as shocked and delighted at the turn of events my emotion over Cori's brief swim through death incurred.

"Can I fuck you, Cori?" Her eyes met mine a moment, and she pulled her head back and then down, continuing to pleasure me with her mouth as she thought the offer through.

A few moments later, she nodded, and I pounced. I pulled my dick out of her mouth swiftly.

"Get down on all fours," I commanded. She obeyed without hesitation, baring her pussy and her ass to me deliciously.

I sank down and ran a finger through her already slick folds, wet with desire and water. I rubbed her clit, pulling her nearly to the edge as her panting filled the shower. Water dried everything else, so I needed her absolutely dripping with cum for me.

Just as she was about to orgasm, I pulled my hand away and lined myself up. I pushed into her. Gods– she was tight and soft and so much more than I imagined.

"Fuck," she moaned as I felt one then the other piercing hit her most sensitive spot. I took shallow thrusts at first, hitting her g-spot again and again until she came loudly, so loud she was nearly screaming as her pussy tightened around me.

"Can I bite you?" I asked, growing breathless as she squeezed me with her orgasm.

She hesitated and then nodded.

I leaned over her back and buried myself to the hilt in one swift movement, leaning down to sink my teeth into the side of her neck. Just like I imagined, she stiffened with pain a moment before relaxing with pleasure, cumming again as soon as the venom traveled from my fangs to her pussy.

She was relaxed enough for me to take her like I really wanted to. I continue to drink her blood down as I fucked her like I'd been waiting my entire life for this, and maybe I had. Maybe I'd been waiting a hundred and fifteen long years for all of them, for my life to finally have meaning and love – an abundance of love.

Her sounds filled the shower as I slammed into her again and again, denying my own pleasure until I felt a third orgasm building in Cori as her moans grew more frantic and her pussy tightened around me. Yes. Yes. *Yes.* We came together in a rush. I spilled my seed deep inside of her as she clamped down all around me and nearly screamed with pleasure.

I pulled my teeth away and licked the bite wound, healing the spots instantly.

"Fuck," she whispered as I stayed seated inside her, waiting to go soft before I pulled out – though it seemed just as likely I'd grow hard again instead.

I was tired though, exhausted from the last two days of the power exchange, of all the kingly duties I never actually wanted to do. But this duty? The duty to fuck my queen? That was a duty I could get behind.

I looked up from Cori to find Cas, Van, and Ambrose covered in their own cum. Clearly watching this had done it for all of us. Cas had two dicks? Fuck, I needed to see both of those in Ambrose's ass at the same time.

"A coronation," I panted as I pulled myself out of Cori finally. "All of you need to be crowned as my queen and kings."

"What?" Ambrose said as he collapsed against the shower wall, sliding down to sit beneath the warm spray with his head upturned towards the water and his eyes closed.

"Everything about us is historical, the first of its kind, but you are going to be my spouses and I am going to have you crowned before we leave Rome. I will not be persuaded oth-erwise," I replied as I stood up and offered Cordelia my hand.

"We are creating quite the power vacuum," Cas said breathi-ly, his voice still thick with the pleasure of cumming *from two dicks*. I wish I'd had the creativity to imagine that was even possible.

"That was inevitable. The moment they said we were to marry, they sealed their fate," I responded.

Cori was standing now and leaning against me, my arms wrapped around her as she shook with the aftershocks of three orgasms in quick succession.

"Yes," she breathed against my cheek. "Yes. I'll be your vam-pire queen."

"No objections here," Van added. "They knew the risks when they made this arrangement. We are all heirs to incredible political power, and they concentrated all of that power into a single marriage contract."

"Not to mention the *actual* power all of you have," Am-brose added, his eyes still closed.

"Don't do that," I responded. "*You* are a seer now and an incredibly powerful garden fae. I will not allow you to exclude yourself from any talk of immense magical power."

Not many people used the old terms for different kinds of fae power anymore. We'd left a lot of that in Acadia too, but I felt Ambrose smile at my compliment. He was a seer, and he was an incredibly powerful plant wielder. He was not the odd man out here.

"A seer?" Cas asked, his breathiness replaced with intrigue.

"Yes," Ambrose said. "I saw Queen Rixana come for Valdon. I saw him leave with her before the battle for the crown was even over. It's how I convinced him to yield: the promise of a future after that moment."

"And it happened just as you saw it?" Cas asked.

"Yes, down to every step and every word. My mother confirmed it after the fact," I responded.

"Fuck. We might actually be able to make a difference in this war afterall," Cas said.

"Avengers assemble, win – and fuck each other along the way," I chuckled. "I like that better than the original plot."

I was a huge fan of old mortalborn movies, what could I say? I particularly liked the ones that explored superheroes and magic in ways so similar to the reality of the magicborn. It was no secret there had been smaller, briefer-lasting wormholes before the rift; magicborn had undoubtedly slipped between worlds and fueled centuries of mythology on our existence, but it was incredible to see that come alive on screen.

Ambrose

Watching Ruyek fuck Cordelia was otherworldly. There was a time – well, actually right up until the moment Cori took him in her mouth – that I feared I would be jealous when he touched another of our fiances. But there was no jealousy. It just felt right. It felt like all of the pieces were finally coming together, not like I was losing some standing with Ruyek. We were all to be married. It went without saying that one day we would all take pleasure in each other. Together or apart, it didn't matter. I wanted it.

After the shower, Cori had to be half-carried to the adjacent room with sinks to brush her teeth, and then Van did actually carry her to the bed after drying her off delicately.

"My legs are jelly," she said as Van pulled back the covers of Ruyek's massive bed and laid her in the middle.

Van crawled in behind her, cradling her against his massive body. Cori was a tall woman, but she looked so small snuggled against him. I'd grown so used to sleeping tucked against Ruyek that I didn't really know where to go until he pulled me by the hand to the other side of the bed and motioned for me to crawl in next to Cori. He laid next to me, pulling my body into his arms as I looked into the golden irises of Cori's eyes. I felt her watching me, and I wanted to ask what she was thinking.

Cas shifted his tentacles away and climbed in behind Van, throwing an arm over the dark brown wall of solid muscle that served as Van's midsection. Cori kept looking at me without saying a word, and then slowly she extended a hand and ran her fingers gently over my antlers. I shivered in response, growing hard instantly.

"Oh, I see," Cori said with a smile. "That is a very interesting reaction that I will save for another time."

Her fingers trailed down the side of my face, gentle and soft.

"Can I kiss you?" she asked softly. I was aware of all the eyes on us, on this moment that felt like it should be intimate.

"I– Yes," I responded.

I'd only kissed Ruyek before, and while I felt like a fast learner, what if I didn't know how to adapt to Cori's style? What if I was ruined for everyone else? How did I–

Her lips interrupted my racing thoughts, silencing all my insecurities as she held her lips firm against mine. She didn't part my lips with her tongue. She didn't ask for anything more than our lips pressed together, and then she pulled away.

"Goodnight, Prince Ambrose," she said with a smile before closing her eyes.

"As much as I loathe mornings, there's a lot to do today," Ruyek's voice pulled me from sleep. He was already out of bed and dressed in a very well-cut suit. He flashed his red eyes my way like he could feel the heat of my admiration.

"Good morning, my king." Ruyek smiled.

"Morning." I was all grins in response.

Cori was still laying in bed next to me, her eyes still closed. Cas was behind her now, spooning her and sleeping soundly. Van was standing opposite Ruyek in a pair of gray jogging pants that left absolutely nothing to the imagination and a tight black t-shirt.

I unspooled myself from the most comfortable bed I'd ever slept in and crossed the room to where they stood leaning against a high table with five chairs around it.

"What's on our agenda?" I asked with a quick peck on Ruyek and then Van's cheek. Ruyek didn't seem surprised but Van did. The smile that followed his shock seemed answer enough on whether or not that move was okay.

"My agenda more than yours, sweetling," Ruyek answered. "I have a meeting with my mother to plan the coronation she doesn't know is happening yet, then I need to outline what her duties will be in my absence. As much as I love running this kingdom, I want to get back to Richmond and question the shadowborn general Van was just telling me is locked in the dungeons on Belle Isle. You three can do whatever you want until nightfall. Then we'll be going to Vatican City to find what was so important that my father gave up his throne to protect it."

"Your day sounds riveting," Van responded with a clap on Ruyek's shoulder. "Want to go for a run, Ambrose?"

I nodded with a smile.

"Have you ever seen Italy in the morning light?" Van asked.

I shook my head. I knew that this castle stood where Castello di Lunghezza once was and that it was twelve miles into the city proper, but we'd spent our time here on vampire time. No daytime excursions.

"Enjoy that," Ruyek said with a smile that I couldn't quite read. "There are a lot of trails leading directly from the castle, and all of them are rather secluded. Funny thing about vampires, we don't often go jogging in the morning. And while the mortalborn do that sort of thing, most of them keep a wide berth around this castle unless they're here to ask for royal favors."

Mortalborn stories of vampires were far more like the shadowborn with their tales of being turned into the monster that bit you, but old customs died hard. Most educated mortalborn knew their folklore about vampires missed the mark by a wide margin, but the fear of them persisted; whereas fear of witches, fae, shifters, and mer had subsided over the last century. Vampires were still the boogeymen that would suck you dry –

unless you were one of the mortalborn who was into that sort of thing (and there were certainly plenty).

Ruyek kissed Van and then me on the mouth, dipping his tongue into both of our mouths (to my horror, since I definitely had morning breath) before leaving us alone. I got ready quickly before joining Van back in the main bedroom.

"Lead the way," I said with a smile. I'd chosen a pair of red basketball shorts and a plain white t-shirt for the run.

Van led me out into the morning sun after a number of long hallways and doors without a single window. Ruyek's family was incredibly serious about keeping the sun far away from them. We jogged down a dirt path that led into a copse of trees. The trail continued through the trees and then down a hill. The entire countryside here was Italy straight out of a travel magazine. Rolling green hills, tall thin cypress trees, and smaller, more robust olive trees.

He set a running pace that was likely far slower than he preferred to run, but it allowed me to stay next to him. Up and down the hills, down long dirt roads and along the occasional ruins of streets made for cars, we ran.

My chest was burning, but it felt good. I'd built up a lot of stamina on Malden Island, but the only stamina I'd found in Ireland was the ability to go round after round with Ruyek in the bedroom. Van looked over at me as I briefly remembered some of those long, pleasurable nights. His nostrils flared a little, and he looked down at my crotch.

I stopped running immediately, gasping for breath. "Can you smell it?"

"Uhh – I smell a lot of things. I need you to be more specific," Van answered.

"Can you smell me thinking about sex right now?" I asked, all embarrassment gone as I looked up at him. He was a full head taller than me, and somehow, that made me even more turned on.

"I can smell your arousal, but it doesn't have to be a thing. I can smell everyone's arousal. It happens in the oddest of situations. Don't worry about it," he responded before taking off again, me a pace behind.

I know he said it didn't have to be a thing, but it definitely felt like a thing. While I had no idea where we were going, he was turning and leading like he had a destination in mind. After another thirty minutes of running, we crested a hill and he paused.

Below us, surrounded by hills, was the ruins of some ancient mortalborn city. Pillars of stone stood opposite each other in a line to the center of the town. In the center, there was a circular building with no roof left but very clear archways cut into the stone around the wall that still stood. Four columns held up a triangular patch of roof with what must have been a statue at the top. Only legs and a torso remained of the figure.

Broken statues and crumbling walls covered the empty space surrounded by hills. And while I knew next to nothing about Roman architecture or mortalborn history, it felt important standing here. For the first time in my entire life, I felt alien amongst the ruins of a world that existed long before we came through the rift. I was an alien. I was born in Ecuador, but this world, these ruins, were proof of eons of life before we showed up. And for some reason, that made me ache.

A rush of emotions coursed through me as I reached down and picked up a piece of a broken clay pot. What would Earth look like if we weren't here? If we hadn't come to this planet? Would they have destroyed themselves in their third world war, like the scientists who opened the rift had undoubtedly been working hard to do? Would someone have built a weapon powerful enough to wipe all mortalborn from the face of this planet? Who would be here to touch this pot and take in the remains of this ancient city if they'd succeeded? Where did we fit into all of this? Were we saviors or colonizers? Heroes or villains?

"Careful," Van said, kneeling next to me. "I feel like I can read your mind right now. Your face gives everything away."

"I don't often feel like an alien," I responded, wiping a tear from my cheek as I spoke.

"But we are. It's important to know who we are to this planet, to this world. This isn't our home, and I bet if you asked Ruyek if he wanted to stay here in this world where the sun is deadly, he'd want to go back," Van said softly.

"No one ever talks about going back." My eyes are still locked on the piece of pot as I talked, like I might fall completely apart if I met his eyes.

"I do. We are. Right now, we're talking about going back," he said, his voice quiet, as if the ghosts and the broken stone walls might hear him.

"I didn't think going back was an option."

"It's not an option anyone has ever presented to us, but it doesn't mean it isn't an option. Our parents, our elders, are very careful with what they offer to us as solutions to the shadowborn problem. There's entire worlds of information they are keeping from us." Van reached out and lifted my chin as he spoke, forcing me to meet his feline gaze.

"But how? We came through with millions of magicborn. How did everyone agree to keep our generation in the dark? Was it an order? It doesn't add up," I argued, pulling my chin away from his grasp, plopping down in the dirt, and bringing my knees up to my chest. I continued to run the pad of my thumb over the cracked, ancient clay; somehow, it felt soothing to touch something older than the oldest living magicborn. It was so rare to have that opportunity on this planet.

"I don't know what the average magicborn tells their children about Acadia or the shadow queen. Neither do you. None of us live in a home with the freedom of information a layperson has. We are royalty. Our education, every aspect of our lives is carefully controlled. I think that's why I went to a mortalborn college. I didn't learn anything new about Acadia, but I learned a great deal about the mortalborn and their histories.

"I learned that even if the witch queen sells us as the saviors of a broken, wartorn planet, she's wrong. We are alien invaders who happened to be more powerful and conniving than the native dominant species. Nothing more, nothing less. Did we save the mortalborn from themselves? Maybe. Would they be extinct if we hadn't stepped in? Maybe. Who can say? We can't. They can't.

"What we do know is *that* war was not *our* war. This planet is not *our* planet. It's easy to say we saved an entire species when no one lived through the alternative. This world had wars just as deadly before, and it always recovered. Who can say they wouldn't have found a way to relative peace again? Can you say that? That it was impossible for the mortalborn to thrive without our intervention?" Van's tone was so serious, and I realized after a moment of silence that his last question wasn't rhetorical.

"I guess I can't," I responded.

"In so many ways, I envy the mortalborn. We have so many centuries to reinvent ourselves, to grow and learn and figure out who we will be. I'm twenty-eight years old, Ro. If I were a mortalborn, half my life may well be behind me. I'd like to think I'd be a father, a literature professor, maybe a writer. I wouldn't have centuries left to sort out my purpose and who I want to be.

"The brevity of mortality is a gift. You don't have time to waste. It's a purposeful, mercilessly short shot at happiness, and we will never know that kind of drive – to have only decades to pack everything you want into your life. Can you imagine that kind of freedom? To know the here and the now might be it?" Van's voice was impassioned, almost feverish, like he'd thought about this a lot.

I wondered if it was condescending to think of mortalborn lives as quaint and full of purpose. Certainly, plenty of mortalborn wasted their short stint of life. But didn't just as many magicborn waste centuries of life?

"Do you want to be a mortalborn?" I whispered, like saying the words allowed was a breaking of some sacred oath.

Van stood up and paced around in the most feline way, somehow rhythmic and smooth like he was dancing around me.

"I know that you think I'm being ridiculous. Who would trade centuries for decades? But when I was at university, you should have seen the way the mortalborn spoke about literature and history, about morality and philosophy. They spoke like they knew they were running out of time, like they had to make their point right now because they would be dead in the blink of an eye. They didn't measure their words or hold anything back. They were honest, Ambrose. They were honest in a way that I've never known many magicborn to be. I wish I could explain–" Van paused and looked around. "The university– I can. We can sit in on a class. Have you ever attended a college class, Ambrose?"

I shook my head.

"We have to. One day, we have to sit in on a literature lecture. I know you don't speak Italian, so one of the universities in Richmond would be a better choice than one here. They have courses in American History."

America – there was a word I hadn't heard in a long time. The United States stopped existing the moment the witch queen won her seat of power.

Van spoke like a man possessed, like this was the single best idea he'd ever had.

I would go, of course. All of us would. If this mattered to Van, it mattered to me.

"I'm in," I responded, finally setting the piece of clay pot back on the dusty ground. "I'm always going to be *in* with you, Van."

Cordelia

"Hold formation!" Nadella's voice was so desperate, so raw and terrified. "Cori! Cordelia!"

But I couldn't listen to her. A dragon was headed towards Manhattan, pulling away from us to burn the city to the ground. It has happened before. Never on this scale, never New York City, but a city had been burned to the ground by the shadowborn forces before. That couldn't happen tonight. I couldn't let that happen on my watch.

I pulled away and moved Atreyu after the dragons. He didn't hesitate. He never did. Facing certain death, Atreyu would still follow me. We'd been born under the same moon, raised alongside each other. I spent more time in the stables than I did in my own room.

And so we dove after the dragon and its rider, a blonde woman I'd seen before. She had to be important in the shadow queen's army. I pulled at my core, drawing out more power than ever before. My ice reacted, covering my hand and my battle-ax, rising its head like a winter serpent ready to strike.

The dragon stopped midair, and I struggled to get Atreyu to respond that quickly. We stopped far closer to the dragon than we'd been before, just in time to see the massive creature swing its head around to face me.

I didn't hesitate. Ice erupted in blades and spears, piercing the feathered wings of the dragon. The creature bellowed in pain as its black blood leaked like the shadows of its rider into the night.

Fuck. I only had a moment to react as the injured creature erupted in flames. Winter. I thought of every memory I had of frozen rivers and snowy days, of a frozen Arctic and the icy tundra that lived inside of me. A shield wouldn't work against dragon fire, but I had to try. I had to try to save myself and my sisters chasing after me towards certain death.

The fire surrounded me, boiling my ice as it sank into my skin – *into* my skin. My body did not boil, but I felt the fire inside of me. My skin did not flake off from my body or char like it should have. Atreyu was screaming, my sisters and their mounts were screaming, but all I could think about was ice. Ice inside me ending this nightmare. I was going to die, but this shadowborn had to pay. In an instant, she'd obliterated my mother's entire line, all of her children would die here tonight. I thought about my father as fire erupted all around us, and I thought about how much I didn't want to die, how much I believed my ice could save us.

And then I awoke. I was wrapped in strong, warm arms that smelled like salt water and summer, like I was laying on a warm beach in the sun. The safety of that scent and those arms washed over me as I trembled.

"Bad dream?" Cas asked, his voice gentle.

"The worst, on repeat these days," I answered.

"Manhattan?"

I nodded against his chest. I knew he understood. I knew that even if we'd come to a place where we could be happy together, we were both still grieving. I'd moved through the guilt phase of loss about as gracefully as a bull in a china shop. There were so many moments on Malden when I just wanted to walk into the sea with rocks in my pockets. Sometimes, there were still such moments.

I turned around to face Cas. I wanted to feel something other than this loss, this grief.

"Do you love me?" I asked tentatively.

"Of course I love you. I thought I made that clear," he answered, his tone kind and soft. It wasn't an accusation. It sounded like he wanted me to know how much he was trying to show me his love.

I moved my face up to his, kissing him tentatively, like I didn't know where I wanted this to go – because I didn't. I wanted to feel loved. I wanted to feel full of the love between us, rather than the mourning that still clung to us like shadows.

He kissed me back, and I felt him harden against me as he rolled me onto my back and covered his body with mine. I was still naked from the night before and as he moved my legs open with his knee, I realized he was too.

His knee?

"No," I said, breaking our kiss. "I want you as you really are, not like this."

"Cori, we don't have to do that. This feels good too. I've only ever been like this with non-mer. It feels—"

"Does it feel as good like this as it does in your mer form?" I interrupted.

"This isn't all about me. It feels good both ways, and I don't want to hurt you," he responded; his ocean blue eyes looked so worried as he looked down at me.

"You won't hurt me, and I want you like a mer woman would take you," I insisted.

"Are you sure?"

I nodded, but he still hesitated a moment before shaking his head. He crawled away from me and reached into one of the bedside tables next to the bed and withdrew a bottle of lube. He came back to me and started kissing me again. I closed my eyes as we kissed, but I felt his body changing around us. Tentacles covered my legs and the bed, long beautiful black and blue tentacles.

"Do you need to be in the water?" I asked. I'd seen him in his mer form out of the water plenty, but I didn't want to deprive him of anything.

He shook his head and looked down at me. My breath caught as one tentacle lazily spread me open before stroking my clit. My head fell back on the pillow as Cas settled one of the suction cups on his tentacle over my clit, making a seal that made me more sensitive than I'd ever been before. He pumped his tentacle up and down, pulling on that sensitive bud with every movement.

Two more tentacles encircled my breasts. Each one squeezed gently at first before amping up the restriction, making blood rush to my nipples. Cas leaned his head down over my nipple and sucked the overly sensitive flesh. Fuck. He continued to suck and pump my clit, pulling me closer and closer to orgasm. I felt him pushing into me with a fourth tentacle, and I came loudly, screaming *Cas* as he obliterated me with pleasure.

He pulled his tentacles away and moved down my body, his face hovering just above my pelvis as he smiled up at me.

"I want to taste you," he purred before plunging his tongue into my slickness.

He licked my clit first, slowly and leisurely before moving his tongue lower and dipping it inside me. I squeezed around his tongue instinctually, wanting to feel full. He responded by placing a finger inside of me and moving back to my clit. He rubbed my g-spot with a long finger as his tongue traced circles, and just when I felt like I was going to cum, he started moving his tongue slower, gently as he pulled his finger out of my vagina.

My breathing was still heavy when he pushed a finger inside my ass. I was reminded of that same thing I told Van when we'd almost gone there: I'd never really done this. I'd thought about it plenty, but I'd never felt comfortable enough, trusting enough, to let someone take me that way. But now? In this moment? I felt ready. I felt hungry for it.

I tightened around him as he pushed his entire finger in.

"Relax," he said.

I breathed deeply and tried to unclench as he pushed another finger inside of me, slowly spreading them open, scissoring me wider and wider. It felt good in such a foreign way, like it shouldn't feel good, but by the gods, it did. He stretched me again and again, adding lube before filling me with a third finger and then a fourth. My own juices would only take us so far, I supposed.

"I want to touch you," I said as he pulled me back to the brink of orgasm by just finger fucking my ass. "Lay back," I instructed.

He moved his large body around and lay back on the pillows while I crawled over him. I ran my hands over his tentacles and felt him shiver as my hand explored inside the mass of them, feeling the heavy pouch against his body. A small slit was open atop the pouch, straining to stay closed as he grew harder under my touch.

"Are you okay with this?" I asked as my fingers danced along the seam.

He nodded, his eyes closed as I pushed the slit open wide enough to reach in and feel his two cocks. They were both so big. The one on top was longer and thicker, but the one on the bottom still put every mortalborn dick I'd ever seen to shame. I reminded myself I'd taken Van's knot when the *How are these ever going to fit?* fears started to sink in.

His tentacles danced around me, pulling me close as my head moved down, and I took the top penis into my mouth. He drew in air sharply, his body taut as I moved my hand up and down his second penis as I sucked the first.

I felt his pleasure building, like he might finish right here, but then he pushed my head away. His eyes were black with desire, the blue pushed to a thin ring as he looked at me.

"Lay down," he said in a voice that wasn't commanding but that made me want to follow anything he told me to do.

I watched as he lubed up both of his penises, and anticipation sank into my lower belly like a heavy stone. I wanted him. I wanted this. I wanted it so badly.

It took a moment for him to situate himself so both of his penis were pushing against my holes. My breathing was ragged as he moved, pushing himself in. Every part of me felt stretched as his wider cock pushed into my vagina and the bottom one pushed into my ass.

"Relax," he whispered.

I knew I was clenching. I wanted this, but I'd never done this.

"Please relax." Kisses down my neck joined his pleas as he whispered *relax* again and again until I finally felt myself unwind a little.

He pushed in a little deeper. He was only an inch or so in, and I felt so fucking full. I was going to combust when he took me down to the base. He pushed in again, slowly and tentatively as my body stretched around him.

When he was fully seated inside me, leaning heavily forward so that his body was flush against mine and both penises were inside of me, he paused.

"Are you okay?" he asked.

My breathing came in short, heavy breaths. I could only nod because I felt like I might burst if I moved – like he was filling me beyond capacity, but it felt so fucking good. The stretch of my ass burned, but I wanted more. He pulled back slightly to pour more lube between us before sinking back in. He started with slow, gentle thrusts, opening me and filling me with each movement.

I could see the muscles in his neck straining as he held back, trying so desperately not to hurt me. I shifted, moving my ass and vagina up at a slight angle so I could wrap my legs around him. He turned my hips upward with his tentacles, pulling me even closer as he started to pick up his pace. Fuck. Fuck. He was so fucking deep.

My breathing quickened as he hit parts inside me I didn't know existed. In and out, deeper and faster until he was fucking me harder than I'd ever been fucked. It felt so strange, the stretching and the pain mixed with a pleasure I couldn't even describe. His tentacles reached back up to my breasts, squeezing them so tightly I knew they'd leave marks as the blood rushed to my nipples.

I came in a rush, screaming into the massive bedroom as my body squeezed tightly around his cocks. He pushed into me a few more times with deep, brutal thrusts before he followed me over the edge. I felt warm cum fill my ass and my pussy. Between Van, Ruyek, and Cas, I was incredibly glad the pill seemed to work for most powerbound witches. I had to be full to the brim with their cum.

The soreness set in as he pulled out of me, panting heavily as he rested his forehead on mine.

"I never–" He breathed heavily. "I didn't know it could feel like that. That was–"

"Amazing," I supplied, turning my mouth to press against his.

"Transcendental," he responded.

His skin was so hot, but I knew that I was running cold. My ice was so close to the surface after all this sensation. We lay like that for a while, him on top of me, kissing me gently and tenderly until I felt him hardening again.

"Round two?" he asked.

I was so fucking sore, but I wanted him. I wanted more. I could already feel myself healing from the first encounter, so why the fuck not?

"On your back this time," I instructed.

Cas happily obliged, both dicks standing at attention as I lathered him in more lube and mounted him. I moaned with pain and pleasure as I sunk down on both cocks slowly. Fuck. I was very sore, but I needed more. I needed so much more of him – of Van, of Ruyek and Ambrose.

I moaned loudly as I pushed my body flush against him. He felt even better at this angle, something I didn't think was possible. I moved myself slowly, pulling him out inch by inch before pushing myself back down. Soon enough, I had a rhythm as I rode him, shoving myself all the way down, enjoying utter fullness only a moment before pulling myself back up again. A tentacle snaked between my legs, finding enough room to create a seal around my clit again and start pumping.

Holy goddess, everything was getting so sensitive so quickly. I came after only a few pumps of my clit, covering us both in more wetness as Cas put his hands on my hips and started guiding me, slamming himself into me harder and faster than before, obliterating any hesitation left between us, any shadow of doubt that we were meant to be this way, to be together.

He was mine. All of the princes were mine, and I was theirs, and I was done with hesitation. I wanted to feel everything this relationship had to offer. I wanted all of them inside me, fucking me, until either the world ended, or we closed the rift. For however long we had each other, I needed this.

He came again with a roar, spilling himself inside me as his nails dug so deeply into my hips he drew blood. He dropped his ass back to the bed with a heavy sigh. I was so full of his wetness that I feared I might have wrung him dry and put him out of commission for a while.

"Let me bathe you," he panted, his chest moving up and down with heavy breaths as I pulled myself off of him with an uncomfortable pop as he left my ass.

I was jelly, liquified in every manner of the word. I couldn't walk. There was simply no way. "Only if you carry me there," I said, my own breaths coming rapidly.

He scooped me up with a grin and carried me into the bathroom.

Savanna

We walked most of the way back after exploring the ancient ruins of the city. Ambrose and I hadn't had any time alone together to just be, and I felt better knowing who he was. He was funny and kind, soft in ways that Ruyek and Cas weren't.

I'd felt drawn to Ambrose as soon as we met, but now I felt like I genuinely liked him. It was good to know that the love I felt extended beyond whatever fate drew all of us together. I enjoyed the company of my fiances, and Ambrose was refreshing after the stress of the battle and the journey here with no idea what was really waiting for us.

Ruyek wouldn't journey to the archives until the sun completely set, so we had time to amble along together, talking about our very different (and yet, somehow very similar) childhoods. The Fae Court and the Shifter Territories had different customs, but we had both grown up as princes in a world ruled by monarchs.

The black basalt castle came into view through the trees that surrounded it. The original mortalborn castle had been pale stone, but Valdon tore it down to build his own stronghold. The once-historical monument had become a place for seasonal festivities and parties in the decades before the war that tore the world apart. When we arrived, it was completely abandoned, and Valdon said Italy reminded him of home in a way he couldn't describe. So, he designed a black stone castle without a single window in the entire structure. The tops of the turrets had statues of creatures left behind in Acadia keeping watch: centaurs, dryads, satyrs, nagas, sea serpents, halflings, redcaps, and a massive ice dragon made of polished black stone, all visible from the ground.

A shiver ran through me as I wondered anew if I would ever see the glory of the world we left behind. A red world with innate magic that transformed the landscape in unnatural ways. What would it feel like to look up and see two moons staring back at me? More importantly, what would it feel like to stand in the sun with Ruyek? To watch him close his eyes and feel the red rays of a safer sun dance along his skin?

"You okay?" Ambrose asked.

I realized then that I was staring up at the massive statue of the ice dragon. Its feathers were thicker and longer than the two dragons perched on the roof looking down at us. Isolde and her mate Drystan were watching us intently as we approached. Drystan, in particular, seemed to have a laser focus for us, watching every move we made.

The sun was heading towards the horizon, but there was time to rest before what would undoubtedly be a long night of research. I shook off the visions of Acadia and followed Ambrose into the castle. We'd barely reached our shared chambers when Ruyek sent one of his guards to fetch us for a council meeting.

Cori and Cas were sharing a plate of fruit at the round table in the corner of the massive room when we entered. The scent in the air made it clear they'd united while we were out. That information made me smile; all of the walls between us were truly crumbling.

The guard was polite enough to give us some time to shower and change into business casual attire. Cordelia and Caspian apparently conspired to be the sexiest people alive when they selected clothing from the large wardrobe that contained clothes in all of our sizes.

Cas wore a black silk shirt unbuttoned over his chest, revealing the ripple of his muscles. His sleeves were folded up neatly to his elbow, revealing the blue underneath his skin in all its glory. His shirt was perfectly complemented with tight black leather pants and black boots. His thick mass of dirty blonde waves were unbound with a few small braids neatly twisted through his locks. A thin line of dark eyeliner highlighted the deep blue of his eyes.

Cordelia chose a dark red sleeveless dress that hugged her body all the way to her waist before draping into a looser skirt with a slit that came to the top of her thigh. Easy movement, but I swear if she bent the wrong way, we'd see whatever underwear she'd chosen for the occasion. Her nipples were erect beneath the top of her dress – braless too then. A string of onyx stones hung around her neck with a line of stones cutting down to the top of her cleavage. She wore black boots with a small heel beneath her silk dress and her thick black curls were unbound beneath a thin golden circlet.

"Are we wearing crowns then?" I asked with a smile.

"Shouldn't we? This council meeting is most certainly to discuss our coronation," she responded with a smile of her own. She radiated heat, as if Cas had so thoroughly fucked her that she was still taut with the pleasure of it.

"Fair enough," Cas answered before piling several boxes on the bed. "Take your pick. Ruyek apparently decided we needed nearly a dozen crowns to choose from."

In the end, we were all dressed in red and black silk and leather, wearing simple golden crowns without jewels or embellishments. The show of wealth and status wasn't needed here. The whole world knew who we were. Ambrose wore a tight red shirt and black leather pants while I wore a completely unbuttoned black shirt and black pants.

We stepped into the hallway a united front; from the complimentary colors to the power that rolled off of every one of us: we were ready to take our places as kings and queen of the Vampire Kingdom.

Ruyek sucked in a deep breath as we stepped into his council room. An intricate map of Acadia hung on one long wall and a map of Eurasia hung on the other: the old world and the Vampire Kingdom. Behind Ruyek, who was seated in a high backed chair at the head of the table, was a painted mural of a red sun over a dark landscape with two moons reflected near the edge of the wall. Fitting for what looked like a war room.

"You should have told me you came here to seduce me," Ruyek said with a teasing lilt to his voice. "I would have cleared the room before you arrived."

"Here for business first, seduction later," Cori replied with a smirk. Seeing her coming out of her shell was absolutely world-altering.

"Promise?" Ruyek asked.

"Promise," Ambrose answered breathily, like he was already imagining a night dripping with debauchery.

"Council members," Ruyek said as we all settled into chairs around the table. "Meet your new sovereigns. They will serve on the council, and they will be crowned as monarchs of this kingdom."

Every vampire at the table straightened, with the exception of Ruyek and his mother (who was seated to his right and absolutely beaming at the idea, it seemed). Non-vampires and vampires were equally matched in number at this table. It was a normal state of affairs to have few incumbent council members after a shifting of monarchs, but it was still odd to be seated at a vampire council meeting comprised of so few vampires.

"Your highness," one of the councilmen said.

"Let us hear your objection, Aurel." Ruyek rolled his eyes and leaned back in his chair as he addressed the man.

"It's just that—" Aurel's words trailed off as he seemed to search for the right words. "It's just that your arrangement is novel, your highness. I don't know how the people will react to the crowning of non-vampires. There could be discontent."

Ruyek's smile fell as Aurel spoke and shadows poured from Rue's body in waves, coming to sharp points like hundreds of black blades around him.

"Ruyek," Cori whispered, her voice like a plea.

"No," King Ruyek snapped, and he was every bit a king at that moment. "No. I will not concede this. Anyone discontented is free to challenge me for my throne. That is the tradition of our people, is it not, Lord Aurel?"

"Yes, your majesty." The lord's eyes were downcast as Ruyek addressed him.

"This world is changing, and if you recall, it was none of us who sought to change it. The broken traditions lay at the feet of my father. He was our king when he engaged me to a witch princess ten years ago and now, a monarch from every magicborn royal family. And while that may sound like a criticism, this most recent engagement is fated. There is something about this union bigger than you or I or the contentment of our people. You will crown my fiances and I in two day's time, and then we will return to the Witch Queendom to ensure my father is behaving and to prepare for our wedding. My mother will rule in my stead, as I trust her judgement more than you should ever have trusted my father's. None of this is up for council debate. These are orders, Lord Aurel. Do you accept them?" Ruyek's red eyes nearly glowed as he stared the ancient vampire down.

It was the other councilman who responded. "We have no objections, your highness."

Lord Aurel only nodded, his eyes still on the table as Ruyek's shadows stretched towards him a moment longer before the air in the room seemed to shift and a smile returned to Ruyek's face and his shadows retreated into him.

"I leave the preparations for the coronation to the three of you." Ruyek looked from his mother to the two vampire councilmen. "My fiances and I have immediate business to attend to in Vatican City."

With that, Ruyek stood and years of royal tradition pulled every butt in the room out of its seat as we all stood and slightly bowed our heads.

"No," Ruyek said. "You four do not bow to me. Not now, not ever. Do you understand?"

His eyes traveled from Ambrose to Cas to Cori and finally, landed heavily on me. And while I understood he was making it clear we were equals, his command was electric. It had a gravitational pull and all of us straightened and nodded.

We shared a meal in our chambers before changing into more practical clothing for the flight to Vatican City. It would be only a few minutes from the castle, but the air was already cooling as night approached. We all strapped on flight leathers and weapons. Ambrose chose only a few knives while Cori strapped her battle-ax to her back, a short sword on each hip, four knives total in her boots, and a small blade to either wrist.

"Are you preparing for war?" Ruyek asked as he strapped a broadsword to his own back.

"If we've learned nothing over the last few months, I hope it's that war is always imminent. We can feel safe inside castle walls, but every trip outside is a risk. I won't be caught unprepared again," she answered.

Ruyek nodded and added a few more knives to his own leathers in response to Cori's thoughtful warning.

Cordelia's pegasus and the bay pegasus that was quickly becoming Cas' personal mount joined us outside the castle while the dragons just stared down at us.

Ruyek looked very tersely toward the sky like he was having a mental conversation with Isolde. A few moments later, she deigned to meet us on the ground, her mate in tow. Dystan, her mate, stepped closer first.

I felt my mouth fall open as he pushed his massive feathered head against Ambrose's side. Was he – was he choosing a rider who was *not* vampire? Had that ever happened before? The vampires and the dragons were a centuries-long treaty and partnership. Honestly, at least a thousand years.

"What's happening?" Ambrose asked, putting my thoughts into words.

"Well, I'll be damned," Ruyek said with a small chuckle. "Drystan is choosing you, if you'll have him."

"Choosing me?" Ambrose asked.

"He chooses you to be his bonded rider." Ruyek's smile grew as he watched the red dragon continue to press against Ambrose like some massive dog seeking affection.

"And if I don't choose him?" Ambrose's voice was quiet, so quiet and full of fear as the dragon continued to make contact.

"He'll probably eat you, so I think it best you accept," Ruyek responded as he swung up on Isolde's purple and black back.

Ambrose reached a tentative hand out and touched the dragon, running his fingers over the feathers I knew were thick and hard like armor, soft only on the underside. We all watched in awe as the massive beast laid down on the ground, flattening himself as much as he could.

"He's helping you mount," Ruyek said as Ambrose shot him a look of confusion. "We all know you have no idea what you're doing. He's being kind about it."

Ambrose rolled his eyes at Ruyek before slowly climbing up the dragon's wing and settling just behind his shoulder blades. He'd definitely need a saddle for any further trips.

"Hang on," Ruyek said a moment before Drystan shot into the air and Ambrose screamed with fear.

I shifted into the ice dragon I'd seen memorialized on top of the castle. It was a heavy form, and my blood ran cold like my heart pumped rivers of ice.

"Badass," Ruyek said as we both took to the sky, he atop his own dragon while I met him wingbeat for wingbeat in this foreign body. It felt wrong for this world, like this night was far too warm and uncomfortable, despite the cool breeze.

Only a few minutes later, Ruyek led us to a smooth landing in St. Peter's Square, which was notably not a square at all, but rather an open oval around the Vatican Obelisk.

Caspian

"We can cover more ground if we split up," Ruyek said.

"Have we learned nothing about splitting the party?" Van said with a smile.

"We'll all be in the same vicinity this time," Ruyek responded. "Cas, Cori, and I will go to the king's archives beneath the Sistine Chapel while Ambrose and Van go to the royal archives under St. Peter's Basilica. Visiting the royal archives only requires the blood mark of the king — that's the key."

I watched as Ruyek pulled a knife from his boot and sliced open his hand. Dark blood trickled slowly from the wound. He stepped forward and rubbed his hand across Ambrose's forehead before doing the same to Van. To their credit, neither of them flinched as blood dripped down their faces.

"Anyone who sees you will not stop you. The command in my blood will be felt by every vampire you encounter."

"St. Peter's Basilica isn't a small place, Rue. Where exactly are we going?" Ambrose asked.

"There's a staircase in the Papal Altar. It will open when you are close enough for the magic to recognize my blood. If you wipe off my blood, you'll be stuck there until we realize you're stuck and come to your rescue." Ruyek reached a hand out to grasp Ambrose's, covering his palm in more blood. "You will be safe. If you need me, call for me, and I will find you."

Ruyek didn't need to explain what that meant. His mind and Ambrose's undoubtedly formed a very close connection over the last few weeks, and he would hear if Ambrose reached out mind to mind. One day, we would all have that level of closeness, of telepathic power. Our connection to Ruyek would make us more powerful.

"Do we need bloody makeup too?" Cori asked as Ruyek let go of Ambrose's hand.

"No. Only my blood, fresh from the vein, will allow us into the king's archives. You just need me," he answered.

The five of us headed in the same direction, parting at the base of St. Peter's Basilica. Van and Ambrose kept straight while we veered to a doorway to the right. Before the magicborn, such a door likely didn't exist, but we watched as Ruyek sliced his hand open anew and pressed it to the door. It opened and he led us through dark hallways and doors until we stepped back out into the night.

The courtyard we entered was nondescript, just like the pale stone building in front of us.

"This is it?" I asked. I expected something far grander.

"It's the inside that wows. If you ever doubted the artistic superiority of the mortalborn, the Sistine Chapel will set all that to rest. We have power; that is our art. Mortalborns are born with art and music in their veins. It's their own magic, I'm convinced of it." Ruyek's voice held such reverence for the mortalborn, and I wondered if his father had ever regarded a single mortalborn with such awe.

"Let us not forget their actual magic," Cori replied. "The magicians may have something to say about art being the only magic of the mortalborn."

"The magicians have a lot to say about everything. I maintain my position, even if some mortalborn have gotten very clever in recent history."

Ruyek led us into the chapel. His guards had already cleared the building for us. Only vampire guards met us, all of them armed and dressed in black armor. I stopped walking as I took it all in. Rue wasn't lying. Six and a half centuries had come and gone since the building had been painted, but still, the colors were vibrant and alive.

I felt Cori stop next to me too, both of our heads swinging around to take in the grandeur. I looked down as Ruyek chuckled. He was facing the pair of us, looking at our faces as we took in the magic, yes the *magic*, of this place. He was right. This was unlike anything that existed in Acadia. I might not have been born there, but I knew enough about Acadian culture to know magicborn would never spend years creating something like this.

"Acadia was a different reality," Rue said in the uncanny way he always seemed to read our minds when we weren't careful with loud thoughts. "It was always a fight for our lives, for power, for the survival of our races. There was no downtime from those fights. I think that's why our elders collectively left so much of our history behind when we came here. What history was worth keeping?"

"There is plenty of history in this world that is not worth keeping, but still, it is our duty to keep it. If people died, were murdered, enslaved, or ill-treated, remembering honors them," Cori said.

"Does it?" Ruyek twisted his lips like he was thinking. "What does our remembering do for them? They're dead."

"It reminds us they lived, that we remember they lived and existed – even if there were others who thought they were worth forgetting. Their children, descendents know that we do not forget, that we are their memory keepers," Cori answered.

"I suppose," Ruyek said, not unkindly or flippantly, but rather, like he was actually thinking it all over and seeing history in a new light. "Shall we?" He gestured towards the altar at the end of the room. There was an open doorway between what seemed like ornate fences separating the rest of the chapel from the altar.

We followed him, but my eyes continued to scan the walls, taking in the centuries-old art that persisted in a world so different from the world of its original creator. What would Michaelangelo think about a world so technologically advanced? What would he think about a world ruled by monarchs from an alien planet? Of magic existing in ways only folk tales and myths spoke of before us?

My musings were cut short when we reached the altar. Cori stepped closer to me, her hip touching mine as I watched Ruyek kneel down and examine a rune on the ground.

"Fuck," he said.

"What's wrong?" I asked.

"This is going to take a lot of blood." He gestured towards the rune. It was cut deep into the stone with intricate swirls and dips.

As I looked at it, I began to understand. Rue would have to fill the entire rune with his blood, blood that was much more precious to a vampire than to any other magicborn. His healing could heal his cuts, but his body could not make more blood. He'd have to drink it to recover.

"Do we have to do this?" Cori said softly, stepping forward and kneeling next to Ruyek.

"We have to have answers, or we may very well all die." Ruyek was never one to mince words. He was silver-tongued and witty, but he was straightforward when it was important.

Cori didn't stand as Ruyek pulled out his dagger again and sliced a straight line from the base of his palm through his wrists. He held the gushing wound over the rune, closing his eyes as he bled into it.

Halfway through, he had to slice the same wound open when his healing powers clotted the blood and tried to scab over. It did not stop bleeding this time. Even when the rune was filled and the floor around us began to shift, Ruyek pulled his arms away and held it firmly to his side in an effort to put pressure on the wound. He'd lost too much blood, and his body was struggling to heal.

Cori reached a hand out to steady him when he swayed where he stood.

"I'm okay," he said, his eyes unfocused as the altar swung out of the way and a descending staircase was revealed.

Ruyek kept his arm pressed to his side, blood spreading across his shirt as he led the way down the staircase. Cori walked one step ahead of him, her arms out like she was ready to catch him if he fell. I walked a few steps behind, my mind focused on Ruyek's stumbling progress rather than the dark staircase that descended lower and lower under the church.

Finally, we stepped on solid ground and Ruyek led us down a long hallway. There were no candles or torches, just darkness that our magicborn eyes allowed us to navigate. A door stood at the end of the hallway.

"Well, at least I don't have to slice myself open again," Ruyek said as raised his bleeding wrist above another symbol where a doorknob should be. His blood bled into it, cascading down the door until the rune was full enough of the king's blood filling it.

The door swung open silently. Ruyek swayed as he stepped through. Cori rushed forward to catch him, but he fell heavily, pulling her to the ground with him. She shifted him onto her lap, holding his head in her hands.

"You need blood," Cori said. The red in Ruyek's eyes had gone black and his pale skin seemed even paler than usual.

"That's the whole ruse. My father always brought a few of his favorite vassals along with him for his visits here. I've never been one to keep mortalborn chattel for my own needs. He knew I wouldn't do it when I inherited, that this journey would kill me without vassals," Ruyek's black eyes stared up at the ceiling and he breathed heavily.

"No," I demanded. "We have blood, Rue. We can help you."

He shook his head. "Not like this. I don't want your blood out of pity or fear. I want you to want me, to want me to drink from you, to be blind with desire when it happens. Not like this. It can't be like this."

"I do want you," Cori whispered. "You've already drank from me. You know I want you."

He shook his head again, but she ignored him and reached for a knife in her boot. He shook his head again, much weaker this time, but when she sliced her wrist open and held it over his mouth, he shuddered. Her blood dripped into him and he licked his lips greedily.

"I want you," she said softly. "I will always want you, Ruyek."

Whatever speed Ruyek had left, he used as he struck. His fangs sank in her wrist and he drank deeply. Cori closed her eyes with a heavy sigh, and I imagined what she felt like with his venom coursing through her veins and bringing every nerve ending to life.

He drank and drank until I knelt down next to them.

"Enough," I said. Ruyek didn't look satiated, but he couldn't take more blood than Cori could handle losing.

His eyes flashed angrily, hungrily at me before his mind kicked in and he pulled his teeth out of Cori's wrist, licking the wound as he moved away from her.

It was my turn. I took Cori's knife to slice my own wrist, but before I could, Ruyek sat all the way up and pulled my wrist away from the blade. He sank his teeth into me and I stiffened at the pain. The pleasure followed only a heartbeat later, filling me with desire. I felt my dick stiffen in my pants. I was in my humanoid form, so only one dick this time, but it got so hard, I felt dizzy.

I didn't stop Ruyek as he pushed me down and mounted me, didn't stop him as he held my wrist with one hand and pulled my pants off with the other. He paused and searched my eyes for consent. I hesitated only a moment before nodding. I'd never been a bottom before, but I wanted it. I wanted him.

He pulled his flying leathers down and paused drinking long enough to rub my blood all over his dick. Then his mouth was back on my wrist as he pushed my legs up against my chest. I breathed heavily, ready and a little bit afraid as he lined up. The fear gave way to pain as he pushed into me.

"Breathe," Cori said, crawling over to us and running her hands through my hair. "Let yourself relax."

I breathed deeply, in and out, and willed my body to relax. He pushed in further as my body responded, burying himself in one quick thrust.

Fuck. He felt so good, even if the stretch burned. He met my eyes again, and I nodded *yes* to his unspoken question.

He took one last long drink before pulling his fangs away and licking the wound. He leaned over me, pushing my hands over my head and holding them down as my body responded by opening up further for him.

And then he unleashed himself. His thrusts were deep, hard, and fast. He was relentless, a force that seemed to tear me open and expose every part of me to him in a way I hadn't before. This was a reckoning, a claiming like I was sure he'd claimed Ambrose while we were apart. He'd fucked Cori in the shower, but this was different. He was absolutely feral this time.

Cori's hand reached between us as his brutal pace pushed his piercings against my prostate again and again until I was leaking pre-cum without any dick stimulation. Her thin fingers stroked me gently as Ruyek's breathing quickened. A few more strokes and I was cumming all over myself. My body squeezed with the orgasm, bearing down on Ruyek until he followed me over the edge. I felt his cum pour into me, warm and wet as it leaked out around where we met.

"Fuck," he panted. "You feel so fucking good, Cas, so tight. I didn't expect this. I don't know what I expected, but this was effervescent."

He pulled out of me and gently lowered my legs to the floor. Under normal circumstances, I'd want to clean myself up after such an encounter, but something about his cum and my blood dripping down my legs was sensual. I pulled my pants back up and found my feet without wiping a single drop away (though plenty had pooled on the floor).

Ruyek did the same, pulling his leathers back up as his breathing evened out. "Thank you for the blood and the–" He looked between me and Cori. "For this."

I answered by leaning forward, grabbing his face in my hands, and kissing him. My tongue parted his lips and explored his mouth. I pushed my tongue against his razor-sharp fangs, slicing myself open so my blood could fill his mouth. He moaned and reached his arms around me, cupping my ass and pushing our bodies together. He was hard again and so was I.

Later, I said in my mind, knowing he would hear me. *When we're back home, you can have anything you want.*

The unspoken part was the reminder we had some very important business to tend to here, so important he'd nearly died to get us inside the king's private archives. He pulled away, healing my tongue as we parted.

"On to the business, I suppose." His smile didn't reach his eyes, like pulling away from me was the absolute last thing he wanted to do, no matter what was at stake here.

Ruyek

What felt like only moments ago, I'd felt my lifeblood pouring out of me, my heart slowing. After drinking from Cori and

Cas and then devouring every part of Cas' body, I felt like my body was buzzing with electricity. Every part of me was alive and burning. It was almost too distracting to focus – *almost*.

The room wasn't a particularly large chamber. Books lined the walls and papers were strewn across a long rectangular table near the back of the room. A chest was open and full of Acadian gold and rare gems. Apparently my father had kept a lot of secrets in this room. I wondered casually if he'd ever even allowed my mother to see this place, but I knew the answer and I vowed to bring her one day, to show her that which was unfairly denied to her as Queen of Vampires.

We pulled books from the shelves and sorted through papers on the table. Cori scanned maps and military stratagems with her phone, archiving them so we could sort through them later. That was all very exciting, but none of it had anything to do with the shadow queen.

I was about to give up on finding anything actually useful when I felt my entire body jolt with awareness as I fumbled through the chest of gold to see if anything was hidden beneath all this extravagance. My fingers touched a wooden box.

I reached in and pulled it out. It was made of Acadian willow. I could tell from the feel of it, from the innate magic that radiated from it. The dryads were the trees and the trees were the dryads in a way that made Acadian wood feel alive.

Another rune was carved into the top of this box, and there was no other lock or opening mechanism. Fan-fucking-tastic. I reminded myself to punch my father in the dick the next time I saw him. I sliced my arm open again with the blade on my hip and my blood pooled in the rune.

The bleeding stopped on its own this time, almost perfectly in tune with the rune being full enough to make the wood shudder. The wooden box parted and swung open with an audible click.

The box was filled with – letters? I felt Cori and Cas close in around me, kneeling next to me as I took the first one out.

Val,

I don't know what to do anymore. She visited my castle, demanded I end this. She left me a potion to drink that would take care of everything. I swore that I would, but you and I both know I can't. If she was truly a god, my deception wouldn't deceive her. But we both know she's not. She's something else entirely.

I will continue to hide. Autumn has glamoured me, and you know she is unrivaled in so many ways. I am starting to believe she is a royal bastard. Satia herself doesn't rival Autumn's powers.

I will send word when it's time, and you must come to the cabin. I don't care what your father says. You will not make me do this alone. That is an order, Valdon. You cannot leave me alone with this. This is our family, our future.

Before then, I hope that you find a reason to visit. I burn for you.

Rix

I knew Cori and Cas were reading over my shoulder.

"Satia, like King Taron's mother? The former fae queen?" Cas asked.

"I assume so. I had no idea Autumn was that old. She looks far younger than Rixana," I answered.

"She's a master at glamour, apparently, and my mother's servant of many centuries. There's no chance she didn't tell her about the shadowborn general." Cori's voice had an audible frown in it, though her face remained neutral.

"She's talking about the goddess, calling her a false deity," I said. I met Cori's eyes. "Are you okay with this? With reading this correspondence between our parents?"

It made me uncomfortable, but I knew I couldn't stop. We all knew Rixana and Valdon were lovers. We didn't know the depth of it, and it made me mildly uncomfortable to think about my fiance's mother fucking my father, but this wasn't new knowledge.

"Do you think she was pregnant with his child?" Cori asked softly.

I nodded. That's exactly what I thought.

"We can continue," Cori responded with a nod.

I pulled the next letter from the box after setting the first on the pile of gold.

Valdon,

I will never forgive you for not coming to me. Never. You are dead to me. Even though you clearly don't care about my well-being or hers, the delivery was smooth. I've named her Soraeda. Autumn has agreed to stay with her, along with a wet nurse and ten of my guards.

I don't know what happens next, but I know that she must stay hidden until she's old enough to defend herself. She will come for her if she knows she's alive. Do you think she's afraid of her? Is that why she told me to get rid of her? Half-breeds have existed before, but Soraeda feels different. Her power is already brimming at the surface. Can you imagine what she could do after the ripening?

She has your hair and your nose, but I still hate you. I do not forgive you for not coming to us. I don't care what Del was dealing with. I don't care that she lost your child. I don't. I can't. I hate her, and you can tell her that.

I do not forgive you, and I do not forgive her. I never will.

Rixana

"Soraeda?" Cori whispered. "I–I know that name. I think I was her for a moment, when I was dying. I was in a memory or something. My mother was comforting her, telling her she loved her, but she had to go."

"We share a sibling then," I answered, shuddering at the thought.

"Don't act like every royal family in this world and the old doesn't have a healthy dose of nearly-incest. Keeping the blood pure and all that. You two do not share blood. You are not related. Don't go there with your thoughts," Cas reminded us firmly.

The reminder was timely, as I was absolutely going there with my thoughts. I pulled out the next letter.

Val,

I promised her you'd visit again soon. She wants to see you. Every six months isn't enough. You're her father. She's growing angrier about it. She nearly killed one of my guards in the middle of a fit the other day. She can...do something to people when she's angry. She bit the guard and I thought she was dying, even though the blood loss was not substantial. The guard didn't die...but she came back different. Her magic was tainted, dark and full of shadows, and it's like her loyalty shifted. She only cares about Soraeda now. She's desperate to keep her safe, and while you'd think this shift in loyalty bothered me, it doesn't. If she is willing to die for Soraeda to live, then she's exactly the kind of guard I need here.

I don't know anything about your power beyond what you've shown me. I need you here. Your daughter needs you here. You must come to us soon, or I swear I will declare war on your entire kingdom, Valdon. I don't understand what's happening to her or what she can do.

Find a way to come to us within a fortnight, or I swear there will be consequences.

Rix

We all sat in silence, staring at the words on the page. Soraeda was the shadow queen then. The secrets our parents had kept from us was that our *sister* was the shadow queen.

My eyes met Cori's and agony coursed between us. Had Princess Nadella known? Is that why she had allied with her? The attack on New York, the death of four witch princesses – had it really been some cosmic accident? An attempt to bring the shadow queen's sisters to her that had gone tragically awry? Did the shadow queen mourn them? Was the cold evil queen from our nightmares crying in her castle beyond the rift?

This was a fucking lot to take in, to try to make sense of somehow.

Another letter was in my hands before any of us could respond, could attempt to put words to the absolute shitshow we were uncovering.

V,

Soraeda hasn't stopped talking about your visit. You have no idea what it meant to her...to me. I have taken precautions, but I think I am with child again. I don't know how to avoid it with you. You overcome all potions and elixirs.

Only the staff here know about Soraeda, and I don't know if I can risk them further with another child. I don't know what to do.

Why don't you leave her? Your father is dead, Val. You don't have to keep this ruse up. Who can stop us if we want to be together? The goddess is powerful, but if we are joined together against her, we can stop her. We have to believe that.

Please, Val. I need you. Soraeda needs you. We have a family now. You have a family now.

I love you.

R

Seeing the witch queen vulnerable and pleading was uncomfortable. I knew it had to be for Cordelia too. We'd all known her as an unshakeable force, a queen who ruled over all the magicborn kingdoms and mortalborn countries with her own desires and demands. No king or queen opposed her, truly opposed her, when she set her mind to something.

How could this stone fortress of a woman be the same woman begging my pathetic father to be with her? It was unfathomable.

"It's been almost four hundred years," Cas said, like he was the one reading thoughts. "They were different people then. We have to allow space for that reality and this one to coexist."

"It doesn't seem possible," Cori said. "My mother has never begged anyone to do anything. How could she have – how could this be the same woman?"

"Maybe that's why she's unbreakable now," I answered, the thought coming to me as I spoke. "Maybe he broke her so thoroughly she became someone new, a wall of ice that no one could penetrate. Ruthless because of what my piece of shit father did to her."

The next few letters were more of the same. More letters about Soraeda's powers frightening Rixana. More letters begging my father to give a shit. The last letter was the only one that was markedly different. It felt like a final letter too, like a goodbye.

King Valdon,

She came for them. She blasted the entire house apart. I lost four guards, but Autumn escaped with the children. She disappeared into the Fae Wild and did not return. She told me she'd found a doorway to another world, a world where they could be safe. All I can do is hope she was right, hope that my children are alive. Hope that they understand why I could not keep them with me.

I am only writing to inform you of these events because I feel you deserve to know. Even if you don't care about whether we live or die, I care enough to tell you.

You are not welcome in my castle, King Valdon, unless invited by royal decree. I will remind you that I am Queen of Witches, not a common king's whore. If you come uninvited again, I will consider it an act of war.

Queen Rixana

"A door to another world?" Cas whispered. "Did Autumn bring them to Earth?"

"I think that's a very good question that we need to ask her as soon as we return to the Witch Queendom," I answered.

I was shaken though. I knew I wasn't hiding it well. So was Cordelia. The very fabric of our reality felt torn in two. How could we not know this? How could none of the other royals? After five centuries, had no one discovered this truth?

My mother's words on the night of the witch princess' funeral filled my head: *Why should we bear the burden of a war we did not start?*

My mother knew then. Maybe all of them had figured it out, but Rixana was not a woman you'd want as your adversary. If she'd decided her half-vampire children were a secret, then they'd remain a secret. Or, at least that's what our parents' generation of leaders had decided. I just might be angry enough to land on her front lawn and scream the truth so loudly every soul in D.C. could hear me.

Ambrose

When we arrived in St. Peter's Basilica, we climbed down
into the recessed floor of the Papal Altar. We were still covered

in Ruyek's blood and the magic in the doors was so thick it felt like it was physically touching me, examining me for king's blood. When the probing was satisfied, the double doors swung open.

We descended into a well-lit staircase. Magic balls of light hovered against each wall, and I wondered who was sustaining them. Valdon was a well-known adversary of magicians, so this had to be some poor magicborn fae or witch's constant power expenditure.

"Wasteful," Van said as he examined the lights.

He was right. There was no way any mortalborn was allowed here, and magicborn could see in the dark. This felt like an idiotic show of power and control.

I'd tell Ruyek when we met up again. He was king now. Things would change. Things had already begun to change.

The staircase went down and down, with two landings along the way. At each landing, the staircase shifted to the right, curving underneath the stretch of staircase above. Finally, the monstrosity ended, and we found ourselves on solid ground.

A single door in the middle of a white stone wall stood at the bottom. There was nothing but a few feet of stone ground and this floor-to-ceiling block.

"There's no handle," Van said after examining the door.

"It should recognize the blood on you, according to Ruyek," I said.

"Well, it didn't, and I was pretty close."

Maybe *close* wasn't close enough. I stepped forward and pressed my hand to the wooden door. It was Acadian wood. I could tell by the way it buzzed with magic and life as it warmed beneath my touch. I leaned my bloody forehead against the wood and closed my eyes, willing the wood to accept the blood I brought.

He is the king now, I thought, *and he has chosen us to come. We have King Ruyek's permission to enter.*

Nothing happened, so as ridiculous as I felt, I continued to talk in my head to the wood.

He's my fiance, you know. Both of our fiance. In two days, we will crowned as kings of these lands.

That thought gave me an idea. I pulled a dagger from my armor and sliced the skin between Ruyek's dried blood. Our blood ran together, warming his dried blood as I pressed my hand back to it. The wood shuddered then, like I'd hit it with a battering ram, and then it swung open.

"Did you just use blood magic? Without Ruyek's assistance?" Van asked, his mismatched eyes large with shock.

"I think I did. I was talking – well, I was mind-speaking to the wood and the idea came to me. We will be kings in two day's time. Ruyek has already spoken his intentions. The land listens. Maybe it didn't want dried king's blood today. Maybe it had to be fresh."

"You did blood magic, *and* you responded to wood because of your innate plant power. Anyone who ever doubted your magical superiority among the fae would shit themselves if they could see you now." Van shook his head as he finished speaking, like he was trying to shake off the shock.

"Th-thank you," I stuttered.

Ruyek complimented me all the time, but he knew me in a way that Van didn't yet. This felt real and raw, without the influence of sex or desire lacing it. He meant it. He thought I was a superior fae wielder, and I believed it for the first time in my life.

Van stepped past me into the royal archives, and I followed. Holy goddess–there were thousands of books here. The overwhelm when the doors parted was instantaneous. How were we ever going to find anything of significance in a collection this large?

"We start with what sticks out," Van said after regaining his own composure at the thought of the task ahead. "Most of these are likely historical accounts of vampire king's lives and conquests. There's likely some book on blood magic and vampire law. What we need is going to be older and may never have seen a printing press."

"Like handwritten texts from old mortalborn monks?" I asked.

"Exactly like that. The shadowborn might have been around for centuries, but their dominion is far closer to recent history. Our people were fighting for their lives, so there might not have been a lot of time to study shadowborn or rush to the printers for informational texts," Van responded.

Right. Look for what stands out then. So, we began. We combed through books as quickly and as thoroughly as we could, casting aside the histories and the biographies. I did grab a thick text on non-vampire usage of blood magic for my own use. I stacked it on one of the many empty tables in the massive cavern of a room.

I saw Van set aside a book on the anatomy of shifters. The writer and the viewpoint seemed to be vampire when I looked through it, so it should certainly be an interesting perspective to see himself through.

Just when I thought there was nothing useful left in this library, I reached a long low shelf near the back of the archives. This shelf was set away from the others where a table might have been more appropriate, and it was only two shelves high.

The very first book made it obvious that these books were very different from the rest of the library. Just like Van had guessed, it was in loopy handwritten Acadian. The book had no title stamped on the outside, but there was a cover page that read *Study of a Shadowborn Woman.*

I flipped to the first page. The writer described himself as a scholar and explained that the vampire legions had captured a female shadowborn. The rest of the book was far more ominous. Descriptions of torture littered the pages with intricate drawings to match.

Notes such as, "Fire burns her, but she heals quicker than most magicborn" and "I left her to the pleasure of soldiers for sixteen years. I am told she had more daily visitors than a common whore, and still, she did not quicken with child, even with fertility elixirs. It may be true that the shadowborn are sterile" were written next to the drawings.

The writer described her "species of origin" as "witch" and her powers as "fire power."

I shuddered. If this was how prisoners were kept, no wonder the shadow queen hated us so much.

Several images of every part of the shadowborn woman's anatomy were drawn. To my eye, she was just a woman with nothing extraordinary beyond her powers. An entire chapter was devoted to the woman's mind.

The following note was written next to a drawing of her stretched out on a table with her arms and legs bound in iron: "I believe there is some truth to the hivemind of all shadowborn. She is connected to someone and that someone is far more powerful than any vampire I've ever met. When I tried to break her mental barriers, a presence attacked me and drove me half-mad with mental torment. It took the fae healers weeks to set me back to sorts. I ensured the prisoner paid in blood for what she did to me."

Something about the woman tied to the table looked so familiar. The artist, whether it was the writer or someone else, drew extremely lifelike drawings. I flipped back to the anatomy drawings with fresh eyes. There was no drawing of her full face, but there was a drawing of her eyes and then another of her nose and mouth.

Cori had shown Ruyek mind to mind what the shadowborn general they'd captured looked like, and in turn, he'd shown me. If the image I received was accurate, the prisoner beneath the castle on Belle Isle was a dead ringer for the woman captured and tortured by the vampires in Acadia.

I flipped to the end of the book, skipping over pages and pages of torture, cruel experimentations, and even descriptions of the sexual exploitation of the prisoner. I didn't have the stomach or the heart to continue reading what was done to her in the name of studying the evil shadowborn so they could be better defeated.

The last two pages of the book were written in a different hand than the rest of the text. Some other author described the last days of the original writer. Apparently, the woman had tricked the man somehow, convincing him to set her free of her iron chains and to stop putting iron into her food every day. For a time, she worked alongside him like a lover. The king warned the writer that she was "not a house cat" and "could not be tamed."

Yet, the man continued living with the prisoner like some sort of lovestruck moron until she regained her full strength and killed the man. She burned him within an inch of his life with her fire power before chopping off his arms, legs, penis, and finally, his head. She took his head with her when she left. Assumedly, the passage explained, to ensure even the strongest healer in Acadia could not piece him back together. She returned to the barracks where she'd been kept a sexual prisoner and burned the building to the ground with nearly every soldier tucked in for the night. And then, she was gone. Returned, undoubtedly, to the shadow queen.

Good for her, I thought.

It was getting harder and harder to see who was right and wrong in this war. People had died at the hands of the shadow queen, but people had suffered and died at the hands of the vampires in the name of fighting the shadowborn too. I was sure the fae, witches, shifters, and mer had their own bloody hands in terms of similar atrocities against the shadowborn.

I set the book on top of the bookshelf and reached for another. The moment I touched the soft leather spine, I was somewhere else.

I looked down at bare feet to see a mossy forest floor. Bare feet that were most certainly mine. The air around me felt off somehow as I looked around the massive trees around me. Massive trees that looked and felt very much like Acadian wood. The bit of sunshine raining through the trees was red in hue and the entire world seemed to have a layer of red saturating it.

Was I in Acadia? I breathed in deeply again and every breath felt like power, like wild magic filling my lungs. This had to be Acadia.

"Ambrose?" I snapped my head to the source of the voice.

Cordelia stood about twenty feet in front of me. The top of her fighting leathers was off her shoulders and unzipped. They hung down with the arms tied around her waist. A plain white t-shirt covered her midsection where her flight leathers would have been. She still wore her double-headed battle-ax across her back, a short sword on either hip, and there were several knives strapped around each boot. For all the casualness of having her fighting leathers half-off, she looked ready for battle.

"Are you okay?" she asked when I did not reply.

"I–I don't know," I said.

She closed the distance between us and took my hands in hers. "I miss them too, but you have to believe they'll find us."

I had no idea what she was talking about, but I felt my head nodding.

"I know," my mouth said without any direction from my brain.

"We don't have time for this," a voice called from further ahead. I looked up to see a blonde woman with eyes I recognized.

In my mind, I asked: *Is that the shadowborn general? The prisoner?* But my mouth said: "We're coming, Aleria."

Cori took my hand and led me towards the woman. The feel of the moss beneath my feet was incandescent, softer than any carpet I'd ever felt, and buzzing with fae magic.

"The Lake of Memory is just ahead," Aleria said once we reached her. And yes, she was definitely the woman Cori had in her dungeons right now, and quite possibly the same woman held captive by the vampires in Acadia. "Don't get too excited though. It isn't a lake at all. It's a hot spring that smells like rotten eggs and will dry your skin out if you stay in too long. But, the magic is still there. We can find out what we need and get the fuck out."

Cori squeezed my hand, and then the world was spinning. I stumbled when I found myself back in the archives with a book in my hands and Van's hands on my shoulders.

"Are you back?" Van panted, his eyes wild with concern. "Your eyes rolled back in your head. You were shaking. Did you have another vision?"

I could only nod. Van helped me into a chair a few paces away. I was still reeling. He knelt next to me and ran his hands up and down my sides. His touch calmed me.

Finally, I spoke. "I think we were in Acadia. Cordelia and me. And – the woman – the prisoner on Belle Isle."

"The shadowborn general?" Van asked.

"Yes, but she wasn't a prisoner. She was traveling with us. I think we were friends or at least working together. I don't know." My body's shakes subsided under his touch, but my voice was still shaking. "I need you to read that." I pointed towards the book I'd just gone through, and he immediately acquiesced and crossed the distance to grab the book.

Cordelia

Ruyek brought the letters with us. He found a regular box that didn't require his blood to unlock. We had read them, but we were sure Van and Ambrose would want to as well. He also handed a book to Cas on Phorcys (with the explanation: "In case you want to know what I know about your dear old dad"). Van and Ambrose were still in the royal archives when we finished, so we walked into the St. Peter's Basilica and found a bench.

I pressed myself between Cas and Ruyek, each of my arms looped around one of theirs, and took in the art while we waited. Cas' head turned and twisted as much as mine did as we tried to make sense of this kind of beauty. This kind of magic.

Finally, Van and Ambrose climbed up from the recessed floor and appeared in front of the Papal Altar. Ambrose was pale, like he'd seen a ghost, and Van held three books under one arm.

"Find something useful?" Ruyek asked, standing to inspect Ambrose. Clearly, he noted the lack of color too.

"We did, but I think Ambrose needs to rest. He had another vision, and this one was a lot to unpack. And this book?" Van held up a book without anything engraved in the cover. "You're all going to want to see this, but it's seriously fucked."

"Is the vision why you're so shaky?" Ruyek asked gently, his fingers lifting Ambrose's chin so their eyes met.

"That and the book. I just want to go home." Ambrose wrapped his arms around Ruyek.

"Sleep or pleasure?" Ruyek asked with a wolfish grin.

"Pleasure would certainly take my mind off a few things. Maybe we can wait until tomorrow to dive into everything we discovered." Ambrose gave Ruyek an absolutely pleading look.

"What do we think?" Ruyek looked around at all of us. "Let me direct tonight, and everyone goes to bed satisfied."

"Are we going to be putting on a play then?" Cas asked with a grin.

"Well, there are a lot of moving parts when there are five of us, so it might feel like that. I want Cori and Ambrose to be so stuffed they can't sit down tomorrow. Any objections?" Ruyek's eyes met mine and his lip curled up even higher.

Heat pooled in my belly, and I knew I was already getting wet at the thought. I'd already experienced so much pleasure today. Cas had fucked me this morning and watching Ruyek fuck Cas in the archives had been its own kind of release.

Van turned his nose to the side like he was scenting me, like he knew I would be dripping with anticipation by the time we got home.

"Yes," I responded breathily. A single word answer was all I could manage as my mind ran through all the different things Ruyek might have planned.

Ambrose managed to ride his newly-bonded dragon home without issue. Either he was a natural or the dragon was making the transition very easy for him. I instructed the mortal-born in the stables to bathe the pegasi in the morning, and I brushed Aldric's mane before heading in after my fiances.

All four of them were sitting in bed in their underwear when I entered the massive bedchamber – and all four of them were hard and straining against their briefs. I tried not to pay them any attention as I walked into the bathroom and stripped. I rubbed a soapy washcloth over my pits, ass, and pussy before drying off and stepping into the room completely nude.

"Fuck," Ruyek moaned as he looked me up and down.

"So what's your game plan?" I asked, trying to sound like I wasn't brimming with excitement at the thought of whatever was going to happen next.

"I'm not going to tell you every step before we even start, my queen." Ruyek licked his lips as he looked me over again. "But, first things first, I need you to come lay on this bed so Van and Cas can devour you. Hands, tentacles, and mouths only though. Do not fuck her, even if she begs."

"Not fucking her seems like the opposite of the point," Cas said.

"Trust me. Everyone is going to fuck tonight." Ruyek grabbed a large bottle of lube and tossed it on the bed.

I walked to the end of the bed and did as he instructed, climbing up to lay my head against the soft down pillows while Van and Cas whispered about logistics. My attention was pulled away as Ambrose moaned. Ruyek had him on his back. We all forgot about my pleasure as Ruyek's fangs sank into the head of Ambrose's cock.

A sharp intake of air was the only proof it hurt at all, and then Ambrose was moaning again as Ruyek drank him down. Ruyek pulled his mouth away and met my eyes before looking at Cas and Van.

"There is a distinct lack of pleasure happening right now for our queen." Rue's voice was a reprimand, and it moved both of them to action.

Van kissed and sucked his way down my body, nipping lightly at my skin. Goddess above, why had Ruyek said they couldn't fuck me? The memory of Van's knot inside me made me so wet. His tongue found my clit with that familiar pull of his feline-esque tongue. The nodules pulled against my clit better than any mortalborn tongue could.

Fuck. I couldn't cum that easily. I swallowed down my pleasure, wanting it to build up more before I came. I wanted a tidal wave, not a ripple.

I glanced over a moment to see Ruyek pushing Ambrose face first into the bed. Ambrose turned his head to meet my eyes as Ruyek pushed into him, and forest green eyes rolled back in his head. Ruyek ran his fingers over Ambrose's antlers, making him shiver.

"Someone is distracted," Cas said. He had shifted into his mer form, and I shivered at the memory of his tentacles and two cocks.

Van pushed himself up a little as he continued to devour my clit, pulling me closer and closer to an orgasm I couldn't deny myself. He gave Cas enough room for two tentacles to get between us. One pushed against my pussy while the other pushed into my ass. Clearly, he'd been kind enough to lube his tentacle up because it pushed into me easily.

Just as the thicker part of his tentacle started to push into my ass, I came. I was far louder than I intended to be, but the feel of Van's tongue and Cas' tentacles stuffing me was overwhelming.

"Get on your knees," Van said after I'd composed myself enough to be open to fresh commands.

Ruyek was pounding into Ambrose as I repositioned. Van moved around me and lifted my shoulders up enough to position his crotch under my face.

"Remember not to take all of me. You do not want a knot in your airway," he said.

He didn't have to say anything else. I pulled his cock into my mouth and pushed him against my throat. He was big enough that I wasn't actually afraid of taking him all the way at this angle.

I stiffened when I felt a tongue on my asshole. Cas was rimming me, and I had no idea how to respond.

"Relax," he breathed against the tight hole.

I focused on sucking Van's dick as Cas continued to lick and nip at me. I'd never experienced anything like it before, but it felt good. It felt really good. I moaned around Van's dick as a tentacle sucker formed a seal over my clit and started pumping while Cas devoured my asshole, pushing his tongue inside of me and bringing me entirely new sensations.

I came again, but Van was biting back his own orgasm. Maybe he didn't want to have to wait for his knot to deflate before sticking his dick in one of us. Ruyek came loudly next to me and collapsed on the bed just as Van pulled my mouth away to prevent himself from cumming.

"I need a moment," Ruyek panted as Ambrose dropped his body back to the bed.

We all needed a moment, but it was a very brief moment before Ruyek stood up and wiped his dick off.

"Round two," Ruyek said a little less breathily than he'd been after cumming. "Van, I want you to take your huge dick and your knot and fuck Ambrose until you both cum and our boy sees stars. Cas? You're with me. I'll take the front, you take the back."

I shivered as Ruyek laid back on the pillow and pulled me towards him. Van moved to where Ambrose was already laying and gently flipped him to his back. I climbed over Ruyek. I remembered the feel of his piercings inside me, and I did not fucking hesitate to climb over him and sink down on his dick.

He closed his eyes when our hips were flush. His breath was heavy and his chest shuddered when I started to move, angling myself so his piercings took turns stroking my g-spot. Just as I was about to cum, Cas pushed against my back, laying me flat against Ruyek's chest. I kissed Ruyek gently as Cas positioned himself behind me.

I had no idea what was going to happen next. Cas had two dicks, and I was fairly certain I could not take both in one hole at one time. Luckily for me, he must have agreed as only one dick pushed against my asshole. I breathed deeply as my body shifted to let him enter. Fuuuck – it was such a tight fit.

"You feel so good," Ruyek whispered before he kissed me again. "Let me bite you."

"Anything you want," I panted as I felt Cas push all the way in, his second dick resting on top of me.

Ruyek turned my head enough that he could sink his fangs into my neck. I went taut and then loose as pain quickly gave way to pleasure. Cas started to move, and I could tell by the way Ruyek moaned against my neck that he could feel Cas through the thin layer between them.

"I'm about to cum," Van said beside us, and I heard Ambrose's pants pick up in intensity. I knew what that filling up felt like, what the stretch that burned and hurt and felt so fucking good as Van's knot stretched him more than he'd ever been stretched before felt like.

Cas started to go faster as Ruyek drank from my neck, pulling my blood into him in a way that felt just as intimate as sex. Cas came in a flood and I felt his second dick spray cum across my back. Ruyek pushed into me once, twice, and then he came too. I was absolutely dripping by the time he licked the bite marks on my neck and both of them pulled out of me.

Ambrose

"I'm about to cum," Van said. He pulled out and thrust in deeply with a low moan. He was holding my hips so tightly it hurt as his warm cum shot inside me. I was already full of Ruyek's cum, but Van had taken me to entirely new depths. He'd fucked me on my back first before telling me to get on my knees, a position that made him feel even deeper.

I felt his knot begin to swell inside me – stretching me painfully. I panted, waiting for the pleasure, my eyes shut tightly as he grew and grew inside me. Just when I thought he'd rip me apart, I felt his knot stop swelling and he shifted so I could feel the pressure against my prostate. The pain gave way to pleasure as he let go of my hips and rocked himself gently, hitting my prostate again and again until I was cumming all over the bed beneath us.

I constricted around him as I came, but it didn't hurt. All the pain had bled into pleasure. As soon as I finished cumming, he started rocking again.

"I can't," I panted as the pleasure started to feel like too much.

"You can," he responded. "I've done this before."

I fisted the sheets as he moved, feeling like he was unraveling me, like he'd destroy my pleasure center if he kept going, but then I was cumming again, and this one was more intense than any orgasm I had ever had before.

"Fuck," I panted as he finally stopped moving.

"That second one is the best one," he said between heavy breaths.

I had heard everyone else in this bed cum sometime during all of that pleasure, but my attention was firmly on me and Van. I could feel my heartbeat where we met, like that had become the center of my body. As he stilled inside me, the pain ebbed back in a little, but I couldn't deny how much I loved this. How much I loved him pushing me to my limits.

Finally, I opened my eyes as I felt Van deflate enough that he could pull out. I shifted to my back just in time for Van to lean down and kiss me wildly, his rough tongue exploring every part of my mouth until I moaned his name. How was I getting hard again?

I had missed so much pleasure during my years of waiting for Nadella, but somehow, now that my fiances were the ones who were taking me to all the places I never knew existed, it felt like it was the right decision (even though it turned out far differently than I anticipated). Every night with them would be a smorgasbord of experiences. It would never get old or boring, even if we spent seven hundred years together. Somehow, I was more sure of that than anything else in this life.

"We aren't done yet," Ruyek said as Van pulled away from me. "How relaxed do you feel, Cori?"

"I think I've cum like six times, so pretty relaxed," Cori answered contentedly.

"Everything still loose and wet?" Ruyek grinned.

She nodded in response, her golden eyes going black as we all waited for Ruyek's next set of instructions.

"Mount me again," Ruyek said to her. She didn't hesitate. She climbed over him and easily took him all the way to the hilt.

"Ambrose, it's your turn to fuck our queen, but her ass is tired. Get behind her."

I did as Rue said, but my hands were shaking as I touched the skin of Cori's hips. I'd never been with a woman. I wanted to. Gods, I wanted to, but I didn't know what to expect.

"You ready for the big stretch, baby girl?" Ruyek purred as Cori laid down against him again, resting her head against his chest.

She nodded like she knew what was going on, but I still had no idea.

"Lube yourself up and slip in right next to me," Ruyek said to me, his eyes locking on mine. "She's ready for both of us in the same hole."

My eyes widened as Cori breathed in deeply against Ruyek's chest.

"Trust me," Ruyek said as I hesitated. "We won't hurt her."

I did trust him. I trusted him more than anyone else in either world. I spread lube all over my cock, but I reached down to insert a finger inside of her first. She was already stretched so tightly from Ruyek's cock inside her. The fit didn't seem possible, but she moaned as I inserted a second finger inside her, stretching her as much as I could with my fingers.

"If you want me to stop, I need you to tell me to stop," I said as I spread more lube between us.

She nodded against Ruyek, but her eyes were closed. I know she was trusting Ruyek too. I was convinced she'd never done this before either. I pushed against where they met, slowly and gently, but her body opened up for me, responded and let me in as I pushed in deeper and deeper.

Fuck. Fuck. Fuck. She felt so good. Ruyek felt so good. This was so tight and warm and wet, and I felt like I could cum without moving as I pushed all the way into her. Cori breathed in and out quickly beneath us, like she was still adjusting to the two of us.

"Are you okay?" Ruyek asked as she stroked her hair. She nodded again.

"Fuck both of us, Ambrose, but do not cum. Cas, you're on deck. We're going to need both of your monster dicks."

We all obeyed. I started to move, my dick rubbed against Ruyek on one side while Cori's pussy pulsed around me. I felt Cas situating myself behind me like he knew what Ruyek wanted from him.

"I have to stop or I'll cum," I said mid-thrust, forcing myself to still. I had to squeeze my eyes shut to keep from going over the edge. If I looked down at where Ruyek and I were both fucking Cori, I'd come at the sight.

"Good boy," Ruyek growled. "Cas, Ambrose is ready for all of you."

What did that mean? I felt Cas push me down against Cori's back as he spread lube all over my ass. My hole was so sensitive after Van stretched me, but I refused to protest. I trusted Ruyek. I trusted Cas. I trusted that I could handle what came next.

Cas started with three fingers, not bothering with one or two. I was already stretched from Van's knot. Cori and Ruyek were still beneath me as Cas put in a fourth finger and then his thumb. He was nearly fisting me when he finally pulled his hand away and poured more lube on me.

"You ready?" Cas whispered.

No? Yes? I nodded my consent.

Cas pushed one dick inside of me only an inch or two. It felt good. Gods, it felt so fucking good. I wanted him. I arched my back up as much as I could without pulling out of Cori to give him better access. And then his other dick pressed in, stretching me as Cas worked his finger around my asshole, making enough room that the heads of both dicks could push inside me.

I could barely breathe as I became aware of every part of my body. Cas had one hand on my hip and two dicks pushing inside of my ass. He struggled after he got a few inches in, so he poured more lube between us, and then he put both hands on my hips and shoved himself inside of me.

I shouted with pain and pleasure as he buried both of his very large dicks inside of me. I was never going to recover from tonight. Colors would be duller. Sounds would be shriller. Tastes and smells – everything would be *lesser* after this experience of otherworldliness.

"Fuck all of us, big boy," Ruyek said.

He didn't have to specify that he was talking to Cas. We all knew. I was vaguely aware of Ruyek's hand stroking Van's cock where he lay next to him, and then, my awareness narrowed down to Cas pounding into me with his two dicks and my dick being pushed deeper and deeper inside of Cori and against Rue.

Cas did not hesitate. He set a demanding pace and he fucked me like it was the last time he'd get the opportunity, like this moment was everything we'd ever share in both worlds. He pushed my body beyond every limit I ever thought I had, absolutely rearranging my insides as he fucked me.

Cori moaned loudly beneath me as he slammed into me – into *us*, again and again. And then I felt her cumming, clamping down on me and Ruyek as her body tamped down with the orgasm. She pulled me with her, Ruyek too. We both came so deep inside her, I felt like she'd feel us for days. I knew I'd feel tonight tomorrow, magical healing power or not.

Cas pumped once, twice, three times more before he came, and I imagined both of his dicks painting my insides warm and wet and white just as Van came from Ruyek's stroke, splashing cum all over me, Cori, and Ruyek.

We all collapsed in bed, crawling until everyone's wet, sticky bodies were pressed against each other.

"I told you to trust me," Ruyek chuckled as I started to drift off to sleep.

We were way too exhausted to clean ourselves up, and I loved the thought of Rue, Van, and Cas' cum dripping out of me as we slept while Rue, Cas, and my cum dripped out of Cori. Fuck. I was the luckiest man in the universe.

The next morning, we all pored over the letters and books together before trying to figure out how I had a vision of the prisoner, Cori, and me in Acadia.

"Were you held against your will?" Ruyek asked. "Maybe the prisoner imprisoned you both and kidnapped you."

I shook my head. "It wasn't like that. We weren't prisoners. We seemed to be traveling partners, maybe even friendly."

"Even knowing of her torture and trauma, I can't imagine being friendly with the woman who attacked us the night my sisters died and then attacked Atlantis the night Cas'– the night Queen Morgana died."

"I know," I agreed with a nod. "The vision didn't make any sense."

"It was just you and Cori? I wasn't there?" Van's voice was soft, maybe even sad. After what we'd talked about yesterday in the mortalborn ruins, the sadness made sense.

"It was just a moment, Van. A glimpse in time," I responded, putting my hand on his forearm in an attempt at reassurance.

"And I think the goal is for none of us to end up in Acadia," Cori responded.

Van just stared down at his hands in silence.

"It seems that goal isn't achievable," Ruyek responded.

"Is a vision set in stone? Unchangeable? Is there no free will?" Cas asked.

Ruyek sighed. "Yes and no. There are the kinds of visions that the witch queen's fae seers have: cryptic and prophetic with no moment in time attached, just an understanding or words that must be deciphered. And then there are the kinds of visions Ambrose has: clear moments in the future. Something could certainly alter the fate that led to that vision's occurrence, but we have no idea what steps or decisions led Cori and Ambrose to Acadia. There's no real information we can use to unravel its meaning in order to change it."

"That sounds rather hopeless," Cori said.

"Ambrose has visions for a reason. Why he saw that moment in time will make sense one day. Just like everything we learned in Vatican City will make sense one day." Ruyek's voice was contemplative, like he was already trying to piece it all together.

"That was enlightening." Van laughed dryly, but I could see the wonder in his eyes, the hope that we would go through the rift and still somehow protect Earth – that he would see Acadia.

It didn't seem worth mentioning again that he wasn't in my vision, and none of us seemed to be looking for him, Ruyek, or Cas. Why we were in Acadia was mystery enough, but why Cori, me, and a shadowborn general were in Acadia without the three of them was quite another one.

"So. Back to the business of things: the coronation and then the wedding?" Cori asked. "I don't know if I've shared how much I loathe planning royal events. Planning the wedding with my mother involved is going to be a nightmare."

"We all want to get married, yes? It's not just the prophecy anymore?" Ruyek asked.

"Do you really have to ask?" Cas smirked.

"Yes, Rue. We are all in this," Cori added more softly.

"Remind me *why* the wedding was planned for the autumnal equinox?" Ruyek asked.

"I think the seers just thought it was a good omen," Van said.

"So there's no prophetic reason why they chose that date? Interesting." Ruyek looked between us, meeting each of our gazes. "Do you trust me?"

"Quite emphatically," Van answered for everyone, his feline eyes holding Ruyek's sanguine gaze.

"Good. Let me plan this next one, at least. I just need everyone to be open to take your measurements this afternoon. I'll send in my father's tailor."

"Rue, if he's still in your employ, he's your tailor now. None of this is your father's anymore," Cori said.

"Fine then. I'll send my tailor to find you all this afternoon. Do stay inside the walls so the poor man doesn't have to face a blistering death to locate you." Ruyek stood up and kissed each of us on the forehead, lingering a bit on mine before he left us alone.

Savanna

The tailor was so old that he actually looked old. "Old" for magicborn was a relative term, of course. His black hair had streaks of white, and wrinkles framed his eyes and his mouth. He appeared in his sixties or early seventies by mortalborn standards, but I'd guess he was closer to nine hundred and nearing the end of his natural life. He was kind though, a softness that seemed rare amongst vampires. Ruyek wasn't cruel, of course, but he still had an edge to him. It was one of the things I loved about him, but it was also very vampiric to be thorny and sarcastic.

The tailor was different. If his eyes weren't red and his fangs didn't show when he smiled broadly (which he did often), he might have been mortalborn. He found me, Ambrose, Cori, and Cas all lounging in the sitting room area of the king's chambers. Cori and Cas were still poring through the books Ambrose and I had brought back, while Ambrose played a game of solitaire with a set of rainbow playing cards.

I was the only one just existing. I was watching my lovers relax and thinking about what a quiet afternoon in fifty years might look like, wondering if we'd all be just like this: content doing our own things in a shared space. It was a kind of easy intimacy my mothers had, a kind of gentle love that I'd always hoped would exist for me. And here it was.

Ruyek was off planning a coronation and running a country, but then, he was the first to ascend to kinghood in our group. Although we were all close behind with a coronation a little over twenty-four hours away. It would be at night, of course, and Ruyek had hinted at a few outdoor locations for the event, but he'd never clarified which he'd be choosing.

After the tailor left, Cori offered the idea of a late afternoon nap. Somehow we were still following a diurnal schedule despite being in the Vampire Kingdom. We'd gone to bed sometime around dawn and woken up in the late morning. None of us needed a full eight hours of sleep like the mortalborn, but we still needed *some*.

Cori's yawn and offer was too much for me to refuse, and soon, we were all spooning in bed together. Ambrose and Cori were the little spoons, and they both faced each other while I pressed my body against Ambrose's back and tried not to remember how good he'd felt around my cock just hours before. Cas held Cori close, cradling her head in the crook of his neck and looking truly at peace for the first time in a long time. He and Cori finally looked like they'd found a way to put some of their grief in a place that did not constantly sting.

I heard Ruyek crawl in behind Cas a few hours later. The room was in heavy darkness, and he moved so like a shadow that I didn't notice him until his weight shifted the bed. We only slept a few more hours before growling stomachs woke all of us up.

A servant brought in massive plates of pasta and bread and two large carafes of blood. Cori's smile was electric, playing across her face like some distant sun we all yearned to bask in.

"We finally get Italian food in Italy," Cori said. "Please tell me there's dessert too!"

Ruyek told the servant to bring gelato, cannolis, and tiramisu within the hour. He took care to point out the vegetarian dishes for Ambrose before we all dug in. We ate and laughed through several plates of food (and in Ruyek's case, nearly fifty ounces of blood), finally slowing down after several scoops of pistachio almond gelato, a few cannolis, and way too many bites of tiramisu. The contented fullness seemed to sober all of us up as Cori brought us back to all the anxieties of being at war.

"Is the coronation location secure enough?" Cori asked quietly. "I don't know if I'm ready for another shadowborn attack, Rue. I need just a few more moments like this, like we might just be normal people choosing to live our lives together. I need time to forget all that is at stake here."

Ruyek reached a hand across the table, gracefully avoiding a wrist full of sugo di pomodoro with a quick rearrangement of dishes.

"The location is secure. It should be a big thing like my father's and grandfather's coronation, but the fact remains we are at war. I have invited our families, my two remaining vampire councilmen, and a single loyal vampire camera crew who are under strict instructions to not share the footage or the location until after the coronation and after we have safely left the vicinity. No one knows the location except for me and my mother. Everyone else will be translocated from the castle grounds when they arrive. I have done everything I can to keep us safe."

"But your people–" Cori whispered, "–they'll want to be there. They'll at least want to see it live. Don't we owe it to th–"

"We owe them nothing. We have given our lives to the service of countries and cultures that are alien to us. You are power-bound, Cori, and while I remember a red sun on my face, I have spent over a century on Earth. I was a toddler when I left Acadia. I am of this world far more than I am the old one. If they do not like my attempts to keep us safe, or they think it dishonors them, they are free to raise a challenger to my throne. I accept the mantle of responsibility that comes with my crown, but I cannot live my entire life for others. We've all given enough, and you know we will give much more before this war is over. We will be on the frontlines. We will stand first, die first, and that has to be enough for them. If it isn't, then they can find themselves another monarch to die on some Acadian battlefield for them." Ruyek's speech was quick, like he was desperate to say his piece before he lost the nerve.

"So you do think this ends in Acadia?" I asked, trying to cover up the small bit of hope that swelled inside of me at the thought.

"I believe in Ambrose's sight. I don't know how or why, but I don't think this war ends here. I don't even know if it ends with the shadow queen," Ruyek replied.

"The goddess then?" Cas asked.

"The goddess, your father, the shadow queen and the missing brother Cori and I didn't even know about until the archives. None of those players are on Earth. They're all through the rift." Ruyek's eyes landed very seriously on me, like he definitely heard the hope in my tone, and he was trying to remind me that our foray into Acadia would not be a simple vacation to the motherland.

"You think we'll die on some otherworldly battlefield then?" Cori asked, her voice sober despite the copious amounts of port she'd consumed with dinner.

"I think we're all willing to die to end this." There was pain in Ruyek's voice, but also acceptance and the responsibility he took on for his people – further proof that his sacrifices, our sacrifice, had to be enough without a public spectacle of a coronation.

"I was really looking forward to at least a few centuries of what happened last night," Ambrose said with a small smile.

"May we be so lucky as to defeat all the big bads in the known universe and live to tell the tale. Your lips to Moirai's ears." Ruyek smiled softly.

Moirai – the goddess of Fate. An old god that most of our ancestors had cast aside for the goddess that usurped them. How easily all histories were erased, rewritten, and then forgotten. As it was in the histories of Earth, so it had been in Acadia. It really was a conqueror's universe.

We won't be conquerors, Rue's voice said in my head.

My walls were down, and apparently, my unrealized fears of becoming our enemies was being projected.

I don't want this throne, or any throne. I will keep it to protect my people from all the darkness that awaits, but I swear to Cas' watery sire, I will cast it aside when we win. I will be the last vampire king.

He didn't sound like he was joking. He had made up his mind long before this mind-to-mind conversation.

They don't know that. Why aren't you telling them too? I replied, my midnight lion form standing in front of the mass of humanoid shadows that was Ruyek.

They're not ready to hear it, he said, his shadows swirling around me like a caress.

And I am?

I know we are of like mind. What would either world be without kings and queens? Ruyek asked.

Historically, more stable and a lot less bloody. The democracies of this world only grew weak when they began to exalt their elected leaders like the monarchs of old, I said.

Precisely.

And then he withdrew from my head and suggested we all take a dip in the hot tub before sleeping. Everyone agreed.

When we awoke, Ruyek was gone again. He left a note on the bedside table to be very nice to the people making us up for the coronation and promised we'd see him before the ceremony. Not long after we were all awake and moving, servants came in carrying trays of food and drink. Charcuterie were set up in each room along with wine, juice, coffee, and water.

An entire team of vampires entered the room by early afternoon. They were all carrying bags of supplies and four servants were carrying garment bags. Every one of us endured waxing, shaving, and makeup.

Ambrose looked stunning with a little green glitter on his eyelids and mascara to highlight his naturally long, thick eyelashes. The color perfectly drew out the vibrant green of his eyes. Cas' blue beneath his cheeks was accentuated in a way I'd never considered, but he looked like a mer prince out of a story book with blue eyeliner against his ocean eyes.

They chose a spattering of gold dust for my eyelids and cheeks. Somehow, it made my feline eyes and high cheekbones sharper. They chose a pearlescent sheen for Cori's eyes, paired with perfectly placed cream highlighter and liberal use of mascara and eyeliner, giving her a bit of a smoky eye effect.

Yes, I absolutely loved makeup and knew more than most mortalborn men would admit to. Toxic masculinity wasn't a thing in a household with two mothers, and outside of the vampires, masculinity was far from fragile in magicborn societies.

Every single one of my mates were gorgeous. *Mates*. I'd never thought of using that word before. It was an old Acadian term that didn't hold much meaning on Earth. It had something to do with the soul of our ancestral planet tying lovers together with Moirai's blessing. With the fall of the old gods, the term and the soul-deep connection had become a thing of a myth.

But it *fit* for us. We were prophesied and my heart raced with every look and touch my fiances shared with me. And if we were fated mates, blessed by Moirai, didn't that make our odds of surviving this war better? Why tie us together if all of this was leading up to our deaths?

Power, a voice inside my head said. It wasn't my voice and it wasn't Ruyek's. Maybe it was the voice of reason I was desperately trying to shush to imagine a life together with the people I loved, a life that wasn't cut short in service to a world I didn't even know. I longed for Acadia, but I was a stranger to her and she to me. The voice had a point I didn't want to acknowledge though: tying us together concentrated world-shattering power against a being who subjugated the old gods and made a world of magic wielders bend the knee.

Not today. I couldn't think about the possibility we were all brought together for a single purpose that had nothing to do with our happiness or longevity. Today, I was going to be crowned a king alongside my lovers, and I was going to steal a night of happiness from a dark reality.

The garment bags came next, pulling me from my thoughts. I was fitted into a black tuxedo that fit my body better than any suit or tux I'd ever worn before. A gold waistcoat hugged my body over a white shirt. They chose a matching gold tie for me, but across the room, Ambrose and Cas were fitted with their own color schemes: Cas in ocean blue and Ambrose in a deep, vibrant green. Cori had been pulled behind a screen for her fitting, so I couldn't see what she was wearing.

Ruyek joined us when we'd all been fitted into our tuxedos and shiny black shoes. He had a smokey eye and a thin line of red glitter on his eyelids. His waistcoat and tie were a dark red: the colors of his kingdom. He directed the servants to leave us with a simple command.

"Keep her behind the screen," Ruyek said with a smile. "The mortalborn say it's bad luck."

"Ruyek!" Cori's voice snapped from behind the screen. "Is this a wedding dress?"

"A wedding dress?" Ambrose asked, confusion written across his face.

"You all agreed to marry and Cori was stressed about wedding planning. High profile events are dangerous right now, so two birds, one stone as they say." Ruyek's shit-eating grin made me want to devour him.

"Is it bad luck to fuck you before our wedding?" I asked, a growl lacing my voice.

"I think it would be bad luck if you didn't," he replied.

A moment later, I had him pressed against the wall. Ambrose kindly brought me a bottle of lube just as I yanked his pants down. I had no time for warming up, and Ruyek had always liked a bit of pain. I was slamming into him a moment later, our moans filling the room.

"I have to stand behind this screen and listen to you two fuck each other?" Cori said, a pout clear in her voice. "Seems incredibly unfair."

But she did stay behind the screen, and a few minutes later, my knot was stretching Ruyek's ass as he panted through the pain and pleasure of the stretch.

"Fuck," Cas whimpered. I looked over to see his cock straining against his pants.

"Married, yes. Let's definitely do that as soon as possible. I'm in," Ambrose said with a nod.

"I'm in," Cori said behind the screen.

"I've been in for a long time," Cas replied.

"Van?" Ruyek whimpered.

"Isn't what I'm doing right now answer enough? I want to fuck all of you every day, and I want to spend whatever time we have – two years or a thousand years – with all of my mates." I bit at Rue's neck as he tightened around me in response, and an orgasm spilled out of me.

Mates. The word hung in the air between us, but nobody challenged it and nobody questioned me. It was true. Somehow in this world far, far from Acadia's soul and Moirai's blessing, we were mates.

Cordelia

The sound of Ruyek's moans as Van pulled out of him had me nearly dripping. I understood the mortalborn wedding dress first look tradition, of course, but it took everything in me not to step from behind the screen to watch my lovers – my mates – devouring each other.

"Do you need to clean yourself up?" Van asked Ruyek.

"And miss the feeling of you dripping down my legs during our wedding? Absolutely not. I want to think of you every time I move tonight," Rue responded, his voice husky with the sound of lust and satisfaction.

I shuddered. I should have forgone makeup and fucked my fiances with that time instead.

Fiances. Mates. *Husbands*. This was our wedding night. June seventeenth – our anniversary for as many years as fate allowed us. I wanted to ask if Ruyek had invited his father, not because I didn't want him to be there, but because I didn't want there to be a power struggle tonight. I wanted to be married in the calm, quiet ceremony I was promised.

But Ruyek had asked for our trust, and I easily gave it to him. I had to believe he wouldn't do anything to ruin tonight. All the safety precautions, the secrecy of the location. I didn't even know where our wedding was taking place. I did trust him. I trusted him to keep us safe tonight and to make this a wedding we would all cherish for the rest of our lives.

"Give us a five minute head start, Cor," Ruyek said, shortening my name in a way no one ever had before. Cor, not Cori. I liked it though. It fit.

Two servants entered and scooped up the long, heavy train of my dress and directed me to lift the front as we left the room. The dress was elegant and beautiful in a way I never imagined it could be. The pearl white shimmered beneath a silvery overlay of lace cut into the shape of intricate, delicate snowflakes. They surrounded the bottom of the skirt and the long, cathedral train, then formed a belt of winter around my waist. There were more spattered across the skirt and the upper bodice before forming lace sleeves from just below my shoulders to my wrist.

My hair fell in thick ringlet curls down my back with a delicate, silver crown of snowflakes atop my head. I felt like the ice princess everyone called me. No – the ice queen, the first vampire queen without a drop of vampire blood in my veins. The only queen who could trek across Antarctica and close the rift torn into the side of an ancient, frozen glacier.

It was always me, wasn't it? I was born with the ice of two worlds in my veins. Maybe it was Ruyek, Caspian, Savanna, and Ambrose too – but I was born to close the rift. Whatever that looked like, whatever that meant, I existed for that task.

The thought made me shiver as we left the room and headed down the hall. If I was destined for such a monumental task, did I exist for anything more than that? Was that my only destiny? Maybe that meant the task would destroy me. Closing the rift may very well drain me of every drop of magic inside me, leaving only a husk behind in the snow. Or maybe that meant the rest of my life, my fate, was my own to decide. A life entirely unwritten or planned for, a wild card with endless possibilities.

The first felt more realistic. Great magic came with a great cost, but the second made me warm all over. Ambrose had seen me in Acadia. That had to mean something, right? Maybe the next part of my life would begin with the closing of the rift, or maybe what happened next was entirely up to me.

We stepped through the side door Ruyek had directed us to and only a single fae man with skin the color of night and ears with fine, high points was waiting there.

"Are you ready, your majesty?" the man asked.

I nodded. I was ready. Whatever happened next, I was ready.

The two servants stepped back with matching smiles as the fae man took my arm. There was no fabric beneath the lace sleeves and I felt his warm touch against my skin. It grounded me as we disappeared into a howling void before landing gently on smooth ground.

I looked around me. We were in the Roman Colosseum. A long aisle of soft earth and white flowers stretched from the tourist overlook across the ruins. Red rose petals lined the middle of the aisle, the place where I would step, as if the roses would carry me to my fiances. I looked up as a thought hit me. Red roses. My mother's symbol was a black rose, and somehow, it felt like this difference was intentional. I wouldn't be the kind of queen my mother was. I'd be someone else entirely.

Rue, Cas, Van, and Ambrose stood at the end of that long aisle, a vampire woman standing between them in heavy, red robes. Seats were erected along the aisle. All the members of the royal families were there. My mother looked back at me from the first row, sitting between my father and Valdon. Each of them held one of her delicate hands in theirs. How different would both our worlds be if she'd been allowed to walk down an aisle to Valdon hundreds of years ago?

My eyes and my thoughts moved from my mother to my mates. The fae man holding my arm squeezed once before translocating away.

I felt like my heart would beat out of my chest as I looked down the long aisle, every eye on me. There were no extras. Harmonie was blessedly not there and neither was a magician representative. Only our direct family, the two vampire council members, and a number of guards posted in all black around the perimeter.

Twinkling balls of soft, golden magical light illuminated the ancient space. It was perfect, a combination of everything mortalborn and magicborn in one.

Like you, Ruyek's voice whispered in my head.

I pulled back enough to let him all the way in.

I feel like I'm going to pass out, I whispered back, an icy wind blowing around us in the tundra of my mind.

Would you feel better with a battle-ax strapped across your back? Ruyek chuckled.

Much.

In a blur of motion, one of the vampire guards stepped from the shadows behind me, my favorite battle-ax in his hands, the black belt replaced with a white one carved with the delicate shapes of snowflakes.

You never cease to amaze, Rue.

That's the goal, my queen: to amaze and please you for the rest of this life.

The guard stepped behind me and tightened the belt between my breasts. The feel of Acadian wood at my back steadied me. I took a cautious step from the smooth ground of the viewing stage to the soft earth of the aisle. I understood now why my silver slippers didn't have heels.

One step in front of the other – I focused on the weapon at my back and my men at the end of the aisle. My men. My fiances. My mates. My husbands. My future. My everything. All the noise of my restless thoughts silenced, and I realized there was soft music playing. It wasn't the traditional mortalborn wedding march, but the violin version of "Hymne de L'Amour."

When I reached the four of them, I stepped directly in front of the vampire woman. Ruyek and Cas framed me on either side. The music stopped as Ruyek took my left hand and Cas took my right. Each of their other hands grasped another, so that all five of us were connected by touch, like I was the centerpiece of this magnificent marriage. I didn't always feel like that, but in this moment, I did and it felt like it mattered.

"We are joined here today for two purposes," the vampire woman said, her red eyes looking directly at mine. "A coronation and a matrimonial blood ritual."

I turned to Ruyek.

It's not as scary as it sounds. You know all of our customs are grounded in blood magic, Ruyek's voice reassured me.

The woman started to speak in Acadian, reciting the coronation rites to the crowd. Would they all accept us as their monarchs, bend the knee, rise to fight if we called upon, and die to protect us if Kali asked for a sacrifice.

The crowd all replied in the affirmative. The woman told all of us to turn and face the crowd as she told them to bend the knee, kiss the earth, and swear their vows to us. My eyes shot to Valdon, the only person who lingered a moment before lowering himself to the ground. He was still so angry, so hurt, even at his son's own wedding. Another father might have been proud his son had outgrown his shadow.

Every monarch, prince, and princess of Acadian blood knelt and kissed the ground. Only vampires were usually invited to a vampire coronation, and I was certain no other king or queen of another kingdom had ever sworn allegiance before.

The woman lifted each of our stylized crowns from our heads, one by one, and replaced them with heavy black crowns encrusted with garnets. We came here as princes and princess of all of our cultures, but we would leave here as kings and queen of the Vampire Kingdom.

We turned back around to face the vampire woman.

"Is the coronation usually this short?" I whispered to Ruyek.

"I decided none of us wanted to be here all night. There will be enough blood shed soon," he whispered back.

The wedding ceremony started without much transition. The woman continued in Acadian, asking all of us if we swore our allegiance to one another until Nefthys welcomed us into her bosom, if we swore fidelity and commitment before the eyes of the old gods, the new, and the gods and goddesses of Earth (an addition to the original wording, I assumed).

We did. I squeezed Ruyek's hand as she pulled a blade from the pocket of her robes.

It's symbolic, Ruyek whispered in my mind, but I felt the others connected to us, like he was reassuring all of us mind to mind.

The woman sliced her own hand, her words describing blood binding and the sanctity of marriage. Just as her blood hit the earth beneath us, Ruyek moved as fast as a viper, his teeth piercing my neck without warning.

I cried out in shock, but the pain lasted longer this time, burning as he pulled my blood into him. When he pulled away, he did not lick the wound.

"Now, you are marked as mine," he whispered in a husky voice before turning to Cas and striking again. One by one, he marked all of us, his venom burning deeply and painfully to overcome our natural healing as blood dripped down all of our necks.

"Mine," he growled as he marked Ambrose last, all of our blood staining his mouth and lips a deep crimson.

The vampire woman proclaimed us husbands and wife a moment before the fae servant who brought me here appeared next to us and whisked us away.

Fear settled in as we translocated. I had no idea if this was planned or an ambush. I didn't know where we were going, and all I could think of was ice. A crack in a long glacier outside of McMurdo Station. The blackness that swirled in the rift, in the wormhole between worlds.

Panic filled me and my breathing came in too-quick bursts, and then we were still again in a well-lit room with a massive bed against one wall. Wait. These weren't Ruyek's chambers.

"You redid my room?" I asked, a bit incredulously.

"As if I'd allow us to spend our wedding nights in separate chambers, my queen," Ruyek said. "I've just had a larger bed installed. You can decide if you want to tear down some walls and open the whole space up or not."

"I'm home," I whispered. The fae servant was already gone, but I almost felt bad for how terrified I'd been of him when we translocated us. "Why are we in Richmond?"

"The wedding will be broadcasting right about now, and I wanted us far from Rome just in case any shadowborn were watching and waiting," he replied.

"You didn't tell us the bite was going to hurt this time," Cas accused, smoothly moving the conversation away from shadowborn attacks.

"Where is the fun in you knowing?" Rue smiled, a wicked one full of teeth and fangs. "Does it hurt now?"

"Yes, it does," Ambrose said. His fang marks were already nearly permanent from all the biting Ruyek did when we were apart, but this one was different.

My neck still burned, but the familiar desire of vampire venom was spreading through me too.

Ruyek snapped his head towards me like he knew what I was thinking.

"Vampire bedding is very traditional, you know," Ruyek said as he walked towards me, stepping into my space.

"Traditional with four husbands and one wife in a single marriage? Do tell how we are going to manage that," I asked, trembling as his blood-stained lips hovered over mine.

"I think we should all take turns filling you up. One at a time until you are swimming in our cum," he whispered.

"Who's first?" I half-pleaded.

"Is it selfish to say me?" he asked, but I wrapped my arms around his neck and pressed my lips to his in answer.

My tongue swept into his mouth, the metallic taste of all our blood filling my mouth and somehow making me even wetter. Ruyek placed his arms beneath my ass and hoisted me up, carefully stepping around my train as he carried me to the bed.

"I want to rip this dress off of you," he whispered.

"Do it," I answered. "We'll have the pictures and footage to remember it by."

The sound of ripping material filled the room as the weight of three other bodies joined us on the bed, but I only had eyes for Rue. He threw the fabric to the floor before ripping my lace underwear off and quickly tearing his tux off.

There was no warmup, no lead up, just him pushing into me so deep I lost my breath. We stayed like that a moment, our hips flush against each other before he started to move. His piercings rubbed against every sensitive part of me, and I felt an orgasm building as he reached his hand between us and rubbed my clit with his thumb.

I came apart just as I felt his fangs ripping into the unblemished side of my neck. It burned again, but he continued to pound into me, mixing the pleasure of sex with the pain of his venom burning new holes in my neck.

Mine, he whispered in my head. *Mine. Mine. Mine.*

His voice growled across the ice shelf of my mind as he moaned against my neck, cumming inside of me just as I came a second time.

There was no time for recovery. He moved off of me and Ambrose took his place.

"Don't be gentle," I panted through the aftershocks of orgasm.

Vines snaked out around us, pulling my wrists over my head and opening my legs wide as he pushed inside of me. I was soaked with my cum and Ruyek's, but I wanted more. I wanted Ambrose. I want all of them.

"Fuck," he whispered as he found his own pace. He was long and wide, stretching me as more vines encircled my breasts and squeezed.

I cried out and the vines slackened.

"No," I panted. "Fucking hurt me, Ambrose."

The vines tightened again and just as the skin was stretched nearly to breaking, painful pinpricks pierced the side of my breasts. Gods. Thorns. Ambrose's vines were covered in thorns and my blood as he continued to fuck me.

Ruyek moaned from where he lay next to me like the sight of more blood was driving him wild.

Ambrose's vines pulled my legs wider and further back until my ass was lifted off the bed, and he fucked me at a deeper angle.

Fuck. Fuck. Fuck. We came together, and his vines slackened as he collapsed on top of me.

"Cori," he panted as his lips found mine. The kiss was gentle and tender after such a brutal joining. I loved every side of Ambrose: the soft, tender kisses and the thorny vine restraints as he fucked me raw.

He pulled out of me.

"Do you need a break?" Van asked me as Ruyek leaned over and licked the bloody thorn wounds clean and closed.

"Yes but also no," I managed through heavy breaths.

"Pick one," Van said.

"She doesn't need a break," Rue commanded, his eyes on mine.

"I don't need a break," I repeated.

Van flipped me over as soon as I finished speaking. He held my legs together as he pushed into me.

"My wife," he whispered.

He felt humongous from this position. Even with the lube of all of our cum, I felt my body stretch around him. He fucked me slowly at first, agonizingly so. He pushed in deep before pulling almost all the way back out and pushing in again.

"I don't like your traditional rules," Van said to Ruyek as he fucked me. "Give me the lube."

"Fine," Ruyek answered before rummaging in my drawer.

Van pulled out of me, and I felt lube dripping down my back as he rubbed it all over his dick. A moment later, he was rubbing his fingers over my ass and slipping a finger inside me.

I gasped at the intrusion.

"Is this okay?" he whispered as he leaned over me and pushed his large finger in deeper.

"I did say I liked pain," I answered as a second finger joined the first.

Far too quickly, he pulled his fingers away, but then he was pressing himself against my ass and pushing in as my own rapid breaths filled the room. He didn't pause as he pushed in, and I felt my body's resistance break as he started to move inside of me. He reached under me and lifted me enough to rub a finger against my clit.

I felt the orgasm building just as his own breathing started to pick up. I came loudly, a guttural scream filling the room as my body clamped around his growing knot and he spilled into me. He leaned forward and kissed my neck as he swelled and swelled until I was whimpering from the pain of the stretch and the pleasure of feeling his swollen knot through the thin wall separating my ass and vagina.

I moved beneath him, rocking myself against his knot until I found the spot that pulled another orgasm from me. His sharp teeth bit into my neck as we stayed conjoined. Shifter's teeth were sharp, but the rip in my flesh was nowhere near as tidy as the two fang marks Ruyek had left on either side of my neck.

I heard Ruyek gasp next to us.

"Savanna, King of Vampires, are you drinking our queen's blood?" Rue asked, delight clear in his tone.

I didn't need Van to answer. None of us did as he lapped at the blood spilling from my neck. Somehow, the thought had my vagina pulsing for more, just as Van deflated enough to pull out of me.

Cas flipped me over again when Van pulled away.

"Are you sure you're up for this?" Cas asked, his tentacles wrapped around my wrists already.

"If you don't fuck me, I'm going to punch you," I teased.

He chuckled darkly in response. I tightened as he settled between my legs. My ass was so deliciously sore from Van, and I didn't think I could take Cas in both holes right now. He looked down as I clenched and Ruyek handed him the lube.

"No ass?" he asked.

I nodded as he lubed all five of his fingers up before pushing two fingers inside of me and easily finding my g-spot. Gods above. The bed beneath me was soaked, but I felt myself getting wetter as a third and then a fourth finger joined the first two.

"What are you doing?" I moaned as his thumb pushed into me.

"Getting you ready for the only way you want me right now," he answered as his fingers curled inside me.

The stretch of his knuckles as he slowly worked his fist inside of me burned and then it felt like every nerve in my body sparked to life as he moved his fist in and out of me. It was too much. I was going to come apart and fizzle out like a sliced cord. I came and continued to cum as he fisted me.

I thought the waves of pleasure would never end, but then he pulled away and I felt the tide ebbing.

I was panting like an animal by the time he carefully pushed one penis and then the other inside of my vagina. My body ached, but the lube and cum around him made the fit possible.

I was nearly liquid with pleasure; both of his cocks pulsing inside of me as he pushed my knees to my chest and fucked me until his growl of completion brought forth my final orgasm.

Cas collapsed next to me and my men moved to touch me. Ruyek pulled my head onto his bare lap while Cas held me on one side and Van held me on the other. Ambrose settled his chest between my legs, laying his head against my stomach with a content sigh.

"We're married," I whispered as I closed my eyes. "I'm your wife."

I was certain everyone knew that *your* encompassed all four of them. I was theirs, and they were mine. Married. Mates. Forever.

Ruyek

I didn't open my eyes the moment I awoke. Instead, I kept them closed tightly against the rays of the sun dancing on my eyelids – sunlight through filtered, safe windows. A gift, just like all of this. I thought of Cordelia walking down that aisle in the wedding dress I'd designed and brought to life overnight for her. If the best moment of my life was the moment that flashed before my eyes before I died, that moment would be it: Van, Ambrose, and Cas surrounding me while our wife walked down the aisle to us.

My eyes opened suddenly as I realized something was different. I was curled up between Cas and Cori, who were still sleeping. Ambrose was asleep too, his body half-covering Cori. Van was awake though, and I found his eyes wordlessly.

It's different now, he said in my mind.

I jolted. He spoke in my mind. I was the only magicborn capable of mindspeak in this room.

Your thoughts are so loud right now, Rue. I can hear everything. I agree about Cori in her wedding dress though. I'll never forget it. Van's midnight lion sat in the dark shadows of my mind, looking more like a golden retriever than the prowling beast he usually was.

You're very proud of yourself, aren't you? I asked, my internal voice clipped.

I am, actually. In all seriousness though, I think it's our mating bond.

I felt my shadows solidify into something shaped like me as I stared down at the hulking lion trespassing in my mind.

We don't know anything about mating bonds, I reminded Van. And we didn't. It had been a very long time since one had been officially recorded, and even in Acadia, they were more myth than reality.

What I do know is I can see into your mind, and I can also see into theirs. I feel them, like I know where they are, and I know that they're sleeping and safe. The midnight lion rubbed its head against my shadowy leg.

Maybe it's because you're a King of Vampires now, I answered. That seemed equally as likely as a mating bond that allowed non-vampires to have vampiric mindspeak.

Could you feel a tether between us before now? Van's voice echoed in my mind.

Of course I couldn't. That's not a power that vampires possess, but as I reached out with my senses, I could feel all of my mates, my spouses. I felt like they were tied to the innermost part of me.

A mating bond is a soul bond, Rue. We are bound together. Our souls, our minds, our bodies. Do you believe me now?

I thought for a moment. *Was it the wedding or the bedding that solidified it, you think?*

The lion shrugged. *Maybe both.*

Maybe both.

The other three soon awoke and discovered our connection, and the amount of frolicking in the shadowy abyss of my mind was enough to drive any man crazy.

"Enough!" I said aloud after Cori's icy wind warred with Ambrose's incessant flowering in my head. "I'm getting a migraine."

And I was getting a migraine. I was used to walking in other people's minds, but I was not used to having four people running all over mine.

"Now that we're here," I said more calmly after everyone retreated from my head, "I think it's time we make use of the prisoner rotting in the cells beneath the James River."

"Oh shit." Cori giggled, and the giggle was so uncharacteristic that I felt like falling to laughter myself. Cori had come so far from the darkness she'd been entrenched in after her sisters died.

"What?" Cas asked.

"I think we need to have the sheets changed." And there she was, one of the great loves of my life giggling at the amount of cum encrusted in the sheets. "I'm literally still dripping."

"Shower first then," I said with a smile.

Somehow, we managed to shower without fucking each other again. Talk of the prisoner had sobered us up a bit after I'd instructed the servants to clean the sheets and the mattress. I told them to purchase a mattress pad today because this would absolutely happen again.

"You don't all have to go," Cori said after we were dressed. Ambrose in particular looked pale at the thought of mind-walking a woman who had already suffered so much in imprisonment.

"I know you won't do what they did to her," Ambrose replied quietly. "I just can't help but wonder if we're on the right side of this thing."

I watched as everyone's focus narrowed to him, to that thought.

"The shadowborn have killed so many innocent people. Magicborn and mortalborn," Cori argued, incredulity in her voice.

"The East End of this city is a scar, a reminder that anyone who does not bow down to magicborn royalty will be obliterated," Ambrose said. Said very carefully, I might add. It wasn't magicborn royalty who destroyed the East End, it was Queen Rixana in particular.

Cori's expression changed. "I–" she started to answer, but then her shoulders dropped. "I guess it seemed like a necessary cost when thinking of my mother's actions, but it has never felt that way thinking of the shadow queen."

"The shadow queen is your mother's daughter. It tracks that she'd have inherited some ruthlessness when it comes to achieving her goals," Cas said.

There it was: the truth we'd exposed but barely been able to talk about. The shadow queen was mine and Cori's sister, the child of two of the most ruthless monarchs in centuries. Rixana and Valdon, both of them so sure their decisions were the right ones, and that anyone who disagreed was an enemy to be removed.

Cori's golden eyes met mine. What could we even do with this information? It settled uncomfortably between us. Sharing a sibling was odd enough, but the real discomfort was the reality that all the living magicborn royals had to know who the shadow queen was and they never deigned to tell us. They didn't think that bit of critical information was important in a centuries-long war against the forbidden love child of two ruling monarchs.

Cori nodded, resolute in something. "We need more information. Whatever our next steps are or aren't, we need more."

And so, we all descended through the damp darkness of the tunnel system beneath the castle on Belle Isle.

The magic that held the river at bay was intricate. I studied the seams of it running along the clay tunnel as we walked half a mile under the water. Was it fae or witch? It didn't matter, but their magic signatures were usually very distinct, and I couldn't differentiate here.

Finally, we reached the iron cells. They were clean and well-lit, but they were still damp cells beneath a river. Electric torches burned along the walls and a single cell at the end of the long line of them was occupied. It didn't look like the prisoners of the mortalborn when we entered this world. There were books and a table, and the prisoner was laying on a gurney hooked up to an IV with tubes running out of her mouth.

Ambrose stopped walking at the sight.

"They're keeping her asleep and nourished for now," Cori said. "We don't know if we could contain her at her full power."

Two guards stood outside her cell, both of them women wearing black leathers and broad swords on their backs.

"Has she been undisturbed?" Cori asked, authority in her voice as she approached.

"Yes, your highness," one said.

"I believe it is your majesty now," I replied with a smile. "She is Queen of Vampires, as you must have heard."

"They do not serve the vampire kingdom," Cori added softly. "I am their highness as long as my mother reigns."

"If you say so." I shrugged.

The guard unlocked the cell at Cori's instruction, and I stepped inside. They locked the door behind me without need for orders.

They're still afraid of her, you know. I projected my voice into all of my mates' minds.

As they should be, Cori responded. *She is the head of the shadow queen's armies. All of us should be.*

And she survived vampire torture. I mused. She was powerful, more powerful than I was giving her credit for, perhaps.

I settled into the bench along the wall and reached out for the prisoner's mind. I was apparently still connected to my mates, because Ambrose's voice echoed in my head: *She has a name, you know.*

Fine. Aleria then. I'll be sure to think her name as I invade her private thoughts.

Ambrose's flowers seemed to waver at my words. It was true though, and he had to accept that this was a violation. It was a violation we believed was justified, but it was a violation nonetheless.

Her mind was still when I entered. Walls were up, but nothing was moving. Black flames burned somewhere behind her walls, but I couldn't sense her. I walked around a fortress of black obsidian stone, searching for a crack or a fissure. Even unconscious, she was formidable.

My shadows curled tightly around me as I felt something behind me. It didn't feel like her, though, it had a different magic than the one burning inside the obsidian walls.

Then I knew. I'd felt her before.

Soraeda. My voice was resigned. I should have known she'd come.

Ruyek. Brother.

I turned to face her. How had I not seen it before? She was a perfect mix of my father and Rixana. Her black hair had the slightest hint of red undertones and her eyes were golden, but red flecks surrounded her pupils. She was pale and angular like me and my father, but her lips and the shape of her eyes were all Rixana.

It's a bit uncomfortable, you know. Thinking of you as my sister. I have been an only child for over a century.

You've never been an only child. You were just lied to. You were always the youngest of three.

Our brother. My voice shifted. I'd barely thought of him. *Is he dead then? Where is he in the annals of history?*

You'd know better than me. He didn't come back to Acadia when Autumn and I returned. Even the mortalborn know who he is. Her eyes bore into my shadows until I solidified, facing her in my physical form.

What do you mean? The mortalborn know him? What the hell was she on about?

He's a time jumper, shows up all over mortal legends. I haven't seen him in centuries and not for lack of trying. I can't find him. I imagine he's living in some different time, hiding from all the chaos this age has unleashed. It was simpler before my mother led our kind through the rift.

Which kind are you referring to? Vampires? Witches?

She laughed at my questions. *You still don't get it, do you? There is only one us. The magicborn. The rules they've used to separate all of us, the categories they put us in were only ever to stifle our powers, to maintain their positions as gods and goddesses. And she knew that, and she took advantage of their own pride. Her army is composed of magicborn never limited to one breed. Fae-witches and vampire-mer. She wants me too, but I have opposed her from the beginning.*

Is she the goddess you've been on about for centuries?

On about? The goddess is a genocidal tyrant. She's wiped entire populations, families, and rare faeries from existence. Anyone who opposes her is destroyed.

Anyone but you, I corrected.

Well, she's afraid of me, and I also think she's bored. She wants to see what happens when I finally come for her. She's always loved the drama of wartime.

So, the goddess who'd taken down the old gods was a lover of drama and wartime games. I could almost understand the kind of boredom true immortality would bring. Before my mates, the years had started to wear on a bit even for me.

Just then, I saw something else in her face.

You're lying! My accusation sizzled between us like a slap. Her eyes grew wide and then narrowed.

Omission of wartime secrets with someone I do not count as an ally is not lying.

Oh, gods. I laughed long and hard. *You're just like them! The miserable people you call parents, the snake of a father we share. I should have known.*

Anger seemed to boil to her surface and she took a step forward.

I am not here to fight with you, King Ruyek. I am here to ask for an alliance.

What the fuck? An alliance. After everything she'd done, everyone she'd murdered. She wanted an alliance?

Fuck that and fuck you. My voice roared between us.

After everything you've learned about Rixana and the goddess? It isn't enough for you to question what side of this war you find yourself on? Your people subjugated an entire planet of lesser beings–

–lesser beings! I interrupted, my own anger reaching a fever point. *Your sister is half-mortalborn, or have you forgotten?*

AND there are magic-wielders among them now. They may be a young species who has not come fully into their powers, but you were the one just talking about how we're all the same inside.

I said magicborn are the same. Mortalborn are something else entirely, and I do not hold it against Cordelia that her father is one of them. That isn't about this. This is about saving Acadia.

Saving the planet you drove us from?

You cannot believe that, Ruyek! I was fighting for my birthright and creating an army to storm Tirnanahg. The people who left were cowards, not refugees. I asked them to join me, and I retaliated only for moves they made against my army, my followers.

How can I believe anything you say when you are so clearly still lying?

And you are keeping my general, a woman who suffered greatly at the hands of our father, prisoner without due cause. You're not innocent here, and I am offering a choice to join me. We can finally be a family.

I stiffened. I didn't know Soraeda, and I had a family. I'd just married the four people I counted as my family. I didn't need someone who shared the worst parts of my bloodline to use that connection to manipulate me.

I repeat: fuck that and fuck you. Acadia is your problem, not ours. I was lying too. I fought a shudder at the lie. We'd all just admitted that Acadia was likely endgame, but I wasn't going to be railroaded into joining a woman who was just like my piece of shit father.

You really think that, don't you? She chuckled. *Then you're a fool. Cordelia is a weapon, and if I can't persuade you to join me willingly, I will have to use other methods. I need her for my war. Your war against me is nonexistent. I have only ever been after powerful beings who could help me win.*

And there it was: the truth at last.

I attacked, pulling my shadows back and throwing them at her. She staggered with the shock of it before roaring into the space between us.

You have no idea what I'm capable of, little brother. Her shadows grabbed me, lifted me up. I fought back, taking swipes at her. She recoiled at my strikes, but she did not lose her grip on me as she pushed and pushed–

And then I was back in the cell. I reached for the prisoner's mind again, but a solid wall prevented me from even tip-toeing in. Soraeda would not allow me in again. I knew that somehow, and she was coming for Cordelia.

Cordelia

Ruyek was shaken when he looked at us from the bench
of the cell. His eyes found mine, and I felt something from

him, like his emotions were being broadcast down the bond between us.

"Why are you afraid?" I asked, my own voice shaking. I'm not sure I'd ever seen Ruyek afraid before.

"Soraeda was there. She wanted us to join her, and I refused." His voice trailed off as he looked at the prisoner lying in the bed in front of him.

"But why are you afraid, Rue? What's happened?" Cas this time, his face painted with concern.

"She's coming for you, Cordelia." Ruyek's eyes stayed on the prisoner. Aleria, I reminded myself. Somehow, we'd be friendly with this woman one day. Ambrose had seen it, lived it for just a moment.

"For me?" My voice broke.

"I think she's always been coming for you. In Manhattan, Nadella was going to give you to her." Ruyek moved his gaze back to mine.

"We don't know that. Nadella wouldn't have just handed me over." I couldn't believe that. I couldn't.

"She believed in her cause. I bet she thought you would too, once all the missing pieces were revealed. She wouldn't have seen it as a betrayal, you know. She'd have seen it as bringing you to the right side of this fight." His red eyes were heavy with concern, with fear of whatever was going to happen next.

"She can certainly try to take me, but I will not live my life afraid." Anger coursed through me. I wouldn't lock myself in this castle. I wouldn't live in fear. I was tired of fear. Fear had consumed me since my sisters' deaths – sisters that might have known all along that I was only ever a pawn on this game board.

"Actually," I said with a nod, "I think we should go out tonight."

"Cori–" Ambrose started.

"No!" I interrupted. "She does not get to tell me how to live my life. I will destroy anyone she sends for me. I am not afraid of her."

"Whatever you command, my queen." Ruyek's voice was soft, resigned.

My stubbornness clearly did not assuage his fears, but I was resolute. I was done living in fear. Done. Soraeda would have to come for me herself if she wanted me, and I would die before she took me.

"The Midnight Art Market!" I said, clapping my hands. "Just a quick flight to Hopewell."

Ruyek had instructed the dragons and pegasi brought here this morning. I wondered how hard it was convincing a dragon to touch someone they didn't know so they could translocate across the world.

All four of my husbands looked at me like I'd grown a second head.

"Soraeda just threatened you, Cori. I don't think you need to lay low forever, but maybe just for tonight. Let's stay in and order Thai and–"

"No," I interrupted Van. "I am going out tonight. If you don't want to come, I'll go without you."

I knew that was a cheap shot. There was no chance they weren't coming with me. Once we were back inside the castle, a servant brought a long black box to Ruyek.

"Thank you," he said with a nod.

"What is that?" Ambrose asked.

"Well, I know many magicborn don't exchange rings, but I'm quite fond of the practice. I assumed Cori would prefer a local jeweler to design our rings, so I placed a call before the wedding and instructed them to deliver them here when they were done." Ruyek smiled as he spoke, the fear gone for at least a moment.

I felt tears in my eyes as he opened the box. Five rings lay inside. Four of them were simple yellow bands with five jewels encrusted in the band: sapphire, emerald, garnet, onyx, and diamond. The fifth was a ring set. A thin yellow gold band with no adornments was nestled against a ring with five stones. A large oval diamond lay in the center; on one side, smaller ovals of sapphire and emerald, and on the other, garnet and onyx.

"I thought the stones and the colors fairly represented each of us," Ruyek said, clearing his throat like our silence was making him nervous.

"Ruyek," Ambrose said, his eyes as watery as mine felt. He didn't finish his statement, but he did lunge at Ruyek, nearly knocking the box out of his hand as he wrapped his arms around him.

"You thoughtful, thoughtful man," Van said as he stepped forward and leaned down to kiss Ruyek's forehead.

I couldn't find any words, but I couldn't wait for my opportunity to kiss Ruyek. My tongue swept into his mouth, and I felt the bite of his fangs. I pushed my tongue against them until a drop of blood swelled and he swallowed it down, moaning at the reminder that he could have any part of me whenever he wanted.

We ate a quiet dinner, talking and playing board games until the sun set and the stars came out.

"To the art market then?" Cas asked, his eyes catching on the ring on his finger and a smile crossing his lips every time he looked down.

"I want to change," I said. "I'll meet you downstairs." They took the hint and left me alone.

I changed into a thin gossamer dress with tiny yellow flowers and green leaves sewn across the light blue fabric. I traded my boots for simple black flats and quickly lined my eyes and added some glimmer to my cheeks.

"Cori," Van whispered on an exhale when I joined them downstairs again.

"Fucking gorgeous," Ruyek said, only a little less breathless.

"I do clean up sometimes," I said.

I grabbed my double-headed battle-ax and strapped it on my back. It still had the white strap from the wedding on it. Even if I didn't believe we were in imminent danger, I didn't want to be caught without it if we were.

The men were all in black joggers or jeans with t-shirts and sneakers; their usual casual wear.

We arrived in the vibrant city. The dragons were circling above the downtown art market when Cas and I arrived on our pegasi. I landed in a small grassy space on the edge of the river (the Appomattox and the James Rivers met in Hopewell) and slid off Aldric awkwardly. I rarely wore anything that required me to ride side-saddle, and it was just as awkward as I remembered.

Hopewell had been an industrial city before my mother arrived, but industry looked drastically different under magicborn leadership. The industrial city had transformed into an artistic oasis, and the downtown strips was home to galleries, craft shops, bookstores, and indie game stores.

In the absence of a work-life balance that tilted hard towards work, the art of actual mortalborn had easily replaced the generative AI thievery of the early twenty-first century. Art was for living, breathing creatives, not computers. Magicborn conquered this planet, but the world that had emerged made it hard to believe our conquering was all bad.

Maybe it was good and bad, Cas' voice said inside my head, and I stopped walking the block to the downtown art market. It was so unfamiliar, having all of them able to mindspeak.

I guess it can be a bit more complex than that. I finally started walking again, leading the way past a historical theater and a microbrewery before turning on East Broadway, the main downtown strip.

The Midnight Art Market was covered in string lights hanging across the road from storefront to storefront. The road had become pedestrian only with the fall of the personal vehicle. Bikes and public transit couldn't travel here either. The stores were open to the warm June night, hundreds of people coming in and out. The vast majority of people seemed to be mortalborn, but I saw at least two vampires and a number of powerbound with slightly pointed ears.

Stalls of local vendors were set on the side of the street in front of the shops, and the smell of a taco truck and a stall filled with baked goods wafted down the street alongside the soft music of a band playing bluegrass music.

"If our families never left Acadia, we'd have never laid eyes on this place," I said to my husbands just as Ambrose stopped at a stall selling flower crowns.

I leaned against Van as we all watched Ambrose barter with the seller. In true Ambrose fashion, he was arguing that the vendor should be charging more for the delicate creations. The vendor disagreed, but she thanked him when he paid triple her asking price. He turned around and smiled at me, his freckles dazzling in the soft glow of the string lights.

He stepped into my space and put the crown on my head. Soft pink and blue flowers were intertwined with baby's breath and small, bright green leaves.

"Are they real?" I asked as he stepped back.

"Quite. I think she's a second generation powerbound with fae ancestry," he replied, matching flowers blooming at the base of his antlers as he looked me over with a smile.

"What gives it away?" I asked.

"Her ears aren't pointed at all, but I could see the plants reacting to her when she touched them. She has garden magic," he replied as he took my hand and led me down the street. Van grabbed my other hand. Cas and Ruyek took up either side of us.

People stopped and looked as we walked through. No doubt the entire world had watched our wedding video by now, but no one asked for autographs or pictures, like this market was a sacred place for all who entered. Artists, poets, and crafters laughed and bartered around us. I watched as an artist traded a painted wooden dragon for an original poem written on a typewriter right before her eyes. Children ran by us blowing bubbles and skipping.

"This could be our life, you know," I said softly. "We can fight in battles and save our world and Acadia, battle gods and shadow queens – or we can close the rift and stay like this. Frequent art markets and raise children in a world that can know peace. This war doesn't have anything to do with us. We can just close the rift and end it."

All four of my husbands stopped walking.

Ruyek spoke first. "You could do that? Close the rift and walk away?"

"Couldn't you?" I asked.

"In a heartbeat, but I've been known to be an incredibly selfish man when it comes to anyone I don't directly love and care for. If you wanted that life, I'd agree wholeheartedly," he replied.

"I didn't know you wanted children," Van said, squeezing my hand tighter.

"I don't know if I do, but I can imagine raising children together. Our children would be surrounded by so much love." I felt tears welling up, but I shoved them down. What would it feel like to grow up in a family that was functional and loving? What a gift that would be for our children.

"Your majesty," a voice interrupted the moment we were all having.

I turned to see General Sabine walking towards me.

"We have to talk," she said, glancing around us at all the people in the street.

"Please, Sabine. I'm begging you to let this wait until tomorrow." I closed my eyes tightly for a moment before meeting her eyes again. She had something world-shattering to tell me. I could see it in her eyes.

"It cannot wait, unfortunately," she said. "Please, let's get out of the middle of the street."

She led us to the end of the market. People were still filing past us, but this dark street corner was far quieter and calmer than the middle of the market.

"Why did you call Cori *majesty*?" Ruyek asked before Sabine could get a word in.

"Rue, you reminded me just hours ago that I'm Queen of Vampires," I replied, a little lost by his line of questioning.

"Yes, and you reminded me that witches follow the witch queen and you are not their majesty. Highness? Yes. Majesty? No." His answer was curt, but his gaze was directed at Sabine, not me.

Sabine sighed and ran a hand over her smooth head. "Cordelia, your mother is gone."

Gone? I grabbed Ambrose's arm to steady me. We had a complicated relationship, but I wasn't ready to bury her.

"Like hells that old bat is dead," Ruyek said, crossing his arms. "Explain."

I cut him a look before returning my attention to Sabine.

"Correct. She isn't dead, but she, Valdon, and Darius are no longer on this planet. She left a letter naming you queen. I need to get you back to D.C. and call the IRC immedia–"

"–they're in Acadia," Van interrupted. "Aren't they? They went through the rift."

"Yes and no. Acadia? Yes. Through the rift? I'm not exactly sure if that's the route they chose."

"What other route is there?" I asked, realizing again how little I knew about anything that mattered. How the hell was I going to be queen?

"The rift is the only portal we cannot close. Portals – wormholes, technically, open up in various places from time to time for short bursts of time. They just aren't usually open long enough for much to come of it. I know your mother had a sense for these things though. She might have found another way through. I can't promise it was the rift."

I looked behind me and saw a bench a few paces away. I stumbled towards it and sat down. This couldn't be happening. My mother – my father, who possessed no magical ability to help him in a place like Acadia – went through the rift or a rift or who the hell knows? A fucking spaceship seemed plausible at this point. I felt panic rising in my chest, constricting my air as all of these realities collided in my mind.

"It makes sense," Ruyek said thoughtfully. "There are legends and stories about us in nearly every mortalborn culture. Surely, they started with some truth. Some fae or dragon slipped through a wormhole and ended up here. No one would forget that sort of thing."

"Cori." Ambrose knelt in front of me. "Cori, I need you to take deep breaths. We are going to get through this."

"We have to close the rift," I panted, rubbing my chest at the pain constricting there.

I knew what closing the rift meant. It meant leaving Acadia, a planet that now housed the only living family I had left, separated from us. It meant we weren't ever going to help Soraeda. It meant giving up on all the great, legend-worthy things we thought we'd do with our collective power.

"Now?" I looked up to see Sabine talking to the sky like a madwoman. "Yes. Okay. Yes." And then she took off running towards the river.

"What the fuck is wrong with her?" Cas asked, but I felt things clicking into place.

My mother had chosen Sabine to train me in syphoning because she knew so much about the shadow queen's powers. And Sabine trained me like she had intimate first-hand knowledge of how to wield my strange new powers, despite not being a syphon herself. The only other syphon we knew about in recent history was the shadow queen.

My panic dissipated as anger and betrayal settled in their place. Sabine, who had trained me to hold my first sword and to land a punch. Sabine, who had been more like my mother at times than my own mother. Sabine, who I thought would one day be *my* general when the crown fell to me–

"She's working for the shadow queen," I said to my husbands, reaching for my battle-ax as I spoke. "And I'd bet my crown they're about to attack right now."

As if on cue, the sound of screams filled the air, coming from the direction of the river. Without pausing, I started to run. I severely regretted not wearing my leather and boots as my black flats pounded into the pavement. But I focused on the battle-ax in my hand and started pulling my magic up from the deepest parts of me. More and more and more I pulled until every slap of my feet on the ground left patches of ice. I didn't need to syphon tonight. My own power would be more than enough.

The screams got louder as my legs carried me closer to the water. I couldn't think about our odds: the five of us against a battalion or an entire fucking army. An ice storm brewed just below the surface of my skin, and I felt the temperature around us dropping as I pulled up more and more power. We would be enough – the five of us against an entire gods-damned army would be enough.

It had to be enough.

The river was down an embankment that kept the city safe from flooding, but the floods were rare and a park with string lights sat near the water's edge. Parents grabbed their children as they tried to run up the paved steps cut into the side of the hill to escape the shadowy creatures crawling out of the river. Crawling out of the river – mer. Species of origin for these shadowborn? Mer, *again*.

We can't win this. Cas' voice was frantic in my head. *Cori, we have to retreat. There are so many of them—*

You are free to leave, I answered back. There was no way in either world I was going to abandon a city in my queendom, a majority mortalborn city just a few minute's flight from *my* castle, to its fate and run away like the coward my mother clearly was.

I looked up as a dragon flew low above us with a rider on its back, trailed by riders on the backs of pegasi. They had sent so many more than they'd sent to Manhattan or Atlantis; they'd sent fewer before and still managed to murder four witch princesses and a mer queen in those attacks.

There is no time for fear, my queen. Fight or flight, and you've chosen to fight. Put it in a box and destroy them. Destroy every single fucking one of them. Rue's voice was in my head this time with the best battleground pep talk I could imagine at that moment.

I watched Ruyek look towards the sky as Isolde descended low enough for him to jump and grab the saddle straps to swing himself up. Drystan apparently knew Ambrose wasn't ready to jump and mount, so he settled in the grass alongside us so Ambrose could pull himself up into the saddle.

"That's an acid dragon," Van said, tracking the green and yellow feathered dragon flying low overhead. "Fuck that. We have three dragons to their one."

He shifted into a massive blue and white dragon with long, layered feathers.

"Ice dragon," I said as we reached the edge of the embankment.

"We can't win," Cas said aloud this time, his voice trembling.

"Then we die trying. No matter what, you do not let her take me. Promise me. I'd rather be dead than her weapon," I said, trying to muster every bit of command I could in my voice, but his eyes gave him away. Cas wanted to promise me he'd do whatever I needed, but we both knew he wouldn't do that. He wouldn't kill me to save me from imprisonment. I guess I couldn't be captured then because being dragged across two worlds to the shadow queen wasn't an option.

My ice started at the base of the hill, below where innocents were fleeing, and it spread out. I pushed and pushed as the ice traveled up the legs of the shadowborn running towards the hill, freezing them where they stood and traveling up, up, up, until they were statues of ice.

"Time to fight, Cas," I snapped in another attempt at command, and this one seemed to snap him into action.

He called a storm. I watched as he wielded lightning strikes against the shadowborn as they climbed out of the river, frying them where they stood. One, two, three fell, and then the green and yellow dragon was spewing a bright green liquid towards Isolde.

She moved just in time, but all the shadowborn beneath her screamed as their bodies melted into puddles of bubbling liquid. Shouts rang out behind us as mortalborn, powerbound, and magicborn from the city joined us with makeshift weapons in their hands. We weren't alone. By the gods, we would never be alone in my kingdom of my people.

A powerbound with softly pointed ears pulled more lightning from the storm clouds overhead just as heavy rain started to fall. She wielded it with far more finesse than Cas did, striking shadowborn as they approached the bottom of the hill we stood on. If nothing else, we had the high ground.

I threw spears of ice towards a mounted shadowborn riding towards us, striking true as the pegasus and its rider plunged to the ground. The rider on the back of the acid dragon boomed a command across the field in Acadian: *To the point.*

My eyes went wide.

They were going to City Point. There were homes there and an old manor turned into a home for at-risk youth, and we were all here, blocks away from where the shadowborn were heading to strike a most vulnerable artery.

I took off before I could really think through my next steps. I whistled for Aldric, and he was there in an instant, catching me as I hoisted myself onto his back. Mounted shadowborn flew overhead, and an aerial battle would just slow me down. I urged Aldric forward with the pressure of my knees, making it clear that his wings were to stay tucked.

His hooves beat against the asphalt of an ancient road as we sped down Appomattox Street before turning left on Cedar Lane. The river was to my left as we ran, and I heard battle cry after battle cry in Acadian through the trees that blocked my view of the river.

Then the trees gave way to open sky and a massive grassy yard with a manor used during another war centuries earlier and the ancient, wooden cabin that stood as a remnant of a general who had ended that war in Virginia. Hadn't nearly every war on this country's soil ended here, in Virginia?

What would it be like to live in a world, in a single space, that had never known war?

I saw shadowborn climbing the steps cut into the hill above the river, moving toward Appomattox Manor, no longer just a historical monument, but a home filled with children. Up ahead, mortalborn were gathering atop the cobblestone road that overlooked the steep hill to the river's edge. I screamed into the night as I veered away from the battle ahead of me and rushed towards the shadowborn creeping ever closer to the manor.

I looked up as a blue and white dragon roared overhead. Van – and Cas was on his back. Van screeched into the night before pouring waves of ice on the shadowborn cresting the hill. He roared again and ice poured down the hill, and it was enough for me. Van would protect the children. I swung Aldric around and rushed back towards the group of mortalborn holding off the approaching attack.

Most of them had crossbows, but I noticed a few very-illegal shotguns and handguns in the crowd. And for once, I was grateful for the mortalborn who refused to bow to my mother's demands as arrows and bullets rained down the hill and the screams of shadowborn filled the night air.

I dismounted and ran to the front line of this battle. Ice poured from my hands down the hill, and long brutal ice shards sprang up beneath shadowborns, impaling them before they had time to react. I poured and poured, erected a wall of icy spears between us and any shadowborn who dared to risk the climb.

Below the hill, Isolde and Drystan were facing the water, breathing fire on the mer as they climbed out of the river. Shadowborn screams of pain were a song that made me shiver, as I remembered just how hot dragonfire burned.

Ice and dragonfire – the world turned into a battle of dragons as the shadowborn fell and fell and fell. It felt like we were turning the tide of this battle, like finally we were proving to Soraeda that she could not take who or what she wanted from this world.

Just as I breathed a small sigh of relief, the massive acid dragon seemed to rise from the black of night, slamming into Van and Cas with the weight of its body. Cas slipped from Van's back, barely holding on with one arm – and then in a swift movement, the acid dragon whirled towards me and I saw its rider clearly for the first time. Sabine sat in the saddle, her floral tattoos illuminated in the moonlight. It wasn't a full moon anymore, but it revealed everything I already knew to be true.

"She trusted you!" Cas yelled, as he pulled himself back into his seat.

"I'm not here to kill her. I'm here to show her her destiny," Sabine yelled back before turning back to face Van. But before she could show me anything, Van sank his massive dragon teeth into the neck of the acid dragon. The creature screamed into the night. He was bigger than Van's ice dragon form, but Van was quicker and angrier.

Van twisted his head, breaking the creature's neck as he flipped upside down and dug his talons into the unprotected belly of the acid dragon, slicing long lines into the flesh. I watched as Cas struggled to hang on as acid poured onto the skin of his arms. And then he was falling. Burning and falling as the acid ate through his flesh. He hit the ground with a heavy thud and the entire world seemed to stop spinning.

Ambrose

Caspian! Ruyek's voice screamed across my mind so loudly I was sure it was echoing in all our minds.

I saw him fall from Van's back. I urged Drystan forward, but Cas hit the ground just before I reached him. Above us, Van was pulling away from the mortally wounded acid dragon. Sabine was screaming for a retreat, but she was too late. Most of her soldiers were frozen, ashes, impaled, or bleeding out from several well-placed arrows and bullets.

Sabine screamed with fury as her mount fell from the sky a few yards from where Van had ripped his body to shreds. The dragon's body crashed into an empty parking lot just as Sabine landed a rolling dismount.

I dismounted Drystan and ran to Cas as the ground began to shake. Sabine poured all of her magic into the earth, and the ground swayed like it was the ocean. The sound of cracking cobblestone filled the air, but another sound caught my attention.

Cori stood in front of the armed mortalborn, staring down at Sabine as fissures spread out from where she stood, snaking towards the top of the hill. Cori looked down at her former general – laughing.

Cori reached down to the ground in front of her and exhaled. Sabine's eyes grew large as Cori kept her hand on the ground. *Oh shit.* Sabine was touching the ground, pouring her power into it, and Cori grabbed the threads of her magic and yanked all of that power into herself.

Everything seemed to still as Sabine's face drained of color, and then her cheeks began to sink in, like all the muscle and flesh into her body was being drained alongside her power. But her eyes were furious as she glared at Cori. Cori, the witch warrior she had trained to hold a battle-ax. Cori, the powerbound princess she'd trained to use this incredible power. Cori was turning all of that training against her.

Sabine collapsed before the last bit of life was drained out of her, and Cori stood. She looked towards the water where the few shadowborn survivors were retreating into the river.

Cori turned from the river to the makeshift mortalborn army standing behind her. They looked at her like she was the sun shining down on them, and maybe she was. Their queen, now barefoot with an untouched battle-ax on her back and gossamer floral dress, had defeated another shadowborn attack very-nearly single-handedly.

"She'll never be anything but a god to them now," Ruyek said as he landed next to me.

"Maybe she is a god," I retorted, remembering myself in time to kneel down next to Cas.

"He's breathing," Ruyek said as I checked him over, "and his wounds are already healing."

We're going to the rift. Cori's voice sounded in my head.

My eyes widened with shock and I looked to Ruyek, but he only nodded. She had spoken to all of us simultaneously.

What about daylight? I asked warily.

It's winter in the Southern Hemisphere. There are zero hours of sunlight this time of year. We will need to stop by Belle Isle to get gear. You have to hike to the rift. No one can translocate directly there, but we are going, and we are going within the hour. Cori did not leave any room for argument. Ruyek scooped Cas up easily and laid him across Isolde's saddle.

Ice dragon Van was covered in acid burns in various stages of healing, but he was still able to fly after us as we turned towards Richmond, Cori right behind us on Aldric's back.

Ruyek

A healer quickly mended Cas and woke him up with smelling salts. He looked like he could use a very long sleep, but Cori told him the same thing she told us: we're going to the rift and we're going now.

She tracked Autumn down easily enough and told her to unhook the prisoner and place her in iron chains.

"She's going back where she came from," Cori said like a woman possessed. Her face was emotionless, and she gave commands so naturally that she reminded me a bit of her mother, as terrifying as that was.

"Can we trust Autumn?" I asked as Cori handed us layer after layer of thick winter gear. Only Van turned down her attempts, since he planned to travel in some form that wouldn't need a winter coat.

"We don't have a choice. Can you translocate all of us there?" Her voice was clipped, like my question was rude. And while I did lean hard into the asshole role at times, this wasn't one of them.

Ambrose helped Cas into his layers – he was still shaking from the battle and quick healing. The latter was only ever a bandaid, never a cure. He'd need more intensive, deep healing when we returned. Just because he was alive didn't mean he was well.

Autumn came back with Aleria in chains. The general was awake and walking. She looked worse than Cas, but she didn't protest when Autumn briefly unlocked her chains to stuff her into a heavy coat before locking her chains again.

"Do you know where to drop us?" Cori asked.

"Are you closing the rift then? For good?" Autumn asked.

Cori's jaw flexed as she looked at the fae woman. "Do you know where to drop us?" she asked again.

"If you are closing the rift, I humbly ask that you let me return to Acadia," Autumn asked, her eyes on the ground as she spoke. I remembered that she'd worked for Rixana for centuries, maybe she too saw the flicker of the former witch queen in Cori's current state of *fuck everything and do what I say*.

"Fine," Cori responded after an uncomfortable silence.

Autumn nodded. "I know where to drop you, and I know the hike."

Autumn took us three at a time, agreeing to take Cori, Ambrose, and Cas first before coming back for me, Van, and Aleria.

"You excited to be returned to mommy dearest?" I asked Aleria while we waited.

"She's not my mother," she said, her Acadian accent thick and her voice hoarse from disuse.

"But you listen to everything she says. Soraeda is kind of your mother," I teased.

"Does that make Queen Cordelia your mother then? You listen to everything she says, even when she's about to make a huge mistake," she bit back, her black eyes boring into mine.

Cheap shot. Before I could hit back, Autumn was back and we were spinning through space and time until we landed into the middle of the frozen fucking hell that is an Antarctic winter.

Van had chosen the form of a massive white cat that looked a little like a midnight lion with white fur and a double coat. An Acadian winter tiger? I had almost forgotten such creatures existed. How many years had he spent pouring over notes on Acadian wildlife to be able to shift into creatures he'd never actually laid eyes on?

More years than you really want to know, Van's voice echoed in my mind.

Fair. *Nerd,* I shot back.

Cas was leaning heavily on Ambrose as Autumn pointed and spoke to Cordelia, presumably about our destination, the frozen wind was so extreme her voice was lost even to my astute ears.

How long is the hike? I asked Cori.

Six and a half miles. Her voice seemed so unconcerned about what she was asking a barely standing Cas to do. Aleria's words struck me anew. What if Cori was making a huge mistake?

Cas just fell from the back of a dragon and endured some pretty gnarly acid burns. No chance we can pop into McMurdo for a bit and let him sleep some of that off? I looked behind us where the old research station was lifeless and dark.

She didn't answer. She didn't even look at me. She simply started walking, and all of us followed. I felt Aleria's eyes on me as we walked, like she'd somehow overheard our mental conversation, and she wanted to tell me she told me so.

We stepped down onto the sea ice that separated McMurdo from the Erebus Glacier Tongue, the same glacier that had been torn in half by the rift. A thought struck me as we trekked through the wind and ice.

If you let her go back to Acadia, how are we getting home? I asked Cordelia.

I have an idea, Ruyek, and I need you to trust me. Okay? Even mind-to-mind, she sounded so curt, so exasperated by my questions.

I tried to remind myself that she was reeling. Her family was gone. Her sisters and now her parents. She'd just expended a hell of a lot of magic to save a mortalborn city from sure destruction, and she was suddenly Queen of the Witches. Her very foundation was crumbling. Maybe she was doing her best, in light of all of this fuckery.

We stopped frequently to rest, Cas looking paler and paler at every break. Three hours into the hike, the air around us seemed to change. It was charged with magic, and it was warmer, like summer was leaking through the rift.

The massive rip in the glacier came into view moments later. We still had at least an hour to reach it, but it was hard to ignore the massive black scar that leaked otherworldly power. Cori paused when she saw it, like she was overcome with a thought before she shook it off and kept walking.

If she was feeling what I felt, it was the pull of home. It screamed my name in the wind and images of standing beneath a red sun flooded my brain, memories of being a child in a world that was not deadly to me.

Home. Home. Home. Home. The wind yelled. *Come home, my son.*

You are not my home. Cori is my home. Van, Cas, and Ambrose are my home, I answered back, as if the wind, the spirit of Acadia could hear my retort.

The air got warmer and the calls got louder as we reached the rift. It was a massive tear, at least fifty feet across and extending a mile in either direction. I could see patches of magic trying to hold it together, but there were far more open holes that poured warmth and Acadian magic into the air around us.

"Send her through," Cori said to Autumn.

She obeyed, reaching the edge of one of those tears in magic and shoving Aleria in. Aleria caught my gaze just before she fell and gave me a grin that almost made me shiver.

"I need all of you to touch me," Cori said.

"You said I could go home," Autumn said, her eyes pleading.

"Fine," Cori said with a sigh before stepping forward, clasping Autumn on the shoulder, and then pushing her toward the rift.

The fae woman gasped in surprise, but then she was smiling as she disappeared like she'd never been there at all. The rift seemed to swallow her and Aleria whole the moment they started to fall towards it.

We obeyed, even though I was definitely having some misgivings about this plan. There was no turning back. We had no idea how to find the other wormholes that sporadically opened up. We'd be closing our only known path back to Acadia forever. We'd be leaving everyone left behind in Acadia to whatever fate Soraeda or the goddess decided for them.

I felt Cori pulling our magic in thin tendrils before channeling it with her own. She wasn't pulling hard enough to drain us like she'd done to Sabine, but she was pulling enough to twist all of our magics into a thick braid of power she then forced into the rift.

The ice around us shifted.

"Do *not* let go of me," she yelled into the wind as the rift crackled and roared.

As I looked down the length of the rift between realms, I saw the ice sewing itself back together like this century-long scar had never existed at all. She pulled and she twisted and she channeled all the unique kinds of power in this world into the rift until only a single hole in front of her remained.

She paused only a moment before closing her eyes and pouring again. Cori screamed suddenly, and I dropped my hand.

When I looked back on this moment, I remembered how fast it all happened. A second? A half second? One breath, Cori was sealing the last stretch of open rift, and the next, two hands were grasping her ankles through the gap between worlds. Shock rippled through us, and all of us dropped our hold on her – all of us except for Ambrose. He clung more tightly as those hands dragged both of them through the rift.

Our magic didn't stop though. Just as they disappeared, the last known gateway between Earth and Acadia closed with Cori and Ambrose in one world and me, Cas, and Van in another.

Author's Note

This book has been a long time coming. This is my third novel, and thank Moirai, it is the first one that will see the light of day. Since I wrote my first two novels about fifteen years ago, I finished two degrees in creative writing and published a PhD dissertation, poetry collection, and short story collection. I have come back to several novel ideas, but life has been life-ing and time is always short. After the birth of River City Siren Press, and the bestselling success of my poetry collection, *Wraith Like Me*, I decided it was time to finally write all of you a novel.

And here we are. I hope you've enjoyed this journey as much as I did, but I also know that it would not be possible without the support of so many people who deserve much more thanks than the author's note no one will read, but it is what I have to offer right now.

Firstly, to my husband who read smut for the first time in his life because he loves me and who will continue to read smut because he loves me: thank you for believing in me and River City Siren Press every step of the way. I can't imagine coming home to anyone but you. I don't believe in fated mates in real life, but I believe in something much stronger – I believe in loving someone so much that in a world of eight billion people, you wake up and choose them every day. On our worst days and our best days, I will always choose you.

Secondly, to my author's group who held me accountable and helped me edit this manuscript when the deadline was looming: thank you. In particular, thank you Jen Desmarais AKA Desiree DuBois, D.M. Mewha, Kate Mathos, GD Ames, Aspen Holden, Marcos F. Eguia, our intern team (Tim, Madeline, and Audrey) and the entire River City Siren Press team. You made this book possible in small and big ways, and you made RCSP possible. I don't know where I'd be without all of you, and I honestly don't want to know. So, thank you sincerely for all of the work you continue to do with me. I cannot wait to see where we'll all be in five years.

To all the people who supported me as a writer on this journey, I hope you know who you are, and I hope you know how much I love you. This list is not complete, but I want to especially thank Anna, Dana, Bud, Jessica, Mom, Dad, Tanya, Nanie, Papa, Laura, Rachel, Jennifer, Analiese, Keatyn, Aunt

Jody, Elizabeth, Sarah, Val, Linda, and Jodi Lea. If your name is not on this list and you believed in me: thank you too!

Last, but absolutely not least, I hope it's obvious that this book is many things, but it is also a love letter to Virginia. I have lived all over this state, and I have lived outside of this state. I have traveled the world, but Virginia has always called me home. Virginia has a siren's call I didn't even know I'd miss until I moved away, but I am so incredibly glad I came back. No place is perfect, but Virginia comes pretty close. I dream of a future where all the equity and community support depicted in this novel exists for Virginians, and I plan to continue to do what I can to move us in that direction. But for now, I love this place for what it is to me: home. I hope you enjoyed it too through the eyes of Cori, Van, Ruyek, Cas, and Ambrose. Richmond, Hopewell, the Virginia Appalachians, and Virginia Beach are all worth seeing in person. You won't regret the trip!

For more books like
Rise of the Witch Queen:

By Geneva Oleander

By Other Authors

Spicy Why Choose
Romance

Fantasy (with Romance)

www.ingramcontent.com/pod-product-compliance
Lightning Source LLC
Chambersburg PA
CBHW061036310726
48969CB00004B/980